GW00455070

THE ENLIGHTENED QUORUM

JAMES ASPLIN

First published in paperback in 2023

Copyright © James Asplin 2023
Illustrations © Sean/Jessika Rose 2023

The right of James Asplin to be identified as the author of the
Work has been asserted by him and in accordance with the
Copyright, Designs, and Patents Act 1988.

All rights reserved. No part of this publication may be reproduced,
stored in a retrieval system, or transmitted, in any form or by any
means without the prior written permission of the author, nor be
otherwise circulated in any form of binding or cover other than
that in which it is published and without a similar condition being
imposed on the subsequent purchaser.

All characters in this publication are fictitious and any
resemblance to real persons, living or dead, is purely coincidental.

CHAPTER ONE

I was three years old when I first saw a creature borne
of the Void.

We'd heard its call, a vaguely human yelping, and had
gotten down on our stomachs to crawl through the grass
of the forest.

"Elena, look," my mother said in a hushed
whisper, "up there, in the trees."

I narrowed my eyes, scanning the misshapen
branches and the deep green vines that entwined their
bumpy surfaces. Then I saw it.

I could have easily mistaken it for a child my own
age, with its baby-fat belly and chubby cheeks. And its
eyes. Huge and bug-eyed, hued in pale green, stared right
at me with youthful curiosity. Then, inevitably, my eyes
started to mark its differences.

Where it should have had an innocent grin
instead was a giant set of bony mandibles peeling back
to reveal rows of razor teeth. With its six twisted and

1

veiny limbs, it gripped the trunk and upper branch for balance.

"It is a spirit," Mum said, rubbing my back for comfort, "we should not approach. We may anger, or even frighten it."

I watched it sit perfectly still, eyes entirely unmoving and unblinking. It cocked its head slightly, studying me, I was sure.

When I look back at that moment, I knew that it could have killed me, killed us both if my mum had been caught by surprise.

It took a long time for me to figure out why it didn't.

T W E L V E   Y E A R S   L A T E R.

The glistening fogs that hung over the valley below were beautiful when the day reached its dying golden hours. The Orchid Sanctuary clung to the side of the mountains above Eleynum's walls, and while mostly concealed from the outside world, the botanical gardens were the only place I could see a glimpse of it.

Though, like a window in a prison cell, this only served as a reminder of the futility of escape attempts. Only a sheer cliff face awaited those who had tried, and if not for the fog, I imagine their skeletons would have been clearly visible if you took a peek.

The stone bench's firm edge dug into the meat of my thigh, reminding me I'd already stayed too long. I kept watching the bright red flowers in front of me, their twisted and spindly heads like outstretched hands, begging me to try the climb down.

My hands were still shaking and the skin around the scraped knuckles was starting to turn red from swelling. I felt my throat swell again and swallowed it down, that urge to cry. It made me weak, that's what father always said, and I needed to fight it.

I needed a distraction. I reached into my pocket and dug out a piece of black-glass I'd carried with me ever since Burcanon. It was simply a small tear-drop-shaped piece of oily black glass, at first glance.

The Void took many forms in our world. Creatures acting as manifestations of emotion, crystals and oil promising great power if used properly, or this simple glass. It was the most common element found at tears, acting as the building block for all that came through.

It was mostly disregarded. But with great effort, it could be manipulated, slightly. Most of the time people can manage to change its shape a little, maybe increase its size. I'd come across a book at my mum's when I was little, an ancient text detailing Gunray glass manipulation techniques. They were mostly a myth now, having disappeared hundreds of years ago, but their methods were fascinating. The glass itself, however, was mostly useless, as Theona liked to remind me.

I laid the droplet down on the bench and took a deep breath. I reached through the layer between our world and the Void's, that invisible screen where realities merged.

The Enlightened Quorum

It was like dipping into a tin bath filled with crushed ice, my nerves flaring with a sharp pain at every stab of cold across my fingertips. The shocks worked their way through my muscles, reaching for the base of my skull.

I pushed back, keeping my breathing slow and gradually gaining control of its energies. It was there, in that layer, where I could see the potential of the glass. It had a chaotic glee to it; in its raw state as unmoulded earth it was nothing, but it could be anything.

I shaped my hands like I was grabbing at silver strings and allowed that chaos into my body. It always sparked with fear when I tried to connect with it, but eventually, those maddening streams started to play.

I tugged at the air and with it started to pull a shard of the glass away, stretching it beyond its limits into a thin spike away from the tear drop. I kept doing it until the tangled mess started to look a little like hair.

It was like Oliver's matted mess, I guess. I was missing him that day like I did most days. I said a quick prayer to Mun, asking them to watch over my brother. I knew all too well what dealing with my father could be like.

I heard Sonya approaching long before she decided to try and sneak up on me. She had a clumsy step as she snapped a fallen twig on her way, her breath coming in short, excited gasps. Then, finally, her hands clapped on my shoulders.

"Boo!" she yelled, pleased with her effort.

I'd known it was coming but I still jumped somehow. Maybe that added to her satisfaction. I shook my head as she fell onto the bench, facing me.

"Knew you'd be here," she said, "you okay?"

I didn't know what to say. How do you respond to a question like that?

"I hate this place."

"I know," Sonya changed tact then, placing a gentle hand on my arm, "I'm sorry I wasn't there to help."

"I shouldn't need you all the time."

"It's okay to need someone," she chuckled then, "I heard you broke Marius's nose, he was complaining about it to Theona."

"He's such a prick," I spat a little more excess blood out.

"An entitled, pompous prick, agreed," she said, "someone was bound to do it eventually."

I nodded, then heard some loud voices from behind.

"Ah shit," Sonya swivelled on the bench, "this isn't good."

When I looked at the approaching group, I saw a bloodied Marius Detarn with his team, 'the Lords' following behind. A cabal of well-off kids who'd all fallen for the same lie and took their frustrations out on everyone else.

Or, in plainer language, a bunch of spoiled cunts.

"What do you want, rich boy?" Sonya stood up, "looks like she beat the blue out of your veins already, so just fuck off and call it a day."

"Makes sense...you Mutts...always stick together," Marius was clearly struggling to breathe through the tissue and binding on his nose, "not strong enough on your own."

"What'd you just call me?" Sonya's rage radiated off her in thick waves.

I went to grab her wrist.

"Don't, please."

She pulled her arm away and stepped towards them. Marius didn't back down, he stepped forward, almost bumping into her.

"Mutt."

"I didn't know Sonya would be here," one of his friends spoke up, "Marius, let's go."

"She's weak," he hissed back at them, "and Elena's a freak," he placed his hand on his belt, "we'd be doing the Sanctuary a favour."

"Yeah?" Sonya smiled, "you know, you walk around here like you own the place, but why do you think you're here? The rest of these pricks are rich, but you're the only one from a 'great' dynasty."

"My father sent me here to gain experience," Marius cocked his head, "where's yours? Dead out in the wastes like the rest of the Mutts you left behind?"

"Face it, Marius," Sonya leaned close to his ear then, speaking softly, "your daddy doesn't love you."

I couldn't help myself and laughed a little. Marius snarled, sizing us both up. Then he ripped his knife out and stabbed Sonya in the gut.

The Enlightened Quorum

It had happened so fast, I barely realised what had happened before she cried out in pain and his friends were shouting in confusion.

I think even Marius hadn't really realised what he had done until a moment after, his eyes widening with adrenaline.

Sonya didn't hesitate long enough for him to make his next decision. She grabbed his wrist and wrestled his hand away from the blade, punching him in the throat and chest as she did it. Marius fell to the ground in a trance, trying to cover his face as Sonya kept pounding at him like an enraged ape.

"Get off him!" a girl from the group, Greta Errant, slapped her hands together.

She started to make signs with her hands, thick milky Void energy spilling through her fingers. She started to pull a razor-thin string of purple light out of the air, bringing it back to slash Sonya across the back.

I rushed forward, feeling the cold course through my veins as I made a quick mark with my right hand. I grabbed the whip as it came down, my arm numb with an icy protective shield. I ripped it away from her, quickly slashing the ground to the side in a wide arc, setting it alight with lilac flames to block the others from intervening.

Greta growled as she cast again, infernal flame jetting towards me. My arm barely held up, and I was thrown back from the impact, my skin burning like I'd been out in the sun for hours. She leapt on me then, gripping my throat with her flaming fingers.

7

It was all too much. My skin screamed for the pain to finally stop, and I was quickly losing air. I felt like I was drowning all over again, feeling the panic set in as my breath was taken from me.

I felt the hateful bile build up inside me, the venomous words that were all I had left. I screeched at her.

It came out in an unintelligible howl, the words infused with white-hot energy. They barraged her face, peeling skin from one side as she turned to shield herself. But I couldn't stop. I rounded on her writhing on the ground, letting it all go. I unleashed black flame on her, setting her clothes ablaze and searing her flesh.

The others quickly came to aid her, and when I saw them using spells to stop the flames and cool the screaming girl down, I pulled back in horror.

The binding mark on my hand sparked and stung, cutting the stream short, but not my connection to the Void. It still pressurised my fingertips, fighting the binding. I gripped my wrist as the searing pain grew worse by the second. A soft hand enclosed mine, cooling gel oozing from its pores.

Theona must have heard the commotion and come to put a stop to it. I saw Theona's face staring down at me with the cold and laborious eyes of a scholar, not a soldier built for battle. The pain abated, but she still held my wrist tight.

She threw me to the ground and then stood over me. I saw her hand on the hilt of her blade, ready to cut my throat in an instant if I kept fighting. I was a rabid dog to her at that moment, and I couldn't look away.

Greta's wailing filled my ears like water, blocking everything out. Distantly, I heard Sonya saying something, but I couldn't focus. Everything was just so loud.

CHAPTER TWO

The hanging crimson light above the steel table didn't reveal much about the Red Room, but it showed just enough to know all its secrets at a glance. I think that was intentional, the Warden's order wanted their prisoners to know exactly what was in store for them.

The flakes that danced in the heavy air may have looked like dust at first, but I was sure that they were particles left behind by others who sat in the same chair as me. The metal surface of the table was scratched and warped, nail marks gripping the edge in ghostly fear.

The walls were clean, but their memories still haunted the place, imprints of bloodied hands barely visible in the scrubbed veneer. And at the edges of the room, were thick grates with the subtle splashing of the drains echoing from below. It certainly made the wet work easier to clear if you could simply let it wash away.

I wasn't bound by chains but the binding tattoo on my arm and interlacing my hand still singed my skin, reminding me that I could not fight even if I wanted to.

The door hissed as it was pushed open, the airtight seal letting only a little breath in as Theona entered

10

and quickly closed it again behind her. Her footsteps were muffled slightly by the clear barrier separating us. She sat down in front of me, opening a file.

Theona had trained my father during the last years of the God-King's reign and now sought to train me too. She was old in the sense that she had lived for a long time, but her face was barely marked by the passing of years. Despite being long past it, she still looked like a woman in her forties, with hair that seemingly shifted in tone every other week. My father had joked that she was a Phoenix-Blood, capable of reincarnating at will. But they were just stories.

She placed a blue shard next to her, positioning it slightly so that it lined up perfectly with the edge of the file. It was a listening stone. With training, It was entirely possible to mind-meld with a target and share thoughts and feelings directly, but the connection was always unstable and could cause major rifts, so infused stones were used as a circuit breaker in case of overload.

"Emotionality test," she said with a calmness I always found to be more sinister than soothing, "starting now."

I waited, staring at her blankly. I tried to stay as still as I could, knowing one wrong move would be the end of me.

"Who are you?"
"A soldier."
"Where are you from?"
"A forgotten place."
"Why are you here?"
"A chance."

11

"**A chance for what?**"

"A chance to serve."

"**Why is the sky blue?**"

"The sky is blue."

"**Repeat.**"

"The sky is blue."

"**Who do you serve?**"

"Eleynum."

"**Who rules Eleynum?**"

"The people."

"**Repeat.**"

"The people."

"**What do you desire?**"

"To serve."

"**Who do you serve?**"

"Eleynum."

"**Who do you serve? Connect.**"

"I serve the people."

"**What is your greatest weapon?**"

"My heart."

"**Repeat.**"

"My heart."

"**Who are you?**"

"A soldier."

"**What is your greatest weakness?**"

"My heart."

"**Will you ever love?**"

"Only if it serves."

"**What is your father's name?**"

"Kaurus, the Justice."

"**What is your mother's name?**"

I paused then. The answer was Mun, but it was strange. I rarely thought of my father during the baseline, after all, I barely knew him. But my mum had been a constant ever since I lost her, and yet, I couldn't see her. I tried to picture her, but her face was scratched from my memory. I looked down at the table, my leg starting to bounce as I tried to focus.

"What is your mother's name?"

I desperately searched the table for an answer. I knew it was there. Somewhere. The more I rifled through the stores of my mind, the more lost I felt. The faster I ran to her, the further away she got. I looked at Theona then. Not through her like I had before, but staring right into her eyes, begging for help. But I knew she wouldn't.

"Mun, the mother."

"Repeat."

"Mun, the mother."

Theona waited a long time, never letting me out from under her gaze. I felt the crushing weight of her judgement, suddenly deciding that she was going to finally kill me. Then she placed a hand on the listening stone.

"What do you think?" she said.

The stone wiggled and emitted a piercing set of scraping sounds. It was like someone had started strangling a small rodent as squeaking pricked away at the inside of my ears, slowly inserting a needle into the base of my skull.

"Yes, I agree," Theona then placed the stone inside of her toolkit again and closed the file, "it's over, you passed."

13

I let go of the stale breath I'd been holding throughout the exchange, letting my stomach finally settle.

"Why did you hesitate? About your mother?"

"I don't know," I cleared my throat.

"Do you remember her?"

I looked down at the floor.

"When we use the power gifted to us by the Fallen, you must be careful not to lose parts of yourself, lest you become a beast and put us all in danger," Theona's voice was flat and unyielding, "rest, recentre yourself, it'll come back with time."

"Can't you just tell me? I don't want to forget her."

"No, you must find yourself," she leaned forward, resting on her thighs, "I cannot have you fighting with dynastic heirs. I promised your father I would look out for you here. The Detarns may not give a fig what happens to Marius, but they do care about their name, and if they decide that you are worth the price there will be nothing I can do."

"He fucking stabbed Sonya," I looked away from her in embarrassment, "I'm sorry, but how are we the ones in trouble here?"

"Because you lost control," Theona's rage was like dark waters under the moon, mostly quiet, but easily pulled into devastating waves, "Marius will face his own punishment, but this is a test to ensure the safety of the Sanctuary."

"He always gets away with it because of his name," I slowed myself then, suddenly aware of how erratic I seemed, "I always have to be better. Even when people like him provoke me."

"How did he provoke you?"

"He was calling me a liar."

"About Burcanon? Why are you even telling people about it?"

"You don't believe me."

"I never said I didn't believe you, but no one else here will and it's dangerous."

"I know what I saw. And I won't let him push me around."

"They might push you, but don't give in. I can sense your power, power forged in the fires of pain, but if I were in command. I would prefer control and discipline over raw strength. This gift will destroy your enemies, but it can also annihilate your physical form and massacre those around you if used wildly. Remember that."

"Will Greta be okay?"

"A couple of days in the healing chambers will see her right, but had I not stopped you, I fear what you might have done. And what I would have had to do to rectify it. Do you understand?"

"Yes," I said, "I understand."

Theona gathered her things hastily and turned on her heel, then paused.

"It's wrong, by the way," she said.

"What is?"

"The baseline. When we ask what you are, the answer to give is 'a soldier', but you're less than that to them. You are a weapon, and weapons can be decommissioned when they are faulty," she sighed, "just, please be more careful."

"I'll try."

"It was a good punch. You've been practising," I caught her flash a brief, small smile, "Take a day or two to rest, then come and see me for training. The guards will take you back in a moment."

I watched her leave, knowing what was about to happen and I braced myself. Grates were pushed open at the corners of the ceiling and blue smoke started to hiss through the vents. I felt the hunger pangs kick in already, my stomach suddenly burning with emptiness. My limbs ached after a time, and I decided it wasn't worth fighting it. I let myself go limp, letting the hunger drain me completely.

CHAPTER THREE

B U R C A N O N.

\- \- \-

F O U R   Y E A R S   A G O.

It was the same dream again. The same uncanny nightmare that smothered me in my sleep every night. I always felt so disconnected from my past, like I was watching another version of myself at a distance while also reliving the pain of that day over and over. I looked at my small sweet face framed in hazy pictures and saw a stranger. What stared back at me was a dream.

But I watched in quiet horror as Sonya dragged me by the hand towards the drumming beat again, looking for a way through the crowd. I looked at her and I knew what was coming but had to watch myself giggle as I took her hand again and followed her into the jaws of death.

"Okay, get on," she knelt down, gesturing to her shoulders, "I can just about see."

I tried clambering on, and she buckled a little.

"I swear if you get any bigger, I'll need another person to help," she chuckled as she said it, bracing herself to stand.

I gave her a small kick in the side.

"Ow okay, I said if."

She lifted me above other heads in the crowd, and the band came into sight.

They were dressed in bright pastel shades that danced in the sunlight. The hand drummer had a pale pink sash wrapped around him, with the strings duo dressed in blue and green. The vocalist wore a deep purple dress, and he hummed rhythmically along with the instruments, occasionally bursting into deep warbling verses.

Two dancers accompanied them, one dressed in the dark purple of the Void, so black it sucked in all colours around it. The other was wrapped in brilliant gold, her skin even painted and glimmering in the light.

They circled each other, as the song told a tale of balance, of equilibrium. Of how our energies never died, but simply passed into their next stages, and always returned to the world eventually. The darkness kept trying to grab hold of and smother the light, but she kept spinning and flowing like sand through his fingers.

Every time the darkness seemed to catch her, a strip of clothing fell from each dancer, revealing opposite layers underneath. As the song continued, the dark slowly became the light, and the light faded into night.

As the singer's voice hummed the final verses, and the instruments slowly died until a slow drumbeat was all that remained, the dancers froze, staring at each other, before finally embracing.

We stepped into the small shop, the ceiling clearly too low for most as Sonya kept ducking the hanging ornaments.

For some reason, I expected an old woman, or even a wisened grey man, like something out of a fairy tale. But instead, it was a boy, maybe only a few years old than Sonya, who sat on the mat at the centre of the room.

He beckoned for us to approach, smiling softly as he did. His eyes were a golden brown and kind, warm even.

"Come, sit," he brushed some dust from the larger mat in front of him, "I have fresh tea if you would like some?"

He seemed to ask us both, but somehow, it felt like the question was directed at me. I wondered if Sonya had felt the same and if that was his way, or if he really was focused on me specifically.

"Yes please," she said, speaking for both of us. But he waited, looking at me.

"Would   you   like   some   too?" I wasn't sure how to react for a moment, then nodded, looking down. He then poured the reddish liquid into two mugs, passing them to us.

"It has calming properties, it will help with your premonitions, for that is why you have come."

It wasn't a question, or a confirming phrase, it was a command.

He first looked at Sonya, smiling.

"Tell me, what do you seek?"

"I feel..." Sonya paused, sipping the tea, "I feel lost, I'm not sure what I'm looking for at the moment."

"Our community has experienced a lot of turmoil of late, this is likely causing confusion and unbalance in your mind," he drank from his own mug, "We have a collective desire to control, and your lack of it is causing you to seek it where you can," he looked at me then, "You too are likely experiencing this."

"I'm not Matuni," I said.

"We are all connected to one another, or at least we should strive to be. When these connections are severed, we all suffer. You are in a place that should be your home but is made to feel it is not, that our peoples are different. It is natural for you both to feel lost at this time."

Sonya and I passed a glance then and smiled reassuringly at each other. The seer focused on her again.

"However, I sense you have experienced personal turmoil of late."

"Yes, my dad, he got called to one of the work camps a few weeks ago," she sighed, "I think he's okay, he writes and all. But I'm now helping my mum look after my siblings and I feel...I don't know."

"Did you have dreams outside of Burcanon?"

"I wanted to travel, maybe when the war was over. I don't know."

"You have been saddled with a great burden, and you are young. You feel trapped in a cycle you worry you will never escape."

"No, I don't feel trapped, I love them."

"Your love for them does not stop your feelings, and you should not allow them to be stopped. You need to confront your heart and know its limitations. That is the only way you will continue to love them unconditionally despite your sacrifice. If you deny yourself these emotions, you will only grow to resent them, and that will only poison the well of your family."

"I wanted to do so many things, and I feel like I might never see them now. I'm so angry all the time. It doesn't feel fair."

"It is not. Your father is caught in a conflict that is not his own, and you must direct your anger at the necessary causes of that pain, not your family or community."

"I understand. Thank you."

He nodded then and looked at me, "And you, my child?"

I couldn't help but shake my head and shrug a little.

"There is nothing you seek?"

I looked down at the swirling drink in my hand.

"I see the pain inside you. It radiates from you and warms my tea."

"I'm just sad my dad has to go fight in the war. That's all."

"There is more. The pain was there before he left. There's a hole inside you and you're not sure how to fill it."

"You don't know anything about me," I snapped at him, "war's sad, everyone says that."

"War, and the death and destruction it brings, is the biggest tragedy of them all," He said with a soft smile, "You are right, it is terribly sad."

"I'm sorry," I said, calming myself a little, "I shouted."

"As I said before, we must allow ourselves to feel it all, if we do not, then the Void will plant seeds of guilt and doubt within us, they will grow and twist our insides to fester hatred, the most destructive energy we know."

"I felt sad when he was home too," I blurted out, "he hates me."

"No, Elena," Sonya rubbed my back, "he loves you."

"Why do you think that?" the Seer asked.

"I felt it, whenever he was in the room with me," I dug my nails into the skin of my thighs, "he shouts at me all the time."

"Your father has been moulded into a shape that he does not fit," the Seer then stood suddenly, "he is of Eleynum, no?"

"Yeah," I felt like he was pouring through the cabinet of my mind then, "how did you know?"

"I see their hateful energies passing from him and gripping your throat, they will try and shape you in the same way if you allow them," he went to a nearby table, "they have destroyed so much of the world, but nothing more so than the very souls of their children. Their hopes and dreams are ash in the wind, their connection to the Beyond so utterly obliterated that they will never see its light again."

He turned back to me, his eyes glowing with a vicious fiery amber.

"Your father is a fool, and he will remain so until his dying day and one day your people will join together in one, singular, tormented scream as you stand atop your mountain of rotting flesh," his eyes dimmed then, and he looked down at the ground, "I am sorry, I am tired."

I think he saw then the horror on my face and felt shame, because he couldn't look at me anymore. I didn't understand then what he had meant, my knowledge of the world and Eleynum's place in it was so lacking it was pathetic. I understand now though, and I often dream of visiting that tent again and telling the Seer that I'm sorry for not listening earlier.

It doesn't matter now though. The tent's gone.

Sonya and I left holding hands, reassuring each other silently that everything was going to be alright. That the Seer's prophecy of doom was a mirage on the horizon, and that we would be strong enough to face it when the time came.

We were wrong.

Night had begun its descent on Burcanon and the rich tapestries of the stalls had begun to wind down, people preparing to call it a day and go home.

"I'd better go," Sonya said, letting go of my hand then, "I think Mum said she'd need help with the cooking later."

"That's okay, I should probably go too," I smiled then and felt my cheeks burn a little, goodbyes always felt so strange.

I then heard a faint, piercing buzzing, and I noticed Sonya wincing slightly too. We both looked up above us. Burcanon was mostly made up of simple stone tower-like homes surrounded by stalls and other trading posts, but recently that had begun to change.

Eleynum had moved soldiers into the city a year or so before, and with soldiers came the Inquisitorial Order. They had been placed there under the purview of protecting the city from the war between Eleynum and Adelaston over on the River Moirn.

The reality was that Burcanon sat so close to the Moirn and its natural resources, that both of the rival cities had placed a lot of value on controlling Burcanon and its Matuan inhabitants. Eleynum had just gotten there first.

So, the Order had begun placing strategically advantageous fixtures, taking advantage of the land. One of these had been sets of power relays bolted into the roofs of the structurally dubious buildings.

The machine's amber-gold cores were bound in wrought iron bars like ribs around a beating heart. They belched yellow smoke from their crowns made-up of multiple fume exhausts, and connecting each relay were thick wires that hummed with vicious voltage.

They were connected to machines out in the plains, tapping into Void deposits where strange oil poured into our world from fonts and could be used to power most of Eleynum's technology. And these relays acted as a direct line to the far-away city. Burcanon, I supposed, would see some of these benefits too one day.

But the relays were behaving strangely. They seemed to crackle even more aggressively than usual, their glow less a hazy lamp in the darkness, but now burning with the ferocity of small stars.

Then a shockwave burst from the relay above us, colliding with the others and bursting their internal networks. The golden lava spilt from their insides, instantly corrupting and melting away the weak stone blocks below.

Sonya grabbed me and pulled me back with her, hiding under a small balcony as liquid splashed onto the ground around us. The weeds and small flowers that had fought their way through the cracks in the cobblestone paths twisted in the molten fall and their green stems soon gushed with a hideous deep purple of rot, growing thorny vines that reached for greater heights. Their white petals turned a sickening blue and begged for blood.

"You okay?" Sonya asked, wheezing slightly.

I nodded, looking around to see if anyone was hurt. It seemed in the distance that some rubble had fallen onto a carriage and that maybe someone was trapped inside. But it seemed that maybe the worst was behind us.

Then one more relay sparked with an auditory crack. There was a bright light from afar and I followed it. I saw an unstable machine glowing white hot on a distant tower. It boomed again and soon became impossible to look at directly without burning a hole in your retina.

A beam of energy pierced the glass shell it had been held in, arcing out from the relay like a searing whip and slicing straight through a quarter of the city. It disintegrated anything it came into direct contact with and set ablaze everything in its wake.

It continued its stream up, striking the night sky and rending it with a violet scar. A tear, a giant tear all the way across the sky. I'd never seen or read about anything like it.

I wanted to speak but nothing felt satisfactory. I just stared in paralysed fear at the sheer speed at which the world had ended. Sonya had tears streaming down her face, and I realised when I followed her eyes that, of course, her home was in the direction of the flames. I grabbed her arm, words failing me again. I just stared at her shattered face, knowing that her life would never be the same again. A perpetual scream that leaves a scar of despair.

The machine had finally collapsed in on itself, the darkness of the evening enveloping us once again. But the wounded sky remained, pulsating with an ominous droning. The tear seemed to bulge and swell at the seams, and after an audible squelch, bloody rain came lashing down against a field afar. The red droplets were haunting the silver light of the moon. It was the coming of a great storm.

"Sonya, we have to go," I blurted out, "get to cover...something."

She didn't move for a moment, but then she nodded and turned to me.

"I have to check they're okay," she sniffed, wiping away her tears, "they might be okay."

I cupped her cheek and nodded, feeling my own eyes well at the thought of Mum and Oliver being anywhere near the blast. The fear would be overwhelming.

The tear kept shuddering with a visceral downpour until four giant hooked fingers punched through, grabbing the slit by the folds, and pulling it apart. Sonya and I watched together, unsure when to execute our escape plan.

A titanic shape fell from the sky then, easily dwarfing the city. It crumpled into a heap by the river, but it soon righted itself, and its form was so large that it blotted out the moon, casting only its vast silhouette.

The only feature I could make out was a set of burning pink eyes, hundreds of them, staring directly at us. It heaved with a rasping apnoea and slathered thick mucus from what I assumed to be a gargantuan maw.

It began screaming, short high-pitched screeches in rhythm, before balling up almost entirely. The pale blue flesh on its back started to crack and burst, holes like sewers opening across the mound. Then it squeezed violently, and thick sludge was propelled outward.

A huge globule gushed over the buildings on the far side of the street from us, instantly liquifying much of the supports and walls, causing them to collapse in on themselves.

Sonya and I ducked behind a cart and held onto each other in the gusts of sand that sliced into our flesh. She screamed at the top of her lungs, pulling me in tightly. I couldn't slow down, my breathing just kept getting worse and I soon found myself panting with fear and my lungs ceasing up.

But the initial shock was only the beginning, screaming erupted all around us as the panic sent people into madness. We stood from behind the cart to see a man writhing in the filth, his flesh melting away to reveal bones turning brown and crumbling away like dust. His face collapsed in on itself like a dune but still, he screamed in agony as he was reduced to nothing.

And he wasn't the only one. People all around us were wailing in pain, their loved ones trying to help but staying back from the steaming puddles.

I saw a woman reaching for the convulsing corpse of her child, desperately grabbing at pieces of him in some vain attempt to put him back together, but soon her own fingers melted into the pile too. She slowly died from both the physical pain ripping its way through her body, and the excruciating pain of losing her son that tore through her mind. She screeched and laughed all at once, rolling in the acid until she joined him.

"Sonya I have to go check on them," I said, "Mum, Oliver."

She just nodded and hugged me again.

"You be careful."

"You too," I said, running then.

The sight was too much for me, their faces had looked just like my mum and brother by the end of the horrific scene, and I needed to know they were okay.

I rushed as quickly as I could through the streets, having to take care not to step in any of the bile and avoid the less stable-looking buildings. Someone tried to grab me at one point, but I weaved away from them, continuing my sprint along the road.

Someone else then stood in my way and managed to stop me for a moment. I thrashed against his hands and screamed at him.

"Stop, child!" the man barked, pointing to a building, "it's dangerous!"

When I waited for a second and really studied what he was referring to, I saw that he was right. It was hanging by a thread of wooden beams, ready to collapse at any moment. At the top was a great mess of pulsing white sacs that seemed to only weigh it down further.

Then the mounds shuddered, and one bulbous spot seemed to pop open, and a spindly black shape emerged from it. Soon hundreds, maybe thousands did the same, and huge insectoid creatures buzzed outwards towards the crowd.

I escaped from the man and kept running, taking a different way to my home. I panted heavily as I pushed on, seeing the shapes fly into homes and drag people out by the arms, legs, their hair, wherever they could grab them, taking them towards their disgusting hive-mother.

As I turned left, I knew I only had a little further to go, recognising the street that led to mine by the red post box. It had been hit by a piece of rubble and had been snapped off its post. Things didn't seem so bad here, the buildings only sustaining minor damage.

"They're okay," I struggled to say aloud, smiling for a moment, "I'm coming."

Then I turned right to see the small square my home was located on, seeing the building almost flattened. Most of them here had been it seemed, but I homed in on my home alone. It was a smoking ruin, with several hideous bugs crawling over its roof.

Everything was tinged in cool tones then as instinct kicked in, and the little training I'd had in the Void was immediately forgotten. Its power overwhelmed me for the first of many times, and I immediately screamed at the bugs to get their attention.

But it did so much more. That same wave of energy that would mangle Greta years later in the Orchid Sanctuary shattered their frail bodies and obliterated them like flies under voltage.

I moved like water, gliding forward in fluid motions, barely thinking through what I was doing. I gave into the Void's influence further and landed on the roof, gripping an edge of debris to lift it with ease.

This tiny version of me, this child, she growled with a feral ferocity I'd have expected from a rabid dog. She broke through pieces of the roof with her little fists, tearing the rubble apart in her frantic search.

Then I found them, and the power of the Void was exsanguinated from an internal wound behind my sternum.

My mother was clutching my infant brother in her arms, protecting him from anything that had fallen on them. I reached out to touch her.

"Mum?" She was freezing, and when I held her arm, it went limp, releasing Oliver a little, "No," I sniffed, "Too late."

Oliver started to cry then, looking for me with his innocent eyes, unsure where he was. I scrambled forward and scooped him up in a tight hug, he was still so small then.

I sat there for a long while, humming him into a state of calm as best I could. The sounds of the fighting became an endless drone that could have put me to sleep. Instead, I watched my mum's lifeless body, willing for her to get up and finally leave Burcanon, but knowing that she never would.

Then I woke up and stared at the wall beside my bed, back in the Orchid Sanctuary again. The guilt, the shame, it always felt the same. I once again wondered if there was a way that I could somehow never sleep, but I knew that with all the training in the world, there would still be nights when I would have to face the nightmare again.

I stirred in my cot and watched the ceiling for a moment. A trickle of honeyed sunlight was finding its way through a distant curtain, dazzling a spider in the corner a little, its web's dew now glowing like prisms. The others would start waking up soon anyway, so why not have a couple hours off from sleep?

I watched the spider rub its face and legs, preparing itself for another day of survival. I wondered, then, if I was ready to face mine.

CHAPTER FOUR

I waited at Theona's door after knocking on the heavy wood twice. I'm sure it was only a few moments, but the silence meant that I suddenly became aware of my own breathing, noticing it move out of sync and counting down the seconds with my inhalations. Eventually, she yanked the door open and stood in the entryway to her office, waving for me to move as if I had kept her waiting.

'Office' may not have been an appropriate word for it. There was a desk, and neat skyscrapers of paperwork behind it, but there was also a cot to the side, and the floor was soft and spongey like a dojo. There was even a small table and some chairs to the left of the room, a half-melted candle at its centre. This was the epicentre of Theona-based activity. This was her home.

"Right," she said without a hint of flair or special inflexion, "grab a blade from over there."

"A sword?" I said, admiring the ornate golden hilts on the short, curved weapons.

"Yes," Theona rolled her sleeves up to her elbows before tying back her silver-speckled hair and pulling on some leather gloves, "they may seem simple compared to the weapons used by most today, but there are fundamentals that will lay the groundwork for whatever you choose."

"Okay," I picked one of the old blades up, admiring its lightweight, "are these yours?"

"My family's," Theona had already tightened the straps on her own sword, "my grandfather was a Knight-Paladin under the God-King."

"What happened to him?"

"Same thing that happened to the rest of them," Theona blew a strand of hair from her face when she'd finished stretching, "he died."

I unsheathed the sword to look at the carvings on the edge, and I found that I struggled to understand most of the runes. It was traditional Atrean, a dead language even before the fall of the God-King's empire. By the time I saw those runes, however, it was lost to history.

"Swordplay is as much a mental match as it is a physical one," Theona slowly circled me as she spoke, "you will need to learn to exercise patience, restraint, and cunning, in order to beat me."

"I can't beat you," I said, stepping away from her, "I have no idea what I'm doing."

"Then you will leave here beaten and bloody every day until you do," Theona's eyes were dark, her usual golden brown almost oily in the dim lighting, "you are not ready."

That first session was the worst. Both in skill and in the scars it left on me. Theona didn't hold back, smacking me with the flat of the blade at every chance she had, even slicing me with the edge on occasion when I made an especially egregious error.

Now that I look back, I realise that she never once went easy on me. She simply expected me to learn and catch up, and I did, for the most part. But the better I got, the deeper I went, focusing almost entirely on the sword.

It got to a stage where I barely slept, dreading the next day, knowing my wounds would open again, knowing that if I gave up and didn't go, she would simply come and find me, dragging me back to that dingy room. I stopped eating properly after a while. I felt so sick at every moment that it didn't seem to matter, and Theona explained that food and sleep were things I would go without some days anyway and so it was important to learn self-control now.

After some time, eventually, I managed to land a hit on her. It was a simple thing really, she'd blundered with a strike and I'd managed to sidestep with just enough time to glance a hit off of her waist. I found myself smiling like a child with something to hide, feeling immense pride and vindication wash over me.

Theona turned slowly, and I don't know why I'd been foolish enough to expect any form of praise, but her face was that of a mannequin. She stared at me for a second, unblinking, and then she punished me.

I remember feeling so confused at the moment. I thought that she might be impressed at my sudden improvement, and my commitment to her and the lessons. I thought, at the very least, that she might be frustrated but pleased.

Instead, it was as if I had insulted her and her entire line. She started by cleaving across my cheek with the blunted blade, still rending it open with a pain that knocked me flat. Then she was on me.

After some time, she finally relented, standing up to leave me on the ground, curled up like an infant.

"Never let your enemies have a moment's rest, foolish child," Theona hardly even looked at me, instead focusing on the blood staining her gloves, "you'll never be ready."

Maybe she was right. I hid my face from her, I couldn't let her see the tears in my eyes.

"Go, training's over for today."

I gathered my things in a hurry, still averting my gaze, and rushed from the room. I'd managed to find a small empty study room to finally cry alone and in shame, letting it all out so that I could face the others in the food hall.

"Sweet spirits in the sea," Sonya said like she was out of breath, "Elena, you look awful."

"Thanks for the words of encouragement," I groaned as I sat across from her, "you're as stunning as always…although, I did hit my head pretty hard."

"Seriously," she leaned forward across her broth, wincing slightly from the bandages on her stomach, "what's happening? I've barely seen you since the fight."

"Sorry."

"Look it's," Sonya exhaled, softening her tone, "it's fine, I've just been really worried about you. Something's up."

"It's training," I took a sip of water, the smell of the broth making my mouth water in the same unpleasant way it would before I was sick, "don't worry."

"With who? A fucking bear?"

"Theona."

"What?" Sonya put her spoon down, "this is too far, Elena. You need to back out."

"I can't," I had to push the bowl away from me, "she's helping me prepare for the Bid."

"It's like two years away," Sonya gingerly put a hand out to rest it on my wrist, "at this rate, you'll die before you even get there."

"I have to survive it. I have to."

"You will," Sonya sighed, "have you heard from them recently?"

"No, it's been months and no letters or anything," I looked around the room then, speaking quieter, "I need to make sure he's okay. Somehow."

"I'm sure they're just busy, your father sounds like he's got a lot to deal with and Oliver's probably at school a lot."

"Dad left me here so he could take care of his favourite kid," I kept scanning the room, "and that's what I'm afraid of. Oliver's sensitive."

"That's not true Elena. You need to eat something and get some rest."

"You don't get it, Sonya," I saw her then, standing at the edge of the hall. Theona was staring right at me, "I have to go."

I heard Sonya trying to call after me but I left the hall as quickly as I could without making my limp worse. I turned a corner and walked straight into an elderly man. His outer shell was flabby and well-fed, but underneath was a wall of stone that I bounced off of straight away.

I looked up and immediately caught my breath, bowing low to not stare.

"Where are you going in such a hurry child? Are you hurt?"

It was Donlan Calthern, lord commander of the Warden Order and the head of the Orchid Sanctuary. I'd only seen him when he was giving speeches at special assemblies or at a distance when he left the sanctuary.

He was an enigma to me. His features should have, objectively, been considered handsome and well-sculpted, but they seemed off. It was like I was looking at the pallid and decomposing flesh of a skin suit pulled over a much uglier man. His wormy lips pulled back in an unnatural smile.

"You must be Elena, correct?" he smiled when I backed further away, "I have known your father for years and I can see him in you," Calthern cocked his head, his nose wrinkling slightly, "and a great deal of your mother, too, I assume."

I'm not sure what gave it away, whether it was the tone of my skin or the hue of my eyes, but something about me screamed 'Matuni' to him and he was making it clear that it disgusted him. I tried to think of some way of responding but nothing sounded convincing, so I simply nodded instead and tried to take another step towards leaving the conversation.

"How are you finding it here at the Orchid Sanctuary, Elena?"

"I am learning a lot, sir," I said, "Theona – I mean, Inquisitor Faygalen, she's been giving me private lessons."

"And why is that?" his face had barely moved an inch for the entire conversation, "are you special somehow?"

My first instinct was to protect Theona, but then I realised that maybe this was a way out. Maybe Calthern could get word to my father, and he could come and get me if he knew what was going on.

"She felt that my skills were inadequate for the upcoming Bid," it was too late now, I had to try it, "she has been teaching me patience and self-discipline through sword work. It has been…challenging."

Calthern's gaze slid over the surface of my skin, marking the wounds that were out in the open with a marked detachment. Then he was suddenly beaming again.

"Excellent, I'll make sure that your father knows Theona is looking after you well," he then moved his right hand out from under his cloak to place it on my shoulder, "I wish you luck in the Bid."

The hand was typical of Wardens, but it was my first time seeing one so close. It was grey and loose as if the flesh was about to slough off of the skeletal fingers at any moment. It was covered in light blue bristles that seemed to shiver and sway as soon as they touched me.

I knew that with it, he could control my every action by activating the binding mark on my own hand. And he knew it. Whether he had any real intention of telling my father what was really going on was irrelevant. I was never leaving here either way.

"Your father, devoted to his work as he is, does not have the resources of some others here," he brushed my cheek with his thumb, the smell of rotten meat permeating the air, "But I will do what I can to help you get selected by an excellent party. Perhaps one day you can work for me alongside your father."

"Do I have to be an inquisitor?"

"Yes, child," he finally removed his hand then, "After all, what else could you do?"

Those were the words that had dogged me ever since Burcanon. What else could I do? This was my life now. I was doomed to be the instrument of a city I had never set foot in, a city whose values seemed to make less and less sense every day, a city doomed to collapse under the weight of its own greed, just like the seer said. Burcanon had proven that the machinery they used was dangerous, and there was even more of it in Eleynum than I could ever imagine.

I found my feelings crawling up the shredded walls of my throat again, threatening to spill out in a mutated mass. I nodded and quickly bowed to Calthern, making my way past him.

I was on auto-pilot for the journey, avoiding eye contact all the way and pushing my emotions back until

The Enlightened Quorum

I had finally reached the gardens. I made my way through a winding path through the fields of red buds, seeing the bench from a few months ago, where I had last lost control.

I let go then, expecting a torrent of tears and a horrible sickness in my stomach. But there was nothing. I focused on crying, willing myself to let it out now that I was finally alone. They never came. Instead, I kept coming back to thoughts of Greta, imagining melting her down into fats and acids, my rage finally untethered. And I felt nothing.

The bench was cold as I sunk into a pile on top of it, hunched over and resting on my knees. It was over then, I realised. I was done. If this was all my life was destined to be, then I didn't want it anymore. I wanted to simply fade away, never having existed in the first place.

But that was impossible. I was alive, every frayed thread in the patchwork of my body reminded me of that with the dull aching of my injuries. I was painfully aware then of every hair touching the back of my neck, of every itch from my healing cuts, every deep and staggered breath I took. The noise gnawed away at my sanity, driving me further towards the edge.

The sheer cliff face below seemed inviting then, every black-bladed edge offering a tempting bargain. I thought at first of jumping, but that seemed terrifying. Perhaps if I leaned forward? No, I would keep moving back. I realised that if I simply stopped trying to steady myself, the wind might make my decision for me. That seemed like a nice way to go.

As I scanned the rocks aimlessly looking for a solution to a problem that ultimately relied on me making one final decision, I saw a small nook. It was intriguing to me, I was sure I had never seen it before. It was a dark cave slightly concealed by the waterfalls.

It seemed like a good place to end it, and I figured that if I failed to reach it, I would die anyway. At least I would finally achieve something in my final moments.

The start of the climb was the most difficult part by far. I felt my insides lurch and twist as I slowly lowered myself off of the ledge and onto sharp footholds below. The wind was already nipping at my fingertips, threatening to throw me to my death. I waited a little moment, hoping my urge to be sick would pass soon.

Shimmying along the edges was easier than I thought. As long as I looked at where I was going and stayed focused on my balance, I found that the sharp rocks supported me fairly well. The difficulty was finding appropriate areas to descend towards the cave, as every time I did was fighting my insides as well as the burning cold that clung to my fingers.

Soon, offshoots of the falls were on me. Icy streams collided with my shoulder and back, freezing the joints in place, making every move a challenge. It was hard to breathe properly, my lungs were already tight from the temperature but every time I tried to inhale I would inevitably swallow some water.

But my greatest fear then was the rocks. I kept thinking I would lose my grip or slip on the wet stone, or that the sheer weight of the water would eventually drag me down with it. Every time I lost my footing for even a moment, I was starkly reminded of my mortality then and wondered how much I really wanted this.

"Please," I said to the universe at large, whatever gods might inhabit it, "please give me something."

I rested my forehead against the rocks, hearing nothing but the crushing water around me.

"I'm tired," I shouted, my lips quivering as I did, "I'm tired of losing!"

I felt my body's senses slowly fading, all feeling now obliterated.

"Fuck you," I was whimpering and defeated, "I deserve this."

I exhaled and closed my eyes. I knew then that no matter how much I wanted to die, I was too much of a coward to end it. And I hated myself even more for it. But it was acceptance, at least, and an acknowledgement that I was not going to die that day.

It was a matter of principle at that stage. An insistence that, no matter what, I would reach that cave. I cried out in pain as I started to move again, every part of my body screaming for me to stop.

I kept moving lower and eventually reached a lip of the cliff face above that blocked the waterfall. I wiped my eyes and took an unimpeached look around for the first time.

I hadn't realised how far I had come, how much I had already overcome in this foolish defiance. The cave was so close now, only a few more meters would see me there. And when I reached the opening, I placed a foot down on the solid ground for the first time in what had felt like hours. My leg buckled slightly, so I carefully manoeuvred myself inside, before collapsing onto the hard ground.

I lay there breathing like a fish out of water, my chest heaving and falling in heavy movements, gravel swayed just slightly by my panting.

I finally managed to push myself up into a sitting position, crossing my legs. The cave was small, and stone collapsed at the other end where there may have once been a tunnel. Now all that was left was the blank stone insides of the mountain, a dark room for a lonely mind.

I looked outside, past the waterfalls and out at the valley below. There were great streams below that filtered through vast forested veins in one huge body.

It would have been breath-taking, had I much left to give.

CHAPTER FIVE

Over the next couple of months, I found myself needing increasingly more time away from everyone, and the cave provided an excellent opportunity. The second time I attempted the climb was almost my last, but soon I found myself growing stronger and more confident.

I would spend hours sometimes just sitting in the centre of the rocky chamber, listening to the rushing waters and enveloping myself in their sounds. Soon I hardly noticed my own breathing and just allowed myself the time to reset.

I was doing much the same that day, pinching the corner of a letter until it started to crumble. I looked at the scrawling handwriting and the minor misspelling of the address and couldn't help but laugh. I wondered how he had gotten it to me.

Letters were an obstructive and irritating way of communicating, but there was no way of reaching beyond the confines of the Sanctuary with listening stones or other artefacts. So, this was the only way he knew how.

The Enlightened Quorum

I pressed my thumb under the seal, trying to carefully move along its seam but quickly tore the corner, ripping the rest off in frustration.

Dear Elena,

Sorry it took so long to write this. Dad kept promising to do it, but he's been really busy, so I just wrote it myself and got Took to send it. Sorry if there's any mistakes *_*

How is the Sanctuary? I'm so jealous, it's really boring here. Dad's sort of trying to teach me stuff but keeps saying I'm too young, so I just read a lot. I think I've read like hundreds of books, so I'm definitely beating you.

I miss you. When do you get to visit? You better show me some moves when you get home. Please write back.

Oliver

My brother was always the smart one, his writing was already miles ahead of mine at his age of eight. I couldn't help but read it several times, just taking in every moment I could with him.

I would have to consider my reply carefully. It was no secret that all communications going in and out of the Sanctuary were thoroughly investigated by the Wardens for security. I decided to focus on something else for the moment.

45

The Enlightened Quorum

I reached for the small pack I had come to take with me on each of these trips, unrolling it fully. There, among some other basic supplies such as food and water, was one of Theona's swords. It was a simple hand-me-down, one I suppose she didn't mind me losing or breaking somehow.

But I found it enchanting.

The training had only gotten harder. Theona grew increasingly cold and distant, hitting me harder and cutting me deeper each time. But I could see the peak ahead and I refused to give up when I had already lost so much of my time and spirit.

The short blades had become such a nauseating part of my existence, that my only way out was to dive headfirst into oblivion. I had to focus all my energy on studying her, learning from her, and embodying her. And I had done it.

The sword, as simple as its wooden handle and beaten steel blade was, had become an extension of myself. A foreign limb I had come to bond with. And Theona knew it. I saw the flashes of fear in her eyes as my deflections kept growing swifter, and my attacks deadlier. She knew that, with time, I would soon outclass her, and I had all the time in the world. And it scared her to death deep down. So she kept punishing me for it, hoping to destroy the essence of my soul, and I would never give her the satisfaction.

Then I heard a snapping branch.

It was a distinct crack that cut through the now barely perceptible splashing that rumbled in the background. Who, or what would even be close enough to make such a noise? I grabbed the sword up off of the ground and quietly unsheathed it, proceeding to stay low as I moved slowly towards the ledge.

There was a faint crack as a pebble hit a lower rock. Something was climbing the cliff, the same as I had. I leaned forward to peek at it.

It was a boy, probably around my age. The skin around his knuckles had grown a pale brown as he held himself securely in place, and a long braid hung below his shoulders. Matuni, maybe? What was he doing out here?

"Who are you?" I shouted down to him, "stay where you are for a minute."

He didn't seem shocked or even a little bit surprised by my presence. When he looked up at me, it was almost lazy and impatient, as if he had been waiting for me to say something.

"I don't want to stay here too long," he chuckled as he said it, "I'm feeling a little faint."

"Who are you?" I said again.

"I'm Bhari," he squinted slightly as the sun caught his face, "can we talk up there?"

"Why are you here?" I moved my sword into view, "the area's restricted."

"I saw you climbing in there and I just thought," he shook his head, "I thought, wow, I want to meet this person. So I climbed up."

"Up?" I looked past him, perplexed, "from down there?"

"Yeah," he slipped slightly again, "I'm falling here."

47

"Alright," I sighed and stood up, "come up. Do you need a hand?"

"A little," he said, his confidence waning, "thank you."

I grabbed his outstretched hand and helped pull him up onto the ledge. He immediately lay on his backpack, taking deep breaths.

"Unfortunately, didn't realise until, too late," he panted, "I hate heights."

"Don't know many who love 'em," I said, sitting on a nearby rock to rest the sword on my knees, "so, what were you doing in the valley?

"I'm uh, a writer," Bhari propped himself up straight, "I like poetry and stuff."

I nodded, smiling a little. I also liked poetry and stuff. I could imagine the peace of the valley helped clear a lot of unhelpful or unhealthy blocks. I thought about venturing down there someday.

"You Matua?" he said, using the Vhoran words for the community of clans, "You look like it."

"It's hard to answer," I shrugged, "my mum was, but she died," I went further, "at Burcanon."

"So, you're empire now," He nodded towards the sword, "Huh?"

"Oh, no," I looked down at it again, "This is training, I'm going on a trip soon and I have to be ready. My teacher says this is the best way."

"I don't see swords as much these days," Bhari then managed to place himself cross-legged, his breathing a little more regular now, "pigs tend to use clubs, fists," he looked out of the cave entrance then, "bit of light maiming is better than killing I guess."

"Which district are you from?" I think I already knew, but I couldn't assume.

"Darius."

The word hung there for a while. The Darius district had been the subject of a great deal of reports lately. The people there had become embroiled in all but all-out revolution, with tensions simmering to near boiling point, and crime growing at an almost unmanageable rate.

"Yeah, you're the only Matua I know that isn't from there," he stood up for a second, and I tightened my grip on the hilt, "why is that, by the way?"

Bhari then took a seat on a rock opposite me, gently taking his pack off of his shoulders. I couldn't tell him about the Sanctuary, how so many children from Burcanon and other war zones had been placed there to study their potential after exposure to the void.

"My father's an inquisitor," I said coldly, "he pulled some strings, I guess."

"So what is this place? You said your teacher was showing you some tricks?"

"It's a school for people with connections to," I paused, remembering that the Matuni used a different word for the Void, "The Beyond."

"Of course," his eyes became sharper then, "You're a piglet."

"I'm training to protect people," I gritted my teeth, "I'm sorry criminals are ruining it for the rest of you in Darius, but Inquisitors are meant to help."

"You don't even believe that, do you?" he scoffed, "you saw Burcanon, you know what their perversion of the spirit world is doing."

"They tell us it was the Matuni's perversions that caused that tear."

"And you believe them?"

"No," I snapped at him, "no, I know what I saw. I know they're lying about that."

"What did you see?" he leaned forward then, "Please, my brother died there."

"We all lost someone that day, Bhari," I took a deep breath, "it was their machines. Their magic. It caused the tear. I know what I saw."

"You know, if you shared that with others," he said, excitement spreading across his cheeks, "we could really turn the tides for the movement."

"Feel free to share it," I said, "I thought everyone knew."

"Why are you still here?" Bhari's voice was soft then, kind, "you seem so sad."

"I'm angry," I looked away from him then, focusing on pushing the tears back again, "my life was taken from me that day, and I've been trapped ever since. The Quorum's words are the only thing I've ever known, their laws the only ones I can recite," I swallowed mid-sentence, "I shouldn't complain. I have it easier than most."

"Well," Bhari thought about it for a second, "I would say we are simply different prisoners under the same heel."

He stood up again, slinging his pack across his shoulders.

"Come with me," he said with a smile, "You're worth more than this."

"You don't know me. You don't know that."

"Yes, I do."

"How?"

"Because everyone's worth more than this," he said, "Come with me."

"I can't."

"Why?"

"I have to do this, trip, I guess. It's the last step, and I have nothing else," I took a breath, "I feel like I can do more from within the Order than I could away from it."

He nodded, then spoke up again.

"Maybe this isn't the time. Maybe when you're back from your trip?"

I laughed at him then, looking away.

"Maybe."

"Maybe's good enough for me," Bhari made his way to the ledge, then looked back one last time, "I'll come visit again, it was very nice meeting you, Elena."

"Yes," I smirked, "it was nice meeting you too, Bhari. Don't fall."

"I'll try my best," he left with a wink, climbing back down nervously.

I found that I missed him a little even moments after he had left. Whatever the Sanctuary had in store for me, Bhari would be welcome company while I prepared.

CHAPTER SIX

"Come in," Theona's voice sounded through the door, "quickly now."

I pushed the door open and made my way inside, standing to attention once I'd closed it again. Theona was sat cross-legged at the centre of her office, a set of rolled fabrics and pouches in front of her.

"Come, sit," Theona said, smiling for maybe the first time in months.

I didn't want to question her niceness and potentially deal with the other side of her, so I sat down across from her wordlessly.

"Elena, there's no easy way to say any of this so I might as well get to it," she straightened her back a little and looked right at me, "the Bid is tomorrow. They are sending you out in groups of twelve to different locations in order to test you."

I felt my ribs twist and snap around my lungs, puncturing them with the shock. I had prepared for this moment for a long time, but it still felt like too much all at once. I opened my mouth to start forming questions, but Theona raised her hand.

"Please, we are not meant to be discussing this. I have been given secret orders that I must now relay to you, so please save your questions. Understood?"

"Yes, I understand."

"While everyone will be told that the mission you will be given is the test, this is false," she pulled a roll of paper from within her coat, "we have identified traitors amongst the recruits. Those in contact with terror groups and spies from other cities. They must all be eliminated."

Theona handed me the note.

"Inside you will find the name of your target."

I rolled the note open to read the name.

Greta Errant.

I looked back at her, and I couldn't help but feel utter contempt and disgust for her at that moment.

"This is a test of loyalty, to see who will betray their team," I put the note away, "it's sick."

"I can assure you, Elena, if Greta Errant returns from this mission alive then it will be safe to assume that you yourself are a traitor too and that will leave us no choice," Theona's face was blank, "we will be forced to eliminate you, and your family."

"What?" I yelled on impulse, "that's completely insane."

"The Sanctuary has already been compromised, if we allow this rot to fester anymore then all of Eleynum will be under threat. Do you remember your oath? You are sworn to the people of Eleynum."

"But you know my father-"

"His reputation will be tarnished by your failure. He will no longer be trusted among his peers."

"I can't kill Greta."

"You don't have to," Theona sighed with frustration, "But you now know the consequences if you do not. Do not fail, if not for your sake then for your brother's," she cracked then, "I don't want to lose you, child. I've come to care for you as if you were my own daughter. Please come back safe, Elena, and make sure that Greta does not. No matter what."

"You don't give a fuck about me," I tightened my grip on my knees, "you hate me."

"I pushed you, to achieve your potential," Theona looked lost then, "I pushed you too hard. I did the same with your father, and he ordered me to give you the same training. I regret it deeply."

"Father...father told you to do that?"

"Yes," she sighed, "you know his way. He believed that this was the only way to get you to where you needed to be for the bid. But my methods destroyed him," Theona managed to stomach looking me in the eyes again, "truthfully, he is my greatest failure. And I do not wish to see the same happen to you. You must do this."

"I can't kill her."

"This is your true test," she said, "will you comply?"

"Yes," I still didn't believe the test was real, but I had no choice but to agree.

"Say it again."

"Yes, Inquisitor," I said, louder.

Theona smiled sweetly and then went to unroll a pack in front of her, displaying a wide range of tools and weaponry.

"You will now pick your hunting gear, and choose wisely, for you will be expected to use it on your mission."

I saw many typical items, such as special gloves designed to pulverise, rip, and tear flesh, a barbed whip, hatchets, and knives of all kinds. There were even firearms, though not typically used against Void creatures due to their regenerative abilities, they were still useful in certain encounters. I also noticed an assortment of traps, bombs, and defensive mechanisms.

A part of me almost didn't select the old sword, just to spite Theona one last time. However, it really did feel like the best option for me and so I went for it, but Theona stopped my hand.

"No, not that one," she said, reaching into yet another bag, "I was going to wait until after to give this to you, but I want you to be safe, so you can have it now."

She handed me a razor thin scabbard and hilt as black as soot. It was a little longer than the short swords she had been teaching me with, but it was still incredibly light, almost weightless. I grabbed the hilt and slowly unsheathed a blade like paper and oily in tone. Even lightly touching the edge stung.

"That's Crystalarian," Theona said, "cut from Void stones. That's about as sharp as it gets," She lightly touched my wrist, "Elena, you've done very well with your training, but you are still a long way from being ready. Right now, you are fire, uncaged and wild. But you must become like water, always moving, always changing, always...adapting. That is your true purpose. And this blade will serve you well if you can learn that."

"It's amazing," I said, sliding it back into the scabbard, "thank you, Theona."

"Do not thank me yet," she looked down, "this will be hard, but by the end, perhaps a Great Dynasty will choose you and you will have a much easier life. I only hope my training has been sufficient."

I didn't know what to say then, I eventually just smiled and put the sword away to continue looking over the rest of the equipment.

Tomorrow would be the beginning of the end.

"Sonya," I hissed in her ear with venom, seeing as this was my third attempt to rouse her, "hey!"

Her eyelids tore open with an audible smack and the whites of her eyes glistened for a grain of time's sands, before she lunged forward while she slid a knife silently from its sheathe. Sonya blinked a few times, arching her back like a cat, focusing on me.

"Elena?" Her shoulders dropped a little and she left the knife under her bed, "what time is it?"

"Mid morning?" I tried to smile as if it was funny but I knew from the narrowing of Sonya's eyes that it really wasn't, "sorry, I needed to tell you something."

"Bridge?"

The bridge in question was located in the Old Gardens, a section of the sanctuary where the flora had been blighted by Mania long ago when the God King had still used it as a personal palace. It had since been abandoned, the soil too firm and corrupted to grow much at all other than a few resilient weeds that had begun to take on the sickly lilacs of the Void. The small decorative canal that the bridge had once crowned had been blocked and sealed, the gates to the gardens locked with a basic gate that had rusted away at one stage. No one had bothered to replace it. The Old Gardens were a reminder.

We nestled into the dent we'd hewn away at over the years with the smalls of our backs. The ground fizzed and hissed at us as it broke away in greenish chunks. It was probably unsafe, but Sonya didn't care, and neither did I, I suppose.

"Fuck." Sonya let her head fall lightly against the earthy pillow behind her, breathing in the silence between us after I had explained what Theona told me.

"Yeah."

We listened in on the conversations of insects, pretending we understood the whistles and clicks as well as we understood the task ahead of us. It was strange to think what manner of creature could survive the volcanic soil, and whether I would even recognise them after their exposure. Mania had a way of twisting and breaking the rules we humans set out for the natural world and the shapes it should take.

"Well, I knew this was a sign."

Sonya dug into the inside pocket of her coat, pulling a thin silver roll from within. It crinkled a bit as she held it up.

"What is it?" I leaned in a touch, just to get a better look, and realised it smelled like acidic herbs and dead wood.

"Widow Wind," Sonya smirked then, twizzling it in her fingers, "one of the rich kids got it from somewhere, didn't like it, so I asked for it."

I tried to shake my head like a stern and disapproving prefect, but I had to in order to hide my smile. She laughed then and I let the mask slip too.

"We'd get in trouble."

"Ooh," Sonya bunched her hands into fists, mockingly rubbing tears of air away, "we wouldn't want to get in trouble."

"Yeah yeah," I grabbed her wrist and pulled it towards me, prying her fingers open, "I didn't say I wouldn't do it."

"That's what I like to hear."

I would hope that at this stage, it would seem obvious that the sanctuary didn't allow us to have matches or lighters and so on. The argument being that tools like this would make escapes far easier. A moot point, ultimately, as fire was a fairly common manifestation of the Void, but the restrictions seemed more about the potential inspiration said tools might give as opposed to their usefulness. And the binding marks kept our power in check well enough.

However, no one was around, so conjuring a small flame to light the end of the rolled paper was simple enough. The smoke was sour and harsh on the back of my throat, the first few attempts striking involuntary coughs out of me.

"Open your mouth a little."

"What?" I managed between two small hacks.

"Like at the corners," she pointed to the ends of her lips, "just take a bit of normal air in too."

As much as I felt like the whole world was watching me look a fool while doing drugs for the first time, I had to begrudgingly admit that Sonya was right. I found I could inhale the burning air and hold it for a moment before letting it go again, and felt my fingertips buzzing after a while.

I felt very light, which was strange because as time passed my legs seemed to weigh more and more every time I tried to shift them to get the blood flowing again. But it was as if my mind had finally taken a breather, sitting on the benches a moment and having some water. It was usually a constant nagging hatred that seemed to whittle away at the stem of my brain, and while I could still hear that voice rattling against its cage, I found I could throw a sheet over it and muffle its screams.

When we'd finished the Widow Wind, we didn't say all that much at first. We didn't need to, not really, but there came a time where it seemed absurd not to confront it.

"So, who's name did you get?" Sonya was resting her head in my lap, stripping a string of dead grass in her fingers.

"Should I tell you? I don't want to think about hurting someone."

"Sounds like you got me, then."

"No," I laughed but I knew that she had no reason to trust that, "I swear. It's Greta."

"Gods."

"Yeah."

"You don't think it's real though?"

"No, I think it's a test."

"But what if someone takes it seriously?" Sonya turned to look at me, suddenly tired and sad like a grieving widow, "you have to take that part seriously, at least."

"You're right," I couldn't hold her stare, "I'll be careful. And I'll look out for you."

"I don't need you to look out for me."

"I know I just," I swallowed, "I can't lose you too."

"Kaurus, Elena, I could die tonight," she rolled her eyes, "we did just take illegal drugs after-all."

We made the effort to recognise it as funny, despite it all. But there was a deflation in the inflexion of the giggles, a wind escaping the folds of our throats.

"Do you ever think about, like," I tried to think through my words but the processes were sluggish.

"Like?"

"I'm getting there," I leant back against the crevice as my back twinged from idleness, "I guess like, the point of it."

"The point of what?"

"I don't know, life, I guess."

"Okay, you're having an existential crisis," Sonya lifted herself into a lazy sitting position, "now I'm aware that these are fairly regular for people in our line of work but it's only been a few minutes."

"No, I mean," I looked down to hide my face, "you just said you could die tonight. We could both die tomorrow. They say we're maybe not even the only ones, that maybe this is just one planet of an uncountable amount with people on it."

"And it makes you feel small."

"Yes!" I clapped my hands over my mouth to capture the shout too late, "shit."

"So, if we're so small, so meaningless, what's the point? Is that what you're saying?"

"I think so," I shifted in place, "I just feel like, if tonight's the last night I might see you, then I don't really know what the point is in seeing tomorrow at all. It'll be too painful."

"What are you saying, Elena?"

I started but I lost the words in the reeds along the way. The ones I gathered back up felt wrong as soon as I started saying them.

"If it could happen tomorrow, then why not tonight?"

"Nah."

I opened my eyes again and saw that Sonya was now staring at the ground with her lips closed tight.

"I'm sorry, let's talk about something else."

"Nah," she said again, "fuck that. If we could die at any minute then what's the point in doing it now? We should treat tonight like it's the last."

"What?"

"Fuck it, if it could all be over tomorrow then let's take every second and enjoy every fucking bit of it."

"Yeah," I sat up straight and felt, and I mean really felt, my heart beating against my chest, "I like that."

"Me too," Sonya smiled at me, her fury dying down, "so don't worry about me. Focus on surviving, and I'll do the same. And if one or neither of us come back, then we move on. Otherwise, we'll be together again, and then we'll keep going like that until the time comes."

I glanced at her mouth before admonishing myself and moving back to her eyes. My mouth was dry then, and I placed a tentative hand on her leg, a maelstrom of surprise and terror moving through me as I found her taking it.

Sonya leaned towards me, and our breathing synced up in its short and nervous gasps before we kissed under the light of a waning moon like it was the last chance we'd ever get.

My fingers didn't feel quite as electric as they had on the Widow Wind, but Sonya's fingers still sent shockwaves through mine as we walked back towards the bunkhouse. She glanced at me for a moment and grinned, speeding up her gait suddenly to outrun me.

"Wait," I laughed at her as she stumbled a little, "don't leave me here!"

"Oh what? You gonna miss me already?" Sonya giggled as she turned to run fully, but the thunderous gunshots silenced her.

I felt my heart leap away from me as I made half a move to duck, watching Sonya do the same as the sounds rattled the corrugated wall beside us. It was a short, deadly burst, and it had come from the West where the gardens were located. Sonya and I felt for each other's warmth just to check we were both okay. She was shuddering as if she'd been sat in the cold for a few hours, but that checked out, so I thought she was fine.

"We need to go," Sonya said, yanking me by the wrist towards the bunkhouse entrance, "before anyone sees us."

"It's too late for that, child," A familiar, deadly soft voice whispered to us.

Theona had clearly seen us from afar but I'd had no idea she was there, her presence jolting us both almost as much as the shots had. I stood in front of Sonya.

"Come with me."

Theona was resting her fingers on the hilt of her bade, a silent request not to make the night bloodier than it had been already. We obeyed.

She took us to the mess hall, where Donlan Calthern was sat across one of the benches, attempting to look relaxed and approachable, but really looking like a mannequin in a haunted house set up to scare children. He was chewing at an apple with great care, and I realised then that his gums were bleeding as he did so.

He didn't acknowledge us at first. We stood there for a while before Theona clamped down on our opposing shoulders, forcing us to kneel a few metres away from his boots. Then, as if he'd been unplugged and plugged back in again, he threw the apple in a bin at the end of the long table and brushed his hands.

"So girls, sneaking out at night is it?"

"I caught them on their way back from the Old Gardens," Theona hissed.

I watched the older man study his grotesquely rotten hand, seemingly admiring its sluggish sheen. He surprised me, surprised all three of us, I think, with a shrug.

"It's the night before the bid, they're allowed to get a bit rattled."

"Sir, the girl needs discipline."

"Yes," Calthern snapped at Theona, and I somehow heard her fold in on herself, "I'm getting to that."

"We're really sorry sir," Sonya said hoarsely.

"I know you are, but unfortunately an example must be set," He stood up and stalked over to us on silent steps, "I am not unreasonable, however. I will need to split you up."

As much as we both wanted to protest, we knew that there was likely no other way. We had gotten lucky that night.

"I think you both have great skills to offer the order, you especially Elena," Calthern peeled his teeth then, "just like your father, in many respects. I'd like you to come work for me after the bid, you'd be well looked after, and you'd be carrying out the most important work in the city. What do you think?"

I couldn't think of anything worse in that moment. But I selfishly considered the option anyway.

It made sense in the ways it should have. I would have some level of power and privilege that I could maybe do something good with it, even if it was just to look after Oliver and Sonya.

But I knew that that was a lie. The core instinct at that moment was survival, and I knew that working with Catlhern would give me a few more years at least. If I wanted it to.

"Sorry sir," I forced out of my mouth, "I think maybe I'm not the right person for that."

"Well, I have a way of getting what I want," Calthern grinned again and flexed his glistening fingers, "eventually."

The doors were thrown open then and rain splattered the soldiers who had barged them apart. They wore long waterproof ponchos as they carried in a sack between them. I watched the water drip from it and leave a trail behind, but as their shadows lifted away from the spatters, I realised they had a muddy brown tinge.

The soldiers dropped the body bag on the ground next to Calthern and a small hand flopped onto the wooden floor with a wet slap, a gaping hole just below the wrist spilling even more fluid into the seams between the boards.

"Sorry sir," one of the sanctuary guards pushed out through panting breaths, "she was trying to escape."

"So you brought a body to a mess hall where children will eat the next day?" Calthern didn't look at his subordinates, still focused on me and Sonya, "shame on you."

"I thought you'd wanna see it straight away, sorry again."

Donlan Calthern sighed and shrugged again, as if he was some kind of clerk who'd received ten times the paper clips he needed, instead of a man whose bread and butter was death and decay.

"You see, girl? This is the price of dissent."

CHAPTER SEVEN

We'd been briefed the night before. A Void oil outpost near the Burcanon wastes had gone dark, all the signal lights irregular and the messages strange. A group of us, all recruits, had been sent to investigate.

The train's tracks must have been bent again because the bench, our side this time, threatened to tip us into the row of recruits opposite were it not for the tight harnesses strapping us in.

The twat across from me, Frendon, made his caustic whooping noises again, finding the whole thing amusing and assuming the rest of us did too. He refused to wear his padded hood, assessing that 'they were useless anyway', treating us to the sight of his bare grin every time he made an attempt at humour.

Annoyingly, he was right. The netted covering was similar in design to what a beekeeper might wear, both aesthetically, and in the fact that it offered about as much protection from toxic fumes.

But I didn't keep mine on for that. I knew that the air here was slowly killing me. It was to protect my skin from the acidic flecks that flurried in the hot gusts, the flakes that would start off feeling like pin-pricks, but in storms would peel a prime cut of your face off and melt it like butter.

Of course, Frendon didn't know any of this. It was only his first day out here, being a couple years younger than the rest of us. And if he wasn't careful, it could be his last. The cramped metal unit came to a squealing halt before the doors leading out the back were pulled open.

"Everyone out," said the Warden, Barns, a couple of Constructs standing by either side of him, "We've got a long day today."

The Constructs were beings of wrought iron and wood, empowered by batteries using Void energies. They stood, unfeeling, uncompromised, in the dust that barraged their cold flesh, painted in the blue shades of the Detarn dynasty. They weren't much use for complex tasks but were excellent at simple, heavy labour.

And the storms were brewing that day. As always in the wastes, the sky was etched with faint purple veins lining the yellowed clouds, flashes of crackling reds lighting their bloated corpses at random intervals.

The trees around us swayed with their clawed limbs beckoning us further in, leaves splattered in wine and sickly pastels. I stepped off the ramp and onto the pale blue dust, fastening the straps on my hood as it puffed into the air.

"Right, line up," Barns barked, "Frendon, get that hood on, I'll not have my pay docked to cover your funeral."

Frendon's smile had been smeared off by the sight of his new workplace. He was twelve, and he'd never seen anything like this.

"We've found the broken drill," the winds battered my ears and made it hard to hear Barns clearly, "we're to connect the pipeline to the South-West Quadrant and start it flowing back to the capital. Some of you…" he was lost to the howling, "…of operations. The rest are on the pipeline. Don't be a pain in the arse, watch each other's backs, and let's get this done quick."

He started splitting us into two groups. I could see another two tanks arriving, the engines chugging and shaking their frames as they dragged trailers of materials behind them. I went with Frendon, Marius, and a few others I'd gotten to know, to the train bringing the huge pipes and connectors with it.

It took hours to unload them, ears battered by horrific squeaks and the grinding of metal. We soon set off into the depths of the forest. The trees were encased in pallid hardened flesh, grey and quivering in the intense light, cast almost blue by the infected clouds.

The forests of the wastes seemed to breathe like ragged lungs, heaving the winds at us, and then sucking us further in. The air was heavy here, and with the hoods, it was like I was slowly drowning. The ground was getting muddier the further we got in, clasping around our ankles. Soon though, up ahead, I could see the font.

It was in a hole in the ground, acrid fumes coming off it in long whisps. At the bottom, forced into a kneeling position, was the source. A person hunched over and spilt the thick blue liquid from their gaping mouth. Was it a person? Didn't matter, I supposed. I couldn't be sure anyway. Wiry silver strands had torn through its body, light pulsing along its ghostly flesh like moonlit ripples in the sea.

We took the giant frame of the refinery out piece by piece, laying them out on the ground around the hole, before setting hooks in place to rappel down. The pure Void, like this, was not immediately dangerous, but it sank into your pores and sapped your essences slowly. Latent emotionality and your vitality would drain into the pool until you become a husk, a Stragan.

So, we took it in turns. Four at a time, for only twenty minutes, before taking a break to work on the pipes. Those of us who went down would get the pumps in place.

I sank into the oil and felt it ooze against me, squeezing the air out of me. It was warm, like a bath of melted fudge. I'd done this enough to know when I'd been in there too long, but it was different for everybody.

Frendon seemed to go to sleep almost as soon as he dropped in, his movements sluggish, his breath heavy. I watched him as I worked, hearing his ragged panting through the hood, now firmly pulled up.

Personally, I heard singing. A distant melody that I could never place. Simple, mostly humming, carried faintly on the wind. I think I knew what, or who, it was meant to be. But I had to remind myself that she was gone and that the Void always lied.

Frendon slipped deep into the sludge, flapping limply as he did. As much as he frustrated me, he was a kid, and I wasn't going to let him go under. I waded through, the others stopping their work and calling up to the rest of the team. I watched him fall beneath the layer of skin that had formed on the top of the coagulated pool, hands punching through.

I reached down and grabbed what I could of him, dragging the boy up. Frendon was trying to scream but his body wasn't obeying him anymore as if he'd fallen into sleep paralysis. I heard his vocal cords tearing against themselves, a hushed breath exploding out through the netting.

The others had gotten to us now, helping to support his weight. We hurried to the ropes and pulled him out of the depths, ooze sloughing off him as he went.

"The rest of you should get out too."

I nodded and we climbed the craggy surface. As I neared the top, her singing had grown faint, and once again, I lost her.

I saw Frendon writhing like a dog having a bad dream, but still no words. The best we could do was calm him down, and stop him from hurting himself. After what felt like an hour, his heart gave out, and he lay still.

"Alright," Marius said, "time of death?"

"15:43," I said, checking my watch.

"Recorded," he replied, "let's do it."

Marius grabbed Frendon's wrists and clasped them together above his head, I did the same with his legs, and the two of us lifted him off the ground. We swayed the dead boy back and forth a few times, before finally throwing him back into the font, where his body sank slowly into the vat.

71

He'd be slowly consumed by it eventually, his body reanimating temporarily with an urge to kill and devour, and then he would dissolve into the Void forever. I regretted how I'd seen him before and felt a retroactive guilt for dismissing him. It was unlikely that anyone would remember him after that day, and that seemed terribly final.

It took a few hours to finish repairing the machinery, but eventually, we were able to finish the job. Even if we were all a bit sick after. The next part of the mission was finding the outpost. It didn't take long. Marius had made a good point that we could just follow the pipelines back. Soon, we saw the outpost walls in the distance.

But as simple as the journey was in the sense that we were more or less following a straight line, the toll of the wastes was a different story. The air was starting to burn the back of my throat at that stage, and I wasn't the only one wheezing by the time the outposts gates became clear.

I'd been surprised by the vegetation of Burcanon, however. The term 'wastes', in my mind's eye, generated images of dusty plains dotted with the skulls of inhabitants past. But the Cavlan forests that, when I was a child, had been a remote grove before, were now starting to creep all way up to the old walls of Burcanon and even towards the pipeline itself.

The trees had once been some of the tallest in the area with a deep red wood that had become famous among traders. When I saw them that day, however, they reminded me of the twisted black legs of the insects that had invaded the city all those years ago. They were covered in thorny vines that tangled amongst themselves to create a death trap for any birds that ventured too close.

All the more eery were the bone-white leaves that now covered the forest, leaking iridescent dew that seemed to shift and squirm in the sun. I heard a faint screaming coming from those trees and hoped I would never have to venture into them.

We got to the gate and Marius stepped up to shout for a guard, or anyone keeping watch. Nothing happened.

"We need to get in somehow," Jack said, "do we blow it? Climb over?"

We all looked around at each other. No one had been put in charge, and most were already shaken by the oil fields. Soon, the conversation descended into chaos. Marius, to give him some credit, was trying to take control, but he was struggling.

Eventually, a figure appeared at the wall, slouching and swaying like a drunk. His hand lifted into the air and clumsily waved at us.

"We're from the Order," Marius shouted, waiting for a response, "we were asked to investigate?"

He waited again. The guard barely moved an inch, and my first thought was that there wasn't anyone there at all, but the shape seemed to sway a little. The figure jerked its head in Marius's direction.

"Hello!" it said, flatly.

"Hello," Marius laughed for some reason, then cleared his throat, "we need to come in."

Another pause.

"Yes!"

It moved towards what I assumed to be the gate switch, but the movement was more of a soft glide than an awkward stumble.

The gates groaned like Oliver waking from a deep sleep, the joints squeaking from dust clogging them over time. They'd been dormant a long time.

"Come in!" the watcher said.

We moved through the archway slowly, keeping our hands on our weapons. I lay my fingers over the sword on my belt, knowing I could flick it free in an instant.

It was a small outpost, granted, but it still housed maybe a few thousand, so the edible silence hit us all immediately. I could feel everyone's energy rising, the collective shift into our connection with the Void. People were standing on their walkways and balconies, but no one moved much. Even machinery and animals, commonplace in these outposts, had seemingly been silenced.

"I don't like this."

"Yeah, there's something wrong."

"Quiet," Marius was a pale, slimy boy at the best of times, but his pallid forehead glistened at that moment, "just be ready for anything."

"Yeah, excellent plan," I snapped, "we need to split into two groups and move those people up there. They're watching us."

"They're just scared."

"Yeah, but of what?"

As we edged up the slope, watching the figures above us, I peered over into a ditch. The pipe running through it was oozing luminescent blue liquid.

"Marius, there's oil in the water supply," I said, watching the shape of an old woman on a nearby balcony, "look."

"How do you know that's not a pipeline?"

"Why would they store any of that near the houses, you idiot?"

A man stepped awkwardly out of his home, taking large deliberate steps to block our path. His face drooped on one side, and his glassy eyes barely moved, except when he made a concerted effort to blink, where they would roll back into place afterwards.

"Hello!" his jaw flapped wildly as he said it, never truly forming the sounds with his tongue and lips.

"Look we're going to need to see the Quartermaster, where is he?"

The stranger looked at Marius, turning his whole torso to look at him properly. Then watched, unblinking.

"Come in!"

"No, we're in charge now, where is he?"

"Come in!" the man stumbled forward, his hand lifting suddenly.

"Hey back off," Marius drew his pistol, "get back inside."

The shambling didn't stop, and as he continued, I realised his feet barely made an indentation in the soft mud, his ankles crushing slightly under the weight of his body. He was like a deflated balloon being blown towards us by a malevolent wind.

"I said get back!" Marius pushed the man over, sending him flying much further than he should have.

He fell into the dirt without a sound, except for the slight wheezing of air leaving his lungs like a popped balloon. And he deflated, his face flattening as lilac ooze escaped his orifices.

"What the fuck?"

Then the rest of them lunged over the railings they watched from, lurching towards us like floppy dolls.

"Spread out!" someone cried, but it was too late.

They came streaming from the houses in thick, gelatinous waves, swimming towards us with knives and tools in hand. I drew my blade and watched Jack get dragged into a crowd. Marius looked at him for a second before scrambling to get away from the onslaught.

They swung with discordant motions, stabbing so furiously they sliced each other apart more often than they did Jack, and fell into dismantled piles around him. But no one could survive a frenzy like that, he was cut to ribbons so quickly I barely had time to move back myself.

It was chaos. Any semblance of a plan had been lost, and the goal became clear: Run, and survive. The group splintered almost immediately, small groups going their own ways. A few of us managed to move down an alley, even more having sacks of flesh dropped on them from above.

There was a wall that looked scalable, getting us to the rooftops, but they soon came pouring from access doors nearby as well.

"We won't make it, we have to fight!"

We set up a corridor as best we could, gunners firing volleys as the rest of us kept them back with our blades. It started strong, but soon the waves were getting thicker and we knew we couldn't keep it up too long.

"It's getting worse," Greta cried as she kept laying down fire, "we have to go!"

Marius looked terrified then, and I realised that any authority he'd held up until then was slipping away from him in an instant. I grabbed him by the arm to snap him out of it.

"This way," I shouted, turning back to a set of stairs leading to a flat above us.

We managed to bar the doors and seal them with magic, but we all knew it wouldn't hold forever. The horde kept throwing themselves against it, their sheer mass slowly growing.

"Maybe we should surrender?" Greta said, pacing back and forth.

"Yeah, I don't think they're negotiating," Marius screamed at her, "I won't go down without a fight."

"I respect it," I said, "really, I do. But we've lost."

"If you want to cut your wrists in that barn over there you go ahead," Marius growled, lopping a shambling citizen in half, "I'm not giving up."

"We can do the right thing before we die," I yelled back, pulling my sword back from a sack's stomach, "we can clear this place off the map."

"The bindings."

"If we push together maybe?"

"Maybe," he sighed, "worth a shot I guess."

He took my hands, and together, for the first time, we connected. Our energies collided into a swirling tornado, dark flame catching in the winds around us.

"I can't believe I'm going to die looking at you," I said, smiling.

"Enjoy it while it lasts, love," he held back a smirk of his own, "good luck, Therin, I'll tell them the whole thing was your fault."

"I won't even mention you in my report."

We laughed for a moment, then continued to focus. My skin burned in the heat, but I felt his own flesh searing and knew it was working. Soon we conjured enough to release an infernal storm.

When I woke, the town was ablaze. The emptied corpses of the townsfolk blew in the wind like ashen leaves, flakes of burnt skin caught in the strands of my hair. The buildings had been shelled out by the raging flames, burned to black embers.

The roof had been torn asunder above us, and Marius lay face down in the harsh sun. I went to try and shake him.

"You alive?"

He was breathing but took a moment to stir. He sat up without a word, looking around at the destruction we had brought to the outpost.

"Well, it worked I guess."

"Maybe," I shook my head, "I still feel something here."

"Me too," he scanned the area, then pointed, "Look, over there."

I followed his finger, seeing the slope that lead up to a tunnel dug into the side of the nearby cliff. Strange effigies were lining the way, little dolls on wooden poles.

"Are you okay to walk?" I asked.

"Yeah, I'm good," he groaned as he lifted himself up, "actually, I'm lying, that hurt a lot."

I stood by him, feeling my own aches and pains. It was like the time I'd had the blue rot, my entire body spending all its energy on fighting the illness.

Greta and Vern both crawled out from under some fallen rubble, supporting each other. It was difficult even to descend the stairs back down from the rooftops.

We managed to regroup with a few of the others and set up a small base of operations in the outpost's local bureau. It was a small office building located at the centre of the town, and if there were any others out there, we'd at least be able to see them coming.

CHAPTER EIGHT

I sat on a short piece of a stone pillar that had fallen through the roof of the bureau during the storm. I ran my battered hand along the shattered marble edge, focused entirely on the textures there.

I'd recovered for the most part from the incident, but I still felt exhausted and the freezing cold that permeated the building overnight hadn't helped with sleep. I then heard a clicking sound and looked up to see Marius approaching, propped up on a makeshift crutch.

"How are you holding up?" he asked, perching himself on a nearby desk.

"Not great," I smiled briefly, "you?"

"Still hurts but I'm getting there," he leaned his head back and puffed a billow of fog into the air, "it was boiling when we arrived, how's this happened?"

"The wastes feel different," I said, "as if the rules don't apply or something."

"Yeah, I get that," Marius cocked his head and I heard movement from the other side of the room.

I followed his gaze to see Greta and a few others making their way downstairs. I wondered whether we had all been given the same test, and who might have my name if we did.

Greta caught my gaze for a moment, and I realised then that there was still some scarring above her left eye. Nothing too serious, but somewhere the healing chambers hadn't really been able to solve everything. It was amazing how much good the Nurse Order could do, but it was still hit-and-miss.

"I feel hollow," I said before standing up to dust myself off, "I've never really killed before. At least nothing like that."

"Getting soft?" Marius laughed but immediately regretted it, wincing and holding his side, "it's normal. But they weren't really people, you know? We probably ended their suffering."

"Maybe," I cleared my throat then and moved to exit the conversation, "thanks, Marius. Rest up."

"You too, Elena," he lay back fully on the desk, "yeah, that'll do for now."

As much as I felt the beginnings of a bridge being built between us, he still made me uncomfortable. His previous insults and attacks would be hard to overcome, and I knew he likely still saw me as inferior in some way. Even subconsciously.

I decided to follow the others and see what they were doing, maybe offer my help. The bureau had three levels, the top floor being reserved for administration and the bottom floor held for public-facing affairs and meetings. Beneath it all, however, was a basement level reserved for the storage of arms, resources, and valuables.

I didn't hear anyone as I entered the basement, but I saw light leaking from a nearby door marked "Armoury." I made my way there to see who might be around.

It was empty, of people at least, as the room was filled to bursting with weapons and armour. Racks of firearms and blades were arranged in tightly packed squares and huge crates of munitions lined the walls.

If the outpost was so well-defended, how did nearly every inhabitant get taken and turned into those...things. It didn't make any sense. I stepped back and looked into the corner of the grey brick walls, scanning along its edge towards a wooden beam above.

At that junction, there were webs. Cobwebs as thick as matted hair. Arachnoid egg sacs wrapped in silver silk covered the roof like clouds. The lights flickered, I noticed then, not alarmingly so, but enough that it made everything clearer.

This place hadn't been used in months. Maybe even a year depending on the abundance of the local fauna. Something had taken hold of this outpost's leadership, and one by one, it had consumed them.

It sounded like a Puppeteer. A rare manifestation of mistrust and deceit.

Something had happened at this outpost, a terrible mistake perhaps, and it spread paranoia amongst the population. I remembered a passage from Vehrka, a Matuan Guardian:

"It is in those small moments, the subtle threat from an ally, the cold embrace of a loved one who loves you no longer, and the gnawing sensation that someone is lying. That is where the Puppeteer takes shape.

Bhari had given me some of his father's old books from Burcanon to read when he last visited me at the cave. It was fascinating seeing the difference in language around the Void, and how the focus shifted from individuals to communities and their shared experiences.

I had to warn the others.

"Hey, Elena," it was Greta's voice, and she was behind me, "don't turn around."

She pressed the point of her knife lightly into the skin on my lower back.

"I'm sorry," her vowels shivered as she spoke, "I have to do it. They'll kill my sister if I don't."

She sniffled every so often, and I realised she was crying. She really didn't want to do it. She could have, easily, I didn't hear her approach after all, but she stopped to say this.

I'm sorry too, Greta.

"You don't have to," I said cautiously, aware of the blade, "Greta, I don't think this is you, there's a Puppeteer out there. I think it took control of the outpost."

"It doesn't matter," she said, "I have to do this either way. I won't let Fern die because of my failure."

"No, you don't," I took a step away from the knife, "I trust you Greta, I know you wouldn't do it, and

I'm not angry that you thought about it, I don't blame you at all. But this isn't you."

"Stop moving!" she screamed then, "stop…stop talking. As soon as I let you go, you'll just kill me anyway."

"I'm not going to hurt you, Greta," I was pleading with her then, slowly turning to face her, "I promise, I promise I won't."

"Don't lie to me," her eyes were bright red with tears running down her face, and she started to sob as I looked her directly in the face, "you got one too, didn't you? To kill me? It's obvious. So don't lie to me."

"I think it's just a test," I stepped back slightly, watching the wavering weapon, "to see if anyone would. I'm not going to hurt you, and you don't want to hurt me, I can see it. We can fix it, if we find the Puppeteer then we can all go home. You can see Fern again."

"Elena," Greta sniffed hard then, and her face almost dropped entirely into a neutral state, "I've already locked the doors, you left your sword upstairs," she wiped her eyes with her fingers, "it's too late."

I darted my eyes to the left, considering my escape through the crates on either side for just a moment, then pushed her back before turning to my right to run back through the racks towards the door.

Greta threw her weight against my back, dragging me down to sprawl across the floor. I felt her grab hold of my ankles as I tried to clamber back up and I knew I only had one chance then. I screamed for help as loudly as I could, screaming again until my throat burned from the effort.

Then she was on me.

Her fingers clenched my shoulders and dug deep. It hurt so much I couldn't help but scream again. Then I felt cold metal slide into my flesh and through my ribs.

I could only gasp for air for a moment; The pain was excruciating, and my lungs felt like they were collapsing in on themselves.

She pulled the knife out and stabbed me in the shoulder too. I could barely even register it my chest was so tight. At that point, my focus was on breathing.

Great cried out in anguish, retching slightly before sliding her fingers through my hair to twist herself a grip. She pulled my head back and I quickly put my arm out before she slammed my forehead down, managing to cushion the blow.

I twisted with all my might to throw her off balance, taking advantage of it and pushing her off me again. She fell back against a nearby crate, dazed for a moment. But that was all I needed.

I smashed her face against the box with my boot, gritting my teeth through the pain to start crawling away from her. When I managed to find a rack to hoist myself up with, I saw Greta holding her bleeding nose and mouth.

She got to her feet and lunged at me, trying to pin my arms down again. But she was too late. I had already pulled the knife from my shoulder, and I held it in my right hand.

I plunged the blade into the base of her skull, and I watched her eye slowly fill with blood. I didn't fight anymore then; I didn't need to. She backed away, trying to feel for the knife but her hands flopped about messily, touching her face haphazardly.

I pushed myself back, sitting back against a rack. I wanted to get further away and not watch her flailing movements, but the pain kept me there. Then, for a moment, I swear she looked right at me, before trying to speak. It was garbled, confused, and slurred. Then she slid down into a heap, her fingers still showing spasms of life, but she was dead. I was sure.

I had to cover my mouth with my icy fingers to stop the crying. I felt like I might be sick at any moment, but the relief of it never came. I watched her shivering corpse without blinking until the others came to get me.

CHAPTER NINE

I was still shaking hours later. I supposed it was my body processing the shock and grief of what had happened in the basement, but my fingers felt fragile when I looked at them. In the folds of skin that seemed to age with each passing moment, I saw her blank face again as she twitched like a rodent crushed in the street.

Marius was talking to the others, having heard what I said with patience I hadn't expected. They'd managed to patch me up temporarily and I was grateful, but now they were deciding my fate.

My lungs still felt like punctured balloons, dribbling over themselves as the field medicine and simple spells slowly worked their magic. They wouldn't fix the wounds completely, but I'd survive for the moment. At least until they decided to kill me.

"I said, didn't I, Elena?" Marius came over, "we both still felt like there was something here."

I didn't look at him but I nodded. I was laser-focused on the floor to distract myself from the roiling waves of acid in my stomach.

"And it seems that, yeah, we all had names given to us," Marius cleared his throat, "but none of us left have each other. We're the survivors."

"Who did you get?" I asked him, snarling slightly, "Jack? That why you left him behind?"

Marius didn't say anything.

"Fuck," I said, shaking my head, "was I the only one who thought it was a test?"

"Look this whole thing was clearly set up to kill half of us off anyway," Marius started to pace back and forth, "we need to kill that thing before it gets any more of us."

"We don't know that it hasn't already," I said, looking at those of us that remained, "how did they all die? Huh?"

"Alright that's enough," Marius said before turning to the group, "I think I know where to start looking. Let's get ready to attack in the morning, I just need to talk to Elena."

They all shuffled off in separate directions, the mistrust already setting in. None of them wanted to risk being alone together again, but they didn't seem to mind leaving me with Marius, because, in their bastard eyes, I was already dead weight.

"I'm sorry I didn't come with you or anything," he said, sitting down next to me, "I could have helped."

"No point dwelling on what-if questions," I sighed, "It was my fault. I fucked up."

"This whole thing is fucked up."

I looked at the boy then. I'd mostly avoided Marius Detarn since our initial conflict. We'd always simply looked the other way up until this mission. But I saw then that he had grown weary.

"I'm sorry for how I treated you before," he said, "I was trying to be someone who might impress my father. But you were right. He's left me here, and he doesn't give a shit about me. Something needs to change."

"Glad you finally woke up," I coughed.

"Took me long enough," he said in reply, twiddling his thumbs, "it all needs to change."

"Yes, it does."

"Elena," Marius turned to me, "if we get back, we need to do what we can. This shit needs to stop."

"There's not a lot that I can do," I looked at him briefly, "but yeah, I'll try my best."

"Good," He looked away again, "I'll keep in touch."

The next day we set out up the hill towards the cave that Marius had pointed out before. I was sure he was right too, the path to it had been lined with strange dolls and there was a terrible presence emanating from the mouth of the mountain.

The dolls were made of sack linings with crude stitching for mouths. I went to take a closer look and realised that underneath the linen flesh, something was moving, like a thousand worms waiting to break from the cross-hatched pores.

As we neared the entrance to the tunnel, we heard a low moaning, followed by shallow gasping. Whatever was down there, it was weeping.

The Enlightened Quorum

Soon, the weeping became words.

"I started so softly, so quietly."

Its whisper sounded out through the ratholes, coming from every direction and none. Like it was inside my mind already.

"I just wanted to guide them, feed them, help them..."

We reached a room dimly lit by fading crystals, all milky from their expended use and barely giving off a pale white light. At the centre of the shimmering hole was the Puppeteer.

It was a spindly creature with long wispy arms, but its belly had once been bulbous. Now, however, it had burst, the ropey guts spilling onto the floor. It whined softly, staring at the wall behind us.

"You ready to kill it?"

"It looks like it's dying anyway," I knelt down.

Its face wasn't so alien to me. Its yellowish flesh was starting to crumble away, but clear tears were running from its wide golden eyes. It stared at me then for a few moments, its lip twitching as it tried to figure out its next words.

"I wanted to rule them. But the children were so sweet..."

"You're a monster," I felt my father in me then, the hatred for such cruelty so overwhelming at times that I couldn't help but speak his words.

"Yes..." it looked at the ceiling then, "end it, please. I don't want to live anymore."

It was a simple thing, really. The Puppeteer was already on its way out, and any one of us would have

90

relished the chance to put it out of its misery. However, as I watched the other recruits take hold of each of its limbs, as I heard its sudden wails of fear, I felt that bile coming back. There was a hole in my mind where the final piece of this puzzle would fit. I realised then that I would never find it.

The simple answer was that this creature, who we started to pull apart with our unnatural strength, simply manifested here because of the highly volatile state of the wastes. But as its face contorted into a piercing scream, the flesh at the base of its many arms tearing like bread, I couldn't help but wonder if that was the assumption we were meant to make.

Marius must have noticed my cold expression in the face of such brutality, for he came to my side to place a hand on my shoulder. I nearly shook him off, but I realised then that he was an enemy of yesterday. The enemy of tomorrow was overseeing a board beyond my perception, and I was simply a piece in their game.

I got out of the transport vehicle and noticed that another group was also making its way back in. It would be great getting to see Sonya again and go over my plans with her. I was sure she would come with me.

I saw one of her team checking something in his bag, kneeling down on the ground to look through it. I coughed nearby to announce myself.

"Is Sonya already in?" I looked past him to the large truck, still seeing others climbing out.

"Sonya?" he said with a ghostly intonation, staring at me in confusion, "No...no she didn't make it back."

"What?" I felt a tight pain in my chest and started to massage it, "what do you mean?"

"I lost track of her," his gaze was blank, "I'm sorry. I think she's dead."

I nodded. What else could I do or say? He might have done her in for all I knew, but the horrors we saw were enough to cast the same expressions he wore then, and I would never know the truth about what happened to her. He would never tell me, even if he knew.

As I left him there in his silence, I slowly squeezed air in my fist like there was a windpipe just waiting to be snuffed out.

I always struggle to pick the moment where I knew, where I realised that the whole fucking thing needed to be torn down and rebuilt from the ground up. But I think that was it.

CHAPTER TEN

The rain scattered across the sea of black fabric shielding the commanders and officials that watched us from the distance. They sat on a wooden structure on cushioned chairs, dry as bone, and impatient.

To them, this was just Tuesday. They had seen recruits come and go, live and die, every year. How many bids had they orchestrated for the corporate dynasties? How many of them lay buried in the foundations of the Sanctuary, only to be forgotten?

I stood with the other newly anointed Inquisitor Squires. My hair was soaked in the lashing waves and even the shirt under my overcoat was sticking to my skin. We had stood in silence for an hour at that stage, staring at the carved statue of Kaurus.

Kaurus, 'the justice', was the progenitor and leader of the Fallen, the old gods. And maybe even of us all if the Enlightened Quorum were to be believed. It was therefore no surprise that he was presented as a kindly old man with the chiselled physique of a warrior. He stared back at us with the vacant steely gaze of an uncaring super-being, and I realised then that the image was ridiculous.

The God-King and his brood were storied to barely resemble us, almost monstrous in their appearance and even more so in their brutality. Why would something even older, possibly older than the universe as we know it, even look remotely like us?

A part of me still looked to him for guidance, wordlessly begging for a sign that I was doing the right thing, but there was an aching fear that Kaurus and the Fallen were not what I had been led to believe they were. And my concern wasn't that they were evil, or that they might destroy me for my shaky foundations, but that they were beyond my petty plights. That Kaurus really was watching me then, and simply did not care for my plight.

Somehow, that was worse.

At the feet of the titanic marble man lay wreathes of red orchids picked from the sanctuary gardens. They were symbols of souls now passed onto the Void, forever in the realm of the Fallen.

The rain may have masked the tears for the others, but their faces didn't lie. And it made me sick. Sonya was dead because of one of them, and I would never know who.

But we all had someone lying in the wastes who would never be buried or remembered. We all had reasons to fear and mistrust each other. We all lost someone that day. The grief was palpable.

I knew that Calthern would be among the crowd. Theona too. They all orchestrated this. And they had the nerve to pretend they knew our pain?

I stared at the wreath I laid for her. Sonya. Intrusive memories of her kept prying away at my defences and I didn't want to see her. I didn't want to miss her anymore. It hurt so much every time her face came into view. It was clear then that I had wasted my moments with her, that I had taken time itself for granted.

"Okay, get on," she knelt down, gesturing to her shoulders, "I can just about see."

I tried clambering on and she buckled a little.

"I swear if you get any bigger I'll need another person to help," She chuckled as she said it, bracing herself to stand.

I gave her a small kick in the side.

"Ow okay, I said **if**."

She lifted me above other heads in the crowd, and the band came into sight.

I wrapped my arms tighter around her neck then, resting my head against hers. And she squeezed my wrist with a touch that said:

It's okay. I've got you.

She was gone now, but I wouldn't let her be forgotten. Or any of the others that died under the boot of Eleynum. They had made a mistake. Sonya was more than a friend. She was my sister, and I loved her. And now they had taken her from me as well. It was the final straw.

My grief had mutated into rage.

The rain was still going by the time I had reached the cave. My skin was laced with frost as the running water started to cool and my limbs convulsed wildly as I peeled the wet clothes away.

I was glad that, this time, I had brought plenty of clothes to change into.

Then it was a waiting game. Bhari would often visit the cave every few weeks, but I knew that he was taking a risk coming at all and so I wouldn't have blamed him if he never had.

A day passed. I knew that I didn't have an endless supply of food so at some point I was going to have to decide how long I would wait. But I had a bit more time still, and I needed to prepare.

I had a fire and started to unwrap some smoked meat and bread that I'd stolen from the kitchens. I grabbed my knife by its red leather scabbard and slowly unsheathed its silver edge to gleam in the light.

I placed the point against the crispy shell of the meat and inserted it to slice the flesh, unleashing this terrible rending sound.

Greta's face appeared then, her eye bursting at the seams with thick blood.

The blade clattered against the rock as I dropped it. I started to wring my hands together pressing my thumb into my palm. I felt the nail pierce my skin, and a rush of relief came over me. It distracted me from her for a moment.

The knife shimmered invitingly then.

I picked it up and sat back against a rock, admiring the way the clear juices ran along its razor edge. I found myself rolling up my sleeve and resting the point against my forearm.

I scraped against the caramel flesh and left a faint line that raised slightly at the irritation. I tried again, pressing a little harder. It took more effort than I thought to finally slice into my layers.

I looked at the scars in the making and felt a strange hybrid of relief and shame wash over me. What had I achieved with that? Not much in the long run, but I felt better in that moment somehow.

Another day passed, and I was starting to get low on supplies. I could maybe wait for another day or two at best.

Come on, Bhari.

I decided to distract myself with the black glass again. Theona's voice rang like a distant bell again, naming it as "both useless and incredibly dangerous." She was probably right, but it felt nice to be able to do something that not many others could.

By the end of that day, I'd grown bored of creating mysterious shapes in the black glass and had almost decided that that would be my last day in the cave. But then I heard his clumsy breathing like I always did. Bhari was making his way up.

I was waiting for him at the ledge to grab his wrists and help pull him in. The boy was panting as if he'd been moving faster than usual.

"Elena," He gasped as he lay on his backpack, "I saw the light, knew you were back."

"It's alright, take a breath," I sat down next to him, "thank you for coming."

"It's alright," Bhari forced himself to slow down, "I'm glad you got back."

I struggled to know how to respond. How did I say that I wasn't glad? That I felt that, somehow, it should have been me out there in the dust. Not her. And the guilt was eating me alive.

"You okay?" he said, sitting up to look me over.

I could only shake my head and look down. He edged forward and placed a hand on my shoulder, waiting a moment before attempting to pull me into a hug. It felt strange, constricting almost. But I let myself stay there for a moment.

"They killed her," I said so softly it was almost a whisper, "my friend I told you about, Sonya."

"I'm sorry, Elena," Bhari squeezed me a little then, "I wish I knew what to say."

"Me too," I pulled away a little then, "it's okay, you don't need to say anything. Thank you."

"What happened?" Bhari didn't know where to look, he was avoiding my eyes but he was searching for a way to help.

"I don't know," I sighed, "it's all vague. We had these orders…I was told to kill a girl while I was out there."

"Did you do it?"

"I thought it was just a test," I tried to scan his face for some way of knowing his thoughts, his inner beliefs about me, and I found I couldn't do it, "she died anyway. But she had my name, so I could have too."

"It's horrible to say, but I'm relieved," Bhari scratched at a layer underneath his hair, "I'd have really missed you."

"Thanks," I said, "I want to come with you."

"Elena."

"I need to get out of here," I felt my throat tense up for a moment, "I have to do something. They killed her Bhari, she was the closest thing I had to family and they killed her."

"Are you sure this is a path you want to take?" he winced, "you might not be able to go back."

"I don't know what else to do," I stood up then, walking away from him, "if I stay here, either I'm going to kill somebody, or they'll kill me. Or I'll just do it myself."

"Elena, don't say that."

"You don't get it," I kicked a stone over, "you're free out there."

"Am I?" Bhari's melodious voice then cut with an icy air, "Elena, I'm begging for you to listen to me just this once. You can ignore every word from my mouth after this, but right now, you aren't hearing me."

I looked at him again as he got to his feet. He paced for a moment with his hands on his hips. His answer took an era to come out finally.

"If you come with me, you're moving from one prison to another. And out there, you'll be worth even less than you are now," he ran his fingers through his hair for a moment, "you don't get it. You've been trapped here most of your life and you haven't seen just how bad the district is. You're walking into danger."

"Okay," I nodded, "you're right. I'm sorry."

"No, you don't need to apologise," Bhari smiled briefly, "you're fine, I just don't want to drag you into something worse."

"I appreciate it," I said, "but I'm getting out of here either way, and I'm going to make them pay. I just wanted to see if I could help."

Bhari laughed and beamed at me for a couple seconds. I couldn't help but turn my nose up at him in bewilderment.

"What?"

"As long as you're sure," Bhari grabbed his bag, "no point waiting, let's get out of this place. I feel itchy just looking at it."

CHAPTER ELEVEN

Pipes billowed blue smoke into the air, pumping power to the people through great iron pipes. All pipes lead back to the Centre, the heart of Eleynum, where the great families sat inside the Kaurus and Mun districts. Their ivory palaces glistened high above the interweaving walls of the city.

I walked through the wired fencing like tall grass in a forest, very aware of how alone I was here. There were tales of void-borne like Stragan leaking through from the Darius district, but I had never seen one. And normally, you heard a Stragan long before it attacked.

As I neared the end of the maze, up ahead I saw a looming neon sign.

D E T A R N

It was embedded in thick steel beams, moulded into a strange, circular shape. The sign itself was a bubbly pink, so invasive it hurt to look at it directly. Beneath the beams, the bricks were painted in pink and blue stripes of the Detarn dynasty.

The homes here were a mark of the new and the strange. Thickly dyed steel walls were like a rainbow right out of a children's book. The colours were overwhelming and oppressive, reminding you of where you were with salivating micro-aggressions. But they were not what made me anxious.

Even when the sun was starting to go down, the crowds were thick and amorphous, the well-groomed and brightly lit middle districts. They shuffled through the square, swarming towards the megaplex to buy from their rulers.

At the centre, surrounded by them, was a large fountain encased in polished silver. Sitting atop two lily pads on the water, a loving gaze on their faces, were the visages of Kaurus and Mun.

As the hive continued to flow around me, a stranger bumped my shoulder, his fleeting thoughts of fight or flight, aggression, and guilt, all flashed around his face before receding into silence again. I could hear the thoughts, all of them, looking at me with pity, with disgust, with shame.

It was too much, and suddenly I was drowning. My stomach tied itself in knots and squished against my lungs, pushing air back out of them as fast as it came in.

A soft hand grabbed mine.

"Elena?" Bhari had come back, "I lost you, it's this way."

He guided me away from the crowds. The docks had cargo trains silently sliding in and out of its loading bay like ants, the tracks glistening with the autumn sweat. The roads had been slowly converted onto tracks over a period of years, and now it was almost complete. Paving the way for the future. It was a momentous sight.

The entrances to the Darius district were embedded into a high wall crowned with barbed wire. The only way in was through guarded checkpoints where people were checked for weaponry and other contraband. This at least kept the Stragan mostly at bay. They were similar in design and construction to the checkpoints surrounding the Kaurus and Mun districts; those, however, were focused on keeping would-be attackers away from the important central network of Eleynum's infrastructure.

We approached the double-stone archway and were directed toward the left, passing by a mere two guards and a basic gate. As I passed through, to my right was a line of people waiting to leave. The barriers had been designed with a snaking pattern, layering the would-be escapees upon each other as they waited nervously to be thoroughly checked over. There were at least ten Enforcers, Eleynum's more standard peacekeeping soldiers when compared with the Void-wielding Inquisitors, on this side of the archway.

It became clear then that these checkpoints served an entirely different purpose to those protecting Elenyum's rulers.

We took a turn uphill, through the tightly constrained blocks of flats, a perma-grime sliding down the walls and into the gutters along the bumpy road. There was little light here, the only glow provided being that of small lamps hung outside of windows and street-level doors. I looked to the power relay above, far advanced beyond those of Burcanon, and realised that it had been smashed.

Just below, etched into the brick of the building in bulging black pain, was a crude drawing of a spider and a loosely legible slogan:

The Quorum's light is only darkness.

It was a royalist slogan. I often forgot that despite their names plaguing the mouths of every Inquisitor, the Matuni and their various rebel factions weren't the only ones at war here. Old Knights of the God-King still hid inside the city, and they, like their old rulers, hated the Void. They were one of the many groups proving to be a perpetual thorn in the Quorum's side after their coup.

I looked through almost every window I could, drawn to those lit by dim bulbs and shadows moving across them. Occasionally I would see small families huddled together, single mothers chasing after their small children while their partners were away, or dead.

Up ahead I could see vagrants shuffling into tight alleys embossed with small establishments, their hands slick with the same black sweat as the grey and brown walls. It was the Boater's Rest, a popular place around here. Its design was evocative of an age past, with gnarled wood beams placed at awkward angles across the bone-white walls. The door was painted a deep mauve, with a carving of a small boater, his fishing pole hanging over the edge, suspended above it. The model swung in the light breeze, making it look as though he sat on choppy waters at high sea.

The Sanctuary had taught me that many who lived here denied the ancient ways of the Quorum, and so were punished for it. As I stared at a little boy at a window, looking back at me with wide, desperate eyes, I'm not sure I believed that anymore.

We reached a small shop on the corner, a bright sign lit above it reading 'Bhen's Odds and Ends.'

"This is my father's shop," Bhari said, "we've had to be cautious around your people, so he might seem a bit off."

"I understand, the way they've treated the refugees is awful."

"Well, it's, it's more than that," he said, "my father was born differently to other men, with a name and identity that's dead to him now."

The Quorum hated many in Eleynum, and people like Bhen were chief among them for defiling the body that the Fallen had given them, preferring them to live inside of a prison made of their own flesh. I hoped that shedding that shell had made Bhen happier, despite the risks to his life. Gender and its binary expression was, after all, a concept designed and enforced by mortal men. If the Fallen could look at the misery inflicted by their most devout worshippers and feel nothing, then I was sure they could let Bhen's change of name and appearance slide.

"I'm sorry," I said, "you can both trust me."

"I know I can," Bhari scratched his stubbling face, "he…well, my dad's a paranoid guy. So, we'll see."

Bhari opened the door, a small bell above tinkling as we entered. The walls were lined with trinkets, some in glass cases, others left hanging by nails smashed into the ageing wood. As I came into the room fully, I could see more on the ceiling, some hanging low enough to wisp through Bhari's hair.

I could see old clocks, tools, and even some weapons so old now that they could barely be used for target practice. It was a suffocating room filled with dust and musty scents that clogged the nose.

A small man stood behind the counter, his long nose pressed up against a metallic sphere as he looked through a monocular. A woman leaned on the table on our side, watching him.

"Come on Bhen, what's it worth?"

"Well," Bhen looked over to us briefly, smiling at Bhari, "not much, unfortunately. But I might know someone who can make use of it. I'll give you twenty for the moment, then depending on what I can get for it I'll try and get you a bit more."

"I need it now, Fiona's not eaten properly in a week."

"I know," Bhen took off the monocular and placed it down, "if you want you can hold onto it until I know for sure, but that's the best I can do for now. I haven't got much either."

She clenched her fists.

"Twenty's better than nothing."

Bhen sighed, then reached into his pocket.

"Take fifty, then I'll let you know if I can do any more."

"Thank you," she reached across and hugged him, "thank you."

"It's alright," he handed her the money, "now, on your way before it gets too dark."

She walked out of the shop, slipping past me at the door. She looked back at me for a moment, eyeing my clothes, then hurried away.

"Alright Dad," Bhari stepped forward, then motioned to me, "This is Elena."

"You were hanging around at that school again," Bhen walked around the counter to inspect his son, "I've told you not to go there."

"I know."

They embraced for a moment. Then Bhen turned on me.

"Who is she then?"

"I wanted to get away from the Order," I said, "I think they're going to hunt me."

It wasn't really a lie; I was genuinely afraid of that.

But it's enough of a deception, isn't it? You sad little liar.

"We can't have runaways here, Bhari, you know that," Bhen rubbed his neck, "I already had the Wolf here making a nuisance of himself."

"Are you hurt?" Bhari placed a hand on his father's shoulder.

"Who's the Wolf?" I asked.

"I'm fine," Bhen sighed, "he was just doing his usual thing, making threats and breaking things," Bhen looked at me then, "he's the Inquisitor General for the district, and he particularly enjoys my company. Seems to think I run some kind of smuggling operation here so when something goes wrong he blunders in here,

107

smashes the place a bit, then makes some idle threats and walks out again."

"They're not idle," Bhari spat, "they burned the Motorium the other day."

"No, they didn't."

"Yes, they did!" Bhari had been calm and mild-mannered until that moment, losing the façade in an instant, "They'll keep pushing you around until they decide to take you for real."

"No, they won't," Bhen rounded on him, "he's an 'orrible an' ungrateful cunt, but he's an old friend. He wouldn't dare."

He turned and winked at me.

He's spied you for the rat you are.

I ignored it.

"Look, you're bad business," Bhen put his hands in the air, "I don't mean ta be rude, nothin' personal, but they make lives round 'ere hellish enough without looking for some Summer girl."

"I can help."

"No, you can't, you're a kid," Bhen nodded, "but…you're a kid. And if you're afraid, then, well," he sighed, "if we can't help others, how much better are we than them, ay? You can't stay long, but a few weeks, sure."

"Thank you, sir," I breathed relief, "I'll do whatever I can to make it up to you."

"Don't get my son killed and you've done enough," he walked towards the stairs in the back, "now, let's eat."

CHAPTER TWELVE

Bhari and I stood by the large window at the centre of his small room. From here we could see but a small portion of the district.

"How does the view compare?" Bhari asked, but I felt he already knew the answer.

Where the Spring and Summer quadrants of the city were tiled gardens of wondrous palettes, the Winter quadrant was mostly warped greys and rotten wood. It was awful, there was no other way to put it. And Darius seemed to be the worst, its strange patchwork of architecture already on its last legs. I even noticed some of them had moonlight casting through the holes of shelled towers.

"How did it get this bad?" I turned to him, "what happens to the supplies sent here?"

He squinted, then let out a short breath as if he was laughing at me.

"What?"

"You mean the poultry shipments that turn up here?" he licked his teeth, and shook his head, "they can barely feed the dogs, and the building materials are used, or useless."

"They can't do that," my voice cracked a little as I said it, "they're supposed to give equal supplies to each district."

"They say they do," he stared at something in the distance for a long time, "they say there's a criminal element, that the rebels steal from them. And maybe it's true," he started to pick at the skin on his thumb, "problem is, I never saw the start of it, and now rebels are stealing the supplies just to try and feed the district. Then they punish us even more severely. It's an endless cycle."

The boy, no, the young man who had seen far too much before his time, sighed, and in the moonlight, I could see silver tears welling at the corners of his golden eyes. The deep gold of the Burcanon tribes. The same gold that Oliver had inherited.

"My other father, Gherek, spoke up," he swallowed the pain down, "he said he couldn't watch me starve anymore, so he demanded they bring more."

I watched him in silence. He kept trying to speak but wouldn't allow himself to cry, so he would start, then stop again, and couldn't seem to get it out.

"You don't need to tell me," I reached out and placed a hand on his back, "if it's hard. I understand."

"No, you don't," he barked, shrugging me away, "I watched them, they kept hitting him, and pulled," he was shaking, looking at his hands, "they tore him apart, like fucking animals."

110

Bhari sobbed with deep expulsion, the wave of pain rushing through him and burning the base of his brain. I felt my own hands shaking but I pushed it away, sending my own feelings into lockdown. I lay my hand on him again, and this time, he took it, and we hugged for a while. I had to half support his weight and felt the tears soaking my shoulder, but I didn't mind.

"I'm, I'm sorry," he said, "I'm sorry Elena."

"It's okay," I squeezed him, "I'm sorry."

"Why?" he sniffed, stepping back, "did you kill my dad?"

We laughed for a brief second, a shameful laugh.

"I'm sorry that they…" and that's when I realised, the looks and the distrust, "that we did this to you."

"You aren't to blame."

"Maybe not directly," I shuddered, "but I've been living a lie. And I was ignorant."

"I don't need you to be sorry," Bhari smiled, "you're here now. You can do more if you'd like."

"I would," I smiled back, "my father pushed our roots away, and my tutors have taught me nothing, I want to know the truth now."

"Good," Bhari looked out the window again, "your father, is he a good man? Do you think he would help too?"

I pondered that for a bit. Was he a good man? In truth, I barely knew him. He rarely spent time with us even before Burcanon, and when he had, he was usually in no mood to know us except to interrogate us. An Inquisitor through and through.

"I don't think so," I shrugged, "he's protected their 'truth' for too long to turn back now."

"I see," he paused, "and your mother? You said she was Matuan too."

"She taught me a lot in such a short space of time, but I wish I'd had more."

He still had the tears in his eyes, but his cheerful mask had returned. He was so full of joy, for someone who had no reason to be. Yet I had all that I could ask for and felt none of it. I felt happier, being around him.

I snaked my fingers through his, feeling the details of his lined knuckles. I watched him, watching my own hand, feeling my breath catch. He took a small, terribly minute step forward, straightening up to look back at me.

His eyes were half-closed, staring at me. I saw the flecks of silver in that deep amber, taking my own step forward and reaching out to touch his waist.

"Is this okay?" I asked.

"Yes," he was still looking me in the eyes, then they trailed down to my mouth, coming back up to me, "can I kiss you?"

Our legs were intertwined, and his hands still traced the lines of my bones.

"How was it?" he asked.

"Hmm," I said, "room for improvement."

"Oh," he laughed, "wounded again."

I kissed him.

"It was our first time."

112

He nodded, closing his eyes. We lay there a while, simply listening to the sounds of our breathing.

Then the screaming started. A single wailing, likely a woman's but it was filled with such deep grief that it barely sounded human. It was hoarse, pulled from the depths of their diaphragm.

Then another, and another, a chorus of anguish. We got up and rushed to the window to see people fleeing, running from their homes. Then a hand smashed into the glass, sending a web of cracks across it.

I grabbed Bhari's arm and pulled him back to duck behind the bed. I watched the pale hand punch through this time and a gangly creature climbed through the hole, rotten skin pulled from its skeletal frame by the glass.

It had once been a woman, I think, its yellow, brittle hair hanging to the floor in sparse strands. The Stragan's eyes bulged from its gaunt face, streaked in bloody lines, as it scanned the room. I heard it sucking air into its bloated belly with raspy breath.

Bhari started to move, but I tightened my grip. He looked at me as though he was going to speak, so I slapped a hand over his mouth. The Stragan stepped forward on all fours, its long nails scratching the wooden flooring.

I put one finger over my lips, signalling him to be quiet. Stragan had poor eyesight due to malnutrition, and silence would help. The real problem was our scent. I raced through the books I'd read, trying to remember their weaknesses. Rage-fire was always a good bet, but I could have incinerated the whole block if I wasn't careful.

If you don't do something soon, that thing will flay you with its hands and feast on your insides. Do it.

I closed my eyes, hearing the breathy moaning getting closer, and reached out into the energies of the Void. My fingers had waves of cold pass over them as I reached through the fabrics of our worlds. Then I dipped into my mind, looking for the right feelings.

I thought of Calthern and the empire of shit that he had built. The Senate and all of their lies and the lives they'd taken. How that hatred fuelled me for so many years and how I'd never been allowed to feel it.

That'll be more than enough.

The burning heat wound around my fingers, searing them with the flames forged in fury. Bhari recoiled in fear, the buzzing of his confused emotions flittering away. I stood to face the Stragan, knowing it had smelled the burning ash.

"Bhari!" I heard Bhen shout from below, "are you up there?"

The Stragan grunted and scattered towards the bedroom door. I flung a bolt of white flame and hit the wretch in the back, sending it crashing through the door in a pile of splinters. It scrambled away and I heard Bhen yell again.

"No," I said in hushed tones, sprinting toward the door.

A firearm boomed through the stairwell, and as I rounded the corner I could see Bhen covered in the tar-like blood of the Stragan, his shotgun's barrel smoking.

It writhed on the ground, clawing at the missing chunk in its side. The noxious gasses and putrid liquids that had built up from decomposition were pouring from the wound. The flame had stuck to its back too, rendering its flesh into a sticky soup.

I bolted down the stairs, realising halfway that I was still mostly undressed and knew I'd feel the sting of guilt later. Bhen stared at the Stragan, frozen. I matched its ballooning eyes that searched for relief as it whimpered in pain. I channelled the flame into it again, a concentrated stream from both hands. Its flesh quickly blackened and crumbled into a dark pile of ash.

I went to Bhen, who only seemed to just realise I was there. I shook him.

"Bhen?"

He cleared his throat and nodded.

"We need to board up any doors and windows, and let any Guardians know what's happening," I shook him again, "Bhen?"

"Yeah," he stood up straight, "thank you, I'll get it done," he looked up the stairs, where Bhari stood, then back at me again, "thank you."

CHAPTER THIRTEEN

Seventeen people.

That's how many had died in the Stragan attack. It had only taken a few, a small group of maybe five, to tear through the flats like foxes in a chicken coop.

I stood in the morning fog in a large coat I had borrowed from Bhari. It seemed to hold the cold at bay, but I still trembled under the folds of thick but poor-quality fabric. However, it was better than wearing my coat from the Order, its insignia a potential death sentence here.

The Darius district seemed to be home to some warriors and old Guardians from Matuan tribes who had managed to drive them away, but they were few and exhausted.

"It's not the first time," Bhari said, "this was the biggest group, but they've come before."

"Where are they coming from?"

"Follow me," he said.

He headed into the smog, moving towards a sanitation plant. It was connected to a network of sewers spiralling underneath us, pumping and cleaning sludge before moving slightly purified water further on.

"They come from underground," he said, stopping before a chained fence, "they use the sewers to move around. I hear them, sometimes."

"Can't the Inquisitors deal with it?" I said, "this Wolf, for instance?"

"They don't believe us," he sighed, "they don't understand the Starved."

"Starved?" I shook my head, "they're called Stragan, they're the wandering dead."

"No," he was stern now, "they're the Starved. Those who died of hunger."

There had been speculation that the Stragan changed depending on the manner of their death. I remembered the thin, bony arms, the bloated stomachs, and the bleeding teeth. Maybe he was right.

"And if no one's getting food..."

"Then more of them will come," Bhari's voice was animated and ragged, like there was a morbid excitement to him suddenly, "you see now, yes?"

"Yeah," I nodded, "I can see it."

"This why I have to do something."

I put my hand on his chest, I could see his darting eyes, the biting of his lips. He was hiding something. He looked down at my hand, then glanced over his pocket for a moment. It was there. With fluidity that caught him off-guard, I reached into the inside of his coat, grabbing his other wrist that tried to stop me.

I pulled a gun, a revolver, from the holster he had concealed with the jacket. He tried to grab it from me again, but I spun away, stepping back from him when he advanced. It was heavy, loaded with six bullets.

"What is this?" I demanded an answer with my poise, "what have you done?"

"Nothing," he cried out, slowing down, "nothing yet. You don't understand."

"This?" I held up the gun, "no, I don't. Tell me."

"We can't keep living like this!" this was the second time I'd seen him explode suddenly, "there's a group. I joined them a while ago. They're fighting back against the Inquisitors, stealing food and supplies to give to the people."

"Terrorists."

"They're good people," he closed his hands, "at least they're doing something about it, what are you doing? You follow me home to play the rebel then walk away once it gets hard. You're a coward."

I tightened my grasp on the gun's grip, knowing it was foolish but feeling lost in his desperation.

"You don't know me," I said with a warning tone, "what I've had to do."

"I know it's not as hard as this," Bhari waved a hand over the buildings behind him, "you'll never get it. You're soft."

"Maybe," I was starting to realise that maybe he was right, "but this isn't the way. What if it gets worse?"

"I'd rather die fighting back than live under their boot," he relaxed his posture, "if you want to keep licking it in the vain hope that they take some pressure off, then you can go back to your life. If you want to make change, real change," he walked up to me and grabbed the gun, holding it up to my face, "then the only road is painted with blood."

He holstered it again. I looked away.

"I understand you're desperate," I sighed, "I know that this seems like the only way. But what if this makes things worse? You can't fight the Order, and even if you could, they're not the worst of it. The Changed will destroy you."

"I know that," Bhari smiled again, "that's why we're cutting off their head."

"Who are you going to kill?" I had this dread that I knew who it would be already.

"Donlan Calthern," he said, "the butcher needs to die. He poisons everyone against us and controls the Inquisitors."

It wasn't what I'd expected, but somehow even more insane.

"You can't," I shook my head, "they'll take revenge in a form you can't even imagine. They'll kill everyone."

"He works for an organisation that wants us dead, we need to send a message that it won't be that easy for them."

I thought about my next response for a long time.

"Okay," I said, "I'll help. Promised your dad I wouldn't get you killed and if you're set on this stupid idea then I'd better help and make sure you don't fuck it up."

"Thanks for the ever-growing confidence," he laughed.

I turned away from him then. I didn't blame Bhari, but I knew the enemy better than him and the fear of the reprisals set me on edge.

When we got back to the square, we saw large boxy vehicles surrounding the area, Inquisitors heading towards the crowds of Darius citizens. They started to grab people by the arms and dragged them towards the vehicles.

"No, not again," Bhari started to make his way over, but I pulled him back towards an alley, "get off me, Elena."

"Don't be stupid," I growled at him, "there's too many of them."

He protested but I flashed a glare at him that let him know he was on thin ice already, and he shrunk from me, suddenly afraid. It was a feeling I was used to at this stage, but it still stung seeing him back off like that.

I bit my lip and focused on the Inquisitors and recognised Theona scanning the groups around her. Another man stalked in lines back and forth, looking as though he might suddenly rip into any one of the bystanders.

"Why are you doing this?" a young girl cried as she held tight to a man being dragged away by an Inquisitor.

"You know the rules," the vicious-looking leader snarled at her, ripping her hands away, "as soon as you used the void you marked yourselves as Quarry."

"It's okay," her loved one coughed, "I'll be okay, I promise."

She hadn't taken her eyes off of her oppressor, watching him closely.

"Come on," I whispered to myself, "don't get yourself killed."

She backed down then, covering her mouth to stifle the sobbing. It was at that moment that the Inquisitor General turned to face Theona.

"Wrap it up here, meet me later."

It was obvious now, as painful as it was. I'd hoped that this 'Wolf' had been anyone else, but I think a part of me had always known that this is what he would become, or perhaps, had always been.

It seemed that Theona and my father, Anders Therin, had already begun their search for me. I'd known that as soon as I escaped that this would be a possibility, but for them to be so close already meant that I was steadily running out of time.

"Where are they taking them?" I asked Bhari, unable to bring myself to tell him the truth, "do you know?"

"No," Bhari ground his teeth for a moment, "they haven't done this for a while, the Guardians keep their powers hidden mostly."

"They've done this before?"

"Yes," Bhari barely glanced at me, "Quarry. If you aren't Order, you're a danger."

I nodded. Quarry were unmarked users, and among most of Eleynum, they were a known but mostly ignored factor. However, it seemed that the belief that Matuni Guardians had been to blame for Burcanon had made the rules even stricter here.

We watched the tanks roll away, filled with a few dozen people and puffing fumes as they went. A few Inquisitors stayed behind to disperse the crowds.

I had to find out where they were going, but that was a task for another day.

CHAPTER FOURTEEN

Bhari grabbed my hand and grinned wide as he dragged me into the thick school of people swarming through the streets. His long dark hair was wrapped in a braid that hung along his back, swaying slightly as he pushed through them.

They were of the Spring class, not Summers, but entitled enough that the idea of Winter children brushing their clothes was enough to send them into frenzies. I laughed in the face of an old man who flustered at the dirt on mine.

"Come, Elena," Bhari cried, "we'll miss him if we're slow!"

"I've only got small legs!" I said over panting breath and we laughed together at that.

Up ahead I could see an open-top armoured vehicle moving closer, looming over the parting crowd. Engines sputtered bright blue smoke from behind its wrought metal frame, encased in deep reds.

We found ourselves being heaved back as the crowd moved aside, but Bhari managed to squeeze through them until we were almost at the front.

I kept an eye on the bracelet of black glass that rattled a little every time I moved. I'd decided that if I kept some on me in the form of a simple bracelet then I might be able to fashion something from it in an emergency. And that day felt like it was bound to end up that way.

Huge soldiers in bulky plated armour were pushing people further like they were blades of tall grass. Pipes weaved their limbs and connected to their helmets, a liquid like dark honey running through them. A few held autocannons in two hands, but many held large mauls or blades, and some simply flexed corrugated fists, knowing they could do more damage with their hands than any weapon.

No one was entirely certain of the process that created the Changed. It was mostly carried out in the Undercroft, a secret area of the city where Eleynum's strongest male soldiers were sent. They were usually trained from birth and, if the rumours were to be believed, pumped with refined oil from the Void to slowly change their physiology.

They were more dangerous than any weapon the city could conceive of and took orders only from the Wardens who controlled them.

Donlan Calthern stood up from the tank, raising his hands to a cheering crowd. I watched Bhari's face, seeing an icy stare at the creatures in decorated armour. He reached into his pocket.

"People of Eleynum," Calthern's voice was pinched and nasally, but he used power drawn from the Void to amplify it, "even on our way here from the

Darius District, several men towards the back of the convoy were attacked with a small incendiary device."

He paused while the crowd responded solemnly, many making the sign of the Quorum. It was a simple motion, where one placed a fingertip on their lip as if to shush someone, then traced it down to their chin.

"Our leaders and teachers in the Senate are trying to deal with this issue, but many among their own ranks and the weak Parliament keep blocking action," Calthern shook his head and covered his mouth a moment, "I said, when bringing back refugees from cursed settlements like Burcanon or Furoran, that the ways of heathens like the Matuni would bring the same ruin to our own glorious city. That we were inviting the wrath of the Gods!"

"Look Elena," Bhari nodded towards a man in the crowd, "the Wolf."

I saw him, the horror story among the Winter people. His grizzled features stared blankly at Calthern, dead eyes scanning the crowd. He'd grown so old since I last saw him, grey now lining most of his beard and cropped hair. I kept an eye on him, slowing my breathing.

"Look upon them," Calthern continued, using his mangled, grey hand to project images into the air around him, "look at their gaunt, inhuman frames. Their disgusting, deviant lives. Not too dissimilar to the monstrous Stragan we see bleeding further into our city, no?"

Some of the crowd murmured in agreement, one or two shouting curses.

Anders, saw me, looking directly into my eyes. He started to advance, slipping through the crowd like a water spirit. I saw Bhari tense, so I grabbed his arm.

"Give it to me," I said, looking back at Anders, "now, Bhari!"

Bhari moved back, his brow furrowed. Then, as I pushed into him with my mind, he relaxed and handed the pistol to me. I placed it into my jacket and then tried to drag him away.

As we broke from the crowd, our hunter formed from the crowd like a dust cloud, standing in our way. My father's prosthetic arm gleamed white like a knife in the sun as he grabbed me by the collar and Bhari by the throat, pulling us apart with his inhuman strength.

He pushed me aside and dragged Bhari into a nearby alley, throwing him against the wall like he was a pillow.

"Wait!" I screamed, "Dad, stop! Don't hurt him."

Bhari looked at me with wide eyes, struggling against Anders' iron grip. My father looked back at me with a burning glare.

"Who's this urchin, girl?" his voice was calm, but the words burned in the air.

I glanced at Bhari.

"No one, I dragged him here," I said, shrugging, "his father gave me somewhere to stay for a while."

"I'll have to 'ave a chat with that person when I get a chance," Anders dropped Bhari, backhanding him across the face as the boy tried to look back, "you go home now, boy, and you warn your...father, that if this happens again, I'll pay your 'ome a visit. I dunno which of you I'll take yet."

Bhari held his quickly bruising face, looking at me once more, before scrambling away into the crowd. Anders grabbed me by the shoulder.

"And you, girl, your punishment'll be severe."

CHAPTER FIFTEEN

Oliver ran and wrapped his arms around me when I entered our home, wordlessly squeezing me for a moment. Then as I went to touch his hair, he moved back and scowled at me.

"I can't believe you left without me."

"I know," I pulled him back into a hug again, "I'm sorry, I was going to come back."

"You still left me," he was trying to pull back now, "you said you'd never do that."

"I'm really sorry."

Oliver nodded, then walked away from me. Theona stood at the door.

"Where have you been, child?"

"It's a bit late for that," Anders snapped, "we'll discuss this another time. You're dismissed."

"But Anders, I…"

"You failed," He pushed past her, "go 'ome."

I wanted to speak up for her and say that I decided to do this. But, seemingly knowing what I was planning, Theona shook her head. She brushed my hair back and rubbed a thumb against my cheek.

"Father," I said, "it wasn't her fault."

"No, it's yours," he went to pour himself a drink, "but she failed in her duties either way."

"But she didn't."

"Don't speak to me," Anders turned, a glass of red vioska in his hand, "I don't wanna hear it. You've embarrassed me. I have to set an example that I won't allow it. Even by my own daughter."

I tried to hold it back, but I felt it bubbling up inside of me. It was my time to do something, to use my power for good, instead of sitting on the sidelines.

"You're fucking monsters."

The words hung in the air between us like flakes of ash. The venomous bile was melting through his iron hide, and I knew this because I could see the spiralling wires of his thoughts spilling from him. He wanted to crush me like the bug he thought I was. Oliver stared at me, his eyes searching for an answer.

"You can't say that to him, Elena," my brother was defensive, but I could see that he didn't understand why just yet, "Dad went looking for you straight away."

I ignored him.

"Do you know what the Winter people call you?"

Anders continued to stare at me.

"They call you the Wolf. You're a demon to them. They loathe you."

"They should. They have to fear me."

"You were going to hurt a child not much older than I am, for no other crime than being around you," I wanted to hurt him, to make him feel even an ounce of the pain Bhari had, "you take their food, you harass them, and you kill them, and for what? You can't even do your actual job properly. Stragan attacked the Darius district when I was staying there, and your Inquisitors are letting it happen. You're a disgrace to the Order."

"They only have 'emselves to blame," Anders boomed, his voice ripping through me, "your fuckin' rabble killed two of my soldiers today, and that's just one day. These people, these fuckin' subhumans, they can't be grateful. They keep demanding more, every day, and I can't give it to 'em," he panted for a second, taking a swig from his drink, "you've no idea what I've done. The sacrifices I've made. You think I enjoy it? It's the only way to keep 'em in check. They need to understand when they've been beaten. You have everything you could ask for, and it isn't enough, is it?"

"I don't want it! It's covered in blood."

Then, suddenly, it came to me. I knew exactly what to say. I knew how to rip his heart cleanly from his chest.

"Mum would hate you."

My father threw the glass on the ground, shattering it. Oliver started to cry, and Anders slapped him across the face.

"Men don't cry, boy. Your sister's poisoned you, made you weak, but no more."

I stood between them, daring him to do it again. Anders took a breath and closed his eyes a moment before glaring at me again.

"You'll learn to respect me, and you won't ruin this boy any more than you already have," Anders went to fall into a chair, "I will be taking control of your education personally," he swallowed, "separately."

"No," I screamed, regret strangling me, "please."

"I told you, girl," Anders looked at me with dead eyes, "your punishment'll be severe. You'll be coming with me, I'm working on a case and you need to learn the realities of this work."

He looked at Theona, who stood at the edge of the room.

"Take him to the Undercroft," Anders stared at his son without fully turning his head, his nose upturned, "he needs to learn strength."

"Anders," Theona started.

"Don't," He raised a single finger, "no more. This is how it has to be."

CHAPTER SIXTEEN
-ELENA-

The Summer districts of Kaurus and Mun were located at the centre of the city. Here, the governmental estates of the Senate and Parliament and their various branches operated a spider's web of neural networks, passing information between them at the speeds of light.

The Great Houses and their subsidiaries all had homes here too, giant rainbow mansions whose stones managed to glisten in the morning dew.

But to get into the Summer quarter was a task all on its own. Tiled walls surrounded it, with murals painted on them by outsiders. My father and I passed one of a child's silhouette reaching for a paper kite bent into the shape of a bird. It was seemingly flying over the wall, its owner desperately clawing to get it back.

Enforcers stood in alcoves placed along the wall, the rooves shielding them from the weather. They wore the colours of the Senate, a pure white with blue stripes across their lapels.

We got to one of the checkpoints allowing entry to the gated community, and a stream of people queuing to enter. Most were being immediately turned away unless they had appropriate documents and identification.

The enforcers recognised my father's uniform as that of an Inquisitor General. He wore a long grey overcoat over a pleated shirt with Calthern's sparrow insignia on the lapel.

"Sir!" An Inquisitor approached from a nearby office, saluting, "do you require an escort or transport?"

"We'll be fine. How's it been?"

"Restless, always is in the mornings. Weather's lovely in the Summer quarter today which is helping."

There was a noticeable shift in temperature as we stepped out of the checkpoint gates, a warm breeze from the Ghurden-designed micro-climate brushed past me. The air was being filtered out by the dynasty's machines and felt light. Gods, it even tasted sweet, with scents of blooming flowers lining the wide streets.

Carriages wrapped in deep red wood and dyed leather moved along electrified rails, carrying maybe one or two people each. Others walked the gleaming pathways. Small shops and centres were spaced evenly along the way, clear blue glass allowing light onto the sterile flooring and colourful products.

It was much the same across the city, but more so in the Summer quarter than anywhere else, everything here was plastered with the crests of the Great Houses.

We made our way through the pearlescent estates of the Mun district, where the Subsidiaries lived. Eventually, we came upon the Snow-Steel manor. It was beautiful in the sunlight, the white gates and the crown atop the roof that resembled a wreath of roses. Out the front, right next to the street, was the start of the gardens that surrounded it.

"You grew up here?" I couldn't believe it. The place was sickeningly magnificent.

"Mostly," my father was chewing on the inside of his mouth, much like I did sometimes, "they took pity on me during my selection."

The God-King's knights were selected by great families in much the same way as modern Inquisitors were, but from what I'd read, it happened much earlier and seemed to be more of a lifetime position. The expectation, as my father explained, was to have total devotion to the dynasty you served, and to form a familial bond between the knights and their masters.

Anders gripped one of the bars at the gate, seeing two Enforcers approaching in the Snow-Steel grey and red, the steel rose pins on their uniforms. They pulled thin blades from their sheaths and laid hands on their pistols.

"You there! You get away from the gate. No entry to the public."

"We have been invited by Mistress Snow-Steel," Anders said in his 'polite' voice, complete with its passive-aggressive and patronising tone, "here's the letter."

One of them took it in a gloved hand and read, before looking us over, lingering on me. Anders grabbed the paper back.

"All good?"

"I'll need to get this checked."

"Alright, on your head," Anders sighed.

"What?"

"Well, it sounds quite serious," Anders put his hands in his coat pockets, "I wouldn't want to make them wait any longer."

He looked at his friend, who simply shrugged.

"Okay, you can come in."

Anders waited for them to pull the gates open, then grabbed one by the collar, the other shouting for him to stop.

"I'm Inquisitor General of the Darius district, boy, you know who I answer to?"

"No sir," he struggled through my father's grip, and I watched his eyes bulge. His friend aimed his pistol at Anders' back.

"Donlan Calthern, you know that name boy?"

"Y-yes."

"So, when I make my report, I'll need your name," Anders smiled, "unless, this won't 'appen again?"

"No sir. I promise."

"Good," Anders let him go, then turned to look at the other, the pistol still raised, "put that down before you 'urt yourself."

The guard shakily put the gun away in its holster and Anders started marching down the pale blue cobblestones, his boots clattering against them with a heavy clacking.

"Why didn't you just tell them you lived here before?"

"Cause it doesn't mean anything, this asserts my authority more clearly. That's your first lesson," he stopped me, putting a hand on my shoulder, "as an Inquisitor, you aren't their friend. They'll hate you, even fear you. They know how dangerous you are. But you need to be in charge because they'll take the piss if you show any weakness. These families only care about their pride, and they'll be expecting me to treat them like family."

Anders took a glove off and looked at me.

"What do you see?"

"What do you mean?" I took a cursory look around, "I see this massive fucking house."

"With the Void, idiot," he took my hand and held it palm up, "what do you see."

It wasn't a question, or even a request, more an order. He was asserting a new dynamic between us, him as my General, and me, the Initiate.

He readied his hand, and I did the same, watching the black mark on the back of it glow white-hot. I reached through and pierced the thin layer of the Void, taking hold of strands of energy. It dripped into my veins and soon clouds of vermillion dust became clear in my sight, spewing from the darkened windows of the manor. The power active here reeked of sweat and bodily odour. It was a distinctive scent of guilt.

"S…something happened here," I said.

"Obviously, what else."

"There's shame here. It's really strong, like a rift."

"Good. What else."

I wasn't sure I could see anything else. I looked desperately, but all I could make out were the faint whisperings of those inside and the guards behind us, and I couldn't tell him about that.

"They don't want us here."

"How do you know?"

"I mean," I was searching for the lie, "you said they'd hate us."

"Yes, they will," Anders placed a finger on my forehead, "there's more sight up here. Use your intuition. They've doubled the guard, you can see them patrolling the grounds. There's sheets in the windows to conceal the interior. Notice that no servants or attendants have come to greet us? A crime's been committed here, and they're not just shutting the rabble out with that gate, but us too. The Inquisitorial Order itself."

"I feel like I more or less said that already."

"Not well enough. You need to analyse everything," he flicked my head, "now, let's get inside."

Anders approached the large oak door and took hold of the bell handle that resembled a rosebud. He pulled down. There was a clanging inside. The door was opened just a bit, and a small face peered out from behind it.

"Hello?" then a girl appeared in full view, "Uncle Anders?"

"Guindolene," Anders nodded, "don't call me that. It's nice to see you again, all grown up. Elena, this is Guindolene, cousin to the Snow-Steels. You might not remember her, but you met as children once."

Guindolene did not move; in fact, she was using the door as a wooden barrier between herself and the outside world.

"Velloah'Ra invited us?" I said, struggling to remember Guindolene. It must have been when we were very young.

"I know," Guindolene stayed, still staring at me, "I didn't know you'd be here too."

"I didn't either," I said, smiling at the withered girl, "we're only here to help."

Guindolene allowed us to enter the Snow-Steel manor, standing aside with her head bowed low. Anders stopped and placed a hand under her chin, holding her head up and turning it from side to side.

"Who's been hitting you?" he asked.

"No one, nothing," Guindolene pushed his hand away.

Dad stared for a while, and Guindolene continued to avoid his gaze.

"We're here to protect you."

The walls were slick with darkness, the floors washed in it; the presence here had a feast at its hands. I followed the trail through a tight hallway, and the scent led me to a thick door.

"Please, don't go in there," Guindolene's hands were fluttering.

Anders ignored her and pressed against the door.

It was the drawing room, once a lively and vibrant place for parties as well as relaxation. Its walls were a drab beige, the old rich reds running down them in long liquid streaks. Elegantly shaped seats were covered with torn sheets, rags with a rotten palette of mould thrown across them. The floor had been stripped of a luxurious carpet, and the bare wood was warped from damp.

At the centre of the room was a malformed growth of vacillating fleshy tendrils and, protruding from the folds, tiny hands outreached in despair. I thought of Oliver and pushed it to the back of my mind.

There was an enormous amount of power radiating from the mound, and energy was being absorbed into it at an alarming rate.

"Ashling?" a thick Therainian accent, it must have been Lady Velloah'Ra Snow-Steel, mother to Valeria, Jortan, and Marcus Snow-Steel, Guindolene's cousins.

I turned to discover the entire family had emerged, and stood at the door, watching us. I remembered each of them from documents my father had shown me, and the wonderful mechanical inventions they were working on. I saw my father stare at Velloah'Ra, his features softening just for an instant, then returning to their iron mould.

"Lady Snow-Steel."

She smiled, placing a hand on her chest.

Then she looked at me, with an inquisitive joy I found unnerving. I wasn't sure how to approach her.

"I did not send for the Order," Josiah, the patriarch of the Snow-Steels, stood rigid with sombre aplomb, then looked at his wife, "what's going on?"

"We cannot hide this any longer," Velloah'Ra turned to him, "and the last time I checked, you are not our keeper."

"No, you can't," Anders studied the rest of them, "you should have spoken to me when this first happened. I can't promise anything."

When I looked at the energies surrounding the manor, it seemed that the growth was feeding off of the family. They radiated intense negative emotions, all pouring into the growth simultaneously.

CHAPTER SEVENTEEN
-ANDERS-

The family's reaction had been as expected. They had watched me circle the growth with the watchful eyes of those who had everything to lose, and no options left. The fucking idiots had only reached out to me a few days prior, but this thing was clearly old. And possibly already nearly finished with them.

They'd soon disappeared, however, and left us to our grim work. They knew more than they were letting on, but my refusal to play their game of words and masks had swiftly crushed their hopes I would go easy on them.

The first task was discovering the nature of the aberration. This exercise would also serve as an opportunity for Elena to learn its capabilities and its dangers. I started by taking a pinch of cursed ashes and drawing a ring around the pulsating pile.

I reached into the Void, cupping fountains of pure rage. I channelled it through my skin; at first only sparks shattered against its flesh until roaring jets of flame engulfed it.

I held the shape, the mark burning. There was a piercing howl emanating from the mound, and it drilled into my ear. Once we stopped, the layers of meat that had been melted off soon sewed themselves up, leaving the creature as before.

If the thing were near indestructible, it wouldn't hurt to push it as far as it could go. I pulled back my metal fist and drove it into the centre of the creature, pulping muscle and sinew. The thick folds of skin were rubbery and weighty as I tried to wrench them apart; inside, lining the guts, were fingernails clutching themselves tight.

The arm was a snowsteel prosthetic, one of Velloah's original designs. I'd never been fully able to separate her roles in my mind and it was infuriating. The arm was a reminder that, despite it all, she had saved me back then.

Soon, the wounds knotted themselves back together again, and old flesh sloughed off in a thick ropey soup. After a few moments, the mound returned to its original form.

"So," I shook slime from my hand, "what do you think, daughter?"

"A curse?" Elena sat at a nearby desk, taking notes, "it looks like it's tied to the family."

"I think so too," I looked closely at the rubbery skin, "it looks old, and I think I have an idea, but I'll have to check."

"What's that?"

"Don't worry, very old story, but worth checking."

I remembered the White Vikar, an ancient tome bound in the pale leathery skin of a Stragan. I dreaded the idea of having to get Theona's help again. We sat and studied the growth for a while, discussing possibilities.

"Uncle?"

I turned to see Guindolene holding a tray with a pot and cup on top of it.

"Thank you," I smiled and placed the tray down.

The wealthy families often had an air of elitism, but nothing represented it more than how they would treat their own who had not managed to make a name for themselves. Guindolene was a warm and healthy-looking girl and I knew from experience that being at the beck and call of those you call family was humiliating. But she, like all of us, needed to make a living somehow.

"What do you know of this situation, Guindolene?" I started to pour a cup of the maroon rose-scented tea, and another for Elena.

"Oh, I don't think I should say anything," she looked down, "sorry, I should go."

"Oh, come on," I offered her my cup, "you have something to tell me, you just don't want to get into trouble."

She took a quick sip of the tea and chuckled.

"You'll have to be my eyes and ears here, none of them are telling me anything, and you'll have a unique point of view," I had dropped the forced politeness I always adopted with these families, "we need an ally."

"They all stopped talking a couple of months ago, as in they were perfectly happy, but suddenly it all just stopped," she gave me back the tea, "I never saw

Valeria anymore, which was a shame, we were really close. Then a few weeks ago, I saw Marcus by the river. He was getting rid of something in a small package."

I took a sip of the tea, it was a bitter floral taste that eroded the edges of my tongue.

"I don't know what happened, but I would bet anything that the package had something to do with it. Marcus isn't usually so secretive."

"Where is he now?" I put the cup back gently, still half full, and noticed that Elena had silently abandoned hers too. Guindolene would need to find herself another profession, it seemed.

"He's in the workshop," Guindolene started scratching at her wrist, "he won't be in trouble, will he?"

"Only if he's committed a crime. Thank you, Guindolene, you've been a huge help."

I turned to Elena and gestured for her to follow me to a corner of the room.

"You go speak to Marcus and Velloah, I'm gonna look around for a bit then find out what he was hiding at the river while they're distracted. You join me when you can."

She nodded and made her way to the garden.

CHAPTER EIGHTEEN
-ELENA-

I walked for a few minutes down a winding path towards the centre of a small grove, where the workshop sat. It looked like a little toy that had been carved by Josiah himself with its intricated details. I looked up to see that the rain had ceased for a moment.

The whirring forge at work and the buzzing of tools could be heard behind the door, so I approached and knocked. The noise stopped, but no one answered.

"Mistress Snow-Steel? It's Elena," I knocked again, "hello?"

Marcus Snow-Steel opened the door, his thick black hair covering most of his face. His smell told me that he had not taken care of himself in a very long time.

"Oh, Elena," he cleared his throat, then smiled, "how are you?"

It was overly familiar and invasive in tone, he might well have remembered me but much like Guindolene, nothing came to mind for me.

"I'm fine thank you," I looked toward the door, "can I come in?"

"Oh," he stood aside, pushing the door open, "of course, sorry."

I entered through the front door, into a warm and sterile area, that was more akin to a doctor's lab than the typical blacksmiths you see in Eleynum's slums. To the left, held in place by a steel circle, was almost a full human body made entirely of prosthetics, and spread around the network of small rooms were tables and workbenches focusing on various areas of production. The heat was mostly coming from the back of the building, where the forge itself was located. This was the only room with a secure door.

"Mother's just through there," he scratched at the new beard scrawled along his chin, "how can I help?"

"I wanted to speak to Velloah'Ra, about the growth."

"There's nothing I can say, is there."

"It's strange," I looked at him, "are you okay?"

"What do you mean?"

"It just feels strange, not seeing any of you in so long. But you all seem exhausted."

He shifted his weight.

"There's been a lot going on, I'm sorry we're not seeing each other again under better circumstances."

"Can I see Velloah?"

He nodded, going back to the prosthetic that he was working on.

I approached the door, pushing it open.

Velloah was sat in a chair, staring at the apparatus. She held a large glass of strenger, her stare piercing the walls. The machine was a relay like the ones at Burcanon, but encased in the finest snowsteel and larger than I was used to. Inside, where the liquid was normally a radiating yellow, it was instead a luminescent lilac. A Stragan floated immobile, bobbing slowly on its pipe strings.

"Mistress Snow-Steel?"

"I hardly even recognise your voice, child," she sighed, taking a sip, "though I suppose, hardly a child anymore."

She turned to look at me, her eyes scarred deep by exhaustion. Then held out her arms, as if offering me a hug. I wasn't sure what to think.

"Come, Ashling is as much my son as any other, and you are my granddaughter despite it all."

I took a breath and crossed the room, allowing her arms to snake around my back. I lightly put one around her too. It felt warm there, a feeling I'd been taught to swear off, but one I craved. I stepped away before the pain got worse.

"Ah," Velloah'Ra placed a hand on my cheek, "his training in effect," she shook her head and went back to her drink, "they've broken you, haven't they? You don't feel anymore, not like you used to. You were such a sensitive, wonderful child."

"He's made me stronger."

"You're lying, and you know it, but it's okay. I understand."

I decided that switching the topic was my only move now, she had control of the conversation already and I had to wrestle it back.

"I came to ask about the growth."

"Do you know what this machine is?"

I looked it over again.

"I know it's a generator but I've never seen one use a whole specimen before."

"Try it."

I approached the machine with caution, taking hold of the bright red activation handle. A circular chamber presented itself, where a power cord or even an arm might be placed.

I pulled it down.

The Synthesiser sparked into life, and the Stragan came alive with it, its muffled screams barely heard through the glass. Its body was torn apart, piece by piece, melting its once human face into a paste that congealed with the water into an icy blue solution.

Amongst the chaos, a small strip of light tore through the liquid for just a moment, before dissipating. The liquid was ready to power machinery.

I looked at Velloah, my mouth agape.

"I've done it," she said, sadly, "perfect Synthetisation."

"Was that a tear?"

"It was," she stood, "well, a minor one, but yes."

I didn't know what to say.

"They want this. They want it all," she looked at me, "I want my family safe. Can you do that for me?"

"I don't know what you're asking me."

"I don't trust them. None of them. I'd hoped there was something human left in Anders. But there isn't. My son is gone. But I can see your heart, and I'm running out of time."

"I don't understand," I knelt down in front of her, "who are you talking about?"

"One day, I'll be gone, we all will be I suspect. When that day comes, and you're looking for answers, come back here. This machine is the key, and this is a test. Do not tell him about it. It won't change much in the grand scheme if you do, but if you don't, then I will leave my knowledge with you."

"Why can't you just tell me now? If people are in danger?"

"Because you are not ready, you never will be but I can't thrust this responsibility onto you now," she smiled sadly, "I have nothing else to say."

I walked out and went to Marcus.

"I know that something happened a few months ago to cause this growth," I was beginning to lose patience with this family's secrecy, "Father's going to search the rivers soon, care to come clean before he does?"

His brow was lined in sweat, and his hands trembled as they held the door.

"I can't," he looked as though something lay in his throat and he was attempting to vomit it onto the floor in front of me, but couldn't muster the strength, "I can't."

It was strange. I'd seen it before.

"You can't?"

He shook his head. I think I knew what was wrong, but I would have to address it later. I turned and left the workshop, knowing what needed to be done. I could hear Marcus sobbing as I went.

CHAPTER NINETEEN
-ANDERS-

"It'll be five for a short trip down the river," the boatman, Samuel, said, scraping gunk from the bottom of his small vessel, "but if you don't know what you're lookin' for I could be out there a while."

I raised an eyebrow, cheeky sod was a swindler it seemed, but it wasn't much to ask for, so I gave him double.

The waters in the district had grown thick and slimy with pollution from the local factories clad in precious metals and grand designs of all shapes and colours. Samuel was using a pole rather than a paddle, breaking through the sludge and dragging us along a murky surface. As we moved, I reached out to the Void, scanning the riverbed for any signs of Marcus's energy. I needed a more precise image. Holding onto the folds of the next realm, I pulled myself further in, partially stepping through the barrier. To Samuel, I would have seemed vacant and lost. But here, my senses were more focused than ever.

I could see the barren land around me, derelict buildings smashed to pieces and scattered around me. The waters ran red, and all the way to a distant swamp blanketed in a milky fog. I used my hand to begin pulling on the ethereal strands like a fisherman, as the boat drifted along.

There was vast melancholy in the networks of Eleynum, many drowned dead, bodies disposed of, and heirlooms lost, but eventually, I managed to find a small, familiar trace of Marcus, and what felt like his guilt and shame. There was a shape beneath the surface. The ground shuddered for a moment, and I looked up at the river, seeing it swirling and dissipating. A giant pustulous hand appeared and waved the smoke away. The monster's shape became clear. A giant, clouded eye glowed, shining a horrendous yellow the colour of infected urine. I knew what it was, and pulled myself out of the Void, sealing the way behind me.

"There, clinging to the reeds," I gestured to Samuel, and he handed me another pole, "just keep the boat still for a moment."

I was able to carefully pry the package away from the fronds of grasping weeds before reaching down to cup it in a firm grip. Its withered paper shell dripped with obtuse drops as it was taken out of the water. I was surprised by its weight.

I laid it down on the deck of the boat but stopped before opening it.

"What is it?" Samuel asked, "Inquisitor?"

I considered merely waiting until I was in private, but I had noticed something about the Snow-Steels that I felt the need to test.

"I'm going to bind you to secrecy about this package, Samuel," I looked at him, "do you understand?"

"I uh," he cleared his throat, "of course, sir."

The Silver Thread of Haprocane, the keeper of silence in the Void. An Inquisitor's best tool for the questioning of suspects, especially in matters that require discretion. I pulled a strand of the thread from my tool belt, and tied it around Samuel's wrist, weaving it through his fingers, all while muttering the binding incantations.

When I cut the thread, it dissolved and was absorbed into his leathery skin.

"Thank you for understanding, Samuel."

I looked back to the package, and ran my fingers along the folds, slowly pushing them back. It soon fell apart; Samuel jolted and nearly capsized the vessel.

It was an infant child; It had been entombed in a fatty and crumbling corpse wax. Its face, though disfigured, was just barely intact to form a crude cast of who it once was. I mostly managed to retain my composure, until I saw its tiny hand, pallid and desperate in its final grip. I had to close the package back up. The deep stench of rot hit Samuel hard, and he quickly began vomiting over the side of the boat.

I used a spell to form a solid black film around the package, encasing it so that it could be preserved.

"Are you okay to get us back to the dock?" I said while Samuel was still spitting remnants of his meal into the water.

Soon he stopped and simply nodded, before taking up the pole again. I found myself cradling the resin tomb as we moved.

"Do you know those men, Inquisitor?" Samuel's voice was hoarse, "over there, they're heading to the dock."

I looked over to see a group of three men in dark clothes. They were not soldiers or Inquisitors. They seemed armed with Snow-Steel technology, one having a similar prosthetic to my own, a blade attached at the knuckles.

"No," I placed the babe down, "stay in the boat."

I stepped onto the platform and laid my left hand on my belt, squinting as they stepped onto the dock. One was holding a revolver, and he stayed back while the other two approached.

"Can I help you, gentlemen?"

"Yeah," the large one looked like a bulldog chewing on a wasp, "this is a message from Ghangris: He says you'll drop your investigation into the Snow-Steels."

"Well, that clearly isn't 'appening," I flexed my snowsteel hand, "it's been a hell of a day, gents. Make this easy on yourselves. Go home, see your families. And I won't look for you when night comes."

He snapped his fingers, and the thug with the revolver raised his weapon and fired. The energies of the void were still clinging to me, and I sensed its trajectory and managed to step just to my side. The bullet whizzed past me, sailing through Samuel's throat. The boatman was immobile in shock for a moment, before clutching the gaping wound as he slowly choked to death.

I lifted my prosthetic and pointed at the gunman. Small chambers opened along the knuckles before razor-thin blades fired and ripped through the thug's stomach and torso. He collapsed into the water, blood pooling around him in red smoke.

I stared for too long, images flashing through my mind of corpses floating in the Moirn all those years ago.

The trance broke as the other two ran forward. I dodged one swing and countered with a punch, shattering a collarbone, before pivoting and kicking the large one's legs out from under him. Pain shot through my leg as the other drove his bladed hand into my thigh.

Like a dog in a cage, I fought back, striking the man still standing in the throat, sending him reeling back with his hands clasped around his neck. I turned on the second, his eyes filling with fear as I leapt on him, punching and tearing at him, the void forming my hands into claws to rend his flesh. When he lay quivering, I approached his friend, still gasping for air.

Blood dripped from me, droplets spattering onto his face. The bloodlust still pumped through me, urging me to kill, *kill, KILL*. And as I contemplated his life, I realised something unfortunate.

I'd stopped resisting that urge some time ago.

I grabbed him by his thinning hair, dragging him across the dock. He was trying to scream, but his crushed windpipe was constricting his voice so it came out in breathy gasps. When I neared the gravel, water lapping up against my boots, I threw him in, wading forward to hold him under.

There was peace then, the silent evening only disturbed by the licking water and the buzz of reed bugs. I watched the golden sun cowering behind the towers of Eleynum, its rays warming my face as the animal struggled against my arms. Sometimes he would thrash out at me so I held him even further under, trying to enjoy the quiet.

I felt his strength waning, his fingers growing weak as they slapped at mine. He was pleading now, I could feel it, praying to whatever Treg gods he had left. And soon, I felt the last remnants of him leak out, and his body go limp, waiting to float.

It was only then I let go, allowing him to rise, face down, bobbing on the water like an apple. I stepped back onto dry land and felt the brutal energies leaving me.

I groaned and fell to inspect the blade in my leg. I could see that it had mostly damaged muscle and the bone didn't feel broken, but it was already bleeding heavily, and if I removed the blade, the wound would kill me quickly. I looked over at Samuel, hanging over the side of the boat. I wish I felt pity, for him, but the man would've likely died to his own selfish desires anyway.

I could see on one of their coats an insignia of a silver spider. I needed to find out where it came from.

CHAPTER TWENTY
-ELENA-

The Nurse Order adepts had told me that Anders would
need to spend the night in the healing pools, large cots
filled with viscous white liquid from the Void itself.
His wound wasn't so bad, but it would need time to
regenerate.

It was the perfect time to sneak away and see
Oliver. It had been three days already and I knew he'd
been sent to the Undercroft, where the Changed were
trained before their final transformations.

It wasn't hard to get there, simply heading to the
Order at night. They would know from my clothes that
I was an initiate myself. But convincing the guards at
the door to allow me entry had been harder.

"Only the Changed initiates are allowed
through."

Only men were allowed to become Changed.
We were taught from a young age that women were too
emotional to survive the rigorous training and
mutations that occurred and that men were the only
ones able to truly cut themselves off from their feelings
and achieve mutation.

I wasn't sure how true this was, as most men I'd known simply channelled that energy into anger, but the truth behind nonsense statements mattered little when it came to being allowed entry.

"My father is Anders Therin," I waited for the recognition to sink in, "Inquisitor General under Calthern himself."

They nodded in unison, their posture rigid.

"My father's been wounded, and my brother started his training a few days ago. I need to tell him what happened."

They looked at each other, and then one grumbled to himself.

"Okay, but wait here a moment."

He went to enter the Undercroft, then stopped and waved for his partner to go instead. He sighed and went through. I could see a glimpse of pale blue light seep from behind the door.

It took a moment. I assumed that he was going to double-check with someone inside. I could feel the agitation coming from the other guard, her desire to simply go home already.

He came back and nodded to me, leaving the door ajar. I smiled sweetly and went through, dropping the façade immediately.

The sickly lights above barely illuminated the dark black halls here. I could only make out sharp edges that looked ready to slice you in half if you were not careful. There was a deadly silence that only served to turn the pulsing in my ears into soft drumbeats.

Soon, however, the sounds of fighting became clear. I came into a large amphitheatre, with seats surrounding a fighting pit floored with black sand. There were a few in the stands, coaches and trainers I assumed, barking orders at the two boys in the ring.

They were bruised and bloody, with scratches and whip marks lining their backs. They both had shaved heads and were caked in dirt. Then as one was thrown to the ground, I realised it was Oliver. The other boy began to punch him in the cheek.

"What are you doing?!" I stepped forward, moving toward the ring. Everyone stopped to look at me except Oliver and his opponent.

"Miss Therin, you will show respect in this holy place!" a master stepped out from his seat, Oliver was still being beaten on the ground, "Darak, stop. You've won."

"Yes sir," the boy got off of my brother, stepping back from him.

I tried to push past one of the Changed standing in my way, but unlike the guards out front, he was made of iron. I looked up at him, his pale face staring blankly back at me. I only noticed at this distance, that their pupils had taken over their eyes, only pitch darkness remained.

"Oli, are you okay?" I shouted.

My brother managed to push himself back up onto his feet, panting as blood poured from the wound on his bruised face.

"I'm fine."

"No you're not, look at you," I tried to approach again but the Changed held me by the arm, "let go of me."

"Stop babying me!" My brother yelled, and his eyes flashed a deep red.

The words stung in a way they never had before. When the emotional imprints were alleviated, I felt my skin burning. There was power radiating from him in hot waves of mutating energy.

We stared at each other for a while, unsure how to proceed at that moment.

"I'm sorry, Oli, I just wanted to make sure you were okay."

"I'm fine. Better than ever."

"Okay, I trust you," I sighed, "Dad's in the Healing Ward, I just wanted to let you know."

Oliver winced for a moment, then nodded and turned to walk away. I watched his small frame melt into the darkness of the chamber and realised the others were staring at me. Burning eyes, insisting that I leave.

CHAPTER TWENTY-ONE
-ANDERS-

Six in the morning, on the dot. I nodded to the lead Enforcer standing by the gate. He waved his neutraliser to snap it out to its full length, the crimson crystal pulsing at the end of the metal baton. His team readied their rifles, pulling their reflective black visors down to complete their pitch uniforms.

Elena was doing that irritating thing where she scratched away at her hands until red marks appeared. I grabbed her wrist and scowled at her, silently ordering her to focus.

"Can you handle this?"

"Yes," she spat back, pulling her hand away.

She was growing more defiant all the time and I could feel my grip on her fading. Soon, she'd learn discipline, because I was running out of time to drill it into her like Theona had with me.

As we prepared, I heard metal scraping from the gardens, followed by cheers and clapping. I felt dark energy spilling through the bars and knew I had to act quickly. I grabbed hold of the gate and turned my snowsteel hand, slowly twisting and crushing the lock before swinging it open.

There was a small crowd in front of the Snow-Steel manor, mostly consisting of the family and a few other high-flying aristocrats. I noticed Valeria had a hand gripping her waist, and cocking my head slightly I could see that it belonged to Jortan Snow-Steel, the oldest son. He looked the spit of Josiah, with pale brown hair and a sneer on his face.

They seemed to be watching Marcus, applauding. He was holding some sort of contraption in his hand. It resembled a simple firearm but glowed with blue energy through thick grills and vents. A steel mannequin stood in front of him, half-melted.

Josiah was clapping Marcus on the back.

"Well done, Marcus," he turned back to the crowd, "there, living proof that your investments are safe. He's rough around the edges, but this boy is remarkable, isn't he, Velloah?"

She nodded, staring past Josiah and focusing on her son.

"Pity the other one has been nothing but a disappointment," Josiah pointed his words at Jortan, who simply shrugged back.

One of the crowd members noticed us approaching. Some of them dropped their glasses and yelled, backing away. I watched Velloah's face pale at my approach, her hands white as they held a drink.

"Marcus Snow-Steel," my boots clanged against the cobbled path, "I am arresting you for infanticide, the desecration of a corpse, and treason."

His eyes widened; he still gripped the machine.

Josiah stepped in close to the black-haired young man then and spoke quietly to him before joining the crowd.

An Enforcer approached Marcus, but he was shaking so much that he pulled the trigger on the weapon, recoiling as it discharged a stream of energy so bright, I reflexively turned away for a moment. I had already prepared some power of my own, ripping a protective layer forth that caused the beam to ricochet and shave off a corner of the manor's roof.

Marcus whimpered and scrambled to run, dropping the machine on the floor, but the Enforcer jammed the neutraliser into the boy's back, causing him to screech in pain. He curled up into a ball, smoke streaming from the wound as dark fluid dribbled through his clothes.

Two more of the Enforcers held him down, one placing his knee against Marcus's neck, crushing his face against the stone, as their leader clasped his wrists and ankles together in chains.

"Please," Marcus groaned, "help me!"

"Get off him!" Elena said, rushing forward, "you're choking him, get off!"

She pushed one of the enforcers off and grabbed the other by the throat, pulling him away.

The pup hadn't yet learned restraint, and now was the time for a lesson. The Enforcers, being aggressive brutes trained by years of war, turned on her. One smacked her back and dragged her away from his teammate by the hair. She tried to fight back but the two of them beat her until she stopped kicking.

"You finished?"

She groaned in response, rolling onto her side. Velloah moved forward to go to her son, but I put my hand out and stopped her.

"What have you become?" she growled.

"Get back, or I'll take you too."

I swung my head for the two men to return to a squirming Marcus, dragging him away from the gardens. Josiah pushed his hair back, his face sprinkled with sweat, watching Marcus.

"What is this about?" he was nervous for the first time, that facade of confidence was thoroughly destroyed.

"I was attacked yesterday, a gang asked me to leave this case alone," I saw Velloah watching intently, "now I can't say for certain which one of you ordered it but take this as a warning: Do not cross me again."

I went to leave, then turned back.

"You ask what I've become? I am law and order, and you stuffy, born-to-rule, sibling-fuckers, need to understand that you're not above it," I looked at my daughter, slowly picking herself up, "you tried to use me, use her. She might be thick enough to fall for it. But I'm not."

The family all shared guilty glances, they stank of it in fact. And Elena, I imagine feeling completely humiliated, fell in line then, skulking behind me.

There was a clanging sound as the shaking and rattling of the gun got worse. I looked at the rest of them as they backed away.

"Move now," they did as I commanded.

I held it by the stock and felt the energy spilling from it. There was nothing for it. I smashed the barrel against the stone, again and again, breaking the frame apart. It stopped.

The crystal burst with a blinding light, the shockwave knocking me onto my back. It felt as though I couldn't open my eyes, but they were instead covered in a white film. I was underwater, sounds around me barely resonating with me. The sensations dissipated eventually, but when my vision returned, I could see an Enforcer on the ground, his back to me. A disoriented Josiah turned him over.

Most of the right side of his torso and face had been reduced to a steaming, pulverised mess, sloughing off of him in thick layers. I pushed myself up, a drilling pain at the front of my brain. But as I went to him, I heard screams emanating from the streets, building up to a cacophony.

I stumbled away from the manor, ignoring the cries of protest from the family. I made my way back to the path outside the manor, seeing crowds stream past the gates up ahead. I pushed forward, wincing from the ache in my leg.

People were running past, many bumping into me as they went. I grabbed a man by the elbow, holding him in place.

"What's happened?"

"A-a horrific creature, there!" he yanked his arm away and kept running.

I went further down the street, pushing through the fleeing citizens.

At the edge of my vision, standing in the centre of the road, over a child frozen in fear, was a pale, feminine figure. It had no arms, and her fleshy hair ended in hooked barbs. Her head snapped to one side, revealing a gaping, fanged jaw, cracking as it unhinged. I started to run towards it.

It screeched, and within seconds, the tentacles spread in a fan, striking down and raising the child above its head. The young girl's scream punctured my heart. I only just got within range as the creature turned and pierced the child with two spikes, pulling her apart to disembowel her, letting the fountain of blood wash over its face. The hideous jaw was wide open, drinking the fluid in, its forked tongue licking at the wound.

"No!" I pulled a bladed disc from my belt, throwing it with full force.

The weapon spun in the air, catching the monster in the jaw. I didn't stop, raising my arm to fire a series of spikes from its knuckles like before. They tore through flesh and bone, causing the creature to drop the girl's corpse. Using the weight of my momentum, I drove my metallic fist into its face, spinning to crash into its back.

The foul thing hissed, its mouth hanging from the wound. It was from the family of Stragan, a collective group of monsters, but these forms were rarely seen. It was known as a Saglere-Fol. A blood fiend.

It swiped at me, attempting to pierce my flesh with the barbed tendrils, and shuddered every time it missed. We circled each other, I couldn't let it hit me, or I would be dead within minutes.

Elena rushed from the left, driving a thin black blade through its side. It snapped at her, and she was able to get away but left the sword lodged in the bone structure. I hit it again to distract it.

It came at me with a flurry of strikes, and I was barely able to keep on top of them, only keeping it at bay with reactionary blows. A small ball rattled across the stones, landing next to its feet. I quickly dived away.

The device exploded, shredding the creature with silver shrapnel. Even tattered and misshapen, it still did not fall. I saw Theona rushing its back, driving another blade through its torso. The Saglere-Fol slammed her back, and I saw my chance.

The ends of the snowsteel fingers dropped hooks on long lines of silver, and I whipped it around to entangle the Saglere-Fol's legs. I yanked it onto its front, retracting the hooks as I rushed forward, and kicked it onto its back. It screeched before I repeatedly smashed into its face with my fist, pulverising meat and bone until it lay still.

Theona was pushing herself up into a sitting position, and I frantically searched her for wounds. There were deep gashes in her chest, her ribs bare beneath them.

"You know I'll be fine," she groaned, "check the girl, that's more important."

I nodded and turned to look at the child's body, walking past a panting Elena.

The girl was on her front, propped up on her elbow, looking right at me with eyes drained of all light. She reached out to me, trying to drag herself forward on her spilt guts. Her jaw opened and closed over and over, her teeth clacking as they slowly fell out, along with strands of her hair. The transformation had begun.

I should have been faster. She hissed as she swiped weakly at my leg. My mark burned, and I reached into the Void, pulling on the strings of anger and pain, turning it into a ball of flame, before dousing her in it. She gave out inhuman wails, writhing as her body was engulfed in fire. She was reduced to nothing but a charred skeleton.

I exhaled and went back to Theona. She was on her knees, making shapes with her hands. They represented the constellations and were the start of her process. Her head snapped back, and she winced in pain, her eyes roaring with fire. Then it stopped.

She fell apart. Pieces of her crumbling away and scattering ash. She was gone.

Every granule was soon sucked back and stacked up on top of each other, twisting and turning to reform Theona completely. Eventually, she was sat there, cross-legged, just as before, but with no wounds, and now pure white hair.

Theona had told me the story of her family, one of the seven who had achieved true immortality. Many claimed it in legends, but the Faygalens and their like

167

were Phoenix-Bloods, descendants of the ancient birds of fire. And it was a tale that very few knew to be true.

"Anders," she sighed, "I don't know how many of those I've got left in me."

I helped her up.

"I should have been faster."

I walked to Elena and dragged her to her feet.

"What are you doing?!" I yelled.

She sobbed, mouthing unknown words, her throat croaking through them.

"What will you do when I'm not here? You have to protect yourself," I continued, trying to slow down, "I'm sorry."

I pulled my daughter into a tight, awkward hug, feeling her sniff against my chest, her hands placed on my stomach. She was trying to push me away.

168

CHAPTER TWENTY-TWO
-ELENA-

I sat down in front of Marcus Snow-Steel in the interrogation room, my eyes raw. I took a breath and clasped my hands, leaning on the table between us that Marcus was chained to. He had been roughed up more after I had been gone, I suppose it was the Enforcer's way of getting their licks in. There'd be no way for me to find out who it was, none of them would talk now.

Marcus looked down, his eyes and mouth bruised.

"I'm sorry for the way they treated you earlier," I leaned forward, "a tear opened, and a girl was killed."

He had a vacant expression.

I wiped my eyes.

The door was opened behind me and was accompanied by boots marching across the room. It was Theona, with Anders following shortly behind. She placed a tray down with a pot of tea freshly brewed. I looked at the set, unsure if I could stomach it myself, but it was intended for Marcus anyway according to my father. Some kind of attempt at humanity between them before he focused on questioning.

"Would you like some?" I bit on my tongue after saying it, unsure why I was keeping up this pretence with him.

He nodded, so I poured half a cup for him, pushing it across the table and unlocking the chains so he could relax. Marcus took a sip and cradled the drink.

"Look, Marcus, I'm going to get to the point," Anders said, sitting down. I still didn't know what to make of him; he'd always been cruel but caring in his own way. Now I was afraid of him, and his subtle movements put me on edge, "you were seen by the river disposing of something. I found it."

Anders had placed the small black tomb on the table an hour before, letting both of us consider it before. He said he wanted me to try and figure out what was inside, and that he wanted Marcus to eat himself alive.

"Have you got anything to say for yourself?" Anders ground his teeth, "infanticide can lead to the death penalty," Marcus still didn't look up, so my father slammed his hand down, "are you grasping your situation now?"

He started shaking his head.

"I can't."

Anders threw his chair back as he stood, ripping the casing off and pushing it across to Marcus. He was horrified by its contents, folding in on himself with sobbing breaths. I turned the wrappings over, already knowing what was inside, but the awful grey half-skull peering out at me still made me gag. My father looked at me with even more loathsome disappointment. I really hated him then. Anyone would have felt the way I did, but it still wasn't enough.

Marcus was still looking away, struggling to breathe properly.

"I can't."

"No," Anders pointed in his face, "no more, okay? I've heard so much of that family's secretive shit, and I've had enough. You're a fucking murderer and that's that."

"I...I..." he shook violently, and his mouth contorted in strange shapes, the teacup dropped and shattered, splattering rose liquid across the floor, "I can't. I can't. I can't. I can't."

"Wait," I knew there had been something strange, "you, can't say anything, at all?"

He nodded.

"Even if you wanted to?"

He nodded again, more vigorously, as if I understood.

"I know what it is," I looked at my father, "he's bound, they all are in some way."

"The Silver Thread of Haprocane," Anders finished my thought, smiling for maybe a second or two, "I'd felt something strange; they were all under its spell. No idea how they got a hold of some but that's it."

"Okay, Marcus," I dragged the chair around and sat next to him, looking into his eyes, "I'm going to release you from it, but it's going to cut the threads from the whole family, do you understand?"

He nodded again.

"You can't tell anyone else that it's been lifted yet."

He seemed to understand. I took a small knife and held his wrist in front of me.

"Sorry, this is going to hurt."

I pressed the blade through his skin, until I felt something small and metallic, prying it from his flesh. The silver thread glinted and started to slither back inside him, but I managed to pinch it, ripping the strand out. As soon as it was free, it faded to a withered grey and disintegrated.

I gave Marcus a moment to breathe.

"What happened to this child, boy?" Anders barked.

"Her name is Isobel," Marcus reached out, almost touching her forehead, then brought his hand back, "she's my daughter. Our daughter. Valeria and I."

"Oh," I felt sick, it seemed rumours of these high-born families and their tendency to claim 'pure' bloodlines had a kernel of truth in them, "how long have you two, well..."

"I know what you're thinking," he winced, "But we're not really brother and sister. I learned that my mother adopted me when I was a year old."

"Right," my stomach still hadn't settled, but I didn't feel as though I was going to vomit anymore, "still, that's a risk factor for tears."

"I understand, but no, we are not siblings by blood," he sighed, "If anything, I think that made it worse for them. Josiah especially."

"He's never accepted you, has he?" Anders said.

I empathised with that. It looked like Marcus had seemed the favourite initially, but maybe there was something else there.

"No, but he was always kind enough until I started spending too much time with Valeria," his eyes were so sunken, it was clear now that he had not slept in weeks, "me working more with Velloah in the workshop was his idea, actually, so I didn't spend any time with her or Jortan."

"What happened to Isobel?"

"I don't know," he looked at me, "you have to believe me, I have no idea, she was perfectly fine, a happy, healthy, beautiful baby, already so full of life. Then, suddenly, she was dead," his lip quivered, "Josiah ordered me to 'clean up my mess.' He was distraught."

"So, you threw her in the river?"

"I didn't know what else to do," he looked back at Isobel, "I had heard that many unwanted babes from poor families had been drowned there and that some orphanages did that too, a horrible idea, but I thought that it might prove to be the perfect place. I didn't count on Guindolene seeing me."

"You knew that she'd seen you?"

"Yes. I couldn't tell her what happened, Josiah had already silenced us all, but I didn't try to dissuade her from saying anything either," he sunk into his chair, "I suppose, in a way, I wanted everyone to know. I didn't want her to be forgotten. It's been destroying me ever since."

Things were a little clearer now. But Isobel's death was still suspicious, and I knew who to speak to next.

"Marcus," I rested a hand on his shoulder, "we're going to keep you safe; I promise."

"He's not our problem anymore," Anders made a move towards the door, "he still committed a crime, he's the Justice's issue now."

"We can't," I snapped, "he's family."

"No, he isn't," Anders cleared his throat, "besides, that doesn't mean anything to you, does it?"

"I understand," Marcus smiled, for the first time since I had met him, "I accept an equal part in all of this, and I know that my being here will keep the rest of them on their toes."

"You don't have to do this," I said, looking again at my father, "what the fuck is wrong with you?"

"Come, Elena," Anders said, "we have work to do."

I sighed, squeezing Marcus' shoulder, and then I went to leave.

"Elena?"

"Yes?"

"Could you," he coughed, "Sorry, I," he held his throat, "I want her to," his eyes widened, "What's happening to me?"

Marcus stood and leaned on the table, holding his chest and coughing suddenly quite violently, blood spraying onto the table.

"Get a medic now!" I shouted at Theona and Anders, for either of them to do something.

I rushed to Marcus's side as he writhed on the table, pushing the tea set onto the floor, scattering more shards everywhere. Isobel's body lay precariously on the edge, her grey arm hanging over the side.

"Hold on," I gripped his reddening face, his neck bulging with bright purple veins, "somebody help!"

"Elena," he gasped, "Bury her, please."

"I will," my eyes darted everywhere, "I don't know what to do, Marcus, I'm sorry."

He screeched in pain, convulsing like a terrified worm in my arms, trying to wriggle free. It was horrible. I looked to the door in desperation, and my father was waiting, watching, but no one else. I started to accept that they wouldn't find one fast enough.

Marcus' breaths came as a bubbling black liquid spilling over his lips and into his dark beard. The whites of his eyes were scorched, the same darkness spreading to his irises, spilling into the blue lakes like tar, before sealing in a film over them entirely. His lungs rattled as the clutch on my arm softened. Soon, he was limp.

I laid him on the table and pushed my hair back. I straightened my coat and noticed something glinting among the shards. Driving them apart, I saw a small metallic object, perhaps the size of a coin.

It was a spider or a model of one at least. It had a small engraving on its thorax, the same as my father had described. I assumed that the tea was meant for Anders, but I couldn't help but feel that they wanted Marcus too.

I stared at my father's blank eyes and felt my hatred persist.

CHAPTER TWENTY-THREE
-ANDERS-

When Elena and I arrived at the Manor, I was greeted by Jortan Snow-Steel, Josiah's elder son. He had the thin mousy hair of his father and a plump face that only accentuated the slope of his weak chin. For whatever reason, he was wearing what looked like a workman's jumpsuit, except that it had been sewn together from tweeds and fine leather, without a mark on it.

"Ah, Inquisitor," his smile seemed to sink into his face rather than lift upwards, in the background I could hear a shrieking, "I am afraid that you've caught us at a rather bad time, I don't suppose it would be possible for you to come back tomorrow?"

"That won't be possible, Jortan," I squinted just for a moment, "I don't really have the time for a chat, where's your father?"

"Oh, see that's just it," he looked like he had smelt something pungent when I had called him by his given name, but it continued now, "Father left, he said that he had some things to attend to and then off he went, leaving us behind," he leaned towards me, and I picked up a whiff of his unwashed body, "if you want my opinion, I think he's making a run for it."

"What makes you say that?" Elena took a step back, "where can we find him?"

"Oh, he has been acting very strange lately," he leaned against the wall, "and surely you are aware that nothing comes free in this city?"

"Oh, I'm aware," I rolled my eyes.

I turned and made my way outside, leaving the sound of what I assumed to be Velloah'Ra's sorrow behind. Elena didn't follow straight away, and I looked at her as she stared intently at the Snow-Steel.

"You should be looking after her."

I nodded at her when she joined me. She was right, of course. Velloah deserved a lot, but the loss she felt seemed cruel. I knew that if I lost my Oliver, I would fall into the Void itself, never to be found again.

It was impossible to track Mister Snow-Steel's emotional signature over long distances and in such busy environments, but I estimated that his factory would be a good place to start our search. As we set off, the rain that had given us a reprieve for but a few days began again, and clouds loomed above with violence in mind.

The Snow-Steel factory was built with bricks of snow, now stained like bone from dust expelled by vents and chimneys. A large silver sign simply stating Snow-Steel Designs was attached to the front, a line of roses separating them.

The factories built here had similar designs, attempting to catch the eyes of every citizen of Eleynum.

I entered the lobby of the factory and approached the front desk, passing a guide showing a group of stuffy-looking suits around.

"Hello," I saw bags under the receptionist's glazed eyes, he was clearly ready to go home, "how can I help you today?"

I heard the guide discussing the new range of weapons being produced, including new types of firearms. Like Marcus's original design, a fancy trick, perhaps useful for Enforcers. But Inquisitors always fought aberrations face to face, ripping and tearing through flesh and bone. Even Elena's blade required too much finesse to be of real use against most creatures. A relic of a time I preferred to forget.

"I'm Inquisitor General Therin," I rested my snowsteel arm on the wood, "I need to speak with Josiah. Immediately."

I was directed to Josiah's office, being told by his personal assistant that he had stepped out for some air. It seemed that he often headed to the roof via what appeared to be an endless staircase.

Near the top, I took a moment to catch my breath, refusing to be seen panting in front of Elena. She was cold in her demeanour, her hand hovering over the sword's hilt.

"Remember, you control the situation. Don't let him talk his way out of this," I said, pulling the hammer back on my revolver.

"I won't," my daughter unsheathed the blade, "maybe don't let this one die."

I couldn't help but smile, her fire amused me. Theona's faith in the girl always seemed over the top, coddling almost, but maybe the kid did have it in her after all. I saw her slowly starting to learn the reality of this awful work she was doomed to carry out.

I kicked the door open and was immediately slashed by a sheet of rain. Josiah was standing at the edge of the building's rooftop, overlooking some of the city. He was soaked.

"Josiah Snow-Steel," I had to shout for him to hear me, "I'm arresting you for infanticide."

"I thought that the boy committed that crime?"

"Why'd you do it?"

"Have you ever met a travelling mystic? They're quite common across the channel," he still didn't look back at me, "I thought I would pay for a fortune, why not, a bit of fun. He told me that my familial lineage was of pure blood and that a creature of great power would be born of the union between my children."

"But he isn't your son? You know that?"

"Alas, the child was only a half-breed. It wasn't meant to be him," Josiah stumbled a little as the wind slammed into his side, "I had to take extreme measures. One can find all manners of medicines in the slums, ones that can make someone more compliant."

"That's disgusting," Elena shouted over the rain, "you let him," she looked down then and held her stomach, "Fuck you."

"We all had to make sacrifices," Josiah glanced behind him, "this was Valeria's."

179

"You killed a child over that?" I stepped closer to him.

I'd never really known Josiah. He was cold with me when Velloah had taken me in all those years ago. I'd always been his servant, nothing more. But I saw him for what he was then, a parasite that had been born with immense power, and wielded it like a child.

"I had to, it was impure," he turned then, "I met a man, an extraordinary man, who explained to me the power that would be born under my roof. He knew it was coming, the growth, and he explained that there would be others looking to take it for themselves. He promised some of that same power to me if I just kept it safe. I assumed he was referring to the same prophecy."

"You could have called me earlier, I could have helped you," I said, stepping closer, "who was this man?"

"He has eyes and ears everywhere. He said the Quorum would send people to kill it, but he promised he would destroy everything I cared about if I allowed that to happen. I couldn't let an impure child ruin the plan!" he glanced back over the edge, "Turns out it didn't matter. This is exactly what he wanted, and my life is over anyway. I've already said too much."

"Look," I could barely keep my eyes open in the rain, "I'm going to find out either way, I can help you," I pulled out the silver spider, "where's Ghangris? Tell me, I'll kill him and then we can solve this, together."

"You really do know nothing, don't you?" he laughed for a moment, "he and his gang said they would 'protect' us. He's nothing."

"So who is this man?"

"You'll find out soon enough," he leaned over.

"Josiah," I moved forward, "step away from the ledge."

"Thank you, Anders," he smiled at me again, "to the grave."

He fell backwards, his coat flapping as he slid over. I barely heard him hitting the road below, his bones cracking, as I stared at the edge. It was a painting meant only for the barest of rooms, long after the one who slept there has passed.

CHAPTER TWENTY-FOUR
-ELENA-

Somehow the manor walls looked worse, with giant cracks appearing and dark liquid flowing from them. The Aberration was growing more powerful and Valeria looked haggard. I went to hug her, feeling her half collapse against me.

"Where are your mother and brother?" Anders barked.

"I'll go and get them," she sniffed.

"Bring them to the drawing room."

"Go easy on her," I said, glaring at him.

He'd been wild-eyed for a few days, the hunt almost exhilarating to him somehow. But now they were almost ablaze, deep golden irises flaring at me as I went to study the malignant growth. It didn't seem to represent anything known to the Order, not even in its oldest texts, according to Theona. She had connected it to vague descriptions from numerous ancient books, but nothing concrete had been found.

Valeria, Jortan, and Velloah'Ra all came in. Anders had them sit down around the rotten table by the door. The Snow-Steel matriarch seemed even older now. She managed a sad wave at me as Valeria helped her down, her face set deep with the lines of grief. Whether it was for Marcus, Josiah, or both, was unclear. I hoped against hope she had no part in his machinations. I couldn't handle losing another person I respected to this black hole of an event.

"Why have you summoned us here?" Jortan's shrill voice was beginning to grate on me.

"I have come to explain your situation," Anders sat across from them, "I have ordered Enforcers to watch every exit, so you won't be leaving, no matter what. Understood?"

"Oh please," Jortan stood, "this is ridiculous, Mother, he is trying to intimidate us, and I won't listen to this. This Inquisitor clearly has no idea what he's doing."

"Sit down," I flared my nostrils, "this Aberration is here because of your collective guilt over the death of Isobel, as well as your family's consistent tampering with the Void."

"How dare you," he went to leave, "her murderer, thanks to you, is dead."

"I'm warning you, boy, take another step and I'll break your fucking legs!" Anders hit the table with a powerful strike, breaking a chunk off it, "I have had enough. You people sit there and expect preferential treatment, and for what? If anyone else in this city had committed rape, incest, murder, and single-handedly caused multiple aberrations, they would have been put to death," he scanned over them, "Jortan, do you have anything to say?"

His fish-like mouth hung open.

"What?" Velloah looked around at her children, "what do you mean?"

"You probably helped them, that's why you haven't told me anything. You're caught up in this incestuous Void-worship bullshit," he shook his head, "you're a fucking liar, and you always have been."

"What's he talking about, Mother?" Valeria looked vacant as she spoke.

"He was everything to me," Velloah'Ra's chin shivered, but whether it was anger or heartbreak I couldn't tell, "why are you saying these things?"

"You disgust me," he pulled the metal spider from his pocket and placed it on the table, "do you know what that is?

She looked at it and nodded.

"No, we don't know anything," Jortan said, swiping it off the table, "a useless trinket."

I sighed. Of course, he would deny it, the others had the sense to know they were only making it worse for themselves. I reached out and took Velloah'Ra's hand, as a tear hit the rim of her thumb.

"I'm sorry I said all that, I needed to see how you would react," Anders said as I squeezed her fingers lightly.

"You don't know, do you? What he did to her?" I said.

"What?" she looked at her son, "what did you do?"

"Jortan?" Valeria wrung a handkerchief.

"Go on, tell them," I watched him squirm, "or should I?"

"This is outrageous," he stood and went to the glass doors, "I won't stand for any more of this."

"He already told you, you can't leave," I turned back to the women at the table, "your father was plotting for you and Jortan to have a child, he was involved with some kind of cult. But when Josiah found out it was Marcus' child instead, they killed her. They were..." I coughed at the end.

"What?" Valeria's voice was strained.

"They were drugging you."

"That's not possible..." Valeria's breaths became shorter, more pronounced, "that's disgusting."

"Jortan raped you, Valeria. Your father knew. They knew the whole time. Then they killed Isobel. They said she was only a half-breed."

They sat there for a while, mother and daughter, processing what had been said. Jortan simply stared from afar.

I inhaled, then sighed.

Velloah'Ra, for the first time, moved with a speed I did not think possible and went to Jortan. She stared at him for a while.

"It was for our own good."

The sound made when she slapped his face was thunderous. He fell straight to the floor, a significant mark appearing on his face.

"You are no son of mine," she stared listlessly at the monster sprawled on the ground before her.

The Enlightened Quorum

At that moment, I saw Velloah'Ra's light go out. The energies that had glowed with the fury of that fateful machine in Burcanon just a moment ago, slowly went dim like a lamp losing fuel before the fall of night. She was a husk, a shell waiting to perish.

I thought then of the machines Velloah had built, of the suffering they had caused so many. She hadn't just armed Inquisitors to crush the people of the city but had abused the Void, causing thousands to die. My mum, to die. The scar that had left would ache every day, and knowing that Oliver likely felt the same pain, made me even angrier. I couldn't be sure that those relays in Burcanon were hers, but there was no doubt in my mind that the machine in the workshop would be even worse.

I wondered then what she had been trying to tell me. Surely the Velloah that had been so kind to me upon my arrival had a reason not to tell my father. How involved was the Quorum in all this? There seemed to be too many threads to tie, a tangled web of lies and manipulation that I could barely keep track of.

But I knew that the answer to my questions lay here, at the Snow-Steel manor. This was a chance to finally avenge Sonya. To show the world the truth about the Quorum, the Senate, and the Dynasties that controlled them. These machines were connected to something greater, far more terrible, and I intended to find out what.

Maybe then, Velloah's soul would find peace.

"Hello."

I turned towards a mysterious voice.

"Please, I only wish to talk," it was a dark figure, he was dressed in a long coat with a hat and scarf that I imagine covered most of his face on his way here. But now it was on full display, pale and sharp in its edges, "please."

His eyes were a strange lilac, similar to that of energies of the Void. I saw that his nails looked like they were hooked and caked in soot. Anders pulled his gun from his belt and readied his prosthetic. I coughed to catch his attention. He looked at me.

"This must be him," I said, "the benefactor."

Anders nodded but didn't relax his position.

"Thank you," the figure stepped into the room completely, his frame imposing yet thin. He pointed at the Snow-Steels, "I'll speak with them first if you don't mind."

I sat down with Valeria and Velloah'Ra. Jortan exchanged an embarrassed glance with me and walked across the room towards the creature to make a symbol with his hands, then bow low.

The Void-borne was far taller than Jortan, and so when he looked down on the mousey man it was almost comical. His disdain spoke volumes.

"I think you might be mistaken, child," he looked at Velloah'Ra, "you've not heard from them?"

"No, I held them off for as long as I can, but they know that it's happening tonight and will be here eventually," she kept looking at her daughter, "I've done everything you asked, at risk to myself and my family."

"I know, and I can't begin to thank you enough," he spoke softly, and his words made my eyes feel heavy.

He reached out and stroked her face, "you've done the right thing, I assure you. Now, take your daughter and go. I will handle the rest."

"They're not going anywhere," Anders said.

"Your soldiers are all dead, Inquisitor," he said, with a grim expression, "or they will be soon enough."

I fought the compulsion to run. I was fascinated that I'd met a Void being capable of conversation, and I began scoping out exits from the room, ensuring that he would not escape.

"We are not enemies, Inquisitor General," he looked at Valeria, "I will show some goodwill."

The creature flashed toward Jortan and grabbed his face, forcing him to the floor.

"No!" I drew my sword, "he needs to stand trial!"

"I can't allow that," he hissed, "he knows too much."

His face buried into Jortan's, muffling the boy's screams. His mother watched, numb. When the creature pulled away, Jortan's skin was like ashen bone, flaking away in dusty clouds. His eyes had been replaced by sunken black pits, his fair falling away from the scalp.

"We needed him," I shouted, looking at Anders, who shrugged, still trained on the creature.

"Now, get out of here," the man said to Velloah and Valeria.

They gathered themselves and, on their way out, exchanged one last look with me. They were searching for something but never seemed to find it. I never saw them again after that.

"I am what your order classified as a Folsesjeger," the man stepped ever closer and found a chair to sit in. His hands shook as he sat down, "I am the last, the rest were killed hundreds of years ago."

"Aren't you concerned I'll just kill you?" Anders said.

"You seemed smarter than that," he grinned, displaying rows of barbed teeth, "there is an opportunity in this if you wish."

"Why are you here?"

"Because that creature," he seemed in awe by the growth, "that is a Folsesjeger nest. I was told of its arrival many years ago, and have waited patiently ever since, and today is the day."

"Okay," Anders pointed at the mound, "I'll make sure that it dies tonight then."

"Ah," he leaned back, "we both know you have not been able to."

I took my own chair and sat down, facing him.

"What are we doing, then?" I sighed, "how did you know it was here?"

"What are you doing, girl?" Anders growled.

"I need some answers," I stared back at my father, refusing my facial muscles any movement at all, despite the fear that I might shatter.

"I have my sources, those wishing to bring the next life. But I have come here to ask that you let me take it," he chuckled, "I know it seems strange. The predecessors to your order, the Paladins, they hunted us to our near extinction. But this is the last chance my species has, and I do not wish to harm you. Nor do I intend to teach it to harm others, we will live peacefully."

Anders laughed from his gut, wiping his face with a gloved hand.

"You know, this week has been exhausting, and I genuinely didn't think it could get any more ridiculous," he looked at the growth, "you know I can't let you do that."

"It is a mistake," the creature stood, "but I wanted to give you both a chance to be different. There are others, already on their way, they will turn it to their own ends and bring an end to this world."

"Like who?"

"The Enlightened Quorum."

"What? " Anders said, "That's absurd."

"Why would they do that?" I followed, "they hated the Folsesjeger more than anyone, children of Darius and all that?"

"It's wrong," the creature cocked his head at me, "we were born from Kaurus. Darius was simply the first."

"I don't understand."

"We fought back, against Kaurus himself," the strange man then leaned forward a little, "the one thing the God-King and the Quorum agreed on, was that we were abominations."

"I mean, of course, you would say that," Anders rubbed his nose for a moment, taking a deep breath, "this is horse shit, Elena. Get away from him. Now."

"They will destroy everyone if they get their hands on the child."

"I can't," Anders said, blades slowly protruding from his glimmering knuckles, "you know I can't."

The Folsesjeger lunged at Anders, finding only the chair as he dived sideways, firing blades into his side before leaping forward to punch. The man stopped my father's fist mid-air and wrapped his arm around his other wrist, holding him in place to drive his forehead into Dad's nose. I heard the crunch and attacked. I found myself suddenly being lifted into the air and then thrown through a wall and into the stair banister.

He was faster than I'd anticipated, already on Anders again, swiping relentlessly with his black talons, but my father's prosthetic arm blocked most of them. I was able to rush forward and use my leg to hook his out from under him, before following up with my sword, only to drive through the floor.

I drew my sword as the two circled each other, watching their movements for any sign of attack. Then the Folsesjeger was between us as we faced him, just out of reach of his talons.

His eyes darted, then stopped on something. I thought at first he was looking at me, but it was almost as if it was through me. His eyes widened, and then he moved.

I realised then that the speed and strength he'd shown before had been restraint on his part. I barely registered him sweeping my father's legs from under him before he was on me too, pinning me to the ground.

Before I could scream and fight back, shards sprayed across us. They were embedded in the ground around me and then tore into the man's back, making him hiss in pain. I thought maybe they were my father's prosthetic, but they were biological, needle-like protrusions. The Folsesjeger rolled away from me, seemingly dismissing us as a threat. Anders was getting himself up too.

I was still winded by the blow but managed to turn my head to look at the assailant. It was quick, maybe even harder to follow than the mysterious man. It was a gaunt human corpse with a long spiked tail swinging wildly behind it. Its mouth was filled with fanged tendrils that splayed when it screamed at us.

With a flick of its tail, the monster flung more pins in our direction.

I crawled behind a nearby table, throwing it over to cover myself from the barrage. The Folsesjeger dashed away from us. I heard the creatures clash, growling as they tore into each other's flesh.

I went to my father as he got to his feet.

"Are you okay?" I asked.

He grunted in response and tossed his revolver, drawing an axe from his belt. The Folsesjeger was grappling with the assassin, inches away avoiding its snapping jaws. Its tail battered his side and left horrible wounds that seemed to heal quickly, but not quickly enough. He ripped a chuck of its flesh from its ribs, causing the monster to howl and recoil for a moment, firing more spines at him.

Then there was a loud crack that everyone stopped and listened to. It was like a giant's femur, a single, fleshy snap.

I looked at the growth, violet light lining a fissure in the fingers that held the flesh together. Thick black pus leaked from the wound, and there was the faint, haunting sound of an infant crying from deep within.

Then I realised that the Folsesjeger was smiling. It was the smile of generations. He'd waited a long time for this moment, and now that it was finally here, he seemed deflated. Not the great threat that his name implied, for a moment.

The monster attacked him again, striking his back with the full weight of its body, pinning him down.

My father, to my surprise, ignored the beasts. He went straight for the growth and started hacking away at it again. As before, it was impervious to the strikes, but it was healing at a slower rate than before, the wounds slithering back together at a sluggish pace.

I watched the creatures struggling, each trying to gain purchase for a killing blow. I saw the desperation in the Folsesjeger, the desperation to live and save the child.

"Don't do it," he shouted, "please!"

Anders kept hitting the mound, now punching with his steel fist as well. The infant's cries became hollow sobs of fear.

It was a moment that came to define life as I knew it. And despite the pain and suffering that followed, and the guilt I feel every day, I think a part of me still believes I did the right thing. And I have to hold onto that.

I ran across the drawing room and held my sword ready. The haunting shape snapped its head towards me, but it was too late. I screamed at the top of my lungs and swung the thin razor's edge through the thick sinew of its neck as I sped past it.

I heard nothing, felt nothing. I waited a while, focusing on the brief dead silence, then finally decided to look upon my handiwork.

It was still upright, on top of the Folsesjeger, but its head had been twisted into an unnatural angle to stare right at me. Its yellowed, bulging eyes darted over me in shock. Its head hung limply from the remaining flesh, fetid blood oozing over its shoulder.

He pushed the body off, getting to his feet. And my father, pausing in his attack, had only hatred for me then. Behind him, the growth opened like a flower in spring, tentacles and strips of flesh peeling back to reveal the child inside.

It was an infant covered in pallid, slimy skin, like a strange type of slug. Its eyes were a mesmerising shade of purple I could not name. My father stared at the baby, cocking his head slightly as it looked back at him in confusion.

"Dad," I said, "he saved me. It's over."

"Please, Inquisitor," the Folsesjeger stepped forward, "that creature was an agent of the Quorum. What they have planned for that child is monstrous, millions will die."

We both approached slowly. My father still hadn't moved. He dropped his axe, and moved towards the child, letting it wrap its hand around his finger.

"In that case," he started, "better end it here."

He twisted his hand and grabbed the infant by its wrist, swinging it from its rotting crib into the air. The baby was screaming in pain as its brittle bones snapped in his grip. It was a world-shattering sound that left a mark on my very soul, one that I'd never be able to quiet ever again.

The Folsesjeger tried to cry out and stop Anders, he'd just begun to beg, knowing that even with his speed he wouldn't get there in time. But even if he had, it was too late.

The man I'd once looked up to and respected, who I'd even hoped to become one day, smashed a child into the wall. It hung limply from his hand after the first strike, twitching slightly and gurgling a little. The Folsesjeger fell to his knees and let out a low, painful, wail, watching as Anders swung the future of his people into the brickwork again, splattering brain matter against it.

And he didn't stop. He kept smacking the mangled corpse against the wall, cold anger seeping from him. The Snow-Steel manor, a place that had been exhausting to stand in before, was now completely draining.

"Stop," I said, quietly at first, "stop."

Anders didn't listen, he kept going, throwing until he was holding little more than a pile of unrecognisable meat.

"STOP!"

The word burst forth from me, more an explosion than a human sound. I felt all my built-up emotion fly forward with it. Anders was thrown back into the wall himself, the wind knocked out of him.

He was as bewildered as I was, staring at me with this horrible concoction of anger and confusion, not knowing what to do. I watched the blood, as red as my own, sliding down the wall into a thick pool beside my father.

When I looked for the Folsesjeger, I was surprised to see that he'd fled. I was expecting the pair of us to die then.

The assassin's corpse then twitched. I stepped back in horror, watching its contorted form start jolting again. Its flesh immolated, melting down in the burning inferno.

Rising from the pile was a larger, longer creature, a charred skeleton rebuilding its flesh. I didn't hesitate. I rushed forward again, ready to strike, but it seemed to sense me coming. With its skin bright red and slick with viscera, the creature lumbered away. A trail of slime was left behind it made its way for the nearest window, escaping before I could catch up.

Whatever it was, it would be back again.

Then I heard the soft gurgling and felt my heart sink. I looked back to see my father puzzling over the source. The infant was dragging itself along the floor, blood and broken sinew trailing behind it. Its shattered skeleton barely held the pile of flesh together, but I saw the veins and strings of nerves slowly entwining again.

The creature's face was half-formed, one of its lilac eyes now staring ahead at its goal, willing itself forward again. My father tutted to himself and walked over to his prey.

"Gods, the stories were right. They are tough bastards."

He raised his boot then.

"No!" I shouted, rushing over, "don't. I can do it."

Anders stepped away, squinting at me.

"You'll do it?"

"Yes," I croaked, "I'll kill it."

"Hm," he nodded, "I don't trust you."

My father did walk away, however, pulling a chair back onto its varnished legs to fall onto the seat with a groan. He smiled and made an exaggerated wave.

"Go on then, finish it."

I knelt down next to the little mound, seeing its pale skin gradually wrapping the squelching meat again. The baby managed an actual cry then, despite it sounding broken and distorted. I realised then that it had a chance at life again, given time, but if I didn't do it, my father would have, and much more painfully. Or worse, he would keep it locked up somewhere.

I placed one hand over its back, and another around its face, and started to whisper to the creature.

"Sleep is but a little death, little one, and you will find yourself among the dreamers. They will guide you to the next life, and you will find peace."

I repeated the phrase over and over, the focus being to soothe the infant with my soft intonations. As I spoke my fingers seeped with soporific mist, inflicting a curse of sleep upon the child.

...patient was then subdued with Endless Sleep, experiencing a gradual shutdown of all bodily functions. Patient soon stopped screaming and seemed to experience little-to-no pain, slowly falling into a deep sleep cycle. At 13:41, patient's heart stopped and after an extensive check, at 13:53, the patient was declared dead.

Field Medical Journal of a Senior Nurse – Lydia Verston

It took some time but eventually, the child slowed its breathing down so much, that soon it stopped completely. I watched its healing process halt, and the flesh seemed to dry rapidly then, turning an ashen grey and crumbling.

But I still heard that breathing, faintly, just resting at the back of my mind. Somehow, it didn't feel as though the child was really gone yet. Either way, its body was dust in the breeze now.

CHAPTER TWENTY-FIVE
-ELENA-

My father had locked himself in his room as soon as we got back, refusing to speak to me or Oliver. For some reason, as I always had, I assumed that he was angry with me. At this stage, I no longer knew why. The sounds of that...child...its bones cracking under the weight of the throw, still crunched in my brain.

"What did you do?" Oliver had his arms folded, a miniature man-child expecting an answer I couldn't give.

"What do you mean 'what did I do?' Why is it always my fault?"

Anders' door opened then, and we both glared at each other before looking to see if he'd come out. He stood by the door, pulling his coat on.

"I'm going out."

Oliver and I now shared a glance of fear.

"What? Where?" I said, standing.

"Out," Anders started to make his way to the exit.

I rushed past him and threw my weight against the door, almost trapping his good hand in it.

"Where are you going?"

He snorted and shook his head, pulling on the handle. When he realised I wouldn't move, he let go and glared at me.

"You can't stop me."

"Where are you going?" I could feel my hands trembling as I said it, "you can't leave us here, not after today."

"Oh, what the fuck are you talking about?"

I recoiled, pulling away from the door.

"Well?!" he rounded on me, following as I retreated, "you're not crying because you killed a monster are you? 'ere's a revelation for you, little one, that's what we do, that's our job, so wise up."

"It was a baby!" I slowed my retreat, just slightly, "we didn't have to kill it."

"Yes, we did," my father loomed in the doorway, his shadow cast over me, "it was a parasite, a plague on humanity, if I'd allowed it to live, we'd have been doomed. I assume you noticed how the other one almost destroyed me? How dangerous it was?"

"He was negotiating with you! If he was so dangerous why didn't he just kill you?"

"Because it knew I could've ended it."

"Why didn't you then? Hm?" I sneered, "because it looked like you lost."

He swung his hand then, the bony back of it striking my cheek. I twisted as I fell to the ground.

"If you hadn't been there, I would've exterminated it! You got in the way this whole time, distractin' me, and now things are worse than ever."

"You can't," I whimpered, "you can't leave us."

"I can do whatever I like," Anders turned, "I've wasted all my good years on you, I'm entitled to time by myself. You two need to grow up."

He stormed out, throwing the door into the wall and allowing it to slam after him. Oliver and I looked around each other, staring at anything but the other for a while, searching for something in the oppressive silence. After some time, he finally cleared his throat and spoke up.

"Why do you always have to push him?"

It triggered something deep within me, a fight or flight reflex that rang the same awful song as when I'd seen my brother among the Changed: I've lost him too. He was the last one, and now he was gone, even looking like my father in his hateful disdain.

"Leave me alone," I felt empty, there was a madness that had taken over and I was simply the passenger now.

"You're always so angry. I hate being around you."

The creature I'd allowed then to take the wheel was twisted, a monster I simultaneously cannot recognise and yet know so well. It was me, it was always me, but I will never wash the hatred I feel for her away. She is a sad and lonely creature whose only plan is to fight and never stop until everyone around her is dead and buried.

If I could step back into this moment and change what I did, I don't think I could go through with it. It is a sin I will never forgive myself for, and yet it is the one that has defined who I am today. I don't know what I am without that twisted growth in my heart.

"If you hate me so much then why don't you go?" I said, facing him again, "first mum, then dad, and now you. You've left me in a hole, and I want it to stop. So just go."

"I never said I hated you did I?" he shouted, "gods, you're such a fucking dick. You always twist my words."

"I'm a dick?" I shouted back, "you're a fucking dick!"

I moved towards him then, watching him retreat back towards the corner.

"You're a fucking coward is what you are, you're always standing up for him and pushing me away because you're desperate for him to love you," I growled, pushing him further into the corner, "guess what? He doesn't, he hates you. You know why? Because you're weak and never challenge him. He despises me, but if there's something he hates even more, it's a fucking coward!"

"I hate you so much," he said with a shudder, his eyes suddenly streaming with tears.

"And finally, he fucking says something he actually believes in!"

"Get out!" he screamed, "you're ruining everything and I don't want you here anymore!"

"You spent so much time regurgitating what he gave you that the pair of you nearly drove Mum into her grave, and now you're doing the same to me," I kicked a nearby table into splinters, shouting in blind fury, "you're a parasite, sucking the life out of everyone around you, you tell me to leave? Why don't you go? Why didn't you just fucking die!"

And without any build-up, I felt the power infuse with my voice again on the very final word. *DIE.* We've all said hurtful things to those we love when we fight, that we don't really love them, or that maybe we even hate them. But to tell your brother to die? That was something I should have known would rip power from the Void itself.

Red spectral tendrils tore forward from my face and sliced Oliver to ribbons, cutting his flesh and energies and making strips of light pour from the wounds. He lay there, crumpled up in that corner for a few seconds, white liquid seeping from the deep gashes in his soul.

His eyes were dead, staring blankly at the pooling floor, and I couldn't help but stare back in pure disbelief for longer than I'm proud of. My brother was dead, and I had killed him.

My brother is dead. And I have killed him.

Then the trembling started. The soft and rumbling storms of grief galloped towards me with searing pain on the winds. I felt it tear through me then as I went to my knees, grabbing my chest as a barbed chord squeezed my lungs to the point of bursting.

I covered my mouth with both hands, stifling a sobbing scream, refusing to let any more of that evil escape me.

Then I heard a faint whistle. Something flying through the air. Before I could react, it pierced the side of my neck, spilling paralysing poison into my veins. I only managed to turn my head briefly before falling limply into the viscous pool around my brother's body.

I saw the sleek shape of the creature from the Manor, the Assassin. It had crawled in through an open window, surely? How else had it gotten in?

As it made its way over to us, its teeth ready to clamp down on my throat to finish me, I saw it suddenly bathed in blinding light. My brother, or maybe his corpse, rose then, his eyes glowing, ready to drive the monster back.

I fell then into a black space, never really falling asleep, but falling nonetheless.

CHAPTER TWENTY-SIX
-ANDERS-

Elena was grey. She wasn't before. All the medicines and arcane liquids being poured into her seemed to suck the colour from her. Her chest pumped in rhythmic plateaus, not genuinely human. It was hard to believe that she was alive. I found a note when I came home that night, stating that she would grow and thrive, that at least she was breathing and that the scene had been made to be as beautiful as possible.

They clearly had no idea what they were doing. It was a mess. The bath was filled with a thick paste that was once my son, his bones floating in a mangled mess. They had expected something haunting, that part they got right at least. Only a fucking monster could do that to my son.

Elena, they may as well have killed her that night. She would never be the same if she ever woke up. They had taken her life away from her in all ways except the literal. As for me, I did die then, when I saw his tiny, skeletal hand, covered in only pieces of him, the rest melted away. I had reached in, trying to put him back together with my one, bloody hand, now even worse for wear than before.

As the sky turned a light pink, an attendant named Fera coughed behind me.

"I'm afraid it's time to leave," she said, her eyes sunken from the late nights, "I'm sorry. I'll keep an eye on her."

"I know," I stood and went to Elena's side, "wake up soon, yeah," I leant down and smelled her hair, noting the lack of her typical floral smell, before kissing her forehead, "you're really late."

The Darius district, named after the Pantheon's fallen child and sworn enemy, lived up to its namesake. With every step my boot heels slid on a congealed broth of mud, oil, ash and coal, the red sand beneath only allowed air for a moment before being buried again. There were no real buildings, just shells of aborted architecture. Smog shrouded any enemies lurking in the dark and carried with it a stench so foul that most wore a cloth over their faces, doused in urine, even that being a precious commodity with the lack of clean water.

One might think that if they wanted to hide, this might be the place to go, but it was a known bed for criminal activity and general depravity, so legions were regularly sent in to disrupt anything they could. only idiots and the desperate operated here.

Bhen was both. I had caught him selling Moirn-era guns to a group of would-be revolutionaries last year, and he had acted as a bit of an informant for me from time to time, only rarely requiring a twisted arm. He spent most of his time in a run-down tavern at the end of a grimy alley.

"Anders Therin," he smiled, "how lovely to see you again, and so soon at that."

"I need information," I took the seat in front of him, "you've had dealings with Ghangris and his gang, and I want to know where they are."

"Look I can't give you that," he sighed, reading my face, "as in, even if I wanted to? They have locations all over the city."

"Where's their next deal taking place then?"

"Beats me," he arched an eyebrow, "that it? You buying anything?"

"No," I stood and stepped towards him, "tell me where they are, before I get nasty."

"I'm not afraid of you," he said, swallowing the lump of fear scrabbling behind his tongue.

I punched him in the collar bone, cracking it along the length before driving my heel into his ankle, twisting it in two. He cried out, trying to grab hold of his foot but being held back by the shooting pains in his chest.

"Where."

"There's supposed," he groaned mid-sentence, "there's supposed to be a natural escalation here, start with something light, you know."

I hit him again in the mouth just before he finished and his teeth sliced his tongue open. He spat blood to the side, turning to me, the whites of his mouth stained red.

"I'm doing this for your own good. And Elena's."

"You're stalling," I tangled his hair between my fingers, yanking his head back, "and you take her name out of your filthy mouth."

"I've been through enough of this to know the differences between Inquisitors," his eyes were wide, "everyone says there's honourable ones, then the others. I just say that there's smart ones and dumb ones."

I placed my boot on his ankle again and he whimpered.

"The dumb ones, they do this. Beat and torture bystanders to get the results that they want, not the right ones. You weren't a dumb one when I met you, you're smart, terrifying even," he cleared his throat, blood trickling over his lip, "in this work, you hear things, yeah? I can't begin to know what you're going through right now, not that you haven't made the same threats against my own fuckin' son. But I get it, I get," he looked me up and down, "I get this. I'm trying to help you."

I let him go, falling back into the chair.

"Once more, where is it?"

"It's at the dock, they got a deal with some group that's been operating a while but people don't know much," Bhen's lip quivered, "take what you need."

I nodded and went to the cabinet to make some selections.

"Next time I see you, I won't be so accommodating. That's even if I see your suicidal arse ever again."

"Dad?"

I heard that familiar, scared little boy. Bhari, the one who'd poisoned Elena against me. I turned to see him standing at the door, eyeing a nearby pistol.

"Stay there lad," I said, "I'm in a hurry, but I won't hesitate to kill you if you try anything."

"Son," Bhen gasped, "don't, Bhari, Bhari, don't!"

The boy went for the gun like I knew he would. I'd readied my own under the table, blasting away at his hand. The boy held his bleeding fingers and cried out in pain.

I sighed as I rounded the counter, stepping past Bhen who was screaming at me to leave. But I didn't. I wanted to hurt that kid.

THE RIVER MOIRN

TEN YEARS AGO

Wills pulled back the brakes and slowly powered down its engine. We stepped out together, sliding open the side door for the rest of them to jump out, locking them again behind us. We headed towards the decrepit old barn, rusted tools placed carefully in points of panic and disarray to achieve the illusion of abandonment.

I walked in and saw my contact, Bhen, sitting at a table, backed by a few of his associates. A feared ring of smugglers, capable of moving anything, and with a reputation to back them up in case it went wrong. Theona and I had come across him a lot before the war.

"Mister Therin," he said, "it was somewhat surprising hearing from you, considering your position."

"I have a job for you."

"Ah, business," Bhen grinned as he clapped his hands together, "come, sit," he looked at the soldiers with me, "you guys, you can relax too, don't worry."

I waved them down and sat, looking at him, his eyes young with an amber flame.

"So, what am I doing?"

"I need you to get weapons to a group of Adelastonian rebels, I've marked their location on a map for you," I handed it across, "this is highly illegal and treasonous, you need to be careful and make sure you're not caught. Whether it's them, or us. They won't give you the time to talk your way out of it, they'll simply kill you and take it. Our guys will put you away."

"That's why you hired me, right? I'm the best," he raised his eyebrows, "I must say, this is juicy, what if someone were ta find out you were sellin' illegal weapons to terrorists?"

My revolver flashed forward, pressing against his neck. The guards on either side aimed their own weapons.

"That's why no one's going to find out, right Bhen?"

He laughed, pushing the weapon down, everyone else's went down with it.

"Of course, I'm just teasing," he stood, "so come on, show me what I'm moving."

We went to the vehicle and I let him inside to inspect the equipment personally.

"Some 'eavy artillery 'ere, you sure you're offloading this to the right group?"

"What do you care? You're getting paid either way."

"Forgive me but, I do 'ave some standards," he sucked his teeth, "just makin' sure I'm not helping a group of extremists."

"They're opposed to Adelaston's government and if their attention is focused on a rebellion, then the war on the Moirn will end, saving soldiers on both sides."

"What if they beat the government though? What're they putin' in place?"

"If Adelaston's pissed its people off enough to warrant an uprising then maybe they deserve it."

"Maybe, just wondering what's in it for you."

"It's just the right thing to do, not that you'd understand that."

"Nah," he dropped into the frozen mud, "it's something more for you, I can tell, I know that look."

I nodded, looking off in the distance at the soldiers watching from the barn doors.

"Okay, yeah," I looked back at Bhen, "my kids live in Burcanon, and my wife's sick. Probably water poisoning. This war is killing those on the frontline, and those at home. Probably affecting Adelaston too. It's personal, sure, but I also want to make sure that my kids are the last ones to lose a parent to this pointless conflict."

Bhen reached out, offering his hand to shake.

"I'll get it to 'em, you can count on it."

I took his hand in a firm grip.

"Thanks."

He turned to the barn.

"Come on then you lazy fuckers," he shouted, "get this shit unloaded," he pointed at one man in particular, "and be careful Dorson, I know what you're like."

"Bhen," I called after him, waiting for him to turn back, "don't think this changes anything if I go back to the Order after all this."

"Wouldn't count on it."

CHAPTER TWENTY-SEVEN
-ELENA-

The bars on the cage were made of rough material like grey wood, tied together with tendons. We had been stuffed into them side by side, hulking forms moving around us. At a table ahead, a grotesque demon sat atop a pile of its own bloated and burst skin, diseased boils fizzing and popping all over its fleshy throne. A large plate was brought forward, and two people lay hogtied across it.

The creature licked its bent, dead teeth, grabbing one with a giant hand like one might hold a hunk of meat on the bone. It rumbled with laughter as it looked at me with disgusting yellow eyes.

"You will be mine."

But nothing came. I was in a room of nothing. No shape, no texture, just, nothing.

"Will she be okay?"

I heard Sonya's voice call out to me from the shadows, her voice sucked away again almost as quickly as it had come. She wasn't screaming, but somewhere, someone a lot like her, was, and it resonated with her desperation for me to wake.

"I don't know, child."

It was Theona. I tried to scream for her, for anyone, to come and find me. But the darkness seemed to press against me, and my chest tightened under the pressure.

"If she wakes, she'll never be the same."

I woke in my bed in the Orchid Sanctuary to the sound of the cupboard door slowly creaking open. I slowly turned my head against my pillow and watched the black space.

A tiny grey and glistening hand slowly curled its fingers around the door. The silhouette it belonged to had the proportions of a toddler but instead of moving in the curious, fumbling way they do it instead jittered like a statue breaking free of its photographic prison.

It stepped into a sliver of silver light and became clear. It was hairless and shiny like a slug and its mouth was similar to a locust's. It was naked but there was no exposed human anatomy. It chittered and stared at me with bulging onyx eyes.

I reached out to the child. It did not take my hand but instead, it began to climb the bed and crawl towards my face. The sheets seemed to stretch as it moved and it was going nowhere despite how quickly it came. I sat up and tried to reach out again.

"Come on. Come here," I said aloud. As the creature began to tire my chest tightened and I found I could not breathe properly. My hands violently shook.

The child stopped and cocked its head to one side again before its slimy skin quickly dried out. Its hand ended in spasms as it raised its palm to me before its eyes sunk back into its mushy skull. It crumbled to dust.

I was thrown back and tried to breathe but it felt like sucking honey through gauze. I gasped and placed a hand on my chest. There was a smell. Sickly and sweet, it punched my nostrils and clawed its way to my brain.

I smell like a corpse.

"I'm sorry, child."

It was the sound of an enemy. The Folesesjeger sat at the end of my imaginary bed.

"I'm sorry that you're suffering from this curse."

I tried to scream at him but my body was slowly shutting down, all of its functions weakening with every moment he remained.

"Your mind and body will start to change. I will help if I can."

I closed my eyes. There was silence.

I woke up to blank space like the first page of a diary Dad got me all that time ago, untouched, yet blotched and spotted. How many years now. It was hard to tell. Time was linear and yet also jumbled, and messy. There were parts missing and others poisoned, blackened, and laid out in front of me like empty picture frames.

When I blinked, the world was around me again. Tall shoots of broken structures encircled a paint-splashed sky, building themselves towards the light, roots seeing light for the first time.

The streets were empty, and I half expected paper and dust to roll past in collected bundles, but it was clinically pristine. My footsteps repeated farther and farther away, dogging me at every turn of a corner.

A sign of life. A young man stood in front of a shop window, peering at a sickly yellow teddy bear. I called out to him. His face was blank, or the features were so plain that he looked blank, but he was faceless. He cocked his head, then walked toward the centre of the square, looking down the well in the centre. He turned his head toward me again, then stepped up on the ledge, falling forward into the hole.

I waited for the sound of his body hitting the bottom, but it never came. I went to see the shop window for myself, and the stuffed bear's black eyes seemed to follow me. Its lips then peeled backwards and revealed a set of pearly white teeth. I couldn't help but cover my eyes.

When I opened them again, I was no longer in a cage, but standing in a stone square, with titanic buildings more fit for giants than man. They were adorned in the spiked architecture of old, but I recognised them as the cathedrals of Kaurus. This was the home of the Enlightened Quorum.

The ground was covered in ash, thick layers clinging to my bare feet as I trudged towards the main church. Halfway up the stairwell leading to its grand halls were two bodies. They were kneeling, holding each other's hands tightly. A great tree of flesh grew from the bottoms of their bowels, bone roots tearing their skin as they reached for nutrients. The fleshy leaves fluttered away in the light winds, scattering into ash.

The stairs collapsed beneath me, cascading me into darkness. I landed on soft cushioning with a puff of grey dust.

It was a corpse, its teeth exposed in a hideous grin, its eyes black. It was gaunt with its stomach and cheeks sucked in on themselves, exposing the claw-like ribs.

It was not the only one.

Piles upon piles of bodies had been stacked in great heaps below the shattered glass windows of the enormous chapel. The ceiling was so far above that it was cast in shadow, and the cadaverous treasures went on forever.

I hugged my chest as I moved among them, finding small paths winding through the room. There was a clatter of bone shattering. I saw an arm fall past me and then its owner crash into the floor, scattering in pieces. I looked up and saw that the mound to my right was tipping, and, in panic, I screamed at the top of my lungs.

I had been so restricted, my throat constricted in fear, that the energy of that release had built over what felt like centuries. The bodies shattered into clouds of sooty snow, the flakes slowly falling around me like flurries in winter.

The wall of the chapel had fallen, exposing me to the pulsating skies. A great pink scar lined the clouds above Eleynum, and many more dotted the horizon for as far as my enhanced sight could see.

Points of energy were dotted across the roofs, green beams feeding into the horrific tearing of the world. In the distance, a skyscraper fell, a huge limb pushing its way through the structure. Ahead, a behemoth reared its frightful head. Somehow, I knew.

This was the end. Of everything. And I somehow felt responsible. This eventuality, which, for the most part, felt entirely inevitable, was my fault. I was going to destroy the world in raging Void fires, calling horrors like I had never seen forth to devour the corpses of millions.

It was my fault. And the beast turned its thousand eyes on me, the red sun blotted by its sickly flesh. It knew who I was, and it wanted my soul more than any other.

One last time I woke. I exited what I thought was an endless dream. But there was no way for me to know anymore. No one could understand the burning scar on my brain, and I tried to writhe away from the boiling sweat on my sheets but my limbs were still weak.

I couldn't move.

"Oh gods," one of the nurses said, "hold on, darling."

I have to help her.

The words were alien to me, some strange multitude of voices I'd never heard. Her hands were ice, and the sensation felt worse than the unquenchable fire in my veins.

"Get off me!"

My words burned her skin, just like Oliver's had burned mine. But this was worse. Where he had scratched the surface deep, mine had stripped the flesh from her arm and the left side of her face. The nurse, this innocent girl, had had her life ruined by my emotions.

Dad was right. I could never control them.

Help me. Save me.

It came again. I realised they were buzzing around her face like hornets, these thoughts were now speaking directly to me.

"I'm sorry," my words were broken, my voice strange, "help her!"

Others came to help the shocked woman, staring at me with great fear in their eyes, the thoughts now screaming at me in an unbearable cacophony.

Freak.

Abomination.

Poor little girl.

They were right to cower. I was only capable of destruction.

I had to stop it. The vision I'd seen, it was more than just dreams. I knew that, if I didn't act now, the Change would come.

CHAPTER TWENTY-EIGHT
-ANDERS-

The decrepit warehouse was almost sat in the waters of the docks, workers covered in overalls and mismatched plates of armour patrolling its numerous entrances.

I surmised that the main opening was at the back, as dim light glistened over the shifting waves, whereas nearly every window backed onto the paved stone of the harbour was blacked out. What Bhen said about this group, that I would never bring them down, seemed so preposterous with this sight that I immediately came to distrust the sense of security.

This was the kind of building that any halfway competent Inquisitor would crack open like a can, and the fact that they were being so blatant about their behaviour meant one of two things.

There was a low wall connected by a gate at the front, so it was simple enough to fire hooks from the snowsteel prosthetic and climb into a small storage room filled with wooden crates and barrels. One sniff told me that this was mostly cured meats and alcohol. Depending on the spirit, nothing incriminating.

A man entered the low light, sighing and scuffing his boots as he moved towards my position. I kept low and took cover, feeling the floorboards bend under his weight and listening as the creaks got quieter.

When I was alone again, I made my way to the door he had come from. It led to a landing that overlooked the main hub of the building.

Spry transport vehicles juddered as their engines puffed smoke into the air, the glass tubes leading from them pumping thick luminescent liquid around their metal frames. Several individuals, looking more like genuine dockhands in their overalls and thick gloves, were hooking generators up to them. I couldn't make out the power source, but it was certainly void material. Where could a gang get their hands on this kind of equipment?

And something stranger still suddenly stood out to me. There were no marks, insignias, or anything at all to denote that the gang were working for Ghangris. Even their weapons looked simple and light-duty. Had Bhen been fucking with me?

Others were loading what looked like massive steel coffins onto the backs of the trucks, requiring two, at least, one holding each end. It was a huge operation, with there being at least a hundred people that I could make out. Standing by the vehicles, hands behind their backs as if the overseers of the whole thing, were figures in red-plated armour and robes. They had long blades at their belts, with an edge likely to cut some unlucky bastard in half.

"Who the fuck is this lot?" I whispered aloud.

There were beams above the loading area and using the banister and the hook I was able to pull myself up onto the narrow walkway. My hands shook as I gingerly grabbed hold of anything I could, using the metal for balance.

As I moved past the generators below, I couldn't help my curiosity and turned to look at the setup.

There was a glass pane on the front of the machines, and, as expected, more bright liquid was inside. It was smoky inside and, while I could make out a shape, it wasn't clear at all. Then it moved, and the gaunt face of a stragan pressed up against the glass.

They were always thin, normally the reanimated corpses of the starved, but this one's cheeks and eyes were completely sunken in, its skin peeling off in strips. It feebly clawed at someone maintaining the contraption, but its other arm had been stripped away to a stump. Stragans in the other generators stirred and showed themselves, even in what seemed like torture still desperate to feast on flesh.

Using live subjects for power had been theorised, but I had never seen it used successfully.

"Wait, up there!"

I heard someone shouting below. I didn't need to wait for the others to clock onto my presence, so I stepped up to balance on the beam and make my escape.

Bullets pinged off the beam below as I made my way across the warehouse. I got into the storage room I'd first happened upon and two of them appeared at the door to fire more shots.

I ducked behind the boxes, hearing barrels pissing onto the floorboards. I took out a metallic disc and threw it to the side and the spring-loaded mechanisms burst. Strips of razor-wire slashed the room, cutting into one of the men. He fell on his side, steam pouring from his guts through his fingers.

The other rounded the corner and raised his weapon. I kicked the barrel downward and pulled the pistol from my chest strap to fire a hole through his throat, standing to shoot at the door to stop any more coming through.

I ran for the window and heard two more shots, feeling them rip through my side and leg as they sent me reeling through the glass.

My shoulder crashed against the brick of the nearby alley, bouncing me into the puddles below. Footsteps echoed against the walls of my mind as my breathing strained.

CHAPTER TWENTY-NINE
-ELENA-

They had isolated me in a separate chamber after what had happened to the nurse. I suppose I couldn't blame them, if I had witnessed such horror, I might have even killed me there and then.

Their minds had been wide open to me, their feelings seeping out in viscous waves and *words*. The most I had experienced before were subtle implications and suggestions, the mere flavour of their core emotional responses. Now it was different.

It hadn't stayed that way. When one of the healers came to bring me food, it had subsided to something more familiar. Perhaps that little touch of the Dream had given me temporary power. Or maybe something deep within me had been awakened, just for a moment.

We must wake it again.

Who is that?

I am you. Your other half. We have met.

This feels different.

We have been permanently separated. Our control is divided.

How do I fix this?

You don't. You can't fix anything. But this is good.

I don't want this.

You don't want anything. You allowed the world to stamp you out until you were nothing. Now I can help you. There is power within us, you just lack the courage to use it.

And you have it?

Exactly.

You only exist in my mind. I'm going mad.

Yes, we are, but madness is a key to the worlds beyond. One such world is coming. So many of us have already seen it. We must not only prepare, but we must be ready to rule it when the time comes.

I turned over in my bed, focusing on the slick black walls of the isolation chamber, watching damp slide along the bricks.

You cannot turn away from me, YOU WORTHLESS PIECE OF SHIT. The Spider comes.

There was a knock at the door. I managed to sit up, just barely, the strength in my arms more or less evaporated by this stage.

"Come," my throat strained, the word hoarse. I swallowed, "come in."

The door opened, revealing a silhouette standing still. As she stepped into the room, Theona's features became a little clearer in the light of the glowing lamp beside my bed.

"My child, I'm so sorry for your loss."

She expresses her own grief and regret and has disguised it as sympathy for yours.

"If you'd been there none of this would have happened."

Theona nodded, taking the hurt and swallowing it.

"May I sit down?"

I nodded.

"How are you feeling?"

She is trying to get information about the incident with the nurse.

"I'm fine," I swallowed, "when's the ceremony?"

"What?"

"For Oliver, when's the ceremony?"

"Elena," Theona was looking for words that didn't exist, "it's been months, they had to go ahead without you."

They have betrayed you. They should have waited, and you should have been there.

"Are you alright?"

"Of course, I'm not!"

I stared at her in silence after the bomb, the room reverberating softly from the pattern of my shamed anger. She squinted, just for a second, studying.

"I should have been there," I said, my voice softer this time.

"They weren't sure you were even going to wake up, you cannot blame yourself."

Yes you can, and you should.

226

"I don't," I glared at her again, "where's my father?"

"He has been in a bad way for a long time," Theona trailed off for a moment, "Not surprising, I suppose, but the Order forced him to take leave."

She looked down, avoiding my wrathful gaze.

"I don't know where he is, I'm sorry."

"No one's seen him?"

"There have been whispers, and I know where he started, but it's been weeks, Elena."

"What do you mean? Where he started?"

"He wanted to look for the one who killed your brother. The last time I saw him, he went to the Darius district to ask questions."

I held back my reaction, knowing that this likely meant people like Bhen and Bhari. I knew that they might have seen him.

Why should they trust you? You lied to them.

They won't, but they're good people, they might still help.

You will have to learn to help yourself sooner or later, rather than relying on others to simply let you down.

I pushed myself up again, my arms wobbling as they maintained the sitting position. Any muscular structure of my body had degraded completely.

Theona put her hand out to touch my leg, then retracted it again as if she had touched a burning stove.

"What?"

"Your skin," she almost whimpered like a dying dog, "it's so cold."

I tried to turn but my legs sat like anchors. There was an attempt at movement, I could feel any muscular integrity left straining to pull me around. Eventually, with some help from Theona, I was able to sit on the edge of the bed.

"I need to find him," I said, "But there's some things I need to do first."

"You can't."

"What?"

"After what happened," She nodded towards the door, "Out there, they won't let you leave."

"Am I a prisoner?"

"No, not exactly…"

"Then I can and will leave."

"I'm sorry, Elena," Theona sighed, gathering her coat up in a bundle to leave, "I think it's for the best. I mean look at you, you can't even walk."

"Yes I can," I placed my toes on the ground, even that small weight causing them to tremble under its immensity, "I will."

"I believe you, but until then, I have to keep you safe. And this is the best place for you," she sighed before standing and walking towards the door.

"No," I shouted, "don't leave me here."

"I'm sorry, I'll visit as much as I can," Theona knocked on the steel plating before she turned back to look at me, "just, just get some rest, child."

I cursed her, cursed her name, any family she might have had, and her Order. I had no doubt that she heard me, and I didn't care. I wanted her to know how much I hated her.

The Enlightened Quorum

Sweat was like glue in the awful material of the hospital bed, my skin peeling away with it every time I had to toss my body over again. I watched the shadows of the room, seemingly growing larger and more suffocating with every minute.

There was a squeaking of springs as something leaned on the foot of the bed. The bone-white hairs of my dead flesh pushed against my shirt, and I felt hot breath whistle through my toes.

Like a rusty marionette, I turned at small fractions, until I was on my back. Long black fingers with long black nails clung like giant spiders to my sheets. With the croaking of popping joints in a wrung neck, strands of wet black hair became visible, masking the widened features of my brother.

His eyes almost came past the boundaries of his skull, the sunken ellipticals of an insect.

"I'm going to eat you whole, Elena."

It was a child's voice. So much younger than even he had been at the time of his death. It almost giggled, before its bottom jaw unhinged and rows of black teeth engulfed my lifeless ankles.

CHAPTER THIRTY
-ANDERS-

The Changed guards admitted me into the Watching Room, a large glass observatory at the top of the Warden's tower. Calthern stood with his back to me, staring down at the city. His city, in many respects.

I took a breath, then approached, kneeling at the centre of the room.

"Stand, come to me," Calthern said as the doors were closed behind me.

I felt my stomach lurch as I stepped onto the glass platform, seeing the stretched image of the ground hundreds of feet below me.

"What did you find?"

"They'd scurried the weapons away into one of their rat holes like you said."

"Did you recover them?"

"No, there was a fire."

"Any prisoners?"

"None."

"Hm," Calthern rolled his shoulders, "that's disappointing."

"I'm sorry, sir," I turned to him, "I did gain some information on the whereabouts of Ghangris."

"Good, where is he?"

"In the wind, but I have some hideout locations."

"That's a start," he faced me then, "but he is of little consequence, you understand? We need the abomination."

"I know, I'll find him."

"Did the treg smuggler turn up anything?"

"Nothin', useless."

"Perhaps we ought to burn the shop anyway."

"Bhen's a broken clock but better to have around than nothing at all."

"I suppose."

Calthern sighed and placed a hand on my shoulder.

"I have a...difficult task, one that only you can carry out."

"Anything, sir," I cleared my throat, "what is it?"

"We caught something in one of our rat traps, fugitives fleeing the city."

"Who are they?" I felt as though I already knew.

"Velloah'Ra Snow-Steel and her daughter."

"And the son?"

"No idea, dead most likely."

"Good."

"Indeed," he smiled briefly, "I need you to question her, and decide her fate."

"You want me to judge her?"

"Yes, it's important for you to make this decision, given your involvement in the case."

I looked away, slowing my breathing.

"I'll do it."

"Good," he grinned, "good, come with me."

The cell door was slammed behind me, casting Velloah'Ra in the pale light of the lamp above set into the blue-black brick. Her eyes brightened as I came to sit down in front of her.

"I'm so glad to see you," she started.

"Don't," I barked at her, shaking my head, "don't."

"Please, you have to get Valeria out of here, she's done nothing wrong."

"I'm here to question you, I'm in control now, so you'll listen to me."

"Of course, I just," she saw me tense again, and stopped herself, then looked at my burned flesh and my battered arm, "what happened?"

"You don't know?"

"No," Velloah'Ra was desperate for clues, "what did he do to you?"

"Were you hoping he'd kill me?"

"No, of course not."

"My children?" I watched her stupid fucking expression of ignorance, "did you send it to kill my son?" I pleaded with her, begging for an answer, "my son!"

My words rang against the metal-plated door, bouncing around the room. Velloah'Ra stared at me, rolling through thousands of sentences in her mind.

"Your family housed that thing for months, helped it with its plans. Why?"

"The city is wrong, they were trying to help."

"You killed an infant to appease it," I rolled over her, to the point where we were speaking at each other simultaneously, "didn't you?"

"I didn't know about that, neither did Valeria, what's wrong with you?"

"And you killed one of your own."

"I had nothing to do with Marcus's death!"

"Your own child, I mean, how can you even look in the mirror without wanting to hang yourself?"

"I do!" she cried at me, swallowing her pain in some vain attempt to control it, "I do, every day."

"Why don't you just save us all the trouble then?"

Velloah'Ra trembled, looking down.

"Valeria's the only thing I have left."

I leaned back, realising that I didn't even have that. Elena lived, just barely, and if she woke up then she wouldn't be my daughter anymore. I had nothing left.

"Please…"

I resisted the urge to hit the table, or her, whichever came first.

"Where are the plans for the generators?"

"Why do you want that?" she shook her head, "please tell me you're not doing their dirty work?"

"I'm obeying orders, the city needs to advance."

"I'm not giving them to you."

"Then where's the abomination?"

"I don't know."

"So what use are you?" I stood up, "I'll make sure it's painless."

"Anders, please," she sobbed, "I can't, I won't, this city is wrong, and they're tricking you!"

"You fooled me too many times before," I looked down at her, "it won't happen again."

I made my way to the door and then looked back.

"I gave you a chance," I whispered, "you failed."

I expected to hear her begging for me to save her again, screaming after me. But there was just one simple word.

"Anders."

"What?" I spat at her.

I stared at the frail woman, a shell of herself. Her kind eyes, those fucking condescending eyes, were dark now. She had finally let me go.

So, I left.

"Did she talk?"

"No, she gave me nothin'," I licked my teeth, "those plans are lost."

"No matter," Calthern sighed, "we'll have to reverse engineer, we're already halfway."

"Did they have anyone else? A serving girl, Guindolene?"

"No, why?"

"I think she might be a quarry, could be useful I suppose."

"We'll keep an eye out," Calthern winced, "what do you suggest we do with them?"

"Hm," I shrugged, "they might not know anything, but they're willing accomplices. Do what you like."

"Are you sure?"

"Yes. I don't feel the pain of ghosts anymore."

CHAPTER THIRTY-ONE
-ELENA-

They came to wake me in the middle of the night, two guards of the healing ward. They refused to offer an explanation for where I was going and had placed a bag over my head in some vain attempt to disorient me. But it was obvious from their energy, and the violent agitation they felt, that they were truly Inquisitors taking me to the Order.

Where exactly in Eleynum I was, ultimately, didn't matter. I was being taken for questioning, and these people looked at me like they would any creature more dead than alive.

They want to tear you apart.

I don't blame them.

They should fear you.

They don't fear me, they loathe me.

I heard the sound of a creaky metal door sliding open. The sound reminded me of an animal's pen, and I wondered if maybe that was where I belonged after all. They sat me down in a chair. The seat was freezing.

They left me there for a time. It was likely only a few minutes, but in that darkness, time was stretched like stringy honey. I missed Sonya. Her sense of humour would have alleviated this cold night a little, and where before her unwelcome hugs would have made me cease up, I think I might have crumbled then just to hold her again.

I wanted to miss Oliver. But every time I thought of him, that hideous creature would return, wearing him like a jumpsuit. I knew it wasn't real, but even as I had started to consider it, I felt that rasping breath brush against my ear.

The hood was removed, and a thin old man sat across from me. As my eyes adjusted to the light, I realised it was the pale features of Donlan Calthern.

"Hello Elena," his smile was drawn onto a canvas face stuffed with straw, "Remember me?"

The Orchid sanctuary felt like a lifetime away then, and I remembered what Theona had said. I felt like I'd fallen through a hole between worlds, how had I lost months? But the Sanctuary was almost a year ago now, and Calthern seemed more ghost than a man.

"Uh, yes, of course, Warden General Calthern," I bowed my head for a moment and felt my lungs twinge as the damp air set into them, "where am I?"

I knew the answer, of course, but I felt an instinct to play dumb. He still saw me as the child I had been.

He leaned a little closer, clasping his hands in front of him. The smile didn't change at all.

"You gave everyone a bit of a scare at the hospital, and I need to figure out what's best for you. Especially with your father gone."

"Where is he?"

"Nobody knows sweetheart, I have my best people looking for him to make sure he's safe so don't you worry."

"Is he in trouble?"

"Of course not," Calthern placed a hand on his chest, and his wormy lips twisted into a frown, "I wanted him to take some time off, to be with you, and recover from your terrible loss. Oliver was such a gifted boy, and I was so sorry to hear of it. But, well, you know your old dad, he doesn't know how to stop working does he?"

"No, he doesn't."

"That's why you have such a good life, you must be so grateful for him."

I forced a smile.

"Yes, I am."

He bared unbearably sterile teeth, almost polygonal in shape with sharp and defined edges from years of overbrushing.

"So, my hope is that we can look after you here, get you rested, and then, when you're ready, you can help us bring in the man who killed your brother."

"It wasn't a man," I started, but Calthern cut across me.

"No, of course, the Folsesjeger are," He spat onto the floor, "abominations."

"No," I felt like I had fluid swimming at the base of my skull, slowly expanding my brain like a thick sponge, "it wasn't him. It was something else, it fought with my dad at the manor."

"Oh," Calthern intended to sound as though he was surprised by my observation, but I'd caught the turning of the corner of his mouth, "interesting."

He turned to one of the guards and beckoned for him to come over. Calthern spoke in hushed tones with his lackey, and I knew then that I had him.

Excellent. The creature made a mistake. Now we know that Calthern is connected, and we can destroy him.

"How can I help?" I said, wearing the mask of the good daughter.

"You see Elena, I always knew you were special, as soon as I met you in fact. I said, didn't I say, Jerry?"

"Yes sir," another of the guards, Jerry I assumed, nodded.

"I said, that girl, she's the future. Truly one in a million. Especially for a Burcanese girl. Most girls struggle with the energies of the Gods, their high emotions you see, and the Burcanese tried to suppress it, so I think you're truly remarkable."

Calthern tilted his head, and his eyes changed. It was so quick, I wouldn't have noticed had I not been staring at them intently this entire time. They had been wide, open, and honest, before. But for a flash, they had died. They were glazed, studying, like a hunter before delivering the final blow. Then they reverted to their cheerful demeanour.

"Theona tells me you've been having dreams, dreams that aren't your own."

She betrayed us again. I'll remind you to kill her when the chance arises.

239

"Did she tell you to take me?"

"You mustn't be angry with her, she's trying to look out for you and thought I might be able to help."

"If she knew anything about me, she'd know I wouldn't want to help a tyrant like you."

You fucking idiot. Now we're dead.

Calthern blinked a few times, then allowed his face to ooze back into its original mould. A blank and dead mask, his eyes watching for the moment to strike.

"I am going to take that as an attempt at a joke."

Well, you might as well go out with some dignity. Give it to him, you fucking coward.

"Take it how you like, I hate you, and I'd rather die than help you."

"I see," He closed his eyes and took a deep breath, "well, I tried. Take her back to the sanctuary. We'll give Miss Therin some time to think before she opens her mouth again."

They hooked their arms under my own, pulling me off of the chair and out of the room. The hood went on again, and I felt myself being loaded into a van. I knew now that I was going to die.

They're nervous, and he said he'd give you time. They clearly need you for something. Stop worrying all the time, it's pathetic.

I realised it was obvious. My father was clearly working for Calthern directly and they wanted to distract me with a lie while simultaneously targeting one of their enemies. They knew I'd be the only one with a chance of finding him and foiling their plans. Otherwise, they wouldn't have bothered with me at all, they'd have killed me there and then.

You're welcome.

As the van started, they removed the hood again. I saw pipes lining the inside of the seated area in the back, and as the engine roared into life, they filled with a viscous orange liquid that I didn't recognise. Most vehicles then were fuelled by bluish oils emitting similarly coloured smoke when burned. This was something else entirely.

"Don't look at it for too long," Jerry said, "you'll go mad."

His colleague chuckled and they settled in.

"Shouldn't I still be blinded?"

"Doesn't matter now, you lost your chance to go back to your life."

I swallowed and jerked sideways when we set off. I thought about trying to attack them and making a run for it, but they'd had to carry me all this way and even staying upright was a challenge.

Use your power again.

I don't know how I did it.

You just unleashed what was already there, use your voice.

It wouldn't matter, as soon as I make my move the driver will come in and kill me.

Do something, don't just sit here like a lamb. FIGHT BACK.

You said they wouldn't kill us?

The Enlightened Quorum

Well, I don't know that for a fact, and frankly, I don't fancy our chances of making it through whatever weird experiments they have planned.

I was thrown sideways when the van halted suddenly. It was normal for me to be scattered onto the floor of the van, but I hadn't expected the other two to come with me.

"What was that?" Jerry growled.

He clambered towards the small sliding plate into the driver's compartment. I heard a muffled screaming, and there was a stinging ring that somehow pierced through my ear and behind my eye. It was like a fight-or-flight response deep within my consciousness.

We need to run, now.

I can't.

THEN WE'LL DIE HERE.

Stop fucking SCREAMING AT ME. What do you expect me to do? Magically get up and walk? By all that's good in the world, get a grip.

The pain subsided a moment but didn't disappear. I tried to drag myself towards the back of the van as Jerry slid the window aside, looking for the driver. There were spatters of blood on the glass, but no sign of him. Jerry grabbed me by the arm.

"You stay here, and stay low," he waved to the other guard, "come on."

One pulled a shotgun off of the wall, and the other drew a thin blade tinted red by the crystals used to forge it. They weren't sure what kind of enemy they were going out to face.

They stepped down and closed the door behind them. This was my moment to escape, but I couldn't manage it. I tried getting to the door, and just about got there, but I couldn't get up to the handle.

After I fell down a third time, I lay there, and the grief collapsed on top of me again. I heard his little whimper again, his small cry for help as the fires of my rage disintegrated him.

It was your fault.

It was all my fault.

It would be better for you to just to die here.

All I do is break things.

It should have been you. Not him.

Why do you hate me so much?

I don't hate you, I want to make us better. We need to be stronger and colder. We can't let our emotions get the better of us ever again. Dad was always right.

It had been at least a few minutes. I wasn't going to get a better chance. I grabbed the rim of the bench and pulled myself up, using it to try and get back into a sitting position. Then I leaned on it and pushed with everything I could to get onto the seat itself.

I saw the handle in front of me. I needed to find a way to get to it without falling and use it to not only support my weight but also lean against the door.

Then it opened. The handle had been pulled down and out by an outside force. A pale hand with long black talons gripped the other door, and a tall figure pulled himself into the van. A bloody handprint had been left behind, and his clothes were covered in it.

It was him. The Folsesjeger. I winced in agony as the screaming got worse, trying to jolt into action. He just looked at me with those sad, lilac eyes.

"Sorry about the mess," he cleared his throat, "I couldn't let them take you."

"I won't let you take me, either, monster."

"You don't really believe that. I can hear the doubt in your voice."

"You feed on people, what else would I call you?"

"I actually try to avoid doing that, but that's beside the point," he put his elbows on his knees and I noticed the talons retracting, his facial features softening, "you don't believe it, because you suspect that you might be the same."

I chewed on those words for a while, figuring out what exactly he meant. His thoughts were muddied, unlike others.

"What did you do to me?"

"What do you mean?"

"You came to me, while I slept. You apologised and said that I would start to change. What did you do?"

His pupils narrowed into vertical slits, and the edges of his eyes creased.

"We connected, in the Dream," he couldn't maintain eye contact with me, "most humans can't, it's very much a 'my lot' kind of thing."

"How do I stop it?"

"You don't, you can only attempt to control it now," he flashed a brief, forced smile, "I want to help you. Your father believes one of my agents killed your brother, and I need to find and stop him."

"Who's your agent?"

"Ghangris, he and his group are helping me in my opposition of the Senate and the Enlightened Quorum."

"I feel like, I think I recognise you from somewhere else."

"You might know me as Hurwin Corvin, a member of Parliament."

"So that's it, is it? You can't beat the Senate at politics so you're beating them with violence instead?"

"I spent years infiltrating this government at every level I could, the Quorum and its followers have too much influence over the city and its people, and these corporate shells disguised as families are only feeding into their plans," he sighed, "they only understand blood, and if that's what they want, that's what I'll give them. But none of this matters to you right now."

"No, you're right, it doesn't."

"Haven't you wondered why I'm being so transparent with you?"

"Because you're desperate?"

"I don't know why!"

He looked down, then threw his head back into the seat, looking up at the ceiling.

"I don't know. It's my fault that this happened to you, it's my fault that they targeted you. I feel this...this compulsion, to help you, as though, if I don't, then everything will end."

I watched him. He was harder to read than the others, but there was also a rawness to him and honesty that I'd never encountered before. He was truly, desperately, asking me to save him. And I couldn't understand why.

"This world is on the brink of complete destruction if the Enlightened Quorum isn't stopped, and your father's been tricked into securing those plans."

"You've seen it too?"

"What?" Hurwin's eyes widened, "seen what?"

"The End?"

He stood up, covering his mouth a moment while he paced the length of the van.

"You saw it? In your dreams?"

"Yes. I think. It felt so real."

"That's because it was, or at least, it could be if we fail to act."

"And how's my father involved?"

"Because Ghangris and his organisation are the only ones with the strength and numbers to stop them, if they're hindered or, worse, destroyed, then the Quorum will be unstoppable. Millions will die."

I shook my head.

"This is too much."

"I know," he came to kneel down in front of me, "I think you and I can help each other. Something happened to you, it's changed you, and I can help you manage it. But you need to help me find your father. Your connection to him is stronger than mine, it'll be faster."

"You won't hurt him?"

"No," he swallowed, "I hate him for what he did. But I promise, you need to stop him for his own sake. Once he outlives his usefulness to those like Calthern, they'll eliminate him too."

"What do I do?"

"Well, first things first," he stepped outside again, and dragged Jerry into the van, dropping him at my feet like a cat with a dead mouse, "we need to get you moving."

"What?"

"You might not exactly be a Folsesjeger, but this is how we feed. He's not dead yet, you'll need his energies to get your strength back."

"No," I recoiled as best I could, "I'm not eating him."

"What?" Hurwin looked horrified, "I don't eat people, I feed on their energies."

"That doesn't make it any better?!"

"Well, it sort of does."

"No," I turned away, "I won't kill him."

"Okay," Hurwin scoffed, "he's going to die either way, Elena."

"I won't do it."

He grabbed my wrist then and held it with a twisting grip that burned the skin.

"You need to be stronger. Any connections you have right now are a weakness, and they'll exploit them relentlessly," he hissed, "you need to be cold, ruthless, efficient…we, you and I, we cannot fail."

"I can't," I said hoarsely, "please."

"That's fine," he was softer this time, "I understand. You'll slowly recover with time, but this would have certainly sped things along."

He hoisted me up suddenly, carrying me like a child.

"Where are you taking me?"

"Some of my agents will take you in, you already know them."

CHAPTER THIRTY-TWO
-ANDERS-

I'd fallen asleep on the way to the Darius District, and, mercifully, it had been relatively benign in my dreams.

Hurwin carried me along a neon-lit street that, as my eyes adjusted, I realised I had seen before. The familiar signs masked in fog lead us to the front of Bhen's shop, Bits and Bobs.

"They work for you?"

"Well," he started, "they work for Ghangris."

"Oh."

"He works for me," he chuckled.

We reached the door and Hurwin knocked on the dark wood, lowering me to the floor.

"Can you walk with me helping you?"

"I think so."

"Okay, lean on me as much as you need to."

The door was pulled open by a Bhen who I hardly recognised. The light in his eyes had dimmed, and there were dark bruises across his face and neck. He also leant on a cane, his left leg barely resting on the ground.

"Elena," his mouth was open, and I wished I could run away, but before I even tried, he wrapped his arms around me, "I'm so sorry."

I didn't know what he was apologising for, and I didn't care. I melted in the warmth of his embrace, feeling my tears flow into his shoulder.

"Oh, I know," he squeezed me tighter, "it's the hardest feeling in the world."

I tried to respond but my throat had swollen in the storm of guilt. Everything hurt, but he soothed it a little bit.

"You're safe now, you 'ear me? You can stay as long as you need to."

I managed a few stifled words.

"I can't put you in danger."

"Oh, for fuck's sake," he held me at arm's length, looking genuinely cross with me, "we're already in danger, love, I'm not lettin' you suffer too."

I nodded, mouthing the words 'thank you' to him. He looked at Hurwin.

"How bad is it?"

"It's not good, Bhen. She'll need a few days, maybe weeks. They were going to take her to the Sanctuary."

"And Ghangris?"

"He's hiding for now, after what happened at the dock. I'll speak with him when it's safe."

Hurwin placed a hand on my shoulder.

"I need to go now, there are other things I need to do urgently, but I will come back."

I nodded again, smiling for a second at him. He looked at Bhen.

"Look after her, and, I'm sorry about your boy."

And with that quick blow, he melted away into the shadows, moving faster than anything I'd seen before. I grabbed Bhen's wrists.

"Not Bhari, please…"

"He's alive, love, don't worry," his lip quivered, "he'll never be the same, but I've still got him, and I can only be thankful for that at least."

"What happened?"

"Look come in, you'll get cold."

He pulled me into the warmth of the shop, a fire roaring in the corner of the room. He quickly threw a blanket around me and showed me to a nearby chair. I sat down and looked around at the assortment of trinkets that dotted the walls. It really was just bits and bobs, consisting of strange contraptions and tools.

I realised then that with the high security in and around the district, these kinds of items were likely hard to come by or taken at random stages and perhaps Bhen provided a good service for that, despite the intentions with those *tools*.

I did spy a golden clock among all the junk though and noticed that it was now late evening. I already felt the pangs of exhaustion rusting my joints with time.

*Only **you** could sleep for months and still have the audacity to complain about exhaustion.*

Fuck off.

"Tea?"

251

"No, thank you," I realised then just how dry my throat had been, "could I have some water please?"

"Ah," Bhen cleared his throat, "not much clean water here I'm afraid, most of it's contaminated. Tea's boiled, kills most of it at least."

"I guess that'll have to do then," I watched him go to the pot, "what happened to Bhari?"

"I um," Bhen could hardly hold the pot straight, tea spilt over the counter as he tried to pour, "I'd uh, I'd rather not explain. Sorry. It was horrible."

"I understand, where is he?"

"Just upstairs, love. He's alright, just, um."

Bhen put the pot down and leaned against the counter, shaking his head.

"Bhen?"

"He can't speak. That lovely voice of his. It's gone," Bhen sniffed, then picked up the cup, bringing it over to me, "he was trying to stand up for some kid. They were kickin' her, calling her rat, treg, all the names, you know."

I took the mug from him, smelling the earthy brew.

"Then one of 'em had the bright idea to start fuckin' her. Right there in the street. Them animals were rapin' some poor girl for everyone to see," he sat down to look at the flames, "she were only eleven. And Bhari, ya see, well, you know what 'e's like. That's why I love 'im so much. He's the best of us, you know? Never were one to let someone suffer. 'e jumps in, e's picked up some plank from nearby. Anyway he's beatin' this man, course it's barely doin' anything. He's only sixteen, and this man were wearin' that pig armour."

"They were Inquisitors?"

"It's high time you learned something, love," Bhen's eyes were dark now, his face grim, "those Inquisitors, are the worst of the worst. The soldiers kill, well at least that's quick. The enforcers beat ya, hurt ya, maybe kill ya, but your bones can heal. Even them Changed, they're not even human, they're more machine than man. There ain't even a soul to judge in there. The Inquisitors though? They know they're stronger than you, they know they're more powerful. They turn up knowing they can turn you to dust, demolish your 'ouse, and burn your family, and they'll get away with it if they can justify it. They're cowards, they're evil. They don't care who sees them. They know the law they wield is unjust."

"I'm starting to realise that my whole life has been a lie."

"This 'ole system's a big lie, love. You were too young to know the difference," he smiled again, "but you're 'ere now, and that's all that matters."

"Did she get away?"

"The girl?"

"Yeah."

"She did," Bhen swallowed, "weren't no good though. She'll carry that with 'er. Some might say that death'd been better."

"But she'll get to live, she'll be able to make better memories?"

"Here? I doubt it. Nah, s'pect that day scarred her as much as it did my son."

He trembled as stared away from me, the orange glow dancing in his glistening eyes.

"I watched it happen."

"Did the Inquisitor fight back?"

"He did. Then, just like all those cowards do, he got the traitors to do it instead," he paused, "they've been uh, recruiting people from the district as a militia."

"And they hurt Bhari?"

Bhen nodded.

"Why would they do that?"

"They're desperate. If beatin' a child's worth a meal or two 'oo am I to judge ay?"

Bhen took a ragged, deep breath, a tear travelling the inlays of his face. After a moment, his voice came through choked, even more of them bubbling forward.

"They follow 'cause they're afraid."

So often in my life, I felt unsure of what to say. Often I would say something anyway, just to fill the empty space. But I couldn't this time. This man was broken, broken by a force so unimaginably huge that I had no idea what to tell him. His son, my friend, had tried to fight back and had even more taken from him. I wanted to do something to help Bhen, the way he helped me, but I just didn't know how.

You're a failure.

"I know."

"What?" Bhen had been staring into the fire for some time now and his eyes were wide and jumpy, "sorry, I didn't hear what you said."

Moron.

"Sorry I, uh," I shook my head, "I'm sorry, about Bhari."

Bhen smiled, making a short laugh.

"Why're you sayin' sorry? You couldn't have changed anythin'. You'd've been right there with 'im, or worse."

"Is that why you have the bruises?"

"No, that were, uh, a different Pig, love."

"Who? What happened?"

"You ain't ready for that right now, you need rest."

"Was it him?"

"Who?"

"My father Bhen," I almost shouted, and he looked a little taken aback, "was it Anders?"

Bhen looked down and then back at me. And nodded.

"Your da's in a bad way, love. Wanted information I didn't 'ave. Weren't takin' no for answer."

"He's always in a bad fucking way," I dug my nails into the arms of the chair, "he left us there, and it's my fault Oliver's gone, all because of him and his stupid fucking Order. I hate him."

"You don't mean that, Elena," Bhen sighed, "he's grieving, same as you," he grinned again, "difference is, e's a bad man trying to live under a bad system, you're not."

"I'm sorry."

"Don't be, what 'e did, nothin' to do with you, alright?" he sighed then, "and look, I hate saying this,

255

but he's not lost. Bhari tried to defendin' me because he's a good boy, and truthfully, I thought your dad'd kill 'im. But he didn't."

"Thank you," that surprised me too, honestly, "I'll try and help him if I can."

CHAPTER THIRTY-THREE
-ELENA-

Elena.

Electricity energised my heart and pulled me from whatever dream I'd waded through before, dropping me back onto the chair in Bhen's shop with a drop of vertigo so pungent it still coursed through my gut as I recollected the room's details. Some way of grounding myself again.

I focused on the silver clock that hung above Bhen's seat, noticing then that he was no longer there. The clock showed that it was the dead of night now, and I wondered if it was still worth knocking on Bhari's door?

Wait, silver clock?

Was it not golden before? You are so very forgetful.

I sat up slowly, then heard a board creak to my left, even though I was sure that the room extended to the right before. Hurwin Corvin, or at least that was the name the Folsesjeger, had given me, halted his approach a moment to hold his hand up.

"I didn't mean to startle you," he helped himself to the seat across from me, "I hope you don't mind, I wanted to guide you here."

"This is the Dream, still," I gripped the edge of the chair's fabric arms, wincing at the scratching sound my nails made against it, "isn't it?"

"Yes," when he spoke his words almost seemed to patter against my chest with small impacts across my ribs like rain, "I know that the first few times can be a lot to take in, and I thought that I could help."

"What is this place?" I rested my feet on the ground only to pull them back in fear from the sodden material, realising that water covered most of the floor now, "what's happening to me?"

"What is your understanding of the Void?" Hurwin didn't seem to pay the water mind as it lapped against his boots, "describe it to me."

"The Matuan tribes called it the Beyond, they thought it was the next life and that all spirits went there one day," I remembered vandalism carried out by rebel groups and the day of Burcanon, "they felt that tampering with its energies lead to vengeful spirits. The Quorum told us that it was the realm of the Old Gods, that they were imprisoned there by Darius and that the powers they grant us are gifts intended to help us ascend and free them one day."

"And what do you think it is?"

I felt the accusatory sting of the response, that no matter what I said it would somehow be insufficient.

"I don't know anymore."

"It's hard, admitting ignorance," Hurwin sunk a little further into the soft armchair, "knowing when you don't know, it's a powerful trait. Where others will continue to make mistakes, you will overcome them."

"So, what is it then? Who was right?"

"Neither, really," he sighed and closed his eyes a moment, "both, maybe. I know it as the Reflection, and it's one of the many planes of existence that exist around you."

"And the Dream is another?"

"Precisely," Hurwin glanced at me again then, smirking a little, "this is a lot to take in, I understand that. And we don't have time to go through everything, we have to snatch these moments at your deepest sleep cycles."

"I'm assuming we can't meet often."

"Never, it's too dangerous. Here, I can show you a lot more than I could out there, in the physical realm. And we're safe here, most creatures of the Reflection can't access the Dream."

"So, are the Fallen real?" it was the only question that felt even remotely logical to ask, there were forces here far beyond even the bounds of insane imagination.

"Well, they exist, but not as the Quorum might believe they do," he waved his hand then, reigniting the fire in the room with his mind alone, "the Void is chaos incarnate, an endless battleground, where those that slay others gain their power and grow stronger. Soon, among all that primordial gunk, a few core concepts and ideas soon took powerful physical forms and ruled over others, feeding on souls to satiate themselves. The Fallen aren't imprisoned, they've grown bloated and stagnant, birthing creatures of their own design to bring them more."

"Like Kaurus did, with the Folsesjeger?"

"Kaurus created us with the intention of sending us into the physical world, to infiltrate and subjugate it, bringing the Fallen a new world to devour."

"But you fought back?"

Hurwin nodded and let the silence fill the room.

"You have to understand the enormity of you being here, Elena. As far as I know, only Folsesjeger have managed to access the Dream, and even then it takes a great deal of effort and training," Hurwin paused again, taking a deep breath, "we decided that we couldn't allow the Fallen to access the physical world or the Dream."

"So, the Quorum want to bring those things through? That's…" the anger felt sickly to me, like my stomach was already unsettled and the acidity was making it all the more volatile, "I don't understand why anyone would want that."

"The Quorum may have been offered some kind of power, or even safety within the new world," Hurwin choked a little then, massaging his throat, "but it's a lie, you understand? The Fallen are predators and nothing more, they'll consume until there's nothing left of your world, and it won't stop there."

"You think that they'll try and access the Dream too?" I felt like my body was trying to throw me off of an imagined roof in the reflection of the dark waters now soaking the edges of the seat cushion.

"And planes I've only glimpsed but can't even begin to comprehend," Hurwin suddenly seemed to grey at the edges of his hairline, and his face started to crack with lines of age, "you see, the physical world…"

"What's happening?" there was a heavy pounding in my ears and behind my eyes, "everything's really loud."

"I think you're waking up," Hurwin Corvin's hand started to collapse into the water like wet sand, "the connection's fading."

"What were you about to say?" I raised my voice to get above the drumming beat of my heart, "quickly. Something about the physical world."

"It's a bridge, Elena," Hurwin's voice sounded around me, bounding off the walls in excited patterns, and when I looked at the seat he had been in, I realised that there was only his black shadow left, "if they get to yours, they'll get the rest of them. We have to stop them."

"How?" I screamed at the top of my lungs, the water rushing around me as if I was back on that cliff face near the Sanctuary, "tell me!"

"I'll try and help you as best as I can, you'll have to trust me."

The water rose so fast then that I found myself being dragged under its foamy surface by invisible hands. I tried to swim towards the roof, but the currents kept punching down onto my chest, squeezing the air out of me and pinning me to the rug.

Electricity energised my heart and pulled me from whatever dream I'd waded through before, dropping me back onto the chair in Bhen's shop with a drop of vertigo so pungent it still coursed through my gut as I recollected the room's details.

Check the clock this time.

I saw that it was indeed the golden clock this time and that the room was the right way round. The room felt familiar and safe, finally. It was late at night, and it seemed that Bhen had taken himself off to sleep and join the other dreamers. I wondered if Bahri might still be awake though.

I stood outside the door to Bhari's room for a while, waiting for some sign that it was the right moment to talk to him. But that sign would never come, and there was only now.

I'd reached the top of the stairs using the combination of an old oak cane Bhen had found in the shop, as well as the wooden beams along the stairs. I was still breathing heavily from the effort, waiting for my lungs to catch up.

I knocked, then remembered that he wouldn't be able to answer either way, so I waited a moment, then pressed against the panel.

Bhari was sat by his window, a journal in his lap with his head bowed low in a deep sleep. The dark locks covered his face now, the braid he'd tied before let loose. His soft skin had been lacerated and bruised in several places, but the healing had taken effect. He was mending, with time.

I cleared my throat, and he stirred a little, and then I cleared it again. Bhari lifted his hair away from his eyes, looking at me through the crust of sleep and swelling skin. Then his mouth moved.

There was sound. For some reason, I hadn't expected any, but it was a rasping, faint whispering. I could see the lips forming around the sounds of my name, so I nodded in response.

"Hi."

Is that really all you can manage? "Hi"?

I shook my head, then came to sit across from him on the ice-cold sill by the large glass pane. There was a draft still from where the Stragan had broken through, and the room's air was oppressive in its frozen grip.

"I'm sorry for what happened before, at Calthern's speech."

Bhari nodded, his eyes glazed and watery.

"And I'm sorry I wasn't here."

He shook his head and tried to rasp again, clinging his throat in pain. After a moment, his eyes darted around the room, and then he moved his hand forward. He held it there a while, then reached out and took my hand, looking at me.

I nodded as if to say that it was okay. We sat there a while, staring at the wooden panels beneath us, or the cold skin of our knuckles, anything but each other.

"Do you know what happened? To my brother?"

I watched him nod, and place a hand on his
chest. This time he simply mouthed the words *I'm
sorry.*

I smiled at him, then found my own words were
struggling again. That horrible growth in my throat
pulsed with the pain. I missed the lilting of his voice so
dearly. How could I even start to express that grief
without insulting him? He was more than what he lost,
but I'd envisioned him reading his poetry aloud one
day, and it seemed tragic that he never would now.

Knowing Bhari though, I knew he'd find a way
of being heard somehow.

"I need to find my father," I felt Bhari's grip
tighten around my fingers, "I need to stop him before
he gets himself hurt. Or, well," I rubbed my hand over
my eyes and mouth with a sigh, "someone else."

Bhari was staring outside again.

"You understand that? Don't you?"

He slowly agreed, still looking away.

"Do you know how to get to the docks he was
seen at?"

Again, Bhari lightly tilted his head in
acknowledgement.

"Can you take me there?"

He stood, still holding my hand, pulling me to
my feet. He let go and grabbed his jacket, throwing it
over his shoulders. Bhari strode across the room to the
door, and turned only once, to look at me, a massive
grin on his face.

There was some of that same boy I'd met all
that time ago.

The Enlightened Quorum

The Darius district was shifting into the night cycle, the shimmering neon signs flickering into place. Fog hung in the air slightly, causing beams to splash across Bhari's features.

Vendors set up small wagons on the side of the road, opening their hatches to reveal luxurious scents of homemade food and drink. It was good to see some semblance of life being preserved here, despite the pressure for them to die.

We reached the broken shell of a dock warehouse, burns across the cracks in the seams of the roof. Bhari approached the door and then turned to me.

"Is this it?"

He nodded, then pushed inside. There was nothing but loose broken structures and a strange, familiar smell. It was the burning of rubber, a deep primordial fluid that I'd picked up on at the Snow-Steel manor.

That is where we need to go next.

There was also a feeling. It was an elevated heart rate, a slight knot in my stomach, and the strange child of dread and wonder. It was how I felt around my father. I could feel his energies here.

What are they?!

He was underwater, the sound distorted and muffled. But the fury was obvious. I saw a flight of stairs to my right, the red tendrils entwining the bannisters in my mind.

Bhari was watching me with those wolfish eyes, studying my movements. I laced my fingers through the wisps around me, the sounds of my father's voice growing even clearer.

Tell me what you're doin' here...

My footsteps twinkled slightly as shards of glass were crushed to powder beneath them. I looked down to see dark pieces scattered across the floor.

I climbed the stairs, gripping the energy-wrapped bannisters. Bari followed close behind me.

I looked up and saw the ghostly shape of a man, his clothes tattered. He was flung forward, tumbling down the stairs like a barrel down a hill. I pressed myself against the wooden barrier to try and avoid him but he quickly passed through my skin, shattering into pale pieces of starlight.

Bhari had moved when I did but didn't seem to notice the man. He just stared at me with a puzzled expression on his face.

No one else will understand this power. Or accept it. You are alone.

I continued my ascent, hearing the sounds of a struggle up ahead. It was so clear to me now that a disconcerting realisation came to me at that moment. I would never be able to tell these two worlds apart again. There was now a direct link between my brain and the Dream, and that terrified me more than anything.

As I reached the top of the stairs, I saw him. The ghostly shape of my father. He held a young man, no, more a boy with a young hairless face, by the throat. Anders pressed him into the wall, the pipes along his metal hand releasing red stem as they increased pressure.

"Why are you transporting them?" he growled.

His face was basked in an orange light now pulsing through the window.

"We're not," the lad choked, "we stole 'em. Please."

"Liar."

Anders beat him, pummelling him with his remaining arm until the boy went limp, and my father dropped him.

"Anders, we need to go."

I couldn't see her face but I would know Theona's voice anywhere.

It was already obvious that she lied to you.

Anders faded into mist, the crumpled shape of his victim collapsing into pulsating particles. I walked to the nearby window to see into the warehouse again, but I couldn't see anything. The light had faded.

As the images and sounds receded, I was left in that cold silence with Bhari, even his breath hushed as he watched me. The smell of burning hair lingered still. Where had I placed that before?

"What am I doing Bhari?"

He leaned against the window sill with me, clearing his throat.

"I don't know what to do."

I wish I could help her.

It was a faint, ethereal whisper, but I knew it. I squeezed Bhari's hand so hard he turned quickly to see if I was alright. I blinked furiously. Was it a trick?

I looked into his eyes.

"Do that again."

Do what? What's she on about?

He could see my eyes widen and grabbed my shoulder, cocking his head slightly.

"I can hear you," I couldn't help the smile, "Bhari I can hear you."

CHAPTER THIRTY-FOUR
-ELENA-

Mind-melding, that must have been the only explanation for Bhari's thoughts suddenly pouring in through my ears and mixing with mine. We must have subconsciously desired to communicate in some way, or perhaps this was another side-effect of the Dream and its influence.

I remembered Theona explaining the risks to me at great length and tried to test if I could block the connection at all but Bhari's voice interrupted my process again.

Where's she going?

I couldn't shut it off. At least, I wasn't sure how at the time, and truthfully, at that moment, I didn't care.

"Oh Bhari, you know what I wanted, when I was sleeping?" I said, beaming at him as I limped away from the dock warehouse.

How the hell am I supposed to know that? What's wrong with her?

"To hear your voice!" I gasped, "more than anything, you were so comforting when I needed you most, and I thought I'd lost the chance to hear it."

She's scaring me now.

He should fear you.

Shut up.

"I get that, like, really, I do, but I'm serious. I can hear your thoughts, and I could see my father in there, what he did."

Filkyr...

"What does that mean? Filkyr?"

Bhari stopped walking alongside for a few seconds, before jogging to catch up.

That should be more than enough proof of your power.

It's the name of the mind invaders.

"I have to say, your flirting was better before."

His face swirled in a strange whirlpool of emotion as if he didn't know whether to laugh or scream.

It's really rare, Elena, seriously. This is dangerous.

"I'm aware," I assumed that Filkyr was the Matuan word for the Folsesjeger, *mind invaders*, those with access to the Dream.

Something that Hurwin said stuck out to me then. He'd discussed the Void and its inhabitants, and how they gained power through blood. I had technically killed the child that day in the manor, and I couldn't help but wonder if I had inherited some of its power.

How are you going to tell Corvin that you ended his species? That it's your fault he's going to die alone?

270

I didn't have a choice.

We always have a choice. It's just like Oliver, you had a choice to stay and continue the argument, or grow up and leave, and you chose the former.

I groaned then, holding my head as the voice continued its barrage against my nervous system.

"Get out of my head," I muttered several times, closing my eyes, "stop."

Elena?

Bhari gently pulled me aside from the road and under a sheltering canopy. Two enforcers rounded the corner then, holding bolt-action rifles in both hands as they continued on their patrol. They stopped for a moment by us.

"Get yourselves home," they waited, "now."

I nodded and let Bhari help me walk away, using the cane to support myself the rest of the way. Bhari tried to take us back towards the shop but I pushed left and carried on down an alley towards a small square.

Up ahead was a train station. The entrance was set in the gaping maw of a stone giant, its features worn with time and words painted across its cheeks. The sign flickered slightly as it swayed in the breeze.

Where are we going?

"I need to get to the Kaurus district," I said, seeing the stairs leading down into darkness, "there's something I need to check."

Are you insane? They'll kill us.

I had to slow myself down. My brain was moving a mile a minute and I needed to think for a moment.

"You're right, I'm sorry, I didn't think," I placed the cane's end down on the top stair with a clacking sound, "I'll go, you go back home."

Bhari shook his head and sighed.

That's not fair.

He saw the grin on my face as I watched him slowly come to the realisation that he was coming along either way.

"I don't want you to come."

I know, but if you get killed then I'll feel bad, and that's an inconvenience to me.

"Thanks."

I started again but was cut short yet again as Bhari stood in front of me.

Forgive me, but wouldn't it make more sense for you to go home if you really can see the past?

"I'm not," I sighed, "I'm not ready yet."

But you might be able to see what happened?

"I don't want to," I swallowed, looking down, "I don't want to see it again."

Bhari couldn't hide his thoughts of confusion or frustration from me, and on some level, I think he knew that. But he still covered it anyway, nodding as he made his way down the stairs.

The lights lining the walls would have usually activated as we approached, but in an unsurprising twist for the Darius district, only half of them even remotely worked, and those that did flickered pathetic waves of light over us.

The Enlightened Quorum

The platform was slightly more illuminated, showing maybe one or two people waiting nearby and a large tunnel spilling blackness into the room.

A train could soon be heard, hailed by the echoes of the tunnels and a warm wind blowing through the station. The giant metal contraption soon appeared behind beaming lights and pipes pumping that familiar viscous orange sludge.

It came to a screeching halt as the brakes gripped the rusted bars of the tracks, slowing until the sounds had died almost entirely except for the humming of the engine.

The doors were pulled aside by Enforcers armed with those same neutraliser rods I'd seen used at the manor. They stood apart, waiting for passengers. We stepped inside and stood among the crowd of the carriage. They were stuck together like glue, with barely enough room for air between them.

Are you okay?

I flashed a glare at him, hoping he would pick up on the simple fact that I couldn't start chatting away to myself in front of everyone. I gave a light nod.

What do you hope to find in the manor? There is nothing left. He made sure of that. Bhari's right. This is a waste of time, and you know it.

Shut up.

You can't keep shutting me out, you're too weak on your own. You know it's a waste of time. You already know who killed Oliver.

I swear I'll throw myself under the train.

*Please do, everyone would be better off without
you. You've already gotten how many killed due to your
dishonesty?*

Please…please leave me alone.

*You killed him. You killed Oliver. You killed him,
and now everyone's going to die because of it.*

I squeezed the grip of the cane until my knuckles
looked like they were about to burst through my skin,
white bone pushing against fragile flesh.

Elena.

I realised that people were leaving the train and
that Bhari was pushing me towards the exit. We were as
close to the Kaurus district as we were going to get and
had to leave.

How much time had passed? The crowd seemed
to drag me away anyway, my surroundings still mostly
liquid to me. Bhari grabbed hold of my hand as we were
swept with the busy hive of people making their way
home or to work. I thought then of the poor souls forced
to sleep the days away and work right through the night,
never seeing the sun or their loved ones. How was there
still so much industrious activity so late into the nights
of Eleynum? Did the labour simply never stop?

Once we broke free, we pushed against the brick
wall, waiting for them to pass before climbing the stairs
out onto the street. I had to wait a moment to catch my
breath, the joints in my legs now screaming at me to stop.

You need to rest.

"Not yet," I had snapped at him. I hadn't meant
to, "I'm sorry. I need to do this. The more time I waste,
the more people are going to die."

This isn't just on you.

Bhari reached out to me, wiggling his fingers.

"Don't patronise me," I said with a wry smile, "I can do this."

Bhari grabbed me by the wrist and slung my arm over his shoulder, supporting my weight with his.

Just let me help you there?

I considered arguing more, but I knew it would be pointless. We made our way towards the wall of the Kaurus district, stopping to examine it. There was the crude visage of a spider scrawled onto the bricks with thick and spotty black paint and a message around it:

We make the bread and still they give us crumbs. Vorak au! Ver al MLA!

Fight on, for the MLA.

"MLA?" I said to Bhari.

Matuan Liberation Army. Ghangris.

I nodded. It was an irregular war, fought on street corners rather than great river plains. It was a war of ideas as well as bullets, and to the Senate was likely little more than terrorist hunting. At least that's how it had been described to me. But it was a war for the Matuni.

The old Matuan tribes had focused on non-violent solutions, drawing treaties and negotiations with Eleynum about their future within its growing sphere of influence. These treaties, however, had never been upheld. Little by little, piece by piece, the Matuan culture had been eviscerated after Burcanon, and those left had started to realise that they were out of options.

Bhari and I brainstormed ideas like crates and nearby debris that we could move to make our way over, but Gods knew how long that would take and guards would be patrolling the perimeter.

Then we heard the rolling of large wheels making their way to us and the hum of a small, weak engine. We pressed ourselves into an alcove, watching for the vehicle.

It was a pleasure carriage, a strange contraption of both the musty familiar and the alien future. They used to be pulled by horses only fifty years ago but now moved freely with the use of Void-energy. But their design remained largely the same, an open-top wooden lounging area for the Summer class to parade their wealth.

A young man sat at the large wheel at the parapet, his eyes drooping after a long night. But there was no one sitting in the passenger seats.

What do you think?

"We can't afford that."

Hold on.

Bhari stepped forward and into the path of the oncoming carriage, holding his hands up in the air and waving them to get the driver's attention. It came to a stop in front of him.

"What you doin'?" the man said, "ge'out the way, I coulda killed ya."

Bhari adopted a puppy-like expression, confused and needy, pointing to me frantically. I realised what he was doing, so I increased the severity of my wincing, the pain of my steps forward.

"I am sorry about that," I had to improve on the elocution of my language and the annunciation of my words, make him believe I was a Summer child, "I was attacked and this...boy, he helped me. I need to get home, would you do me a kindness?"

"Sorry ma'am, can't do it. Need to get this back and go 'ome."

"Please, you would be highly rewarded," I rifled through the names of great families to drop into conversation.

A minor house is more believable. You aren't exactly dressed for the role.

"My name is Emilee, Emilee Citrun."

"Apologies, ma'lady," he sighed, "I really can't.

"Please?" I looked down at my shaking legs, "I can hardly stand."

The man closed his eyes.

"Okay," he nodded towards the seats, "the wife'll kill me."

"I am sorry," I placed a giggle, maybe too forced, "thank you so much," I waved to Bhari, "come on, you deserve a hot meal too."

As we settled into the seats, Bhari gave me a smirk, so I kicked him lightly. The carriage engine hummed again as the carriage lurched forward.

"Remind me, ma'lady, Citrun 'ouse is near the ol' Snow-Steel manor, right?"

"That is correct."

"Terrible business that," the driver said, "the 'ole family, traitors and murderers apparently."

"Yes, I had heard," I supposed that he had heard a lot of gossip from the same crowds, and took it at face value, "a shame."

"Ah well, s'pose your family'll pick up the slack, eh?"

"Yes, quite."

The carriage approached a nearby checkpoint, two enforcers stepping forward to force us to a standstill.

"Business?"

"I'm taking Lady Emilee Citrun home, sir," the driver said, "she was attacked."

The enforcer stepped round to the side of the carriage to leer at me.

"Shouldn't have been out without a guard, should we?" he said, then turning to Bhari, "who's the treg?"

I flashed a glare at Bhari, seeing him tense up.

"He saved my life tonight," I cleared my throat, "a lot more than your people have done. What is your name?"

He straightened up at that, tightening his grip on his rifle. Then he relaxed again.

"Sorry ma'am, quite right."

The other enforcer had stepped around now, their own rifle ready for a disturbance.

"Everythin' alright Janta?"

"Yeah," he flared his nostrils a moment, staring at Bhari, then looking back at me, "all good."

"Are you sure?" his colleague said.

Janta looked back at them, and they exchanged a strange look, before stepping away in hopes that we couldn't hear them. I could only make out a few words, but the emotions between them were obvious.

One recognises you.

Or knows that I'm not Emilee.

Either way, we need to go.

"Is there a problem?" I shouted.

Janta raised a hand to the other enforcer and stepped towards the carriage again.

"Yeah, it's fine, just overly cautious. You have a lovely evening."

The driver kicked the carriage into gear again, moving through the checkpoint, leaving the enforcers to argue between themselves. The curious one was shouting at Janta now.

"I'm telling you," they made their way to the booth, "I'm calling them."

Shit.

I placed a hand on Bhari's knee.

"You okay?" I whispered.

He swallowed, before giving a curt nod.

The carriage stopped for a final time outside of the gates to the Citrun house, large fruit trees leading the way to the doors. Bhari helped me out so I could speak to the young man up front.

"I am afraid I have no money to spare."

"S'alright," he said, glumly, "just, put in a good word for me? This ain't the best of jobs."

"I will," I shouldn't have done it, it was wrong, "what is your name?"

You're only giving him false hope.

"Erik," Erik smiled, "Erik Hams."

"Okay, Erik," I felt sick, "I will mention your name."

"Thanks miss, now you get home and be safe."

279

"Thank you, Erik."

He yawned as he turned the carriage around, making his way back towards the checkpoint to make his way home. I watched him go, with pain in my nose from where I wanted to cry again.

What's the point of that? You lied to him, maybe even risked his life. Crying won't change that.

The Snow-Steel manor was a little way down, its hollowed-out shell once a hotbed for the misery that the Void feeds on, now a lifeless husk wheezing with the dust of the dead.

I'd expected guards for some reason, but there was no one, no life signs at all throughout the entire manor. Perhaps they'd already picked the carcass clean for all that they could.

Bhari pushed against the battered gates, grimacing at the loud screech its hinges made. Strange really, as if the house really had died at its abandonment, and this was the rot setting in.

We walked down the cobbled path, and I noticed that even the beautiful flowers, once a spectrum of colour, now crinkled as they swayed in the wind. Their grey petals were slowly being pulled away, one by one, disintegrating in the breeze.

The rosebud door handle was now slick with oily grime, and it seemed to seep from the very seams of the walls and into the gutters below. It reeked of dead energy, something beyond even the simple spells I could cast. Something long forgotten and with good reason.

Are you sure?

"We have to go in, I have to know what they were looking for."

I'm right behind you.

I lightly pressed against the door, and it creaked as it opened inwards. The ground was covered in black leaves, blown in from the sycamores out the back, infiltrating through the shattered glass doors. The paint on the walls was spilling onto the ground like the makeup of the traumatised on their way home, streaks pooling into thick puddles that squelched as we moved through them. The air itself tasted stale.

The door to the drawing room had been left open in the calamity, and the thick sinews of the growth had long faded by then. All that was left was mounds of stinking flesh, pale in the moonlight.

"I'm sorry."

What?

"I'm sorry you came with me, this place is…it's sad."

I can feel its pain.

"You have no idea."

The gusts whistled as they blew through the thin remains of the doors, pushing us back as we made our way to the workshop. A couple of the ghostly sapphire lanterns were still lit, catching the fog in thin wispy hands. The power must have still been connected.

As we stepped inside the silent workshop the lights turned on without our input. Though they now flickered, and some had been broken in what had been an obvious raid. Papers were strewn across the floor and the various prosthetics Marcus had been working on had either been smashed into porcelain shards.

The door to Velloah'Ra's room had been torn off completely as the idiots had smashed their way in. As we stepped inside the office, I saw that the generator she had been so afraid to give up had been taken, a puddle of bright purple liquid all that remained.

"I don't know what I expected," I fell into a nearby chair, "it's all gone."

Bhari routed through some opened files, kicking over a nearby canister.

"Bhari, leave it, I wasted your time bringing you here. They have the generator. It'll only take them a little bit of time to figure out how it works. Whatever the hell they need it for."

Bhari picked something up and studied it for a moment. He was holding a small blue orb. There was a scent of citrus coming from it, almost acidic when hitting the back of my nose. It was old magic, from deep within in the primordial energies of the earth, the likes of which were only ever manipulated by the Gunrays. Bhari then tossed it aside, sending it clattering off of the table's edge.

"Bhari," I sat up. As I focused on the orb, I felt the chaotic energies of my bracelet resonating with it, drawing me to it, "could you bring that to me? Please?"

He shrugged and went to collect it, handling it with more care this time. I squinted as I stared at the soft enamelled glass. Then I heard it.

There was a whisper, near silent but harsh in its intonation. It was a language I recognised but didn't understand, similar to the Matuni general speech but older, and more aggressive.

The intent of the words was as clear as day in my mind. The words meant nothing, but the feeling behind them held everything.

Bhari handed the orb to me, his hands shaking a little. He dropped it into my outstretched hand and backed away, perhaps having heard the voice too.

The dark bangle started to shake and jump as I held the sphere, pieces of it attempting to latch onto its surface. I reached into the black glass and tapped into its insanity, turning it into a liquid mass that writhed into my fingers like a snake at my command.

Bhari stepped back further; his eyes were wide as he watched the shifting shards. His face was stone then, fixed by the sight of an alien horror beyond his comprehension.

I realised then that I would need to conceal my use of the glass from now on. I'd always thought Marius had been trying to tease me, calling me a freak when he saw me manipulating the material. But I remembered the fear in the other voices, the night I'd killed Greta. Bhari's reaction cemented that this was something that nobody could know about.

I fashioned the atoms into a scalpel-like tool, using its razor-thin edge to cut into the orb.

After a few moments, the tips of my fingers felt slimy against the soft surface, and as I drew them back, I saw glistening blue sweat lining them. The orb's edge had been warped, collapsing in on itself at an increasing speed.

"No," I looked around the room for some kind of fridge or coolant tanks, but it was too late.

There was black glass housed inside, spilling through my fingers like sand on a beach. Before it hit the ground, it was caught in a silent wind, swirling into the centre of the room.

The image seemed to draw on the light around it, becoming blinding as it took the shape of a face. It was Velloah'Ra, or at least, a memory of her.

"Hello, Elena," she smiled, "I'm glad you found my little gift. How can I help?"

I saw Bhari staring in awe.

"How do you know it's me? What are you?"

"I am a remnant of Velloah, stored in the glass for a time," her voice hissed softly as the grains ground against each other, "I hoped that it would be Anders who found me, still hoping that there was some good left in him. But I knew that it would be you instead."

"Why me? You hardly know me."

"I saw great things in you, that day at the workshop," the image was unstable, her features cracking as she spoke, "I knew that Anders was too far gone, but that you had the spark."

"I haven't got a spark, I can't do anything now," I gestured to her office, "and besides, they took it all, all your research."

"Not all of it," her voice crackled, "this spell won't last forever. You remember what I told you? About the generators?"

"You said they were dangerous, that others wanted them."

"More than you can ever know. They don't just create rifts for energy, with the right magnification, they could be used to power the city for an eternity," bits of the glass were falling away now, "the cheap imitations they're building now aren't capable of much, but my machine was able to convert anything. Creatures, or even powerful Void-touched people. They were ferrying stragan into the manor through an underground tunnel system for tests and I have no idea where they were getting them from. The tunnel is in the family burial grounds."

I could see the energy starting to fade, her voice growing more constricted by the moment.

"Elena, I managed to hide the fundamentals of my machine away where they'll never find them, but you need to find out where they're developing them and stop it. When pushed too far, the machines fail and the rift becomes unstable, enough for creatures to come through. They will keep advancing their technology, even if another Burcanon happens. You need to stop them or find someone who can. Please."

"I can't," I shouted, stepping forward, "I don't even know where to start."

"Neither do I," her arm collapsed, shattering into dust on the ground, "every time I tried to look, they found a way to force me back into the work. They have eyes everywhere."

"Who? Who are they?" I thought about trying to hold her together somehow, but I didn't know where to begin with eh construction of the emotions of the spell.

"The Enlightened Quorum, and all connected to them," The collapsing blue shell gasped, "I have a list of names...somewhere...I don't want to die."

"I'm sorry," I tried to hold what was left of her hand, "I'm so sorry."

And that was it. Within a few seconds, the light behind the shards of memory went out, leaving them as lifeless black chips scattering across the titled ground.

Elena, did you understand any of that?

I nodded.

"Mostly, I guess. The Quorum worships the Old Gods and wants to free them from the Void, right? If Velloah'Ra's machines can open tears," I started to limp towards the door, "maybe they've found a way to do it. Whatever it is though, it's dangerous. I saw a vision of the world destroyed by the Void. I've been seeing it in some form my entire life, ever since Burcanon. I knew those machines were fucking dangerous."

We should get you back. You need to rest.

"We can't give up now, Bhari," I said, "we need to find this tunnel and see where it goes."

He gave me a stern and condescending look. I suppose it wasn't his fault, he was trying to help, but it was annoying seeing him treat me like a child, or deadweight even.

"What?"

You're going to get yourself killed. Let's go back.

"You can go ahead, I'll be fine."

I walked out into the crisp evening, noting the flurries of snow caught in the lanterns lining the path leading back to the manor. I shoved my hands into the pockets of my coat, burying myself in its collar to try and fight the winds a little.

The Snow-Steel burial grounds were at the end of a path that branched off slightly, amongst an orchard of violet trees. They produced nothing particularly useful, except strange lilac blossoms all year around and sap that was supposedly used in the family's prosthesis business, but their process was still mostly a closely guarded secret. Though, it would only be a matter of time before another family harvested those ideas for themselves.

There were more graves than I expected here. I knew, logically, that nearly half of the family had died during those months, but somehow it had seemed that death never touched families like this. Now I realised, looking at the field of stones, that there might have been a curse after all.

...curses are a controversial topic among scholars of the Order. It is, generally, believed that Kaurus, in his wisdom, forbade the use of fate manipulation and granted us free will. It was, after all, imperative that we chose one day to free the Fallen of our own volition.

But Ghoron, the Weaver, being ever the naughty and mischievous one among the Gods, has been recorded granting boons of curses to his most loyal followers. Such as at the execution of Vetroclus, Speaker of the Old Quorum, when he cursed the God-King's nephew, Godagon, to suffer eternal shame.

The Enlightened Quorum

Well, it is widely known that Godagon, the so-called demigod, slowly succumbed to a meer whoring and o', did he succumb indeed, his genitals soon rotting off in a foul public display...

On Fate and Curses
Jermane Felsom, Scholar-Supreme 873-885 P.R.

The insane story aside, it did raise an interesting question about fate. Hurwin had also alluded to having predicted the child's birth at the manor. This vision I had seen had seemed so real, and everywhere I turned there were more and more signs that this free will, the supposed gift of Kaurus, may have been a crock of shit. That this apocalypse was fated, and that I was already too late.

I pushed those thoughts aside for the moment and focused on the search.

At the centre of the grounds was the core mausoleum. This was where the central family's bones were kept. Three sections had been recently filled, one at the head and centre of the block for Josiah, another to the left of the empty slot reserved for Velloah'Ra, and another beside him for Isobel's tiny body. Their cases were cast in icy glass, their bones just visible beyond the obtuse screens.

How do we know which one it is?

Bhari was holding onto stoicism as best he could but the snowy winds battered his loose hair and he brought his own coat tighter around him.

"I'm not sure."

Everything was covered in age-old vines and moss, snow lining the tops of the small leaves. Everything except, it seemed, another mausoleum towards the back of the orchard. This one, despite being among some of the oldest stones, was a brighter white in its appearance, the vegetation around it largely having retreated. The names had been scratched and smeared, to the point of illegibility.

"I think this might be it, it's newer than everything else, and the names are meaningless."

There was a small blue slot embedded in the stone, the same spectral glow as the orb in the workshop. Once again, I ordered the bracelet to form for me, creating a tiny pin. It slid into the groove as if it were goo, releasing its nectar to dribble over the nonsense words.

The mausoleum shifted then, squealing as steel ground against the rocky ground. It revealed a stairway shrouded in oily black shadows from below, distant lamps barely fighting it back.

As we descended, I saw tunnels leading off in different directions, these were held up by strong iron beams and illuminated by fitted floodlights.

You're going to get yourself killed, Elena, we need to go back.

"No, alright? No," I hobbled towards one of the tunnels, "you can go back if you like, but I need to see this through."

We can come back tomorrow.

"You can, I'll see you later."

The Enlightened Quorum

I slipped a little on the grimy stones, viscera from the running water seeping through the seams of my boots and into my socks. *For fuck's sake.* I heard him sloshing through the waters after me and couldn't help but smile a little. I'd heard whispers along this tunnel, the kind I'd been hearing my whole life and now felt so clearly with Bhari. It was the faint humming of humanity, and I was sure that it would lead back to the surface. Though where exactly we would emerge would be a tragic answer, knowing that the people there were likely being harmed by these experiments.

The tunnel soon began to incline, an elevation of pressure and a change in scent confirmed my suspicions. Soon, we found a huge iron door locked by a wheel. Bhari helped me turn it, both of us twisting the locking bars aside.

It led out into a dark and dust-filled room, with destroyed old benches in the centre of the room and an old desk to the right. And there was a stench so foul I had to bury myself into my clothes immediately, still attacked by the smell of petrifying meat. I realised, through my stinging eyes, that this must have been some kind of reception area.

However, I soon spied the room sealed by bars to the left. It was empty, but I knew a prison cell when I saw one. I tried to study the room more to see if there were any further clues as to where we were, but the walls had been stripped bare a long time ago.

I noticed Bhari heaving against the door to close it after us.

"Do you think we should leave it open?"

I thought maybe we should hide that we've been here.

"Yeah that's fair enough, I'm just wondering if there are going to be any seals or locks coming back."

You might be right.

"I don't know," I sighed, "maybe leave it just to be safe."

Right.

He pushed it a bit more so that it was at least half-closed, then left it alone.

We went to the main entrance and saw glass panes covered in dark cloth. There were small cracks in the barrier, letting in just a sliver of silver light from the moon-dotted skies. Opening the main doors was easy, somehow, as they weren't locked at all, but that seemed absurd to me. But it was true, the main doors to this building offered no real resistance at all.

Outside, there were the familiar smells of the Night Market of the Darius district. Fried meats, steamed vegetables, and scented oils, all wafted through the air. It was welcome after the double act of a sewer and a rotten prison, though I was certain I couldn't eat for a week.

We were in a small square down the end of a back alley. The buildings here were all hollowed and dilapidated, with only silence to offer. The only noise was the markets with their light string quartets and the shouting of merchants.

I felt the white noise buzz of confusion radiating from behind me, as Bhari stepped outside.

We're home?

"I had a feeling, I guess," I held onto a nearby rail, squeezing the grip until it started to warp from that crushing pressure, "they're taking people from the Darius District."

They'll pay for this.

I watched him walk towards a nearby chair, left abandoned by one of the houses. He fell into it, ignoring the pained creak of its joints.

They can't keep getting away with it.

"They won't, Bhari," I couldn't look at him directly, "we'll fix this."

How? They've been doing this right under our noses, ferrying stragan around like morons.

"I don't know yet, but we will," I stifled a yawn then, and realised that he'd been right all along, "look I…I hate being that person. But there's a positive here. We know now, and we can stop it."

Maybe you're right.

"I don't know how yet, I'll admit that, but I'll come up with a plan," my eyes felt so heavy at that moment, like I could fall against the glass and into sleep there, "I think I do need to sleep. Do you know the way back from here?"

He smiled for a moment, shaking his head. Then closed his eyes. I felt the wave of calm wash over him as he took deep inhalations. Then he stood and put his arm out for me to grip.

292

The Enlightened Quorum

We walked through the market that evening like we did before. The food was worse than before, and a rarer sight than ever. And the people were starving.

And you believed they were bringing it on themselves. You should be ashamed of yourself.

CHAPTER THIRTY-FIVE
-ELENA-

I stared at the grimy floor that buzzed against my hands, the black muck shifting and squelching between my fingers. I heard the frantic gasps and whispers of Magda, my cleaning partner, and looked up to see her hard at work.

She was face-down, like me, and crawling around on her knees. Magda kept hushing herself every time she spoke a little too loud, the harsh and hissing reprimands scattering around the room.

"Blessed are the worms, they look after us on our way home," she childishly repeated, "the serpents of the earth shall one day rise again."

Magda leant down and continued with her work, dragging her coarse tongue across the slick tiles, drawing a long line in the filth. I looked back at my own tile, contemplating joining her in her loathsome task.

"Elena," a familiar voice barked at me.

Hurwin stood in the misty door, particles of burnt flesh from the crematoriums catching in his hair.

The Dream.

"Come on," he said, "this way."

I gathered my grey dress around me and fixed the bonnet as I hurried to follow him.

"What is this place?"

"No idea, you tell me," Hurwin marched through a dark hall, the yellow lanterns casting flickering shadows around us.

Cell doors were lining the hall, thick iron bars guarding small windows into the souls of their prisoners. There was a chorus of screaming echoing through the networks of the asylum, signalling our intrusion.

"This is your dream, Elena," Hurwin opened one of the doors, dust flying from its old locking mechanism, "we only have a little bit of time."

The room was covered in thick padding that had been stained by all manners of bodily fluids. The air reeked with the cloying smell of decay. In the centre of the room was a table and two chairs facing each other, the erratic scratches in the steel reminiscent of the one in the Red Room.

We took our seats.

"So, how are you doing?" Hurwin asked, "anything to report?"

"Did you know?"

Hurwin blinked a few times and searched my face.

"About what, sorry?"

"The Snow-Steels," I ran my fingers along the table, feeling the grooves of ghosts again, "Velloah knew you, at the end. You said she 'did the right thing', so I guess my question is, did you know what she was building for the Senate? About what the mound was doing to the family?"

"Yes."

"Yes?" I rubbed my eyes for a moment, "yes? Yes what?"

"I knew what she was building, and that the child might kill them."

"Did you organise for Valeria to be raped?" I swallowed the thick and stringy saliva that had pooled on my tongue, "what did you tell them to do?"

"I gave them some basic pointers, told them the child would happen regardless, and that they didn't need to meddle in it," Hurwin stopped halfway and sighed, "why are you asking about this? What does it matter?"

"I want to know who you are...what kind of person I'm working with."

"Someone who, no matter what, will stop the destruction of this world."

"So, the cost doesn't matter? People like Valeria, they don't matter?" I reached into the apron strapped across my chest, pulling out the broken orb, "Velloah knew those machines were dangerous, and you didn't help her."

"It was her choice to build them in the first place."

"But you knew what kind of damage they could do?" I watched the Folsesjeger, seeing his eyes narrow at my blustering, "she was willing to do the right thing. To give it all up, and I assumed you were helping her stall the Quorum."

"I was."

"Then why didn't you help them sooner?" I took a beat and a breath, knowing I needed to be in control, "why didn't you stop Josiah?"

"I promised him power if he protected the child, his own beliefs in purity were entirely his own and," Hurwin looked up then, his breathing barely perceptible, "perhaps I could have discouraged him. But the child was my last hope, in truth. I didn't discover the machine until much later on. Velloah approached me. She'd tracked me down after I'd met with Josiah one night."

"But you couldn't jeopardise the plan, right? The mound was already active."

"Yes," Hurwin placed one finger on the table, slowly scraping through the plated surface with a squealing noise, "I'd waited so many lifetimes for that moment."

"If you want me to help you," I grabbed his hand to stop the terrible scraping, "we have to start sharing notes. Because we might be too late already."

"And what notes have you got for me?" Hurwin snatched his hand back, "tell me something I don't know."

"I'm afraid of you."

The Folsesjeger's eyes were covered in creases at the corners up until then but suddenly softened, just for a small glimpse. Then his pupils narrowed like a cat, and he leaned forward.

"Good."

"I tracked those tunnels from the manor, where they were taking the Stragan," I couldn't look at him anymore, "you knew they were linked to Darius, didn't you?"

"No."

"You're lying."

"I knew that people were being abducted," he slammed the table then, "guess what? Not a big story."

"You could have stopped it."

"I only have so many people at my disposal, and if I'd let the Quorum know I was onto them that wouldn't change anything," he stood up, "you don't get it yet, but you will. Nothing else matters but stopping the end. The people of that district will die either way, I have to focus on what will advance our position the best. You're afraid of me? Good, you should be."

"I can't trust you."

"No, you can't," he turned to the door then at a loud thudding sound, "I would kill you in a heartbeat if it got me closer to stopping them. Truthfully, I'm still considering it."

"Why?"

"I don't understand you, or your power. It's different from anything I've seen before, and if you decided to switch sides..."

I heard another loud stomp outside the room accompanied by a low moaning.

"What is that?"

"Ignore it, it's just a dream."

"So, you won't do anything about this? The tunnels?"

"I'll try," Hurwin held his head low, "I'm sorry, Elena. I feel that it's already here, and I don't know how to stop it. Inquisitors like your father aren't helping, moving people around is getting harder and harder. But I'll do better. I promise."

There was a loud wailing outside now and it rattled the foundations of the room. It was joyous and giggly like a small child, but it sounded as though it was inside a small tin, metallic and artificial in tone. A shape covered the door's peephole, glistening in the pale light.

Hurwin had disappeared then, not even a wisp of smoke remained as I looked to where he had been standing. Our connection was severed.

The giant with an infant's voice called to me and spoke my name with its torn and disembodied gullet. It wanted me to come and play.

"No fuckin' way, and that's the end of it," Bhen had been tightening a bolt on a pistol while I'd been talking at him, "and you though' I'd consider it? You must think I'm thick as pig shit."

"But if we don't do something then more attacks will come, like before?"

"That is exactly why I'm ignorin' you right now," he slipped with the screwdriver and scratched the side of the metalwork, "bollocks!" Bhen pulled off his goggles and turned to look at me, "I was told to look after ya, and now you're runnin' off into Pig districts? Talkin' about sewers and Gods know what else. They'll peel my skin off."

"If we wait around for him to do something then we'll have worse troubles," I flashed a glance at Bhari, "you have to trust us."

"I do trust ya, but I ain't playing this game with ya anymore," Bhen went to rub Bhari's shoulder, "I can't see you hurt again, boy. You 'ear me? I love ya too much to see that."

Bhari nodded, glancing at me with shame. I understood. Of course, I did. If I had the chance, I would never have challenged my father on anything ever again if it had meant keeping Oliver alive.

But you'll ruin their family, as well as everyone else's. Because that's what you are. You break things.

I then had an idea. It was a silly, fleeting one, but it felt important to me at that moment. I reached out and grabbed them both by the wrists and attempted to channel the ideas between my fingers.

At first, they simply looked at me with confusion. Then they heard their agreement on my insanity, and looked at each other, wide-eyed.

"Bhari?" Bhen was confused.

Dad? You can hear me?

Bhen covered his mouth and trembled slightly.

"Oh gods, I can," he threw his arm around his son, holding him for a moment, "son, what's happening?"

Elena has a gift.

"It's amazing," Bhen sniffed, then looked at me, "if you think pullin' some cheap trick will get ya your way then I've got news for ya."

You're pathetic. You're only doing this to serve your own ego.

Dad, she's right. If we don't do something, the Stragan will keep coming. We'll all be dead soon.

"I know she's tellin' the truth but there's not much we can do. Orders are to sit tight."

But we can try. We have to.

Bhari and I both stared at him then, waiting for him to decide what was best. Then, finally, after a long while, he sighed.

"I know some people that might be able to help. We should speak to them first."

He walked away, waving for us to follow him as he made his way to a wall behind the shop's counter. As he pressed against it, I realised it was a crawlspace, the light wall lifting away and sliding to the side. There was a small set of steps behind it.

It wound round a few times into a tight space, where after only a few flights we were confronted by a jagged stone.

"What is this?"

"Wait," Bhen scanned the wall for a moment, then seemingly found what he was looking for, rubbing a particular bladed section.

Runes lit up in the stone, carved to form a circle. I recognised the boxy language; it must have been ancient because it had similarities to Gunray characters. Then the stone started to peel away, folding in on itself until another set of steps, all carved marble revealed themselves.

We stepped inside and blue lights powered on as we walked along the tunnel. I couldn't see any fuel or wiring anywhere, however. It was seemingly lit by some kind of magic.

Eventually, we saw lights further ahead, illuminating a circular room with three huge figures working on a giant machine in the centre. When they heard us coming, they each stopped what they were doing and faced us, their hammers and other tools in hand.

"That you Bhen?" The giant's voice was booming.

"Yeah it's me," he coughed, "we need your help.

When we got close to them, I could see that they were at least eight or nine feet tall, one maybe even reaching ten. They were strangely proportioned, thicker and weightier than they were lanky and bald like giant toddlers. They were covered in tattoos of different shapes and colours. There wasn't a lot distinguishing them, visually, besides their height; but the colours and shapes of their eyes were strikingly unique somehow.

It was as if I could read their personalities and intentions at a simple glance, their lives making sense to me from a look.

"Elena, Bhari, this is Carnal, Olrod, and Janak of the Auspin clan."

"Are you?" I felt like I might have finally lost it completely, or that perhaps I was still trapped in the Dream after all, "are you, like, Gunrays? I read about you in books...I thought you were all gone."

"Easier to let 'em think that eh?" the tallest one, Carnal, said, "been hiding a long time. Surprised you know anything about us."

Again, that strange feeling came over me. Carnal's expression was a museum, its halls spiralling for eras. I could see every aspect of their life as plainly as I could see the golden hue of their irises with that spectacular violet centre that hugged the black edges of their pupils.

They seemed cynical, having seen histories worth of their people's blood spilt. They knew all too well what horrors can be wrought upon one's enemies, and they knew that there wouldn't be an easy way out or a right answer to any of what was to come.

How was that happening?

"Sorry, what's going on?" a crack formed along the bumpy ridges of my brain, sharp pain running down the base of my neck, "my head...my head's killing me."

"Is it the face thing?" Olrod approached and knelt down to look at me, her eyes molten like magma and hitting me again.

She knew something was wrong with me, it was written all over her studious face. Olrod knew she was the brains of the bunch and didn't feel any obligation to prove it. She knew that whatever explanation she was about to give me was useless because this was something more.

"Yeah," I groaned as Olrod blasted my eyes with a small torch, "is that Gunray magic?"

"Gunray magic?" Janak stepped over to look into my eyes too, "what're you on about?"

He was concerned. Janak wasn't an expert like Olrod, but as family, he knew her well enough to understand when there was something wrong. He was ready to help but was still figuring out what exactly to do, recognising that, ultimately, he wasn't sure there was anything he could do.

"Yeah, gave me half an' headache and all," Bhen said behind me, "you'll be alright, love, just give it a minute."

"No," Olrod said, finally letting go of my face and stepping back, "can't be."

"What is it?" Janak asked, keeping an eye on me and silently offering a hand if I needed it.

I took him up on it before saying a word and he apparently seemed to understand that subtle change in my expression. I felt like I'd been peeled alive and like my red musculature was on full display.

"Can you hear my thoughts too? See my past?" I asked as Janak helped me onto a huge chair, my legs dangling off the side, "this feels a bit demeaning."

"Sorry," the Gunray shrugged, "best I've got. Any what'd you mean? I could see you felt tired and wanted to help. I keep forgetting you guys don't do it normally."

"What Janak's trying to say, is that we've developed a means of projecting intentions and basic thoughts through facial expressions," Olrod was rifling through a journal and had a pen ready to take notes, "you know, you spend so many years in hiding, eventually you have to find ways of communicating non-verbally. But what you said about pasts is interesting, what do you see Elena?"

"I guess," I watched Olrod again, "I see that you're a scientist, or at least, you were one at some point. You said 'we' earlier intending to catch me out because that originally implied, at first, that you three developed this. But I think, from the way you're eagerly jotting all of this down, that this is something Gunrays have done for a long time and it's now become useful in your situation. To you, it's more efficient if I can just see your intentions clearly."

"Impressive, honestly," Carnal laughed, folding their arms, "most people just get the basics, right Olrod?"

"Exactly," she kept writing for a moment, then started to chew on the end of the pen, "might be your Dream-Walker abilities."

How was she able to break you so easily?

"You see, I found it interesting how well you were able to communicate with me, too," Olrod explained, "humans like Bhen, I still can't trust," she turned to him for a moment, "no offence, of course."

"Yeah, sure," Bhen rolled his eyes.

"I can't see their intentions, you see? But you, I saw right through you. Didn't see as much as you can, apparently, but a lot more than you thought."

I had noticed that the headache was starting to clear then, but I felt vulnerable still. For a few moments it felt as though I had had no control over the situation, but with time, I was starting to feel more at ease with it.

"So where did you hear about us anyway?" Janak said with a reassuring smile.

"Not much, some old books I read," I laughed then, "it was on glass manipulation. You might have saved my life, more times than I can count."

"It's a fascinating art, isn't it?" Olrod had seemed sullen until then but was suddenly radiant and animated for a moment, "many useful applications with the right mindset."

"The stories described you as much more monstrous, giants with death machines," I smiled, "but I'm learning more every day, that they often can't be trusted."

And neither can you.

"Well, some of it's right," Janak grinned.

"We're still miles ahead of the human governments, in terms of our technology at least," Olrod grunted, "the ancestors were able to protect that at least."

"They write it as If they wiped you out. I always wondered if any might have survived, and I'm glad to discover that you did. This is, in some ways, a dream come true for me."

"Same goes for us," Janak said, his face stern now, "Dream-Walkers are rare, and a lot of our Clan's drawings rely on it, so it'll be good to experiment and build something new."

"I don't know if I'm good enough for that yet," I looked down, "but I can never repay you for everything you've achieved so far."

"Hey, smashing Eleynum to pieces and installing Gunray tech again," Carnal cracked their knuckles, "that's good enough for me."

"Right," Janak rolled his shoulders, "Elena, let's go look at this tunnel."

CHAPTER THIRTY-SIX
-ELENA-

"It was here, I'm sure of it," I looked at Bhari, "wasn't it?"

He nodded and went searching around the room.

"They've collapsed it, that's all," Janak grumbled, smelling the broken door, "yeah, that'll do the trick, I'm sure of it."

"Can you get through it?" I asked.

"Yeah, easily, just give me a few minutes."

He drew back his hammer and smashed the useless iron slab away, then used a spell in his left hand to slowly disintegrate and shift the rubble on the other side. Soon enough, he was through.

"How did you do that?"

"Gunray magic," Janak winked, then stepped back to allow us through.

"Here we go," I pushed through, stepping into darkness.

I reached out as I walked for some kind of light switch, only a few feet ahead being dimly lit by the open door. The bricks were slick with dampness.

The Enlightened Quorum

"A dark, foreboding sewer, of course," I said, "starting to wonder why I suggested this."

Did you think that was funny? You're embarrassing yourself.

The ground was uneven and my boots slid across what felt like mud and grime. As we moved further through the network, our hands blindly guiding us, eventually we saw lights up ahead.

Are you sure we shouldn't leave? I don't want to get lost.

"We should see what's down there, if there's nothing, then we get out before we go too deep."

Okay.

He exhaled.

Can I hold your hand?

I stepped forward, grinding my teeth.

Seriously.

He paused,

It might come as a shock, but I'm petrified.

I smiled, shaking my head.

"Fine."

It took a moment to find each other properly, but soon he was gripping my hand, so tight I imagine his knuckles were tearing through his skin.

"It sounds like there's someone down here," as we got closer to the lights, I could see doors lining each side of the hall, "hello?"

The whimpering continued, emanating from some of the rooms. I approached one and saw that it had a sliding viewing slot. It looked like a cell. Several voices spoke in hushed whispers and mutters. The sobbing grew louder.

I looked at Bhari and took my hand back, pulling the pistol Bhen had given me from my belt. He unslung his rifle and pointed at the door. I grabbed the bar and pulled it to one side peering into the pitch-black letterbox.

Spines lined with pale skin stained by dirt, shivering forms holding each other tight in their circle. In unison, their chests pounded and they continued their jabbering.

"There are people in here," I tried to look around the room, being careful not to block the light too much, "I can't see much more. Let's get it open."

"Is that a good idea?" Janak said, "we can go back and get the others."

We have to help them.

"Bhari thinks we should help, and I agree," I coughed at the faint smell of mould, "open it."

Janak nodded and pulled the door open, its hinges snapping easier than they should have. The hairs on the back of my neck stood up.

The door opened and I stepped inside, something cracking underneath. Bhari jumped back. Under my boot was the petrified corpse of a person, their body starved and drained. And it wasn't the last.

They were strewn about the cell, bones mixing in decrepit piles. I turned to look at those left alive, the shapes of their skeletons, the pallid flesh and sunken eyes that stared into the dark. Bhari sounded like he was going to retch from the smell.

309

"Bhari," I looked back into the pitch rows of eyes, their owners slowly turning, "Bhari."

I stepped back and heard another crack. It awoke their lust. The Stragan. They sucked in the air around them, reaching out with spindly fingers.

I grabbed the door and dragged it back, the bones below catching and jamming the way. Hands slashed and tore chunks from my arm. The nearest Stragan, what was once a young girl, her hair dried and white, snapped her fangs at me, her dead insectoid eyes thirsting for me.

"Run, you two," Janak grabbed the door too, holding it closed and leaning away from their reach, realising it was futile, "run!"

Bhari was frozen as I almost yanked his arm from its socket and turned to see another figure approaching from behind.

"Get back, girl," his gruff voice barked, and as he stepped into the light, I saw the husk that was once my father appear from the shadows.

He went straight to the door.

"Move, monster," he barked, waving for Janak to get away.

He didn't give the Gunray a moment before he threw his hand out and ejected black flame through the gap, setting the room inside ablaze. The Stragan screeched in fear as the flames melted their waxy remains. One managed to clamber through the gap, swiping at my father's leg. He simply looked down and stomped on its face twice, splintering its skull instantly.

That's the kind of strength and tenacity you need to take notes on. You're weak.

Even when he was seemingly done with his gruesome work, he didn't stop, continuing to destroy the corpses further. He stared at the burning cinders of what remained, the dark flame dancing in his eyes with a pale light. After a while, he turned to the rest of us. Bhari's grip on my arm tightened even more.

"What are you doing here?" he said, coldly.

"What am I doing here?" I said in disbelief, "what are you doing here?"

"I've been tracking the movements of your brother's killers, lead me to this," he winced then, "I didn't know you were so involved," he shivered then, his scarred lip giving way a little, "or that you were awake. I'm sorry."

I debated telling him then. It was yet another entry in a long line of failures that could have changed everything, but I wasn't brave enough. I couldn't tell him I'd killed Oliver, even after everything. It was too much.

Liar liar, you set your brother on fire.

We stared at each other. There was a desire then to go to each other, to comfort one another. But I wasn't sure how, and I knew he didn't. We simply did what we had both been trained to do: We swallowed the pain and focused on the mission.

"Did you know about this?"

I realised after that I had essentially accused him of genocide. But I don't regret that. I had to know then whether my father was now my enemy.

"This?" he focused again on the charred corpse, "no. I had no idea things were this bad."

Bullshit.

311

Bhari's hatred was acrid in the air, and acidic on my tongue. I could feel it radiating from him, and as much as I wanted to give Anders the benefit of the doubt, a part of me agreed with my new comrade.

"Really?" I shook my head, "you're one of Calthern's closest agents, you really had no idea he was doing this?"

"No, I swear," Anders didn't fight then, he was defeated, "I mean. I had a feeling. I knew people were dying here. But not like this."

"Does the method matter?" Janak barked then, I hadn't seen any anger from the Gunrays prior, "murderers. The only difference is your death machines are more efficient now."

"Yeah?" Anders turned to them then, "want me to finish what they started, Gunray?"

Janak scowled at him and then walked to join me, pushing Anders aside. The three of us stared at him from across the hall. He was a lonely man in that pale yellow light.

"I'm sorry," Anders said, "I'm done. With all of this. No one deserves to be treated like this."

Tell the ones you killed that.

I think maybe a part of my father, for just a moment, managed to feel Bhari's emotions then, because he looked at the boy with tears in his eyes.

"I'm sorry, kid," he watched the ground again, "I know it's not enough, I don't have an excuse," he turned away from us and faced the remaining rooms. I saw at that point that the Stragan were gathered at the small windows, staring at us with their dead, black eyes, "I

wanted to believe in this city so badly. I wanted
something to fight for. I lost myself along the way. Long
before Oliver was taken."

He sighed and took a deep breath.

"Get out of here, I'm going to destroy this place,
then I'll come find you."

I couldn't bring myself to say anything. I worried
that whatever I did might drive him back into the dark
forests of hatred, so I decided that silence was best. We
walked away, leaving him to do more of his bloody
work.

When we got back we explained everything to Bhen,
who sat in solemn silence as he listened to the horror of
what had been occurring underneath the Darius district
for so long. People were taken from their homes and
starved, ground down into mulch to fuel their flames.

When we were done, Bhen then pulled a letter
from his inside coat pocket and handed it to me.

"This were delivered today," he said, "I read a bit
of it, I'm sorry to say. Didn't realise it were for you."

I nodded and started to read.

Spider,

*I'm sorry I did not reach out sooner. It has been difficult
getting messages out of the Kaurus district of late, and
the order has been watching me closely.*

The Enlightened Quorum

I fear for your father. I have seen him slowly become twisted by Calthern in ways I cannot describe and I need your help.

There are things happening in this city that you must know about. I have a plan to stop it, but I am not strong enough on my own and I fear asking your father in case he kills me.

Please, come and meet me on the 12th of Autumn at 9pm. I will be waiting at my home.

Phoenix

"Who's it from?"

"It's Theona," I said, "she wants to negotiate."

CHAPTER THIRTY-SEVEN
-ELENA-

When I entered Bhari's sanctum, it was like looking at a painting from a time far removed from my own. He hunched over a large desk, the honeyed light of the golden afternoon sun trickling in through the netted curtains.

"So the meeting's tomorrow."

Do you trust her?

You don't, and you're a fucking idiot for even thinking this would work.

Bhari kept focused on his work, scribbling frantically, repeatedly crossing through words deemed unfit mere moments after their conception.

"No, but do we have a choice?"

Yes, we can choose to ignore her.

"We need information, if she's even considering giving it up, then it might be worth it."

What is any of this for?

He turned then, setting his pen down. His elder eyes were creased from exhaustion.

"I need to find out what happened to my brother, you know that."

I know. But it feels like we've scrambled for answers this past week and achieved nothing. All we've learned is that potentially thousands from the district have been taken or killed.

He looked out through the crack in the fabric covering his window, nibbling the inside of his lip. I wondered what he saw now when he looked out at his home. If he even saw it that way anymore.

"When we expose Calthern, the Quorum, and their plans, we'll make it right."

That isn't enough. We're fighting an impossibly terrifying enemy, with innumerable heads that simply regrow any time we cut one off.

"I know," it had felt shameful, seeing the world carry on as usual despite the discovery in the sewer, "I wanted that to be the end too."

We need to kill the beast entirely and change things fundamentally.

I noted the words 'change' and 'hope' on the page in front of him, and cocked my head to try and read.

"What's this?"

It's just therapeutic writing. Just a way to get my feelings out, I guess.

"Can I see?"

He smiled and waved me away.

You'll laugh.

"How dare you," I did chuckle then, "I'm a fountain of positivity."

Bhari weighed up his choices and soon handed me the wad of sheets, sitting back.

It's just a lot of anger transmuted into a set of political demands. And it's messy too, I know that it's not my best stuff. You don't have to read it...

I couldn't quite interrupt him, his thoughts were still trailing off in my mind on their diatribe of prefacing self-criticism, but I did give him a look that made him pause and recognise that he needed to stop.

It's a strange feeling when the quiet part is said out loud.

There's an unspoken agreement nowadays, between the oppressor and their slaves, that their prejudice will be implied, only hinted at. That direct violence and hatred are a thing of the past, of old regimes that were monstrous demons beyond our human comprehension.

This, of course, is a fallacy. They were human to the greatest of faults, emblematic of our fundamental problem. But it is easier to characterise them as monsters under the bed because that makes their disgraceful spawn seem so far removed from it that violence is never a possibility under their watch.

But violence isn't the shooting of a child, the beating of the elderly, or the rape of women. It is the unspoken agreement itself, that allows these acts to continue under the veiled guise of order. It is the patience of monsters.

They have waited a desperately long time for us to forget the lessons of the past so that we can remain in ignorance. The machine of violence turns again, stoking a great and impossible flame. And we won't know this until it's too late.

317

The Enlightened Quorum

My friends, our ancestors were forced into cells and burned for their supposed sins, blood demanded by the God-King's cruel hand against the evils of the Void. But we live in those same cells now! These districts are nothing but prison yards patrolled by blood-thirsty pigs who will devour you whole. They are cages meant to keep us docile while they take away our children for grand experiments. They are mass graves, fit only for us to slowly die in.

The Enlightened Quorum and their followers are taking people away into sewers and starving them to the point where they become the monsters they claimed we were all along. They use us to bring about the end of our world and life as we know it. Do you know why?

They know that no one will care if they are found out.

That, my friends, is the fundamental problem. Your neighbour may not kill your children but when they blame you for their starvation they may as well be feasting on their bones. They know how easy we are to manipulate into servitude because as long as they have someone else they can blame, we always will.

I have realised now that removing individuals from their positions of power will solve nothing. The system itself is designed to enslave us, and for those with power to retain it at all costs.

We're told that if we work hard, we'll climb out of the pits they dug, and will claim our rightful places among the Gods. They'll shoot at us as we ascend, then point at those drowning below us. Money has become all but worthless and yet we still strive for wealth. Their game has led to the demise of our natural world and they have the audacity to blame us, the masses keeping them in power to begin with.

I don't have all the answers, I never will. But I am so fucking angry and so completely exhausted. And I know that we all have a common enemy in the Quorum and the Corporate Dynasties. We have to work together to fight back and build a fairer world.

This will require a change so catastrophic that I'll never live to see its completion. It will be a war against not only inequality but the unfair minds of the entire human race. But I believe it is possible. I know that, for all our flaws, goodness is inherent in human beings, not evil. That is something taught to us by the powerful, and we can overcome that teaching.

I re-read it once I'd finished, nibbling on the remains of the details, sucking on the passion behind them. I felt Bhari creeping back into my mind again.

It's bad, isn't it?

"No, not at all," I kept reading, "I mean, it is messy," I said with a smile, watching him look down in embarrassment, "but there's a raw energy to this. I think you should be really proud of it."

There's a lot more. I've been doing this for a while.

"I can imagine," I sighed, putting the paper down, "it's wonderful, and something I'm sure lots of people can resonate with. I think you should put it out there."

They'd kill me.

"Obviously we'd keep your identity secret."

319

You're only pushing him for your cause because you're too much of a coward to write anything like that.
Do you really think it has value?

"Yes, even if it sits here on your desk forever, it's your heart, and of course that has value."

Thank you, Elena.

He stood up and went to hug me, then paused.

I should ask, sorry.

"Thank you," I stood up too, "I've felt…constricted, ever since Oliver passed. It's hard, being open again."

I understand. I'm here whenever you need me.

"Thank you, Bhari."

We spent the rest of the night discussing his ideas further. I realised they sounded similar to the Dhorman rebellion a few hundred years prior, rising up during the time of the God-King. Today, I wish I had known then that he would be the spark, and that the sharing of ideas would achieve as much as, if not more, than the exchange of blood.

CHAPTER THIRTY-EIGHT
-ELENA-

Theona was different. Something had happened between the last time we spoke and now, something that had killed her and forced her to be reborn again. Something she swore was a limited option for her. Each time she came back looking older, more fragile, and like the next time she shattered it would be the last.

Calthern was shouting at her, I think. I could feel the hot blasts of anger bleeding through the window and Theona, usually so stoic, was in tears when she spoke to him.

Can you hear them?

I shook my head at Bhari, then noticed Bhen staring at us.

"He was asking if I could hear them."

Bhen nodded, then pulled his pistol to inspect it. I watched him turn it over in his hands and check the barrel, ensuring it would work well in the event he'd use it.

The Enlightened Quorum

I knew I couldn't trust Theona, not really, but I didn't want her getting hurt either. I hoped he'd show restraint. *Have you seriously not come to understand that people will die? You're at war, you child. Grow up.*

Calthern soon stormed out of the small house, two lackeys from the Warden's order following him closely. I knew they'd kill us in an instant if they saw us, so I waited until I was sure they were far away before signalling for the other two to join me as I crossed the street.

I reached for the Void then, probing the ether around me to see if there was anything that would give me doubt about the meeting. But other than the obvious logic, there was nothing. I knocked on the door.

When it opened, I noticed the tears in Theona's eyes, but her emotions felt strange. She was happy.

"Elena," she stood frozen, then reached out to hug me, "I was so worried about you."

"Funny, you didn't seem worried about leaving me with Calthern."

"I know," she was still hugging me, and I felt tight in her grip, as if I couldn't breathe and the flesh of her arms was searing my own, "I'm sorry. I made a mistake. Please, come in."

I stepped inside, then gestured behind me.

"Theona, this is Bhen, and his son Bhari."

"Oh, are those Matuni names?" Theona beamed at them.

"That's right," Bhen darted his eyes around the room briefly, "thank you."

322

"Not at all!" she watched Bhari step in after his father, and the boy stared at her with flame behind his eyes. She held the stare, watching him like she might watch prey.

She drew the curtains across the kitchen window and gestured for us to sit at her table, bringing lukewarm tea over.

"How are you?" she asked me, without much warning.

"I'm, yeah I'm okay," I nodded, ignoring the tea, "It still hurts."

"One day you'll be able to use that pain for your strength," she said, sipping from her own cup, "but for now, pain is normal."

"Have you seen my father?"

"Here and there, he's working on something secret for Calthern," she swallowed, "he doesn't really have the time for me these days."

She's lying to your face and you're just taking it. Kill her. Kill her now!

"Does he know we're meeting?"

"No one knows about this Elena," she set her drink down, "most of them think you're in with criminals and thieves now."

"Maybe they're right."

"Maybe, but I know that there's good in you yet."

"There's good in me now," I sat up a bit, "Calthern and the Quorum are murdering innocent people in the Darius district. They're going to bring about the world's end."

"No, no, I still believe in their cause," she said.

"You said you'd made a mistake leaving me there?" I said, looking around the small house, suddenly noticing the pictures on the side. None of them had Theona in them, "what is this?"

"I made a mistake by not taking you in myself, I believe your abilities would have helped us tremendously," Theona had a wry smile then, watching us all tense and prepare weapons under our coats, "the world needs to change Elena, surely you can all see that? This is the only way. The Old Gods must return, and to do that, the time of man must end."

I pushed the chair back, watching Bhen and Bhari do the same.

"I trusted you."

"Well," Theona gulped the last of the tea, "that was your mistake, wasn't it?"

The woman who'd been my mentor, my teacher, grinned. There was madness behind her eyes, the thin, golden eyes of a predator. In one fluid motion, she snapped up and lifted the table with such ease that she was able to throw it and us away. I landed on the living room carpet, noticing in my daze the misshapen legs of the elderly resident of the house poking out from behind the sofa. She was riddled with flies and their spawn.

Theona was on me already, holding my arms by the wrist. She jammed her knee onto my chest and crushed the air from my lungs, laughing as she did it.

Bhen stood and aimed his pistol.

"Ge'off 'er ya creepy cow!"

He fired a shot that ripped through Theona's shoulder and sprayed across my face. Theona simply cackled, her lips pulling back too far and revealing rows of fanged teeth pushing her blunted ones out like mints from a packet. She slammed her head into mine.

The room swirled and there was a ringing in my ears as I watched her slither back across the room, evading the shots Bhen fired so that she could pounce on him. She clawed at his face with long sharp nails until Bhari jumped on her, trying to hold her down. Bhen joined him, restraining her arms so that she flailed about between them.

"Elena," Bhen shouted, "gimme the gun, I'll put her down."

I tried lifting myself up, feeling a lurching sickness as my head lulled forward.

"Elena!"

I crawled towards the weapon and then noticed something. It was like a snake out of the corner of my eye. I looked at the pair of them, holding the increasingly twisted form of Theona. Then saw it. A spiked tail.

"Look out!"

The appendage swung round and pierced Bhari's shoulder, pushing him away. Bhen screamed in horror and instinctively went to check on his son, but the momentary release was all she needed. She started to break free to pounce on Bhen again. I yelled as I grabbed the gun and fired at her.

I saw the bullets punch holes in her side, and I knew I had hit her. But she still looked ready to attack again. I wrapped my arm around her neck, throwing myself back to hold her away from the father and son.

The tail swung wildly at me, stabbing at the ground near my face, but unable to get any real purchase.

I held her there long enough to see Bhen holding his son's limp hand, wailing in pain. Bhari's eyes stared back at me. The beautiful hazel brown was slowly turning black, and they were unmoving, unblinking. I knew, at that moment, he was dead.

Theona suddenly panicked and thrashed against me with strength I'd never seen before. She slithered on top of me and pinned me by the throat. Her wide eyes stared into mine with hunger.

"I'm going to devour you, child," she hissed and her mouth split open at the lips, "I will take every drop of your strength."

I recognised her then, the gaunt, starving frame and the spiny tail. She was the assassin, the horror from the Manor. She was there when my brother died. She took his fucking body. It was her.

As I shied away from the spittle splattering across my face, I saw my bracelet again. I used my fingers to take hold of it, fluttering them to draw the glass into my palm and shape itself into an insidious point. Then I drove it through her mouth and into the back of her skull.

She was still for a moment, gurgling softly. Then her left set of eyes started going lazy, veering off in random directions as thick milky blood slid across my hand.

Theona fell limp on top of me. I didn't move her. I just turned my head and stared at Bhari's lifeless eyes.

It was my fault.

Again. Your weakness got someone killed. Again.

I eventually got to my feet and had to walk away from Bhen slowly processing the death of his son, his face unmoving. Then he looked at me as I stepped back.

"Where are you going?"

I watched him and knew that I'd see it in my nightmares forever. He lost everything, and had nothing left to give.

"I'm uh," I inhaled through my nose to find only the pungent rot again, "she took my fucking sword."

CHAPTER THIRTY-NINE
-ANDERS-

It would be the last time I descended the crude staircase, making my way to the Sanctum of the Changed to confront Calthern. I had so many regrets in my life but none would ever compare to turning on my daughter for such a creature.

I entered his inner chamber. He was sat by a large fireplace, a drink in hand as always. I strode across the room and neglected to take a knee, holding my head high.

"I've come to resign. I'm going to spend time with my family."

"You're not going anywhere, the war's only just begun. And your 'family' are becoming an increasing problem for me. I'll forgive this outburst if you turn around and get out of my sight."

"No. I won't do your dirty work anymore."

"You stupid boy," Calthern snapped out of his seat and threw the glass into the pit, spattering flames across the floor, "what do you think you know? Hm?

Found some dirty secret that's turned ya stomach? You're fuckin' weak, only of flesh."

He continued muttering, turning away from me.

"Fine, who needs you. Worthless prick. Fuck off."

I nodded and went to leave, as I reached for the door, he shouted after me.

"They killed her, you know."

My hand hovered there.

Just go, Anders, move. He's tricking you. Elena's safe, I'm sure of it.

"Who?"

"Your fucking girl and her gang killed Theona," Calthern spat the words at me and the springs of his chair creaked as he sunk back into it, "you halfwit. They tricked you, to get to her. And you let it happen, all because of some dead tregs."

I let my hand drop, despite everything in my body screaming at me to just walk away. I couldn't do it. I faced him again, this time going to my knee in front of him like a good dog.

"Are you sure?"

"Yes. She was meeting with them to collect information, to help me, and they fucking killed her. You were supposed to watch her."

"Do you know what they're doing? In those sewers?"

"Yes, I ordered them to."

"Why?" the word sounded so pathetic. What did it matter?

"We must understand the realm of the Gods, and use its power for our own purposes. This is all in the name of progress and you knew, going in, that there would be bloodshed."

"But not like that, sir," I murmured, "they were starved to death."

"Blood is blood, boy. It's only cowards who think it matters how it's spilt."

"I know," I felt drunk, like I might have thrown up at any second, "it all just seems...cruel, sir."

"Life is cruel, my boy, and it's a duty I don't take lightly, but it must be done. You understand?"

I nodded. I didn't, but it didn't matter anymore. None of it did. The last beams of my humanity were starting to erode, and there was a strange bliss in knowing that my time was coming to an end.

"Come with me."

He took me, once again, to the antichambers. But this time, he entered a key code on a black door and opened a passage illuminated by strange purple lights. My eyes burned as I stared at them.

We walked the hallway to a large glass cell, steeped in darkness. Surrounding the chamber were scholars, entering data into their pads and watching intently for any kind of change.

"This might convince you to finally do your duty."

Calthern snapped his fingers, and bright lights were blasted into the glass box, showing a small figure held by the arms in glowing chains. As it lifted its head, I felt what was left of my heart, finally fade.

"Dad?" Oliver said, his voice cracked and strangely plural, as if there were several instances of him existing at once, "Dad!"

I sank to the floor, my chest tightening with stinging pain. I watched his terrified face go through so many different feelings in one leap.

"Please help me!"

It wasn't my son. I could see the pale skin, like that of the monster that killed him. The lilac, slitted eyes of a predator, watching me for weaknesses. And finally, I could feel the massive amount of power draining away my own, even through the glass panes.

"This creature was found in your home, and is pretending to be your son," Calthern stared in through the glass at the struggling child, "maybe it is, or what's left of him. Either way, what we have determined is that it's likely the Folsesjeger turned him and then tricked your daughter into joining his cause."

"Why did you hide it."

"You were in pain, Theona asked me what I thought should be done and I decided that keeping this from you until we understood more was best. I realise now that might have been a mistake, but I had your best interests in mind."

"What is it."

"We're not sure, but it's incredibly powerful, and we believe it is key to the Change."

"Dad," it said, struggling against the chains, "please, help me!"

I stood up and glared, burying my nails deep into the flesh of my palms.

"You are not my son."

It screamed then, keeping up the act, and the energy it released almost buckled the edges of the cell. I knew that eventually, it would break out.

"What should I do?"

"Go to Ghangris's headquarters, finish this once and for all. You'll stand a better chance of surprising them on your own."

"It will be done."

CHAPTER FORTY
-ELENA-

Bhen hadn't spoken to anyone since Bhari had died. It wasn't a shock, but it still hurt. I wasn't going to be selfish and expect him to comfort me, but I felt that we needed each other then.

We hadn't been able to take his body with us, it was too risky sneaking back out again. And for that, we had disgraced him at the same time. Matuan burial rights dictate that the body must be burned, and the ashes returned to the earth. We'd left him to rot in a haunted house.

A few days later, the Auspins asked me to come with them to their workshop. Inside, there was a short figure in a cloak. When she turned, I saw it was Guindolene Snow-Steel.

"Hi you," she hadn't changed, not really, "I've got some gifts for you."

Guin walked over to me, gracefully, and sheepishly raised her arms. I nodded, wrapping my own around the small of her back when she embraced me. She still smelled of jasmine.

"How did you get here?" I asked.

Guin let go and nodded after the Auspins.

"An uneasy alliance," she walked behind my chair, "they kind of hate my family, but I'm glad they helped. I have something I thought could be useful. I'm sorry I couldn't come sooner," she was exhausted, "I've been hiding since we last met."

"You didn't have to do anything, Guin, just being here is enough," I pulled a chair over for her to sit, "where were you?"

"I was with Ghangris's team," Guin was nervous when she revealed that, "Corvin managed to find me and take me to them."

"It's more help than he's been to us here," I said.

"I think he's had a lot on his plate."

"Yeah, sure," I shook my head, "he promised to help me. I've learned most of this new power myself so far."

"I know," she sighed, "you should know, Velloah and Valeria were captured."

"What? Where?"

"Just outside the walls, the Inquisitors were following and ambushed us," she scratched her hand, "I watched as they were taken away and couldn't do anything. I feel terrible, I just left them there."

"You survived, one of you had to."

"It should have been Valeria."

"It wasn't your fault," I said, "it's theirs. Don't blame yourself for their cruelty."

She nodded.

"Well, still, this might help, and might make up for it."

She unclipped the front of the case, opening it wide like a walk-in wardrobe. Inside, hanging on a wire rack, was a full-body frame. It was designed like a harness, made of steel and straps, all connected to a central, glowing hub.

"What is this?"

"It's a design she was working on for the Enforcers, it was intended to give them enhanced speed and strength," She sighed, "But, with our new line of work, she figured it could have a better use. The Auspins took a look and tried to tweak it a little to allow you some more movement."

"I don't know."

"You don't have to say anything."

"Thank you," I looked over it again, "how does it work?"

"They said it would connect with the Dream…whatever that is," she came to help me put the straps on, attaching the artificial joints and skeletal supports, "they said it would hurt a bit, is that okay?"

"Yeah, go for it."

I felt her fingers brush the back of my neck gently before she inserted a set of micro needles into the base of my skull. And it did bloody hurt.

But the pain seemed distant then. I knew it was happening, but I was falling again. The small room started to shift in its details, a chair changing position rapidly and a clock spinning its hands. But after a few moments, everything seemed to settle again, and the piercing headache slammed into me like a train.

"Fuck that hurts," I scrunched my eyes then, cocking my head to the side to try and alleviate the shock somehow, "it's so cold."

"Here," Guin threw a blanket over me, "sorry."

"It's okay, you did warn me after all."

The harness slowly awoke from its own slumber, the pistons and pipes starting to hiss into action. The details of the room still flickered now and then, and I realised that I was seeing the Dream in my mind's eye. The harness must have been correlating with that, my movements playing out in the movie behind my eyes dragging my physical body with it.

"It's…it's incredible."

"Are you sure?"

"Yes," I tried to hide my face from her by stepping into the centre of the room, "I feel good."

I stretched the back of my legs and did some light step-work, my movements liquid just like Theona wanted them to be. This didn't feel like a fix. It felt like an upgrade.

"I'll think about it," I said, then seeing her disappointment I spoke up, "I appreciate it though, Guin, really. Thank you."

"It's okay," Guindolene smiled, "I have something I need to tell you. Ghangris and his group discovered one of their main facilities."

"Who? The Quorum?"

"Yeah. They're bringing Inquisitors, prisoners, all kinds to this area, and most aren't seen again. Our spies report that they take most of the outsiders below the facility and that average personnel aren't authorised down there, their only job is protecting the outer walls," she sighed, "they said that they hear strange noises at night, from below."

"Your spies?" I laughed then, "you joined up?"

"Why's that so funny?" she folded her arms.

"It isn't, sorry, it's just strange hearing it," I cleared my throat and stopped smiling, "anything else?"

Guin winced.

"Are the spies out of action?"

"Last week, just went quiet."

I looked at the Gunrays, the machinery that they had already brought with them.

"Do you think we can get in there? Underground?"

They grumbled and turned, huddling together to speak in hushed tones. Every so often Olrod would speak slightly louder and drippings of complaint could be made out before Carnal hit her lightly on the arm. They argued for a few moments before Janak brought them back to the topic at hand.

They then turned back.

"It'll be tricky, but we can do it."

"Ghangris is planning an attack, but it'll take a few days to get ready," Guindolene stood up, "in the meantime, Ghangris thinks the two of you should meet finally."

I nodded.

"Yeah, I should think so."

CHAPTER FORTY-ONE

It had taken a few hours to get to the Motherbase. It was my first time seeing the intricate tunnel system that the three Gunrays had been building for the rebels. It was a warren of activity, with all kinds of symbols and directions for those who had learned their code.

When we got to a large steel vaulted door, Guin wrote runes on a nearby wall and then waited.

"They're just unlocking it. It can take a minute."

I nodded and waited.

Soon beam locks were pulled away with huge clunking sounds, eventually allowing the door to roll away into a slot.

Inside was an ant's hive, many interlocking rooms all connected via ladders and small stairwells, all open plan so that they could look in on a single chamber. It had a large central table and several workstations lining the walls.

I saw people machining firearms, mixing strange chemical concoctions, and even a communications centre where people spoke in hushed voices and communicated to other outfits with single tones played at set intervals.

And leaning over the central table, surrounded by advisors of varying ages and backgrounds, was what I assumed to be Ghangris.

He was strange-looking. I'd expected a large warrior, a brutal man capable of snapping most others like dry twigs. But he was small and old. Almost kindly if the light caught his green eyes at the right angle, but when a nearby suspended lantern swung away again, the dark exhaustion returned. A man tired of fighting a losing battle.

He saw us approaching, chaperoned by young, ramshackle soldiers. He didn't smile, but I could feel relief washing over him.

"Guin, you made it back," he kissed a small figure on his pendant, "and is this, Elena?"

"That's right, she's come to meet you."

"It's good to see you," he smiled, "Corvin told me about you, thought it best to try and keep you hidden for a while."

"I could have done more," I said, "he could have."

"It's hard to pin him down, not being human or dying the same as us. He sometimes has grander plans in mind that we can't always fully know. But we trust in him."

"Sure," I looked around the room again, "this is impressive."

"It'll do, we've been working on this for a long time," he gestured for us to take a seat, "now, what's the news?"

"From what Elena's discovered, they're turning people into Stragan," Guin said, "there's a good chance they've figured out the generators again."

"And you know this for a fact?" he said, his voice a mere rasp.

"No," I said, "but Velloah explained that they already had some of her designs and that with time they'd figure it out."

"You need to launch the attack," Guin continued, clearing her throat.

"We haven't got the strength, yet," Ghangris flashed a mischievous smile, "but we're almost ready. In the meantime, I'll send this to another cell and see if they can get into this temple and sabotage the Quorum."

"Good," Guin released a little tension, but I felt her anxiety brimming.

"I can do that," I said, "I mean, the worst they'll do is imprison me, right? For the rest of you, they'll kill you if you're caught."

Ghangris weight it up for a moment then grunted.

"No, no I think you're a little too important to risk."

"Everyone keeps saying that," I folded my arms across my chest to try and guard myself, "no one's really explained why though."

"Elena, Velloah said that while the machines need Stragan now, what if they've figured out how to put people in there?" Guin's voice was shaky, "People like you."

A freak like you would overload the system for sure.

I think she's just trying to look out for me.

She fucking hates you.

"Maybe," I tried to focus on the maps in front of me, "okay."

A man came to stand by Ghangris.

"Father?"

"Yes?" Ghangris turned his head slightly, still watching us.

"The Wolf is here. He said he's come to help us."

My father? No...that can't be right.

"The Wolf?" Ghangris darted his eyes around the room, calculating his thoughts.

But of course, it was too late. His decision made no difference because there was an explosive clanging as a heavy door was ripped from the walls. I turned to see the distant entrance to the bunker clouded in smoke. Stepping out from it was a creature. It was taller than any human, and its limbs were asymmetrical and misshapen. One arm was larger than the other, so thick in fact that it almost seemed to drag the limb behind it. Long red hair flowed down its back like a mane.

Was it him? I couldn't believe it, but I knew that it had to be. This is what I had done to him. He'd given into the Void and its hatred.

Ghangris started barking orders frantically, stepping around the side of the table to us. He was frozen in fear for just a moment. The flames of chaos burned

341

the place he'd not only built from the ground up, but also the place he had likely called home for many years now.

I watched the monster move lightning quick, tearing and snapping flesh and bone-like cloth. I grabbed Guin and started dragging her back as best I could, hearing the screams of the dying...they were all so young.

Ghangris fired at the ghoul when and wherever he could but it simply ignored the pain, moving with a ferocity that exhausted me to look at.

"Where do we go?" Guin shouted, grabbing Ghangris's arm tightly.

He turned to her, then looked back at the carnage. And back at the brave young woman again.

"You have to go, destroying the Quorum is your only hope."

We knew he was right, and what that meant. Guin squeezed his hand, before pulling me away to a nearby door, supporting me with her arm. Ghangris placed his palm on it, closing it behind us. It was then sealed with a small spell. It wouldn't hold forever, but it'd give us some time.

Ghangris, the man I'd assumed had been the one behind Marcus's death at one stage, had become a hero so quickly that it made my head spin. I heard his cries as he was torn apart behind the door and felt anguish for a man I'd barely known but had known so much about from afar. Anders, or whatever he'd become, didn't kill the old man quickly either, he made it a slow and disgracefully painful death.

Then he slammed against the door and I heard the vibrations of the magical seal straining under the weight of his attack. Again and again, he threw his monstrous body against it, splintering the spell as he went. I felt Guindoline dragging my arm behind me, but I rooted myself in dismay.

"Come on, this way," Gwen said, "Elena?"

"You need to go," I turned to her, "I can distract him, for a bit."

"No come on I'm not leaving you here," she pulled on my arm again.

"Don't be a fucking idiot," I snapped, then I had to pull my hand away from hers, "there's a chance I'll survive this. You won't."

"That's not him anymore!"

"I have to believe there's enough left," I couldn't look her directly in the eyes, "I'm tired, Guin. Knowing you'll get out, with that information, that's enough."

"If we stand here talking…"

"Then we're both dead," I felt the ground shake again, "you have to go. They need to be stopped."

She knew then that I wasn't going to move, and that what I was saying was correct.

She was always going to preserve herself over you anyway. Nobody likes you as much as you seem to think they do.

Guin nodded and pulled me into a hug. It was brief, so I didn't complain. But I gently pushed back after a few seconds.

"Go."

I heard her footsteps retreat behind me and I felt the desperation inside her. I had to let go at that moment because soon the door was ripped from its hinges, splinters of the magical barrier tinkling as they scattered through the air. Anders paused in his advance when he saw me, a great bulging eye staring out at me under thick folds of bluish skin.

Then he charged, using the larger claw to propel himself over the busted door and lumber towards me. I drew my blade, this time in a smooth and silent arcing motion and held it ready. He reached for me with thick luminous fingers, but I positioned the sword to impale the limb.

He howled in pain as the consecrated steel melted the tendons and withdrew, before swiping at me with his smaller talons. It was clumsy and bestial behaviour, the precise brutality he'd always shown me before gone.

But his speed had only increased, and soon he swiped my legs from under me. I landed on my elbow, crying out for a second before rolling out of the way of another attack. I retreated around the corner, watching him hurl a nearby table out of his way. Anders grabbed hold of the walls to drag himself towards me and barked wildly as he did.

I ducked into a room on my left and quickly drew power from the lights to dim the room, seeing some vague shapes in front of me in the pale green light. I went to a pillar with a glass mirror attached to its side. I smashed the mirror and grabbed a piece of glass, waiting for Anders to make his way into the room. I heard the halted breathing of my father and used the shard to see a glimpse of his stalking form. He sniffed loudly, crawling towards me.

Then he paused and looked directly into my eyes through the piece. Before I could pull it back, he vomited a slurry of white phlegm. It splattered across my hand, hardening almost instantly and fusing it to the stone. I heard him growl as he slinked across the room on all fours.

I didn't think then. I just wanted to run. The instinct was burning in my mind and so, with whatever strength I had left, I yanked my hand away. I felt small strips of flesh tear away, screaming in pain as I sprinted past his hulking form and for the door, bolting it shut. I knew he wouldn't waste any time, so I took a leaf out of Ghangris's book and sealed my father inside the small room.

It was longer than his spell had been, stronger too, and it would take some time for Anders to escape this time. I left him, howling and screaming, as he battered against his temporary prison.

CHAPTER FORTY-TWO

The Enforcers jumped out of their truck, moving towards the apartment building with sinister steps. As soon as they broke the door in and made their way inside, I rushed towards the back of the vehicle in a crouched position, leaning under the chassis. It was a case of looking for a nook of some kind, nicely concealed but easily accessible.

Between two metal bars was the perfect space. I lifted the device toward it, watching it get sucked onto the surface with a clunk. I pinched the small bar-switch, and turned it slowly, watching the crystals on either side pulse a yellow light.

I heard screams from inside the building and fought the urge not to rush in and help. I saw a light from a window to my left, the darkened shape of a witness peeking behind the curtains to the grisly play. For tonight only.

I stood and faced them, making it clear that I saw the sadistic voyeur. The curtains called, hopefully for the last time. I made my way back to the manhole, climbing inside the chamber of filth and sealing it above.

The Auspins were building their device, placing steel blades and serrated chunks into the huge dial like a macabre jigsaw. The drill was almost done.

"It's done."

"Good," Carnal looked around for something, "can you find the scanner?"

I pulled aside the debris they had piled up and found the thick glass screen in its steel box. I brought it over to them, holding it out.

"Thanks."

Soon enough, they had their machine ready. Carnal took control of it, holding handles on either side of the scanner's green display in front of them. They explained that it would mark the location of the device, allowing them to follow the truck's path. Janak and Olrod stood on either side of the machine, dragging huge packs with them.

"It's on the move."

As a group, they activated the drill, turning several dials and finally flipping a switch, causing the teeth to turn inward, the layered dials moving opposite. The spinning increased, growing faster, and faster, until it was almost impossible to distinguish individual shapes, the drill becoming a grinding, churning blur.

Carnal pushed forward, and dirt, brick, metal, anything that fell into the path of the death machine was smashed, torn, ground down and reduce to dust. The residue was sucked into a vacuum and collected in tanks.

The Enlightened Quorum

Olrod and Janak got to work, placing contraptions against the walls of the oval tunnel, unwinding plates to line them. When they reached the top, they pressed buttons on either side. The beams released a liquid silver that reached for each other like lover's hands in the moonlight, sewing together and stiffening.

They repeated this process at set intervals, occasionally placing extra support beams to make sure the cave held. I noticed that the living metal hadn't stopped, creating webbing along the roof between the panels as well.

I wondered what other secret magics and designs the Gunrays had constructed. The Auspins had said that their home had been lost long ago, their clan scattered. These three only had each other, and their inventive minds. It was incredible, though, seeing the potential for future progress.

Olrod was setting her plate, then looked concerned. She tried again, before shouting to Carnal. But they didn't stop. Olrod shouted again, I couldn't make out what she was saying. I ran to Carnal and slapped their arm, pointing to Olrod waving. They stopped the machine, waiting for it to wind down.

"I said stop you fuckin' idiot," Olrod yelled, "my side isn't magnetised."

"Alright, so you do it further ahead then," Carnal breathed heavily through their nose, looking and the screen.

"The integrity's going to be fucked if I do."

"The truck's moving, get on with it!"

"I can't!"

Carnal looked back, then hit the controls with their fist.

"Great, well done Olrod, it's gone."

"Well excuse me for wanting us to be safe."

"Fuck you."

Olrod launched at Carnal, and the two rolled away from the drill, punching each other repeatedly in the face and chest. Janak ran over, attempting to pull them apart.

It spilt over. I think it had been bubbling on the back burner for some time now, but the heat was too high, and now it was pouring out. I fell to the floor, sobbing into my hands.

The fighting stopped, and the three of them approached. Janak knelt down in front of me.

"Elena?"

"I've lost them," I managed through gasping breaths, "I've failed them."

Janak's eyes darted and then he went to the side of the tunnel, pulled out a hammer, and started smashing a hole upwards, digging towards the surface.

"Janak," Carnal said, "we can't be seen."

He came back down, a small light cast on his shoulder.

"Come on," he tried to place a hand on my shoulder, but it seemed to cup most of my torso, "you can find it, go on without us."

"I'd never get in there," I said, slumping into defeat. Then, I thought of an idea, "what does the scanner track? Is it void energies?"

"Yeah," Olrod scratched his head, "well, any kind of powerful energy, but yes, Void mostly."

I went to the tunnel, closing my hand before reaching into the void again, grasping a poisonous handful.

"I'll bring it to you."

"Well done, good thinking," Carnal said, "we'll wait for your signal."

"Good luck Elena," said Janak.

"Be safe," finished Olrod.

I crept through the deserted streets, watching for drones or soldiers. I saw muddied tire tracks on the stone and followed, rounding a corner to see the truck up ahead. As I slowed, I realised I could feel the Gunrays below, their energy immensely powerful. I wondered how exposed we would be if the Quorum caught wind of us. I noticed that the vehicle had stopped for a moment, and could just make out a checkpoint up ahead.

I ran back toward the hole, clambering inside the tunnel, heading for the drill that was already on its way again. Each of the Gunrays looked back at me, smiling, before going back to their work. Olrod had attached some strange devices to her panels, managing to make them work.

"Alright, I think we're here," Olrod said.

"Thank you, for getting me here."

"What? Do you think we're leaving?" said Janak.

"I sort of assumed you would," I smiled a little, "you can go, I'll be okay."

"Hey, look, we like you and your cause but we've got some of our own scores to settle here," said

Carnal, smiling back, "we'll conceal the machines and meet you back here at some point."

"Sorry for these two idiots earlier," Janak was packing some equipment up near the drill, "and I'm also sorry for their rudeness, for not apologising."

"We fight sometimes, but you're right, we almost lost you your chance."

"No," I shook my head, "this has all just been a lot for me to take. I think I was trying to hide it for too long, and it's hurting too much now."

"We think of it like a pipe," Carnal said, "builds pressure over time, and if you don't let some of that out from time to time, it'll explode and be damaged."

I nodded.

"Thank you."

CHAPTER FORTY-THREE

I had managed to find a window into the temple on street level and descended the mostly abandoned floors until, finally, I saw activity.

Sheets hung from the temple's original doors in tattered black rags, the entranceway battered long ago by time. I stepped in, pushing the creaking mass of splinters aside. Shards fell away and wondered wistfully on a wind I hadn't noticed, crumbling to ash as they did.

Purple light hummed as it melted the walls away, firing waves of heat through my body.

Up ahead, a member of the Quorum stood still, a blank red helmet covering their face atop ridged sets of crimson armour. Their fingerless glove rested on the hilt of a curved blade.

"Listen, I don't want to fight."

The edge sang as it was drawn against the ceremonial scabbard before they held it in both hands.

"Have it your way then," I said, reaching for my belt, and taking out the hilt.

The Enlightened Quorum

The sword was easier to store now with the knowledge of how to fold the black glass in on itself. I watched the sword unfold and stretch out, its matte obsidian metal remaining dim in the intense light.

I exhaled, waiting for them. That was how I had been trained.

Their sword flashed for my head, and it was easier to sidestep, biting into their under arm with my own. It cut their clothes to ribbons, blood seeping down. They struck again and this time I caught it with my own edge, answering in kind.

Eventually, they lost their temper, thrusting for my abdomen. I slammed my foot on the metal, and cut downward, moving through their wrist as easily as the fabric.

They screamed, cradling the stump to their chest, their head facing up at me. I grabbed their throat and dragged the energy from them until they fell limp. The pulse still beat between my fingers, so I got to work on stopping the bleeding, leaving them behind once it was done.

I stalked the ceramic halls, careful to step lightly with my weapon ready. Another acolyte appeared on a patrol, seeing me and drawing their own blade. We clashed once, twice. I was rusty, but slowly my memories of Theona's footwork were coming back to me. Every time they tricked me by feinting to the left before following up on the right, I knew to catch them off guard.

The Acolyte came at me again, and I managed to deflect before turning my sword downward and disarming them. I placed the edge against their neck.

"My will is absolute," their voice broke out.

It was a young man behind the mask, barely my age by the sound of it. His hand glowed with the embers of a Void-mark, and with it he pulled a whip of milky water from the air, using it to slap me against the wall. I rolled away when I hit the ground, the wind knocked out of me.

The red warrior brought it down on me, torrents sinking into my ears. I pushed forward with my own hand, sending him flying with a blast of kinetic energy. As I stood up he was already scrambling to his feet and hurled violet bolts my way.

"Stop!" I dodged the first, "I don't want to hurt you."

"You won't," he threw another, dazzling me with its blast, "the Gods have blessed me."

His voice was lifeless and empty, to the point of being barely audible over the large cracks of electric waves. I managed to catch one with my own manipulative power, spinning with its momentum and firing it back at him.

He convulsed as his eyes glowed with sparks. The boy fell to the floor, his body still jolting. A hole was burned by a concentrated light, shooting from his abdomen.

A clawed hand ripped through the cooked flesh, an infantile face pushing through after it. The malformed creature kept dragging itself from the empty sack of skin, unable to free its legs completely. The acolyte's own lower limbs animated, dragging the monster along the floor, the deflated torso dangling behind.

I stood on one of its flailing wrists, whispering a short apology before slicing down, finishing the creature off. I then continued creeping towards the main hall.

The ancient main hall's walls were slick with wet sinew pouring from cracked shells lining the roof. It was bathed in crimson light, as acolytes marched towards an altar at the centre. Atop it stood a man, his arms raised as he emitted a low chant.

It was one of the Quorum's Speakers, the members of the inner circle responsible for spreading their message. Felix Ghorn, I think.

Behind the altar, was a giant stone gate, a huge mound of fleshy pillars behind it.

"Bring the chosen!" Ghorn yelled.

Lights appeared from below, lines of more cultists appearing from them, herding cloth-covered prisoners. They were marched toward the altar, in front of which I could see machines.

I made my way forward, gripping the stone beam tight to peer down. They were the Snow-Steel's generators or some crude attempt at a recreation of them at least. They weren't poorly made, but the technology was clearly not readily available to them.

This must be why Velloah'Ra was afraid.

I have to get down there.

No. Not yet, fool.

What? Why? We have to help them.

We've come all this way. We need to know the truth and see what will happen. Otherwise, you have nothing.

Not for the first time, I began to doubt the Dream. It had guided me so far, but this was…wrong.

You're still naïve enough to think that this is some emulation of the Dream, too childish to accept that I am simply you, your own thoughts, that side of you that you always ignored. We are cleft in twain and you will simply have to accept that one day, sooner or later, you will realise I was right all along. You. Will. Fail.

I watched as the prisoners were pushed into the machines, the doors sealing them in. I didn't know what the purpose was, but I knew what the process would do to them. Then, as I prepared to intervene, the Speaker spoke again.

"And now, the catalyst!"

Soldiers appeared from his right, dragging a small boy with them in iridium chains. As he cried out against his gag, his longish hair parted and I finally saw his face.

Oliver. He was alive.

It was him, I was sure of it. At that moment, my reflexes kicked in and I leapt down.

I landed on one of the central acolytes, knocking them into the ground and out cold. I pushed those to the left of me away to focus on the right, flipping and disarming my first. A blade was drawn in front of me.

"No!"

I was as confused as the cult member, looking at Ghorn, his voice trembling.

"Don't," he clasped his hands together, in an attempt to stop the shaking, "they would want her. Feel her power, children. This is what we have been searching for."

The capsule in front of me had a small framed individual, their child-like palms pressed up against the glass, steam permeating from their slick skin. Their little eyes burned through the sack, pleading to me.

"Oli," I said, "I…"

His eyes were wide with fear and confusion, but he nodded at me. I then focused on the Speaker.

"You're opening tears," I said, "you're trying to create another Burcanon."

"We live in an ugly world. It is time for the Gods to return and claim what is theirs. Burcanon was simply proof that it could be done. The proof we needed, the hope that our work was not in vain."

"And Stragan weren't creating enough energy, so you moved onto humans," I stared behind him now, at what was, now rather clearly, a gate, "how many?"

"How many grains of sand line the beaches?"

"It won't work how you hope," I put away my sword, "you've been sold a lie about the Gods. They're using you," I then realised what I needed to say, "I was there, at Burcanon. I saw it. It was one of them, wasn't it? The Fallen? It was a monster. I saw it."

"I know what it was, I was there too, and it was our beautiful Mother Mun," his eyes glowed in the fiery light, "they are beings we could never understand, but they have dominion over the world, and their faithful shall be blessed, forged into gods in the coming fires."

"You're going to end the fucking world!"

"This world must burn in order for a new one to be born, that is the way of life."

My head was swimming. This toppled everything that was believed about the Fallen and had broken my expectations of how insane the Quorum was. I shook myself of the terror creeping up my spine.

"Whatever you're trying to summon here, you know that they won't be enough."

"How would you know?"

"It would have worked by now," I threw the hilt away, "please, don't waste their lives. Take me instead."

"You would give your power, for them?"

"Yes," I looked back at Oliver, who started to shout again, his words muffled, "a million times."

"This is," he cleared his throat, "a fair trade."

"I thank you for your compassion and mercy," I bowed, "but they're to be released immediately."

"We can't release them," Ghorn winced, "we cannot have our activities here be discovered."

"It's too late for that," I reached into a small pouch for something, anything small and metal, finding a disc used to replace bolts on the harness, "this is a Gunray-designed recording device, everything is being sent back to my HQ as we speak."

Murmuring and hushed exclamations rippled throughout the crowd. Their Speaker looked around at them with a cold gaze.

"More importantly, surely it won't matter? You don't know what I can do, but I can assure you that escaping from here will be as simple as clambering up there and snapping you in two," I glared at the cultists approaching me, "however, once you have my power, the Void will be open to you, and no authorities will be able to stand before the Fallen."

"Then why save them, child? It won't matter."

"It might," I sank in my posture, "they might be able to escape, I'll have made some way to repent for my mistakes. And maybe you're right, the Fallen might be merciful to those I've spared?"

"I can only promise to ask for you, you young brave soul," he licked his lips, "very well. Release them."

More murmuring, then resigned sighs as the chambers were opened, and prisoners escorted out of the giant hall. They let Oliver go, dropping him to the ground. He immediately got to his feet, running towards me.

I thought he might hit me, scream at me, or even kill me. Anything. But he leapt forward throwing his arms around my neck.

"Come on, let's go!" he said through his tears.

I fell to the floor with him, squeezing him so tightly. I didn't say anything for a while, I just patted his back and cried into his shoulder, just to make sure he was really real and that I hadn't snapped.

"I will, but we have to get these people out of here. You have to go."

"No," he said, "No, don't leave me again, please."

"I'm so so sorry," I could hardly speak, "I ruined your life, I won't let that happen again."

"Elena, come on."

I pried him away then, looking into his now lilac eyes.

"Come on, Oliver," I sighed, "do as you're told, just one more time."

He shuddered, finally letting go of my shirt. I left him then, standing to look at Ghorn. He gestured for me to step inside the chamber. I made my way over, but then he raised his hand.

"Forgive me, but I fear that your harness may affect the device."

I stared at him, then nodded, pressing the release on the nape of my neck, feeling the needles and wires slowly withdrawing from my spine. I reached out, and two cultists propped me up, helping me walk to the chamber. Ghorn started his chanting again.

"Children, for those who do not understand, this girl has been touched by the Dream. Something long thought myth by the ignorant but known to us as the last vestiges of the foul children of Darius. This power, its raw strength, will bring the Gods to us at last."

The crowds whispered again, before cheering and joining the chants. The door of the capsule was enclosed around me, cutting the raucous screams to a halt, barely heard through the air-tight seal.

Okay, time to think.

You brought this on yourself.

I don't need you.

Without me, you're weak.

Maybe that's not such a bad thing, after all. At least they're safe.

The Enlightened Quorum

You are bigger than this, more important. If you had listened, you would have been able to stop this.

The machine whirred as the liquid flowed through the translucent pipe webbing around me. Small spikes slowly approached my sides, stopping just short of my arms. I faintly heard the Speaker say something, generating more applause from the crowd, and the machine blasted me with its electrical current.

I felt it immediately tearing my body apart, small intersections of my very being slowly pulled until cracks appeared along the flesh of my arms. The power was drained from me, filling external pumps with white fluid. I saw through the flashes that a tiny light had appeared in between the stone pillars.

Felix Ghorn stood in front of them, falling to his knees and raising his arms. The noise was pulled away, blood seeping through my ears. I watched in frozen horror as the tear grew larger, almost to the size of the pillars themselves like the space between curtains. A shape broke the shining light.

I expected some kind of eldritch shriek or a deep bellow, but it was completely different. It was a husky and heavy panting, almost like a huge dog with rotten lungs. The lustful huffing of a predator.

A child's face pushed through the rift. It was giant, at least the size of a Gunray, but it was the face of a child nonetheless. Its blue eyes were flecked with lilac chunks and didn't have eyelids, the pupils darting everywhere, analysing everyone in the room within seconds. Its body soon followed with baby smooth skin

361

stretched over the form of an insectoid creature, its arms single fingers with scythe-like nails lining them.

Its torso was now in view, long hairs from its back licking the bricks. Its hips remained in the Void, the shadow of a gigantic tentacle hanging from its groin in plain view. It was genitalia covered in barbs and writhing black hands. I had to fight back.

I reached out again, but this time, into the depths of my mind. There, in the darkness, I was able to access the Dream, grasping hold of my cells and pulling them back together. Power surged through me, and I realised that fighting back was the wrong move. I needed to go with the flow. I released all of it, everything I had, all the pent-up and held-back emotions, and pushed it into the framework of the machine.

The piping splintered, ripping a hole in the side of the capsule and sucking air in. Soon, there was an explosion, and the tear was closed in an instant. It shut around the monster, cutting it in two.

Its panting didn't stop, and it became an insatiable slobber. Its eyes stared at me in excitement.

"What have you done?!" Ghorn stamped over to me, kicking debris aside and grabbing me by the hair, "you have harmed the great Vari, you will pay dearly!"

He was suddenly impaled by a grubby finger, lifted into the air by the creature. He began wailing as blood poured from his mouth. Vari's long purple tongue ran saliva along its lips and its jaws unhinging before dropping Ghorn into its mouth.

I closed my eyes, hearing him scream as his bones were crushed between flat teeth, his flesh pulverised into a smooth paste. When I opened them again, Vari was leering at me, dragging itself towards me. Did it realise that the Speaker's arm was hanging by sinew from its bottom incisors?

What a wonderful little morsel...

Its eyes flickered as its head cocked from side to side.

We could breed a God, beyond even Kaurus' imagination.

It dragged itself closer, then seemed to finally notice the cultists behind me. I turned to see that they had thrown themselves on the ground in front of their God of Love, murmuring and wailing.

Are they enemies?

I refused to look at it, the heavy breaths brushing the hairs on my back.

My children will take care of them.

Vari croaked, the humming shaking the very foundations below. Higher pitch wails and moans answered the call, from deep within the flesh mounds at the back of the room. The nests opened up like sores, grotesque hybrids crawling from their brown liquid cocoons.

The cultists seemed to realise what was happening, but all too late. The abominations tore into the crowds, sating themselves in the bloodthirsty orgy that unfolded.

Vari wrapped a finger around me, dragging me away from the horror towards its lair.

CHAPTER FORTY-FOUR

Grunting. Moaning. Crying. That was all they did. The terrors born from Vari seemed to know nothing but pain, yet they continued to serve it faithfully, even acting as outlets for its perverted frustrations.

When will you open the Crossing again, sweet? It had said.

You hurt me greatly with that feat, but I'm willing to forgive and will immortalise you when I am whole again.

"Please," I tugged lightly against the tendrils holding me to the ground, "I'm weak, if I do it again, I'll die."

I know, It licked its lips at that moment, *I can sense it in you, but it is returning. Soon, you will be ready, and you'll give me what I want, won't you?*

I could only nod, stuck in the foetal position.

How long had it been since then? Logically, I knew it was likely only a few hours, but it had felt like days already. The air here was hot and heavy. It even had a stench of sweat.

The Enlightened Quorum

Vari was abusing them again. I could hear its piggish grunting and the wailing of its victim. I heard squelching near me and strained against the fleshy webbing to see what it was.

A pallid shape stared at me under folds of skin covering its eyes like a fat dog's. It only had one arm, the hand spiked and rough. Its neck bloated for a moment like a toad's pustules bursting as the skin stretched. As it stepped out from the darkness, the limbs hanging from its groin snapped into life, revealing a half buried creature screaming in pain as it flailed wildly. The smaller body's legs hung splayed and limp.

I couldn't help but watch, a strange morbid curiosity. I wanted to be sick, but I knew that if I was, I might choke, so I held it down.

I heard the panting overhead and saw Vari dragging itself forward. Its bladed finger crashed into the creature's back, the other its neck. Within seconds it was being pulled apart like slow-cooked meat.

It twitched a little still, barely clinging on and I couldn't help but feel the slightest bit sorry for the pitiful thing. It was hard to justify such a slow and painful death for anything on the planet. Still.

Vari turned its gaze back on me, its excited leer gone. It was now burning with anger and frustration, stooping over me and running the blade along my side.

You are not to make yourself appetising to my children. You are mine, and mine alone.

I nodded.

Remember: If I can't have you, no one can.

365

With that it returned to its grotesque routine, making the rounds of the den to hunt for another victim. I spent some time like that. Simply waiting for either my death. The Dream was returning slower than I expected, and I started to think that it wasn't going to save me this time. Even that horrible voice seemed to have abated for a while.

Coming to terms with my reality was soothing in a morbid sense. To know and accept your death gives you a certain clarity that had been lacking in the months since I'd lost Oliver.

At first, it had been a pain so great that I had shut myself down entirely, throwing myself into the work. That was all I knew. Progress and achievement. But it was dust in golden sunlight, flickering for moments at a time before receding to the shadows again.

On that day it seemed to suddenly click. The outbursts and dangerous decisions suddenly made sense. I had shut it out for too long, and my mind, without the crutches of the Dream, had betrayed me. I curled up tighter in the cold and slimy cocoon. My tears ran along the sheened surface, collecting in a divet of grime.

I heard a shuffling sound and looked up, fearful that Vari had come to inspect the sounds. But it was another of its children, the size of a toddler. It was blind, I think, as it crawled toward me, slowly, reaching out in front of it. Its hands were like Vari's, singular fingers propping its weighty body up.

I should have been afraid, but I think in some ways I would rather that this small thing kill me than

Vari, whose predatory sadism was beyond anything even
Calthern could understand.

"Will it be quick, at least?"

It seemed to understand for a moment, but then it
sat down in front of me. It smelled terrible, or perhaps,
the whole den did, but its stench was like that of a
weekend-aged undercarriage.

"Just get it over with."

The child looked at the bindings, then behind it,
before turning back to me. It opened its jaws, flat and
uneven bones lining the black gums. I closed my eyes,
exhaling.

I heard it sink into the skin, chewing slowly like
a bison, but I felt nothing. I strained my neck to see that
it was grinding the webbing between its rows, eventually
snapping the first. Maybe it made a mistake? It was
blind. I waited, watching, feeling the weight of my
chains lifting bite by bite.

"Come on," I whispered, "just a bit more."

It stopped, turning its head towards mine. I
refused to breathe. My lungs, deflated, started to burn
waiting for it to move. Then, as it became unbearable,
the child turned back to its meal, masticating the last
parts.

As the last strip of membrane broke with a crack,
I wrenched free with everything I had. It bellowed with
a shrill wail, crawling away as fast as it could. I did the
same, willing my legs to carry me just a short distance. I
half-limped, half-crawled into the heart of the nest. Its
walls were covered in a solution of blood and faecal
matter, coming away in putrid strands.

The Enlightened Quorum

I held back the retching, hearing grunting ahead. They were in the fucking walls, huddling, fighting, and fornicating in tight orifices. I found myself slowly slipping into the pained choir as I traversed the maze, my sobbing breaths becoming uncontrollable.

My strongest memory will always be the stench. It reeked like a sewer that had been left to rot like a corpse in a river. The traumatic imagery will be etched onto my memory for eternity because of that fucking smell.

Up ahead, I could see the summoning gate, knowing that I was nearly there. It became my north star, helping me get through the caverns.

I climbed the slope out, my clothes stained from the journey, but the joy of moderately cleaner air is something I still can't describe.

Most of the cultists had been dragged into the brood, but those who had been killed in the initial attack still littered the room. They were mostly in pieces, limbs torn from the sockets by the children fighting over scraps.

My exoskeleton and supplies were left where I'd left them. I came to think of it like a human attempting to understand the daily lives and tools of an ant. Vari probably had no idea what they were. But that was giving it too much credit. It was beyond our understanding, but not our cognition. It was sub-human, a simple aspect of humanity, Love incarnate in all its terrible forms.

The name that Hurwin had used suddenly made sense. The Reflection. It was all of humanity's worst examples of these boundless concepts. Love, motherhood, justice, and so on. They'd been twisted and mangled in the Void, formed into something so much worse. But, like a reflection, while it may appear identical, it is not. Humanity was better than this, or at least, it could be one day.

I put the harness on and let it connect with me again. The Dream was still weak, but it was enough to have full movement again. I searched the bag for the transmitter the Auspins built, the real one this time.

The ground trembled and the Gunray's giant drill tore it apart, then came to a rest. Janak appeared, smiling, and then his skin somehow paled even further after sniffing. The other two covered their faces.

"Elena, what is this?" his voice was muffled.

"I don't," there was a deep bellow from the depths, and I turned to see the spindly shape of Vari pulling itself to the top of the walls, seeing me from afar, "I don't have time, we need to destroy this place."

"What in Karl's name..." Carnal said, standing in the seat of the drill, "Olrod, get the shield."

"Yep," she was already on the move, laying out a large pack and pulling a metal disc, slamming down on it with a large hand, "that's fucking vile."

I saw that he was looking at the rising horde of Vari's children, their vicious progenitor trampling them to get out in front. I couldn't help but agree.

The device rattled, white light running down its edges, before firing a burst of energy into the air that sank slowly to blossom around us, creating a fully enveloped shield. It was awe-inspiring.

"Do we have anything that can kill all of them?"

"Maybe," Janak was pulling levers and release bars on a metal box, "if we overload this with one of the drill's batteries it'll tear 'em apart, but I don't know."

"What he means is, we've never tested that trick on a bloody God," Carnal removed the batteries on the drill's front, its surface smoking when it touched his hand, "I mean, that thing, that's something else."

"It's not a God," I looked at them again, and the children were surrounding the shield, circling its edges, "we were wrong about them."

"Yeah no shit," Olrod winced as one tested the edge, getting blasted back, "but there's no way to know if it'll die."

"Plus, there's the collateral damage," Janak stood back from the bomb, taking the battery held out to him and studying it, "it'll likely knock down whatever's above us."

I wracked my brain, trying to think what it could be. I realised that it was likely part of the Senate building, but an older and less used section.

There is no time to think. Do it.

"Go ahead, I think it will be okay."

"That's not very reassuring," Carnal leapt back as another child reached through, its arm being sliced off in the process, "be sure."

"I'm sure that no one will be hurt," I looked at Janak, "if anyone is, it's still the right thing to do. We can't let it escape."

He nodded, ripping a panel of the bomb and using the wires to connect the battery.

My sweet angel.

Vari was standing behind its horde.

Please, I'll die without you.

I reached out with a minimal amount of the Dream.

You'll die alright.

The device hummed, building in pressure.

"It's ready!" Janak smiled, and then a hand managed to puncture the shield, pulling him towards it.

The creature savaged him instantly, tearing into the meat of his neck without hesitation. Its cutting fangs tore Janak's arteries with ease. Carnal and Olrod had already gone to grab him, to pull him back, but this had only made things worse.

The creature didn't let go, and as his cousins tried to save him, the toothy clamp held his head in place, tearing it off with ease. I grabbed the transmitter from Janak's body, as his cousins wailed in grief, and slammed a hand on the button.

I was blinded by the lights that passed through us. All I could conceive was the crying of the Auspins and the horrific screeches of the children of Vari as they were melted away in the pure flames.

When sight returned to me I saw a field of mangled corpses, charred to crisps and bent at awful angles as their bones had snapped in the heat. In the distance I saw Vari, or at least its shape. At first, I was sure it had survived, but soon its body collapsed inwards, leaking thick green pus out onto the ground that started to infect the surrounding area. It was just like Burcanon, all over again.

I went to Carnal and Olrod. As per usual, nothing seemed to suffice. Loss was an insurmountable conversation.

They just nodded, picking up Janak's body and placing it on the trailer at the back of the drill to take him back. We looked around for some kind of exit, noticing a stairwell at the opposite end of the room.

When we escaped, we saw some of the survivors had waited, including Oliver. He looked terrified but smiled when I appeared.

"Is it dead?"

"Yeah, it's dead," I hugged him again.

Oli, Olrod, Carnal, and I made our way up the stairs, which lead to a rooftop. I saw that survivors were making their escape in numerous directions, either climbing down into the streets to over the walls into neighbouring districts.

I then heard a low growl.

Too late, I turned to see the monstrous form of Anders leaping across rooftops towards the survivors, bearing down on them so fast.

"Hey!" I shouted, readying a collection of void energy in my hands, "up here!"

I fired at him, the blast nearly throwing him off the roof. It gave the screaming groups some more time to get away, but now Anders was focused on us.

He shook himself of dust and like a starving dog lumbered over to us, climbing up to our position. His one massive claw gripped the edge of the building, pulling his hideous wolfish face into view.

He crawled towards Oliver, his eyes even more alien to me now than before. I pulled my brother to me, promising to protect him this time. The shape of my father bristled with an animalistic desire to destroy, his jaws prying open to scream luminous pink spittle in our faces.

Silent as an arrow, Hurwin Corvin skidded in front of us, putting a clawed hand back to lightly push us away.

"I'm sorry I'm late, little one," he looked back at me, "well done. I'll take care of this."

I nodded and tried to walk away, but Oli stayed in place, staring at the creature.

"Dad?"

"No Oliver," I said, "not anymore."

"We can help him!" he said, not moving.

He was the same small boy he'd always been but I couldn't move him anymore. He stayed planted in place. There was an incredible strength there I couldn't even fathom.

The two creatures clawed at each other as they circled, testing, then rushed at one another to slam tougher and start tearing into flesh and bone. Corvin twisted with all his strength, throwing Anders across the rooftop. He skidded in the deep puddles forming in the shoddily built structure, and for the first time, slowed to take a breath. His hulking form shuddered and pale blue blood turned the water a murky and milky colour.

Before I could go to him, Hurwin leapt atop the creature and pinned him down. My father roared and snapped at my new-found mentor, swiping with his talons. Hurwin grabbed the thick arm mid-swing, holding it for a moment, before turning and yanking until the shoulder joint popped out of place. But he kept pulling until Anders yelped and his eyes widened as he struggled to escape.

"You're hurting him!" Oliver yelled.

Hurwin didn't listen. He ripped my father's arm off entirely, tossing it so it slammed into a nearby pool, shrivelling quickly and disintegrating. Anders bellowed in pain, writhing to get his other arm free, but the Folsesjeger kept him in check.

"It's over," I said, "we can bind him and take him back, there'll be a way to save him. Just stop."

"Are you fucking blind?" Corvin growled, then gestured at Anders, "save this? He's too far gone."

The wound where Anders' arm had been pulsed and tendrils burst forth like headless snakes, reaching for Corvin's ankle. The Folsesjeger managed to grab one and step back, gripping my father's red mane to hold his head in place. He wrapped the appendage around Anders' throat, tightening it until he whimpered.

I felt sick watching. His huge, bulbous eye was so strange and yet reminded me so much of him. It was the same pain he'd shown when apologising after hurting me before. I hated him for it, for always trying to go back on what he'd done. But there had to be something in there worth saving.

"Please let him go," Oliver said, his voice cracking with the same pain, "please sir, I don't know you, but you have to help him."

"He's killed too many, child," Corvin looked at me, "Elena, come on, you aren't stupid. You can see it, it's too late. What did we say? No matter the cost. He's dangerous!"

"I have to try, he deserves a second chance."

"After everything he's done? Not just to you, this isn't just about you anymore. He's destroyed our cause, all because of his own ignorance," Corvin tugged on the flesh noose again, "he's a monster."

"But he can change! Everyone can!"

"He was always a fucking monster!" his scream went right through me, and my skin burned a little after it was gone, "he smashed a child into a bloody pulp, the very last of my kind. He'll keep killing until he's stopped. He's controlled you two and forced you to commit atrocities you shouldn't even have had to comprehend. How do you not see it?"

"I know, Hurwin, I understand your pain," I sighed, stepping forward and reaching out, "but I have to try."

Anders strained again, releasing a strained roar as he tried to escape. Corvin held him in an iron grip. Then looked at me again.

"I have to set you free."

Before I could even form the word 'no' in my brain and send the signals to my mouth, Corvin placed his boot on my father's back, pulling the cord tight. Anders' eyes bulged as his oxygen was cut, and they started to bleed slightly in thick blue tears. Oliver screamed as he watched Corvin decapitate our father's misshapen body with his own strange limb, the malformed head rolling in the water below.

I thought my heart might stop then. The pain in my chest was wound so tight that I was certain the strings had snapped, because all of a sudden, there was nothing. A deep emptiness filled my gut, just as it had when I thought I'd lost Oliver. The waters of hope had filled that hole, weakening the shell I'd built these past weeks to protect myself, and now it was shattered all over again.

My father's corpse melted away in purple embers, carried away in the strong winds that whipped Corvin's coat around him. I'd never really known him, and now, I was never going to. I hated him for everything he was, but I grieved for what he could have been. My father was dead, and my world had changed again.

I could barely even register the feelings of fear as a blast of light-consuming energy connected with Corvin's chest, nearly knocking him from the roof. I felt the welling of primal hatred next to me and lazily turned to see Oliver rising into the air, his eyes glowing with that same malevolent black. It was like the moon itself was paler around him, and everything was dark when I looked for any sign of him. Oliver was gone again, I knew. Maybe alive this time, but he was not the same. Perhaps I wasn't either.

Oliver hovered over Corvin, who stared back at my brother with something I'd never seen before in him: A deep fear of a creature he had never seen in his thousands of years.

Oliver attacked again, watching Corvin roll away but continuing to let the dark flame burn through the building ahead of us. When he let go and fired again, I saw that the inferno had already hollowed the apartment block, and its supports were collapsing in on themselves rapidly.

This time, Oliver connected with Corvin again, but the spells were too strong. He sent the Folsesjeger flying into the streets and kept throwing his black flame. My brother rose into the air with angelic grace, scanning the area for his prey, barely acknowledging the raging storm that quickly destroyed the area around us.

I stood with no real urgency. The fires no longer frightened me as much as they should have. I wandered lazily into the street, watching my brother in the sky, throwing yet another jet of destructive energy at a nearby building. I heard crying to my left.

There was a girl, maybe five or six, kneeling by a string of charred corpses in the streets. Their fingers were bent and snapped like dead tree branches, and their eyes melted into their black flesh. She had her hands on one of them, rolling the husk back and forth.

As I approached I realised she was calling for her mother, the reality of what had happened to her only really just setting in. I saw the building next to us starting to collapse, burning splinters falling around us.

It was as if I'd been removed from my body for a while, simply passively observing my life unfold. Then, at that moment, I snapped back to reality. I rushed forward and scooped her up into my arms.

"Mummy," she cried, it was a faint, exhausted noise, and she struggled against me for a moment.

"It's alright," I said to her, softly, "I've got you."

I felt the ground shaking as I carried her down the road, hearing the crumbling stone behind me. I kept running, shouting for people to move and run. Some listened to me, others stayed to help but I knew it would be in vain. The firestorm wouldn't be stopped now. I had to get back to the rest of the group.

CHAPTER FORTY-FIVE

The girl still wouldn't say anything. It had been three hours and she just stared blankly at the wall, her eyes glazed over and barely blinking. Most of the survivors who had followed us were similar, and there was only a handful of them there.

I sat with Guin, who hadn't been sure how to react to what I'd told her. She was just as confused and upset about my father and brother's transformations as I was. Still, having her sit there with me in silence was all I needed from her.

Bhen came into the room, his eyes sunken and hollow. I had seen him drinking late into the night more and more lately, knowing that the poison was starting to take its toll on his body. But I also knew that he didn't care. It never let him forget, if anything it made the pain so much worse, but maybe that was the point.

You've destroyed these people.

"Fire's starting to die down," he said, pulling a chair from the wall, "we managed to contact void-wielders in the district who are controlling it as best they can. Lots of dead though."

I nodded, scratching away at the peeling skin on my thumb.

"There's news though," Bhen scratched his head slowly, "city's claimed its another incursion, soldiers are readying up at the district's walls."

"I wish I was shocked," I sighed, closing my eyes, "Changed?"

"Yep. They're getting ready to clear everyone out. Said it's the final straw. Whole city's backin' em."

"What do you mean?" Guindolene asked, leaning forward.

"They're going to liquidate the area," I said, pausing to let that sink in for her, "they've been looking for an excuse for a long time, and now my fucking brother's given them one."

"Liquidate?" she shook her head.

"Genocide, Guin, they're going to kill everyone," I snorted, "it's clever, really."

They both looked at me in horror at what I'd said. But I didn't have the patience to comfort them anymore.

"They'll kill two birds with one stone. Clear out people they've been looking to exterminate for years and cover up that base. They'll be back to summoning the Fallen within a week. And now, they won't have anyone to stop them."

"We'll stop them," she said," we have to."

"We will," I looked up at the ceiling to avoid anyone's gaze, "let the attack happen. Let them…liquidate, the district. While they're distracted, we'll tunnel under the Senate."

Yes, good. You're finally starting to see the truth.

"And then what?"

"We'll kill them all."

No one spoke for a second, so I looked at them all again, taking in their expressions.

"Them, the dynasties, all of them. Cut off the hydra's heads all at once."

"But the people in the district will die," Guin said with a soft horror I'd never seen before, she was devastated that I'd even suggest it.

This is simply the way it has to be. You are weak, and you've allowed defeat. Now, you must make them pay.

"What do you want us to do instead? We've lost."

"You can't decide when thousands of people have to just give up and die!"

"I haven't!" I yelled, standing up so quickly my chair clattered backwards, "they have, they've been one step ahead the entire fucking time, and now they're setting up their end-game while we sit here scrambling for options. We're done, and they know it. They aren't playing fair, so neither should we," I stood up then, glaring at them all, "we fucking kill them all and we make it right."

"Shut up."

Bhen said it so softly, so quietly I almost hadn't heard it. I turned to him, and ground my front teeth together. I went to shout at him, but he cut me off.

"Shut the fuck up, Elena," he stood, his eyes shadowed by his brow, "you will shut the fuck up, and listen to me now, girl, listen to me for the first time in your life."

I wanted to strike back, to lash out like a wounded dog in the corner, but I couldn't find the words.

"I've followed ya this far, 'cause I trusted you," he looked away for a second, "Bhari, 'e trusted you too. And that boy was far smarter than I could ever 'ope to be. So even now, despite everything you just said and did, I trust you. But you don't get to decide when we're done. We've lost too much to stop now, just to let them finish us off like this. You can give up if you want, sit here and twiddle your thumbs until it's all over. You get that choice, 'cause this never impacted you the same way it does for us."

He saw that I was about to protest again and raised his hand.

"Now, you've lost more than most, I won't deny it. You've earned that chip on ya shoulder. But if you went and gave up, they'd probably put you up in a nice cell. I don't get that choice," he took a breath, "they'd, they'd fuckin' kill me, wouldn't they? Without a second thought and it'd be the same for everyone else 'ere. Now, I won't let that 'appen. Even if I'm the only one left, I'm fightin', 'cause these bastards deserve everything I can give. You know what happens if we don't, the 'ole world ends. So you better climb out o' that 'ole you've dug for yourself and start coming up with a better plan, 'cause I won't fuckin' 'ave it anymore. You're better than that."

I still felt the anger running hot in my heart, but it wasn't looking to break out anymore. It was seeping into my chest, spiralling downwards. I was angry with myself.

"And killing them? That'd be an insult to my Bhari," Bhen let out a brief sob then, covering his mouth to recover, "he wouldn't a wanted that and you know it. We can win this. You can win this."

I never knew how to tell Bhen the truth. That Bhari also followed a path of violence once, deciding that blood was the only key to escape the cells we'd been forced into. Towards the end, he'd come to realise that maybe there were better ways, but it felt dishonest saying that too.

Bhari was ultimately just as scared and confused as the rest of us, and he knew that Eleynum didn't fight fair. I saw then a vision of a future where Bhari's name and ideas were taken and fed to children at night to construct a hero, even if that vision was but a picture of one side of this complicated boy I'd lost. And it felt wrong. He was more than that, and that's what made him human. But in the end, there was no need in making these distinctions. It served no purpose to sour Bhen's memory of his son. I could at least give him that.

"You're right, Bhen, I'm sorry," I went to lean on the table, "the stakes aren't the same for me and they never have been. I thought I was like the rest of you but I'm not. I'm just a spoiled kid playing dress up."

"I didn't say that," he softened his tone a little, "you might not 'ave it the same as us, but you're one of us nonetheless. You fight with us, and you've suffered, you've earned your place here. People respect you. Now you need to get back to what you do best."

"I'm just so fucking tired of failing everyone."

Guin's soft hand was on my shoulder and I looked at her.

"Sometimes you fall down, you know? But you have to get back up. As long as you can honestly say you tried and didn't give up, then you haven't failed."

I nodded, turning back around to face them both.

"Thank you, I don't know if I can fix this," I smiled for a moment, "but I'll do my best."

"Good girl," Bhen nodded, relaxing his stance, "now, what're you thinking?"

"I'm not sure yet, how many fighters have we got?"

"Not many 'ere, most are out helping civilians," then he gasped lightly, "Miss Snow-Steel, I meant to say, those royalists you spoke to, that Knight-Paladin Maxus? Him and a couple of soldiers are here, wanted to meet with you and Elena when you were ready."

"Okay, could you send him in in a bit? Afterwards, send word to soldiers in the field to gather as many people as you can to set up defensive positions around the district," I took a breath and thought for a moment, "tell them the Changed are coming, and that void-wielders are needed. Then ask any fighters here to meet me after we're done with the Knight-Paladin."

"Of course," he said, "good to have you back."

"Need me to do anything?" Guin said as Bhen left the room, "I can help."

"Could you sit with me for this one? They might be a bit more polite if a noble's in the room."

"Wouldn't say I count as a noble," she said, laughing nervously.

I shook my head with a smile, taking a seat again and waiting for the Maxus to arrive.

He soon had the door opened for him by another Knight, walking in with the same pomp and ceremony as he had before. I had to respect it, showing off in the face of imminent death.

"Knight-Paladin Maxus, attending," announced the Knight at the door, before closing it behind his master.

"Mistress Therin," Maxus said, taking off his gilded helmet to hold it at his side, "do you accept this negotiation?"

"Negotiation?" I scoffed, noticing the helmet had recently been oiled yet again, "I didn't realise you had anything to offer."

He barely winced, still waiting for me to officially meet with him. It was all about ceremony for these people, holding onto some dying idea of chivalry that never existed. This 'gentleman' and the Knights he served years back were almost as dirty as the Inquisitors, but he'd never admit to that.

"Oh for," I stood up, "I, Elena Therin, do officially agree to negotiate with Knight-Paladin Maxus and guarantee his safety on my honour as a fellow General. I am attended and witnessed by Lady Guindolene Snow-Steel who will hold me accountable should I break this oath."

385

"I thank you for agreeing to negotiate," Maxus relaxed in the same way that a statue might, just the faintest hint of relent. He turned to Guin, "and may I say to the Lady that I offer my deepest condolences for the ruination of one's house, and pledge my service to you should you require it."

The ruination of one's house. Not the deaths of those you called loved ones, the betrayals of those closest to you, or the complete persecution of you as an individual for simply being born to them. No, no condolences for anything that mattered.

"May I ask why you're here, Maxus? From what I gathered, our last meeting didn't exactly go as I hoped," Guin said.

He allowed himself to take a seat, then finally, after all this time, looked at me directly.

"This is true, our prior meeting was not an optimal outcome for either party, and I would like to try again."

"Why? What's changed?" I said.

"I, well," he shifted, "I have had, a change of heart."

"Go on," I said, leaning back.

"Your group made me realise that, regardless of our differences, your cause is just, and my duty is to the people of the city regardless of their station."

"No shit," I shook my head, "forgive me, but I can't believe that you finally empathising with people who aren't born with the world at their feet is the only reason you're here."

"It is the primary reason, but you are right, it is not the only reason," he almost visibly bit his tongue, "I would say that I always cared about their plight. But I saw returning the royalty to their rightful throne as the only way to save them. But I have to understand that we may not have the time for this. I have received information that I believe you need to hear."

"Okay, look, I appreciate what you're saying, really I do, it's good to see that you've come to your senses," I swallowed some excess saliva, "but we need to move quickly, so can you skip to the important part?"

"I will also say that you are an impertinent and rude madam, unfit for leadership," he scowled, "but you clearly command the respect of these people, and I will try my best to look past your arrogance."

I pulled a painful, clearly fake smile. He could mock me all he wanted, at this stage, I knew in his mind he needed me more than I needed him. Obviously, truthfully, that wasn't really the case. But I wasn't about to let him have the satisfaction.

"I have learned that the Changed use specific inhibitors pumped through their armour, this is used to keep them under control."

"We'd heard reports about this before."

"Yes, but we have discovered that these inhibitors are similar to old medicines used by the Royal Guard to keep their emotions in check. And they have a nasty reaction, to this."

He pulled out a small vial of glowing red dust. It moved around the glass tube and glimmered as the light caught the flakes.

"This was used during the Quorum's uprising, it creates violent mental breakdowns if used in vast quantities against those with these same inhibitors in their blood," he looked at the vial with a grimace, "obviously, the Royal Guard was using far smaller quantities than the Changed will be. And their bloodlust is already strong enough that, if we were to fire these into the enemy lines early enough, we could cause them to fight amongst themselves."

"How long does it last?"

"It is hard to say exactly, and it's dependent on their individual will. Some may still attack, but it will buy you some time and a much-needed advantage."

"So what are we negotiating? We'll make more of this and save the district as best we can."

"You will notice that I have withheld both the recipe and the fact that I have vast stores of this weapon ready to use straight away. It is a timely process to mass-produce this agent, and the materials are not easy to come by."

"Of course," I sighed, "what do you want then?"

"One, if we are to win this fight, we need to cut out their heart. I want you to give me some of your soldiers so that I may seize the Senate while you keep their forces concentrated here."

"Act as a distraction for you?"

"Was this not going to be your plan already?" Maxus allowed himself a small smile, "I may not think much of you, but I respect your tactical abilities, and I assumed you had already thought of this two-front attack."

He was right, I had, and I'd hoped he would support at least one of those battles.

"That doesn't sound like much of a concession to make, especially as you're right, that was already going to be my plan."

"My second demand is this: You will allow us to restore the Royalty to the throne, as the city's rightful rulers."

"And there it is," I looked at Guin, "see?"

She nodded.

"Surely you expected this?" Maxus said slyly.

"I did, but you and your kind's ability to bargain with people's lives never fails to astound me."

"Any promise I make here will have to be carried out, on my honour as a general, and if I break that oath it will be on pain of death," he sobered his expression, "I guarantee the people of the Darius district's safety and better treatment. They will be fed and medicated like any other in the city."

"How can I possibly trust you?"

"Because I will invite you and select others to act as councillors to the new ruler, ensuring these promises are kept."

I sat back and thought about it for a while. I remembered Bhari and the beliefs he held. He knew that the system would never work for people like him, and reverting back to an ancient one wouldn't change that either.

"What do you think, Guin?" I said.

"Truthfully?" she looked down, "I'm not sure we have much of a choice. Stopping the Quorum is the only thing that matters right?"

"But they were almost as bad. I can't just hand power to a new despot."

"You said it yourself, Elena," Maxus said, "the time of the God-King is over. Anyone who comes to power next will be human like any other."

"And what about the other cities? What's your plan for them?"

"My first duty is gaining a seat of power for a member of the Royal House, if we can re-establish a link with the capital then maybe we can restore order to the empire peacefully."

"And if you can't? You'll conquer the others to force them into fealty to the new monarch?"

"You surely understand better than anyone that the madness that has overcome the cities cannot go on? We need a strong, central rule."

"I can't agree to that."

"Well, what do you want then?" he raised his voice slightly, "it has come to asking for concessions from a child."

"Okay, you want to know what I want? Here it is," I stood up, "you can have your fucking monarchy, but they'll answer to the people. A real senate. Elected representatives voted in by those who will actually live with the decisions you make. This monarch will have to receive their majority support when making decisions, and your Royal Household will have to select a new head amongst themselves every ten years so that none of them can get too comfortable on that gilded seat and take it for granted. And, frankly? That isn't anywhere close to what I want, but that's the offer I'm willing to make. Things can't just go back to the way they were."

Maxus visibly shook with frustration, and I felt the cool realisation wash over him. He knew he'd been beaten. He probably would have accepted less, realistically, and I wish I'd asked for more.

"I cannot guarantee their complete agreement," he grumbled, "but I will accept this for now. Might we have an opportunity to renegotiate once the Senate is seized? Perhaps with the family present?"

"Sure," I said, breathing relief, "I'm sure you understand, I can't speak for everyone. Things may change."

"But I hope that you and I will keep our promises made to each other in this room? On our honour?"

"Yes. That is my offer and I will stand by it, and we will renegotiate when we've won."

"Good," he stood up and reluctantly offered his hand for me to shake, "I cannot say I am happy with this, but I am sure that you are not either. And, as the saying goes, if both sides are unhappy, then perhaps a good compromise has been reached."

"I'm not sure either of us had much of a choice," I took his hand for a moment, "don't think that I'll forget how you gambled your fucking royalty on the lives of thousands. You'll answer for that in time."

He didn't respond to that.

"I'll have some of our fighters meet you outside, how you attack the senate is your decision. I only have one request: Keep as many of the Senators alive as your can. Most will be in the pockets of the Quorum and we need to figure out which ones they are."

He nodded, then left the room, allowing his Knight to close the door after him.

CHAPTER FORTY-SIX

The Knights had helped smuggle barrels of the red chemical agent now dubbed Spirit of Vengeance and mortars into the district through underground tunnels built by the Gunrays.

Soon they had been deployed in several key locations, ready to fire on the groups of soldiers preparing their attack on the district outskirts. Of course, the news outside of the walls proclaimed that most citizens were already dead, killed in the initial tears, and so they were acting as a clean-up crew.

I had visited a few groups to explain the plan, telling them to wait on the signal flares for the sign to fire. Bhen and a few others had helped me, going to their own pockets to support people.

We'd also redrafted and edited a version of some of Bhari's writings and spread them as far as we could. The Auspins had fashioned small balloons filled with them, that would float over the walls and burst over pockets of the city.

The Enlightened Quorum

I suppose it was our way of letting Bhari finally have his say and speak to the people in the way he knew how. He deserved that much at least. Maybe it would change a few minds out there, once the dust had settled.

Despite all the preparation, the humidity of fear was palpable. It was hard to breathe around the average person, as they knew that if this went wrong, they might not make it. No one had seen Oliver or Corvin for a few hours now, and everyone wondered when they might reappear. Though sometimes small explosions would occur in the distance and I knew that it might be them, causing more havoc.

Soon though, the time had come. Scouts paced near the enemy encampments and soon saw the soldiers and their Changed divisions advance, filtering through the gates.

I saw one such gate directly ahead, down a long stretch of road covered in smouldering rubble. The huge Changed could be seen towering above their fellow soldiers, the pumps and pistons of their armour could be heard hissing from here as their clanging boot steps rang out like death knells.

The temptation had been to fire as soon as we could, slowing their advance. But Bhen had pointed out that entrapping them in the district, firing on divisions at the back would mean they would be flanked straight away.

We waited, a droplet of sweat worming its way into a groove in my cheek. I exhaled slowly, watching as line after line of soldiers came through those large doors. I could hear gunshots in the distance, and I wondered if they were already killing survivors. I had to hold onto my resolve. The timing of this was everything.

Then it came. A yellow signal flare fired in the sky from a nearby building, popping with brilliant luminescence that cast shadows across us in the street. Then another went up in return and another. I knew it was time.

"First shell, get ready," I said to the nearby crew, watching them load the canister into the tube, "good to go? Okay. Wait. Okay, fire!"

They sent it flying towards the gate, and on impact, it shattered. The Spirit of Vengeance scattered in a thick red cloud over the furthest division. There was faint coughing and screaming but I couldn't see clearly through the smoke. Soon, however, the screaming shifted from surprised cries to horrified, blood-curdling shrieks. Soon the clouds shifted and the lumbering giants could be seen tearing their comrades limb from limb. They had abandoned their weapons, instead using their mighty fists to crush smaller allies and each other into cubes of flesh.

They're going to do that to you once they're finished. They're going to pulverise you all under their boots. You've doomed these people to fates so much worse than death.

"Shut up," I said out loud. The crew looked at me strangely.

"Okay, fire again, bring it in closer this time, hit ones at the front. Then keep it up, just keep hitting them. We want the whole army covered in it."

I heard hiding soldiers clapping as they watched their enemies and tormenters die to their own hideous abominations. I couldn't condone the festivity, but I was glad that they had some hope.

Then there was a rumbling deep underground. I felt Void energy running underneath in high-speed rivers, so fast I could barely keep track. Where was it all flowing? I looked around trying to see what might be coming next, then had to close my eyes as a flash of light dazed me.

It was only a few seconds and soon my eyes adjusted. I looked up to see sickly green beams arcing through the sky, creating a strange lattice above us. There was a distant and alien whispering emanating from these electrical streams, telling of impending doom. People around me were shouting.

"What in the world is that?"

"They're coming from the towers!"

"What's happening?"

I looked for the towers they meant. Several high-rise buildings dotted around the Darius district, and they were right, each beam seemed to be sourced from them. I felt a disturbing heat raining down on us, like the crushing humidity before a great storm.

"Some are coming through!"

I looked back and saw that some of the Changed had indeed ignored the Spirit of Vengeance, or were at least emboldened by it, charging through the bloody mist to advance on the buildings. I saw one rip a door off its hinges, pulling residents inside out. It barely waited a moment before stomping a man into a paste before moving onto his wife who tried to protect him with her spells, tearing her apart.

Those Changed who had kept their weapons fired indiscriminately, sending large rounds through the weak walls of houses to clear them quickly before moving on to the next. Some simply resorted to summoning fire from their fingertips, setting buildings ablaze.

"Prepare yourselves!" I shouted, still distracted by the beams, "open fire."

I went to a man named Trank who had been put in charge of this group. But before I could speak to him, there was a large crack from above.

To this day, I struggle to describe exactly what I saw. A hole in the sky, larger and more terrifying than the one at Burcanon, was starting to open up above us. Nothing was coming through at that moment, but I could see a shifting purple sky behind it, reflecting an ashen wasteland below it.

Trank looked at me in terror, then nodded.

"Go, I'll keep the fight up here."

"Thank you," I shook his hand, "I'll stop this."

"I know."

Normally it would have taken some small effort to reach into the Void with my mind and search for energy signatures, but it was so easy at that moment. My first thought was that it was a testament to my rapid improvement. But that same voice reminded me that it was likely the seeping energies flowing into the world.

I tried to single out the single strongest source of power, hoping that I might find the central hub and a way to bring it all down. It wasn't hard, however. There was a familiar cold fear that I had seen years before. It was Oliver, and he was with Calthern at the centre of the web.

CHAPTER FORTY-SEVEN

As I got closer to the central tower, the sounds of butchery grew worse and worse. I could hear children screaming for help, their parents often wailing in grief shortly after. The Spirit had bought us a little time, but not enough to stop the tidal wave completely.

I heard the pounding of metal boots sounding from around the corner of a small alley and ducked into a house. I stayed low as I made my way through the dusty kitchen, running a hand along the composite counter to keep my balance. The curtains were closed in the adjoining living area, casting it in a foggy gloom.

A heavy crack shook the framed pictures from the wall mere fractions of a second before large rounds ripped the curtains to shreds and demolished the walls of the house. I threw myself to the ground as pieces of the nearby cupboard splintered across my back.

The Changed soldier kept firing until the building was held together by the remnants of its skeletal form, then held fire, allowing its weapon to hiss as it released excess air and heat. I dared to look up then and saw the glowing blue eyes of its demonic helm, fashioned with horns like Furnok, the Soldier. I wondered then what kind of horrific hellspawn the Changed really worshipped.

The creature kept staring at the house, watching for any excuse to fire again. I waited like a stalker in the long grass, waiting for the moment it lost focus.

I hadn't counted on a second one crashing through the front door of the home and standing over me with blood dripping from its feral gauntlets.

I stared up at it in disbelief for a second. I froze.

Like the fucking moron you are.

It squealed like a feral pig, lunging for me with its hand outstretched. I scrambled back and screamed as a second swipe went for my ankles.

You're acting like a child. Fight back!

I tried to make my way to the back entrance I'd come through initially but the Changed snatched me like I was its doll and threw me into the other room. I collided with a small table at the centre of the chairs, crushing it under my weight. I gasped for air as it was smacked out of me, writhing on the ground for a moment. My harness pinched my nerve endings then, seemingly punishing me in the only way it knew how.

The monstrous soldier was a rusting automaton, its movements jagged and heavy. After completing its slow and awkward turn, it marched towards me with its fists ready to smash me to pieces.

I only had one chance. I fled for the door then, watching the other Changed catch my shape and start to aim its weapon. It released the shells and they destroyed the brickwork in the path behind me, I imagined. I didn't look. I focused on the hideous contraption and leapt onto its left shoulder, reaching for the cannon in its hands.

The trigger was almost as long as my hand, taking all of my fingers to grab and yank it backwards. It tried to shake me off but I held tight onto its pipe network, yelling as the gun's machinery punched the inside of my ears with relentless fury. I looked away to see that the disorganised spray had ripped chunks from the other Changed soldier's chest plate, exposing several broken glass vials and the burning red flesh underneath. I couldn't help but smile as it slowly clutched at its armour, looking for some way to patch it up.

My unwilling accomplice abandoned its weapon and tried to scratch me with its claws. I jumped off and let it rend its own steel visage, causing it to scream in pain as its helmet came away in pieces.

It tried to look for me again after a second's hesitation but I had already drawn my sword and ducked under its legs. I quickly turned and slashed across two of the pipes on its back, letting white-gold bile spill across the finely machined plates. They were corrupted instantly, rusting, and falling apart in brown flecks.

I watched both of the Changed reach for their throats as they both writhed in pain, their mutated skin overwhelmed by the air outside and their organs rapidly failing after mere moments away from their stimulants.

"You guys aren't as tough as I thought," I spat at them, laughing as I turned to leave.

In a last-ditch effort as his back disintegrated, the nearest Changed grabbed my wrist and in a fluid motion he clasped my chest almost entirely in his other hand. He laughed with a grunting whooping sound, more a battle cry than anything else. I tried to wrestle myself free from his grip, but before I had any idea how, he did it.

My flesh seared in the open air as it was torn away, but the twisted and shattered bone was ice-cold. My harness ravaged my body as it tried to recalibrate itself, the Dream no longer lining up with reality. My arm was already cascading through the air and slapped wetly onto the stone, but I still felt my mind trying to close its fingers and attack. It was gone.

The pain was something beyond description. I was limp in the grasp of the Changed, my senses barely registering what was happening around me as the fire coursed through my shoulder.

KILL.

I felt the pain well up inside me again, the sight of Oliver's face when I had hurt him so badly. The pain of knowing I had driven him into the same hole that had consumed me. I should have been better to him. I should have protected him. I should have saved him from all of this. That was my responsibility and my failure.

And he was just the first in a long line of miseries you inflicted on this world.

No more.

The pain was energy like all others. In the universe of my own mind, it was the primordial force that birthed most others and felt intimidating, but it was really just me. I closed my remaining hand and bellowed with bloody rage as I began repeatedly smashing it into the Changed.

I started with its exposed beastly face, gaining myself some freedom from its grasp as I bludgeoned its skull. I didn't stop when it fell back. My fist glowed white as I continued to break its chest plating, working my way through the shell to finally start feeling the meaty weight of its chest cavity.

The power slipped away again, as fleeting as it was exhausting. I tried to step away then, but the harness was starting to slow down. It was as if it couldn't figure out my shape with a piece missing, and the rest of the joints began puffing steam and spitting sparks. I heard it faintly squeak rhythmically as the inner workings ground each other to dust.

I picked up my blade from the ground and stared at my arm for a moment. I considered taking it with me somehow, but I was already struggling to stay upright, and any added weight might have spelt the end of me. I used my remaining hand to secrete cooling gel from the Void, slowly clotting and soothing the bloody stump for a moment. The pain remained, but the burning didn't feel quite as intense as it had.

With a strange sense of guilt, I fled, as best as I could.

I limped towards the central tower and felt as weighty and awkward as the Changed then, my steps loud and deliberate. I stood at the bottom of the building, taking a breath. It was a hollowed hospital tower, long since abandoned. The doors looked easy enough to blast loose with a spell, and as I went to cast, I realised my left had been my natural hand with my sword in the other.

The Enlightened Quorum

As I attempted to lift the stump that pang of ghostly recognition washed over me again, my brain still not registering the loss fully. I couldn't help but laugh, honestly, but soon regretted it as the wound stabbed at me again. Using my other hand, I ripped the doors off, the rusted hinges prying loose with little effort.

I managed to climb a floor or two with the stairs, but I soon found that most of it had collapsed in on itself, with support beams poking out of the crumbling wall.

I had never tried propelling myself with a blast of air, but it was the only way I could see to make the distance. I took a couple of breaths to prepare myself, trying not to look at the fall if I failed. Then opened my hand and struck downwards, catapulting myself into an arc.

I felt ill as I flipped over once, crash-landing on the floor above with a fumbled roll. I was grazed, but I was alive.

"That wasn't that hard," I said, turning to see that the next gap I had to traverse was even larger than the last, sighing as I prepared to go again.

It took about twenty minutes, but soon, I could hear the wind howling and knew I was near the top. There was a door ahead of me that was marked 'roof access', and I could see green light pouring through the loose seal.

I stepped through the double doors.

They were both there. Calthern stood with his arms raised to the skies in jubilation, his clothes flapping around him as the winds picked up. Oliver was next to one of the same generators that Velloah'Ra had warned me about, though the design was far different to what she had put together. He was feeding energy into it, the great green beam coursing into the air from its nozzle.

Inside the machine, was what had once been a person. Whether it was a loyal and willing servant of Calthern or a child taken for their abilities, was unclear. But their flesh had been melted down into a thick mucus that powered the machine.

They both turned to look at me, Calthern's eyes wild and deranged. Oliver's were black, the purple light still burning around them. He barely reacted.

"So, you've come to witness the next step in our ascension?!" Calthern shouted over the whirring machinery, "your brother has taken his rightful place here as a chosen child, it is good that you have joined him."

"I'm going to stop you," I drew my blade and stumbled forward, "whatever it takes."

"You're too late," he laughed, "it's already over. This is simply the first step in a chain reaction."

"Seems simple enough to me," I said, "destroy the machine, collapse the arc."

"But this is just one of many contingencies, Elena," he said, walking towards me, "the machines, the slaughter below, and yet more and more carefully laid traps will all lead to our salvation."

"What could you possibly get out of destroying the world?!" I circled him, the pistons of my armour now squealing meekly.

"I will ascend to godhood among the Fallen, it has been promised to their chosen followers."

"The Quorum?"

"You think that they would bestow such a gift on so many? No, only those truly loyal, truly understanding of what is to come will be blessed."

"They aren't gods, I've seen them for myself, your followers hated them."

"Yes, because they do not understand. That is why they will also be sacrificed, their beliefs were a fabrication, a useful tool to achieve true ascension. No one will survive what is to come, and when the world has been cleansed, it will start anew. A bold new future."

He knelt down, closing his eyes.

"Surely, Elena, can't you see that we are alike? You want to break this petty, greedy, unjust world and start afresh too. This is exactly what you want. We must adapt as a species, and this is the only way to make it happen."

"You've manipulated everyone into carrying out cruelty just to kill them all?"

"You think that the cruelty was the work of the Quorum? These people barely needed coercing, their greed, their hatred, and their capacity for violence was already so ingrained in this pathetic fucking city, it was easy to trick them into carrying it out for my ends," he grinned, "that was the beauty of it. It was so, fucking, easy."

I stepped back, feeling sick deep within my soul.

"You're a moron," I said.

He seemed stunned for a moment, then finally caught his train of thought again.

"What?"

"I said, you're a moron," I shook my head, "you think the world is cruel? Unjust? And this?" I gestured to the sky, "this is how you want to deal with it? By ending it?"

"There was no other way, child."

"Yes, there was," I felt even worse, having to take a moment to kneel down and take a breath, "I mean, you had that much power and influence over this city, and you allowed yourself to be tricked into giving it away? You could have faced it, you could have changed it, you could have made things fucking better!"

I placed the blade against his neck.

"You coward. You're a coward!"

"And you are a child, you would never understand the sacrifices we make."

I stared at his face. It looked almost plastic. He was a snake in human skin, barely even alive under there. I took the sword back and went to swing down to cut his head off in one clean strike. But I couldn't move my arms.

I saw Oliver's other hand, using his power to keep me frozen in place. Then he lifted me into the air.

"And you!" I shouted, "what are you doing?!"

"I need him," Oliver was calm as he said it, "we need him. You should hear him out."

"Whatever he's offered you, he's obviously tricking you, you stupid boy," I fought the tears down with my boiling anger, "how could you do this?"

"Everyone's going to die anyway. We have a chance to live through it."

"You would be a God in the new world, Elena," Calthern stood again, allowing Oliver to step in front of him, "It was always your destiny. I offered you that seat next to me, you remember, don't you?"

"And you think I'd work with you?" I felt tears breaking through the mask I'd built and I wanted to tear my own face away in frustration, "You took everything from me. You took my mother, you took my father, I could have protected Sonya if you hadn't split us up and now you're taking my brother too! I have nothing left because of you."

"No, child," Calthern was smiling like he'd already won, he couldn't help himself, "Sonya never went on that trip, did she?"

"What?" I stopped struggling against Oliver's burning grip then, "What are you talking about?"

"I spared you from the truth of that night," he clasped his hands behind his back and turned away from me then, "I saw how much pain you were in, and I must admit, it pained me seeing that."

"No I," the memory of the Old Gardens, the kiss we'd shared, "we went back to the bunkhouse."

"No, Elena. Here, I can see that this is confusing, let me show you."

I saw him raise his grey hand.

"Wait!"

He snapped his fingers.

I fell back then, slowly landing back on the soft dirt under the bridge. My joints felt so tired then, the sounds of the hardy insects enough to lull me to sleep had it been any other night.

"What are you saying, Elena?"

I started but I lost the words in the reeds along the way. The ones I gathered back up felt wrong as soon as I started saying them.

"If it could happen tomorrow, then why not tonight?" I felt my relatively unscathed shell say for me, "We could escape. I know a place."

"Where is it?"

"It's a cave, over by the gardens. The main ones."

I followed her, this younger version of me, seeing her link hands with the girl she thought she'd start a new life with, far away from all this. I felt Calthern's odorous presence close behind.

"So, you took her to the gardens, knowing that if you could make it to the cave, you might be able to get away," he taunted, "there were no shots that night to scare you back to your beds."

We arrived at the gardens and the storms had really started to smash away at the cliffside. I saw the slick, bladed footholds I'd traversed countless times.

"It's over there," my foolish counterpart pointed, "it's safe there."

"Nah," Sonya stepped away from the edge, "fuck that. If we could die tomorrow then what's the point in dying tonight?"

"We can live every day like it's our last," I watched her say that stupid fucking line and I knew then that it made sense, of course I had said it, not Sonya, "we can get out of here, we can make it!"

She clambered onto the rocks as if to coax Sonya onto them by showing an example. As I watched her do it, the dissociation from the events soon came to a close. I did this. It fit together all too neatly.

"Come on, Sonya, you can do this. I've got you."

"Of course, she was never going to make that climb Elena," Calthern breathed into my ear, "you have something special in you, something that treg never had. But you'd made the climb so many times and you believed, really believed, that if you could do it, so could the great Sonya."

Sonya shouted something into the wind but I couldn't grasp it. I watched her start the climb too and I felt my stomach whip itself into a frenzy, knowing she wasn't likely to have much of a grip. He made me watch them for an agonising amount of time, and I could somehow still hear myself as loud as day.

"Come on, you're almost there!"

Then lighting tore open the clouds, blinding the two young girls with its flashing light. And then she was gone.

I watched her tiny body hit the rocks below but I knew then that I hadn't seen that. I'd believed for the whole climb back and the desperate sprint to the offices that she might have survived it, had maybe hit the water and that she could be alive out there.

Then we were in the mess hall, watching my hollowed shell hyperventilating in a blanket, with Theona's tentative arm wrapped around my shoulder. I was babbling incoherently, apologising through the sobs and panicked breaths.

The doors were thrown open then and rain splattered the soldiers who had barged them apart. They wore long waterproof ponchos as they carried in a sack between them. I watched the water drip from it and leave a trail behind, but as their shadows lifted away from the spatters, I realised they had a muddy brown tinge.

The soldiers dropped the body bag on the ground next to Calthern and her small hand flopped onto the wooden floor with a wet slap, a gaping hole just below her wrist spilling even more fluid into the seams between the boards.

"You screamed and screamed that night," Calthern said, suddenly pulling me back to the roof, "we couldn't calm you, or console you. You believed yourself responsible, just as you likely do now. So I carried out a kindness."

Oliver let me go then, and as soon as I hit the ground whatever was left in my stomach punched through my throat and splashed onto the roof's tiling. I knew it was all true then, and the pain of that night had come rushing back in an instant.

I killed Sonya.

"I'll kill you," I barely managed a strained echo of my voice, "I'll kill you."

"Elena," he shouted, "for fuck's sake, what are you not getting? I changed your memories. Why would I let you see me in a bad light that night?"

I tried to clasp my hands over my ears, feeling the pang of remorse as I was only able to cover my right, still exposed to the deafening truth. Calthern grabbed my wrist and pulled it aside, staring at me like my father used to.

"You were nothing but a fucking pawn. You did exactly as I hoped you would. I needed to see how you'd taken to the Aspect, to test your abilities. But you did even better than I expected," he gestured to the screams that continued to surround us, "you riled them up so badly that we have almost willing sacrifices. The new world is coming, and I have you to thank for it."

"No," I felt like I was going to throw up again, and almost considered letting it happen just to spite him, but I wanted to hold onto some kind of childish defiant gesture, "no I tried to stop you."

"You did, but you failed, as I knew you would," Calthern tutted, "you were supposed to be better than this. Your father really was a fucking disappointment in every way, even his seed barely carried any of the power he should have," he looked away for a second, "your brother though, being of, purer stock, he'll be the beginning of an ascended army, one that could even rival the Gods themselves."

"I'll never help you," I spat the remnants of bile that had collected under my tongue onto his coat, "you'll have to kill me."

"Mm, no, I won't," Calthern sighed, turning his nose up at the yellowish spittle that slid along his lapel, "I can make more of you, I suppose. It's surprisingly easy, breeding humans, with the right tools."

I drove my forehead into the bridge of his nose, feeling it crunch beneath the weight of the blow, but pain shot through my eyes from the effort. He got up quickly, holding his head back to try and stem the bleeding.

"Then again, sometimes dogs just need to be put down," he reached out with his hand, gripping the binding on my arm, "I don't need your permission."

I watched him slowly figure it out, allowing myself a sad smile as he cocked his head in puzzlement.

"Yeah, left hand," I pushed myself to my feet, "you're no God. You're a sad and pathetic wretch of a man who lost even that title a long time ago."

Calthern's eyes finally resembled an emotion I could attach to something with a soul. It was a look I'd seen many times now. I watched him slowly piece together the fact that he was going to die.

He started to laugh as his mind was snapped in two.

"You're too late!"

"I don't care," I hissed, and I leapt at him.

"Elena! Don't!"

I ignored my brother's cries as he decided which of us he was going to help. I slammed my hand into Calthern's wrist as he held up his arms as a futile shield, shattering the bones in several places. I hit him again, knocking his teeth rattling in their gummy seats. And I hit him again. And again. And again.

"Stop!"

I wrapped my fingers around Calthern's swollen throat, pressing my thumb into his windpipe to cut it short. I screamed as I watched him flap his arms against mine.

"I said stop!" The icy grip returned then, Oliver's tendrils of energy slowing down but no longer

413

completely stopping my fury, "I need him. I can bring them back. Not that you care."

"Of course, I care!" I kept pushing through to try and finish off Calthern's battered body, "you're naive and selfish, people are suffering down there!"

"It's not fair!" his voice rattled my bones, "why do I have to keep hurting? I just want it to stop."

"He's tricking you! I can help you, just let me go."

"You?" Oliver's eyes brightened for a moment, and I could see him again, that glimmer of my brother, "you did this to me!"

He dropped me then, lifting himself into the sky and removing his attention from the machine. It seemed to slow down a little. Maybe I would have enough time if I kept him talking.

"It was all your fault!"

I tried to reach for him to hold him, but he moved away from me, holding me in place again with his powerful spell.

"You turned me into a monster."

"I know," I wanted to cry, to show him my pain, but it wouldn't reveal itself, "I'm sorry. I'm so so sorry. I didn't mean to and if I could take it all back I would."

"Well, you can't. It's over. I am what I am, and I want to see them again."

"You know it's a lie, come on, you're so much smarter than me. You can see the truth."

He paused then and looked at Calthern, and I had to believe he at least considered it then. But as is often the case with people, he thought things through a little too late.

There was a thunderous clap, and the hole that had been drilled into by the green beams was torn open completely by titanic fingers.

A warty face contorted in a permanent scream peered through the gaping wound at us and released a sonic howl that pierced the inside of my ears. I walked away from Calthern and Oliver and went to the edge of the roof, watching my worst nightmare unfold all over again.

I looked back at the boy who had ended the world and watched my brother make his final decision. He opened a rift of his own, and dragged Calthern's almost lifeless shape through with him, closing it behind him. I was alone.

I watched the giant pull itself through the gap, falling like a twisted newborn onto the ground, accompanied by horrific thick slime. It lay immobile, but the wound split further across the sky, opening wider and wider until the sickly air of the Void engulfed our own atmosphere.

And at that moment, I watched the stars burn out like candles hit by gusts of wind, and the sun *died*. It turned into a ghostly white blemish above, its rot spilling out like ropey guts. The sky bled, turning the clouds red.

There was silence then. It was as if the battle below had paused for a moment as every combatant took a moment to watch the spectacle of the end of the world together. I watched the huge shape slowly right itself with an infantile moan.

Then the screaming started. It was one, hollow wail at first. A woman nearby maybe. She was joined by another, and another, until it was an orchestra of horror. Portals opened all over Eleynum, bathing the buildings in deep purple.

Creatures roamed the streets already, scooping people out of their homes and twisting them like someone might do with a chicken's roasted flesh, devouring them. It was all over so quickly.

Something hit the building at its base with such force I found myself toppling over and before I knew it I saw the ground coming towards me at speeds I couldn't even begin to comprehend. I felt my body starting to tear itself apart. The earth below cracked and pulled itself into a stretched and illogical version of itself, the geometry no longer making sense to me, shattering into mirrored images around me.

I tried to scream but my voice was ripped apart, my body shattering into dust.

CHAPTER FORTY-EIGHT

I scattered forth from the dark cloud like rain, my millions of cells cascading toward a thick milky bath. As we hit its viscous surface, I felt like we were starting to stick a little more but held together by melted sugar.

I trod in the dense slop as I struggled to hold my head above the surface, pulling at the folds of the lake. Bristled appendages slithered around my ankles, slowly twisting to pull me further down. Just ahead, a creature swam effortlessly.

Two in fact, though one sat atop the other, his inflated cadaverous throne, using its disembodied arm as a paddle.

I tried to call out but could not make a sound, as if my vocal cords had been cut to endure silent suffering. But the Boater did notice me and gleefully made his way. I reached for the fleshy grey shaft, only to be struck by its palm. The Boater, seeing not a person, but a rudder for his raft, started weaving silver reed to tie me to his boat's rump. He moaned, his mouth spread in a wide grin, and I saw that he had no tongue or teeth.

417

The Enlightened Quorum

My head dangled in my daze, and I found I swallowed more and more of the awful pool as I trailed behind the rotting lump, almost lulled into slumber by the rhythmic splashing of the paddle, only to wake again when I came close to drowning and gasped for air. Finally, the Boater stopped, wading to untie me. I was dragged, face down, through the depths and into the mud and sharp glass, flailing meekly to turn and breathe.

He left me there a while, my laboured rattles ignored. As I stared at the iridescent glass slates embedded in the mud and recognised it straight away.

Soon the Boater returned to flip me onto my back. There was a knife in his hand, which he plunged into my shoulder. I yelled wordlessly and found a rush of strength, punching the Boater in the jaw, and sprawling his small frame into the dirt. The knife would make short work of him, but I feared pulling it out would lead to my death; the boater appeared, a rock in hand, and brought it down.

I shielded my face with my left hand, hearing a loud crack. Had I not lost that arm? In some faraway war? The Boater and I both stared at the black shale arm and its spiny plates. It was black glass. I watched him grunt like a toad and raise the rock again, and I swiped at him.

The arm broke down into several ethereal tendrils and slapped outward with the screeching sound of glass scraping against itself, striking him in several places. He flung backwards, and I heard him crash into the water.

I lay there panting, squeezing my strange new wrist. It was ice cold to the touch. Sitting up, I saw him floating on his back, rasping as the murky water was dyed by his leaking flesh.

As I got closer, I could see that the power had stripped layers of skin from him in striped patterns. I winced as his breath was increasingly constricted, his jaw hanging lop-sided. My hands quivered as the current coursed through them, my insidious ghostly vines receding beneath the surface.

How long had I been here? It all felt so far away, but I also had this aching feeling, a painful knowing that I had only died moments ago.

That must have been it. I was dead. I'd fallen during the collapse and now I was in the Void itself. It was a strange feeling, grieving myself. I didn't feel I deserved to be mourned, but I mourned the loss of the life I could have had. Had things been different.

But as I clambered back up the dirty slope to get some kind of view of the world around me, I saw the gargantuan corpse of the city I'd once known surrounding me. Its geography had been obliterated and no longer lined up with the laws of reality, generating strange shapes and patterns, but I still recognised it. More by its soul than anything else.

I watched the smoke rising from all directions and heard the distant sobbing of those awaiting their turn on the dinner platter. I knew then that I was wrong. I hadn't died.

The Change had come to pass.
We lost.

Elena's story will continue in:

A SHARED TRAUMA

Coming soon…ish.

-ABOUT THE AUTHOR-

-JAMES ASPLIN-

James grew up in Surrey and after a continuing series of increasingly concerning circumstances, soon decided to move and start over. He has studied at the University of Winchester, and as a part of his master's course, submitted a piece known as *Stains on an Orchid*. This piece was the foundation upon which this very novel was built. Due to the entirety of the world collapsing for a few years, James found himself with plenty of time to actually finish a novel.

He is currently working on the next step in Elena's journey.

Printed in Great Britain
by Amazon

25504830R00239